DARK VICTORY

A Novel of the Alien Resistance

Baen Books by Brendan DuBois

Dark Victory

The Lewis Cole Mystery Series

Dead Sand
Black Tide
Shattered Shell
Killer Waves
Betrayed
Buried Dreams
Primary Storm
Deadly Cove
Blood Foam

Other Novels

Resurrection Day
Six Days
Betrayed
Final Winter
Twilight

Story Collections

The Dark Snow and Other Stories
Tales from the Dark Woods
The Hidden
Stone Cold, Blood Red

Nonfiction

My Short, Happy Life in Jeopardy!

DARK VICTORY

A Novel of the Alien Resistance

Brendan DuBois

DARK VICTORY

Copyright © 2016 by Brendan DuBois

A Baen Books Original

Baen Publishing Enterprises
P.O. Box 1403
Riverdale, NY 10471
www.baen.com

ISBN: 978-1-4767-8092-4

Cover art by David Seeley

First Baen printing, January 2016

Distributed by Simon & Schuster
1230 Avenue of the Americas
New York, NY 10020

Library of Congress Cataloging-in-Publication Data

Names: DuBois, Brendan, author.
Title: Dark victory : a novel of the alien resistance / Brendan DuBois.
Description: Riverdale, NY : Baen Books, [2016]
Identifiers: LCCN 2015039678 | ISBN 9781476780924 (softcover)
Subjects: LCSH: Extraterrestrial beings--Fiction. | Human-alien
  encounters--Fiction. | Imaginary wars and battles--Fiction. | BISAC:
  FICTION / Science Fiction / Military. | FICTION / Science Fiction /
  Adventure. | GSAFD: Science fiction. | Fantasy fiction.
Classification: LCC PS3554.U2564 D375 2016 | DDC 813/.54--dc23
LC record available at http://lccn.loc.gov/2015039678

Printed in the United States of America

10 9 8 7 6 5 4 3 2 1

Dedication:

This is for my older brother Michael,
who's been reading my works for more than four decades,
with constant encouragement and a sharp eye.

Acknowledgments:

First of all, I would like to extend my deep thanks and gratitude to Iraq combat veteran Chris Chesak and former U.S. Army Captain Vincent O'Neil, Company Commander, 1st Battalion (Airborne), 508th Infantry Regiment—skilled authors both—who read the manuscript and offered key corrections and suggestions. Any military-related errors in the book are mine alone. Thanks also goes to my wife, Mona Pinette, for her editorial suggestions and advice, and to my niece Molly DuBois, for giving the manuscript a crucial early read.

And finally, thanks to Toni Weisskopf and Tony Daniel of Baen Books, who helped make a dream of mine from 1970 come true.

"If aliens ever visit us, I think the outcome would be much as when Christopher Columbus first landed in America, which didn't turn out very well for the Native Americans."

— Stephen Hawking,
cosmologist and theoretical physicist, April 2010

CHAPTER ONE

In the rear of the old surplus M35 Army transport truck it's dirty and noisy, since the original engine was ripped out after the war started and replaced by a steam system, powered by either firewood or chunks of coal, depending what the overworked Quartermaster Corps can get their collective hands on.

I'm sitting on one of the two wooden benches, facing the open rear, my Colt M-10 across my lap, assault pack at my booted feet, watching the late May New Hampshire countryside pass by with every turn and rise as we race to the site of yesterday's raid. Canvas overhead flaps and bangs as we move on. I'm tired and pissed off. The war is supposed to be over and I should be worrying about possible civilian life, but here I am, with so many others, out in the field again.

Goddamn Army.

An hour earlier the rear of this old deuce-and-a-half truck had been jammed with the rest of my squad, part of Second Recon Rangers, First Platoon, "Avenger" Company, First Battalion, New Hampshire Army National Guard, attached to the resurrected 26th Yankee Division. The last guy out was PFC Raymond Ruiz and his partner, Apache, who deployed at a covered bridge about ten minutes ago. Ruiz is from a refugee family from Boston—not that I hold that against him—and this is his first mission since he made Recon Ranger. He was eager to get to work and when he got out in full battle-rattle, his brown face grinning widely, I said to him, "Don't have to prove yourself tonight, bro. Just get the mission done and come back alive."

He said something back to me in quick Spanish, and added, "Just want to prove I belong, Sergeant," before walking up a dirt lane near the bridge, Apache pacing him.

Now it's just me and two others: my partner Thor, sitting in the middle of the truck bed, tongue hanging out, panting, watching the farmlands and forests pass by, and Corporal Abby Monroe, combat dispatcher, with her mechanical partner, a reinforced Trek mountain bike.

Abby sticks her tongue out at me, laughs. I laugh back, knowing it's too damn loud for her hear anything I say, so I go back to looking out at the few farmhouses as we rattle on. With my Kevlar-helmeted head turned, the truck doesn't seem that loud because of an old injury that took out a chunk of my left ear, about twenty percent of my hearing, and also earned me my first Purple Heart a couple of years back at the Battle of the Merrimack Valley.

We pause at a crossroads, take a left. At the intersection is a granite boulder with a brass plaque, marking the war dead from World War II, Korea and Vietnam for this small New Hampshire town of Montcalm. Faded American flags hang from wooden dowels shoved into the brown grass. If and when plaques are made to commemorate the dead in this conflict, I doubt there'll be enough brass in the world to get the job done.

The truck downshifts, brakes, and then goes down a narrow dirt driveway. My chest tightens and Thor starts whimpering. The truck turns at a dirt lot and I catch sign of a Creeper raid, the scent of things burnt and destroyed. The truck rattles to a halt and the engine wheezes and puffs. I lean over the tailgate, undo the hold chains, and let it slam down. I jump to the ground, wince at the pain in my sore left knee, which had gotten me my second Purple Heart last year, and then I turn as Thor leaps down. He picks up the ambush smell as well and his fur bristles. With a low growl, he trots off to a nearby field.

I'm kicked in my left shoulder. Abby is at the rear of the truck, glaring down at me with dark brown eyes underneath her Kevlar helmet. "What, the doggy gets first dibs?"

I grab her about her slim, muscular hips, lower her to the ground, and then help her get the Trek out.

"You've got opposable thumbs," I say. "Gives you an advantage."

Her brown hair is cut short and she has on a fatigue jacket with a MOLLE (Modular Lightweight Load-carrying Equipment) vest for her gear, plus a small assault pack, but she has on unofficial black bicycle shorts that show off her muscular, tanned legs. Her legs are splotched here and there with old burn marks and scar tissue. Around her thin waist she has a flare gun on one hip, and a holstered 9 mm Beretta pistol on the other. On her back is a Camelbak water container, the end of the hose fastened near her neck. She's the best combat dispatch biker I know, male or female. I'm glad she's going to be out here tonight, biking up and down the nearby dirt road, ready to get back-up if me and the other troopers find trouble.

She says, "You be careful out there in the woods, Randy."

"Careful's my middle name," I say.

"I thought danger was," she says, grinning, running a finger under her helmet strap. I swing my bulky Colt M-10 over my right shoulder, take in the ambush site. Typical Creeper raid. A silo's been burnt in half, silage spilling out, and part of the near barn's roof has also been scorched. A farmhouse with a wide porch sits to the right of the barn and looks undamaged. Over the entrance to the barn is a rusted basketball hoop, and a light orange ball is stuck in some weeds by a fence.

A voice to my rear. "Admiring the view, Sergeant Knox?"

"Not particularly, Ell-Tee."

Our platoon leader, Lieutenant David May, closes the door of the steam-powered truck and ambles over, leaving his driver, Schwartz, behind. He's about a foot taller than Abby and me, wiry and muscular, and keeps his red hair trimmed high and tight. He's an honest-to-God West Point graduate and shouldn't be riding herd with us Recon Rangers, but last year, his right arm had been toasted off at the elbow during the Second Battle of Saratoga in the upper Hudson River Valley, when the Creepers tried to split off New England from New York State. With that and some burn injuries to his face and torso, he could have gone out on disability but instead he re-upped, and ended up with us instead of a regular Army unit.

I look up at the sky. Mostly overcast. Not many clear days, even now, ten years after the war started. Off to the south there's a relatively large patch of blue sky, and just then, I see a line of flashing lights and sparks as a piece of random orbital debris re-enters and burns up.

The lieutenant says, "Catch that?"

"That I did, sir."

He coughs. "Our grandkids will probably be still seeing that, down the road, no matter what else happens." He pauses, like he's thinking about the possibility of living long enough to have grandkids, or maybe he's thinking about the possibility of *me* having children. "Come on, let's get going. You and Monroe have a busy night ahead of you."

The lieutenant starts walking and Abby and I fall in step with him. While our unit's fatigues are worn and dirty, he always keeps his freshly washed and pressed, like a good West Point graduate should. His fake right arm sticks out at an odd angle. Before the war started, prosthetic arms and hands that looked like the real thing for Iraq and Afghan veterans were created, thanks to computer work and all that. But that had been all pre-war. The lieutenant's right arm is old-school, with cables and hooks at the end.

I whistle for Thor and he trots over, as I take in more of the damage from the Creeper raid. The smell is stronger now, of wood burnt and flesh scorched, the faint scent of cinnamon, the true sign of a Creeper rampage. Even Thor can sense it. He comes up to me, black fur bristling, tail quivering, and I scratch his head. Thor is a Belgian Malinois, supposedly a direct descendant of the dog that helped Navy SEALs kill Osama bin-Laden nearly a quarter century ago, but even if it's not true, he's still tough enough.

Lucky dog back then, I thought, as we walk to the nearest barn. What we were up against tonight would make Osama bin-Laden and his crew look like kindergarten children.

Check that, I think, seeing two dairy cows, burnt black and on their sides, charred leg stumps sticking up in the air by the barn.

Make it nursery school children.

We gather in an open barn, me, Thor, the lieutenant, Abby and the owner of the farm, a stout fellow with boots held together by twine, patched overalls and a checked flannel shirt. His hands are rough and dirty, his brown beard flecked with gray streaks. Fine lines are around his forehead and eyes. His name is Gary Parker and he seems damn glad to see us. He looks me up and down. "That by God a real Colt M-10?"

"It sure is," I say.

"Can I take a look?"

I unsling the Colt M-10 and hold it out. It's a bulky, tubular-looking weapon, with an old-fashioned single-shot breech-loading device that can be clumsy at times, but I love it to death. Which explains what happens next.

"Can I hold it?" he asks shyly.

I shake my head, sling it back over my shoulder. "No, you can't. Sorry."

Parker's face flushes and he looks away, and maybe I should feel guilty, but I don't. It took a lot of training to be able to carry this bad boy, and I wasn't going to let a civilian hold it. The lieutenant coughs and spreads out an old topographical map on a nearby workbench, and the farmer then points out where the Creeper had come out of the woods and where it had gone after hitting the farm.

"Started last night, just after sunset," Parker says. "Came out down by this cut here on the other side of the hill. First thought it was peepers, what we were hearing, that clicking sound, and then we could smell cinnamon."

Lieutenant May says, "What did you do then?"

Parker looks humiliated. "Took the family and went to the basement. Heard the cows crying. Heard the silo get hit, smelled things burning. After a while, popped my head out and saw some smoke, over at the west pasture, where the damn thing skittered away."

My boss drags his prosthetic hook down part of the map. "Here, then. Where this stream bed cuts through?"

The farmer nods, bites his lip. "That's right. I guess I should have gone out and followed the damn thing to see where it went . . . but . . . I was scared shitless. I guess you could say I was a coward."

Lieutenant May carefully rolls up the map with his good hand. "I'd say you were a smart man, Mister Parker. The Creeper came and you did what you had to do to protect your family. To tell us where he went. We'll take it from here."

Parker looks at my one-armed boss, then me, Thor and Abby, and shrugs. "God, I hope so. But damn it, I thought the war was over."

"Oh, it is," the lieutenant says. "Has been, for a month, now."

Another tightness in my guts. Just over a month ago, the President had announced we had won the war, following an unexpected and successful manned raid by what was left of the U.S. Air Force up to low Earth orbit. Our post got the news from a telegraph message that had gotten to the state capitol, Concord. Lots of us had partied into the night and the next morning after the news was read at evening mess, but here I was, about thirty days later, near the Vermont border, getting ready for yet another bug hunt. As the lieutenant had said in our pre-mission Operations Order, this was typical in all wars, and they even had a phrase for it: mopping up. Which is great, so long as you're the mopper, not the moppee.

Mopping up. Sounds so innocent, like being assigned to KP duty, peeling potatoes, helping dress a whitetail deer, or sweeping out the fort's dining facility. But on this cool dusk in May, mopping up meant another Creeper hunt, with a very good chance of me or one of my buds coming back in a potato sack, our remains looking like lumps of greasy burnt charcoal. Barbecue bait.

I look over at the other side of the barn, where a car is up on wooden blocks. A sheet of canvas covers it and Parker sees me checking it out. He grins, revealing a gap at the side of his mouth where two teeth are missing, and motioning me to follow, he walks over, like he wants to make up for his earlier attempt to touch my Colt. He lifts up one end of the dusty canvas, revealing a low-slung sports car, bright red. It has orange and black New York license plates, registration just over ten years old. The tires sag, the air long ago having seeped out.

Parker stares, sighs and drops the canvas. "Jaguar XJ-6. Damn, what a sweet ride."

"How did it get here?" I ask.

"This place was a weekend home for my wife Ginger and me, before . . . Used to make a high-speed run up Friday afternoons, spend the weekend unwinding and relaxing. Then we'd get up bright and early Monday morning, make the drive south back to Manhattan. Lucky for us, we were here when the war started on 10/10."

"Did you work in New York?" I ask, thinking about that ghost city, and all of the ghost cities from the attacks that October 10th.

"Yeah," he says, wiping his hands on his overalls. "I worked for a hedge fund." Then he barks a short laugh. "Now I'm a dairy farmer. Boy, if my parents were alive, wouldn't they be pissed, knowing how I ended up using my Harvard education."

Thor comes up to me and I scratch his head. "What's a hedge fund?"

Another laugh. "Even back then, I had a hard time explaining it. Now? Don't worry about it. It doesn't matter anymore. Seems like an old dream, or a fairy tale from a strange country."

Then he comes to me, shakes my hand. "Good luck tonight, okay? We'll be praying for you."

Not much to say after that, so I go out to the dirt yard.

Out in front of the barn, Lieutenant May says, "Randy, just a reminder. You're one of our best, but remember the Recon part of your job. Don't be afraid to call for back-up, all right? If you make contact tonight, you don't have to take it on your own. Don't be a hero."

My assault pack weighs heavy in my right hand. "Understood, sir."

"I doubt it," he says, slightly smiling, the healed burn tissue stretching, and I try not to smile back. This is where the Creeper had struck, and this is where I've been deployed. Corporal Monroe strolls over, pushing her Trek at her side. The lieutenant says to her, "Safe riding, corporal. Keep a sharp eye out tonight. We've got five other Recon Rangers out in the woods tonight depending on you, especially Ruiz. Don't care how tough he thinks he is, this is his first mission."

"You got it, sir."

"Fair enough." He stands for a moment, staring at us both, and says quietly, "Good hunting," and walks back to the deuce-and-a-half. His driver Mike Schwartz, a PFC who's in his sixties and who's content being a PFC, steps out and opens the door for our boss. They both get in, the Ell-Tee leaning on Schwartz to hoist himself up to the truck's cab. Belching and burping starts up, and the truck starts out of the yard and goes down the dirt driveway, leaving behind a trail of smoke, steam and sparks.

Abby holds her fist out and I bump hers in return. "Don't take a nap on me tonight, all right?"

She smirks. "Dewey in the dining facility slipped me an extra Red Bull before I left. So I'm pretty wired up."

"Good for you," I say. "Dewey getting sweet on you?"

She gets up on her Trek. "Don't worry about Dewey or anybody else, Randy. I'll keep eyes and ears open. You be safe out there, all right?"

I shift my pack from one hand to the next. "That you can depend on. Hey, before you leave. Ranger Ball is two nights from now. Get the first dance?"

A big smile from Abby. "I don't see why not. But only if you do one thing for me."

"What's that?"

A wink. "Don't get crisped tonight."

Then she pedals off.

A moment later the wife comes out of the main house, carrying a red glass of some liquid. She has on work boots, blue jeans and a mended red sweater. Her light brown hair is cut short and as she comes closer, I see a hint of make-up on her face. It comes to me that years ago, she was a rich woman, living a life of glamour and pleasure, and now, she's the wife of a dairy farmer out in the middle of nowhere. One hell of a change. When I was six, I remember my parents promising to take me to Disney World for my birthday the next year.

Last I heard, that and Epcot and Universal Studios is one big swamp.

So we've all had to adjust.

She smiles. "Would you like some lemonade before you head out, soldier?"

Can't help myself. I grin. "That would be great."

I take the glass and finish it off in three large swallows. Can't remember the last time I've tasted fresh lemonade. I hand the empty glass back and see a small girl, peering out the screen door.

"Good luck," the mother says, spotting her daughter, as she quickly goes back inside the farmhouse.

I take a moment as I approach the barn. I drop my pack and gently prop the M-10 against the barn's wall. I pick up the old basketball—its pebbling worn off but still pretty firm—and I make an approach to the hoop, make a jump and *whoosh!* the ball slips through.

I grab the ball as it bounces away. "Knox gets nothing but net," I whisper. "And the crowd goes wild."

Then it's back to the war.

CHAPTER TWO

Back in the barn with Thor I squat down, unzipping my assault pack and checking out my battle-rattle. Good luck from the farmer's wife. Sweet words. I don't have to worry much about Abby, whose brown eyes make me tingle whenever she looks my way. Last fall we were down in Massachusetts, supporting a Marine unit attacking a Creeper base outside of Fitchburg, when Abby was ambushed on a dirt road, riding from one Recon Ranger post to another. Her attackers were a couple of Coasties, refugees from Philly or Manhattan or any one of the half-dozen cities up and down the East Coast that were drowned when the Creeper-aimed asteroids hit offshore on the first day of the war. Abby broke through the ambush and kept focused on her mission. Only when our unit had been relieved a couple of days later did she mention, "Oh yeah, the Coastie ambush."

Their bodies were later recovered by mounted Massachusetts State Troopers, found on the side of the road, 9 mm bullet holes in their chests.

That's Abby.

My battle-rattle is a mix of Army-issued gear with a few personal touches.

I lay out my Colt M-10 on the workbench, and then shrug on my protective Firebiter vest, snapping it into place. Compared to the older Kevlar vests, it's pretty lightweight, but that's because those vests were made to halt incoming rounds or shrapnel from our fellow man. These vests are made of layers of an Insulfex cloth in a camouflage pattern, then some sort of protective membrane and then aluminum foil bonded to woven silica cloth to reflect the cutting lasers and flame weapons the Creepers use.

Still, they weigh in at a toasty fourteen pounds. With another six pounds, I could don the new Firebiter arm and leg armor too, but I find those slow you down too much. Out in the woods, hunting Creepers, I like to be flexible and able to react fast, so I gamble, choosing speed and flexibility over added protection.

Next up, a set of Rosary beads, personally blessed by the state's Catholic bishop, which I slide in under the vest. Every soldier I know carries a set, even if they're Christian, Jewish, Muslim or atheist. Out alone in the woods or fields, I'll take all the help I can get. Stashed next to the Rosary beads, a laminated photo of my family, taken when I was about six by some forgotten cousin at Martha's Vineyard, just before the war started. The photo's about ten years old, and even laminated, the colors have faded. We're sitting on a stonewall. I'm six years old, wearing a Boston Bruins Stanley Cup championship T-shirt, cuddled up next to my mom. She has on a light pink polo shirt and white shorts. She's smiling, her arm tight around me, and she's wearing dark sunglasses. I've wished maybe a hundred times a month that she hadn't been wearing those glasses. I would like to still see her eyes.

Next to Mom is Dad, also smiling, his black hair thick, his beard closely-trimmed. He's wearing an UMASS-BOSTON sweatshirt, where he taught history and was also a captain in the U.S. Army Reserves. Leaning in against Dad, smiling and also wearing sunglasses, wearing a light pink sundress, my older sister Melissa. In this photo, she's about nine.

She's nine forever. She died when the war started.

So did my mom.

Dad knows how they died, but won't tell me much. It just happened in the chaos back on 10/10 when the war began, when I was with Dad and Melissa was with Mom. Maybe a dead airliner fell on Mom's Volvo. Maybe part of the Boston tsunami swept them all out to the Atlantic. Or maybe something even worse happened, killed by one of the thousands of refugees desperate to get out to the countryside.

And now I haven't heard from dad in almost six months. A colonel in the Army's Intelligence Corps, he's supposedly been out on the West Coast, and my weekly letters to him have gone unanswered.

Not surprising, but I still don't like it.

I shift the photo. Two years ago, at an Independence Day celebration at our National Guard post in Concord, I met up with a commander in the U.S. Navy, named Barnes. I found him fascinating, for he was the first Navy officer I had ever met. He was the executive officer aboard the *USS Constitution*, a new steam-powered dreadnought based out of Falmouth, up in Maine. During the party, we were talking and I mentioned Martha's Vineyard, and he shrugged and said, "We steamed by Martha's Vineyard just last month. Poor place got hit from the backwash of the Boston tsunami strike. Nothing there but rocks and sand."

Thor is nearby, whimpering, since he knows what's happening as I get dressed. With vest on, I put on my fatigue jacket, with my name, rating and unit badges displayed: KNOX, SERGEANT, 2nd RECON RANGER. Over my jacket, a MOLLE vest with pouches for my compass, knife, water bottle and holstered Beretta 9 mm pistol with four additional magazines. The pistol is of no practical use against Creepers, and is only there mostly for Coasties, like the ones who had tried to ambush Abby. Speaking of Abby, on the other side of the belt is a holstered flare gun, used to signal her during the night. Fixed to the belt as well is a plastic card showing the three types of Creeper exoskeletons and their apparent missions: Transport, Battle, Research. Apparent, of course, because even ten years later, our guys and gals in the labs still don't have a definite answer of what the bastards are up to or why they came to Earth. The plastic around the edges of the card is splintered and cracked.

That's all right. I never refer to the plastic card, because I know all three types of Creepers by heart; but I've carried the card since my first solo deployment, and that's a lucky streak I don't want to break.

A couple of more things. Knee and elbow pads if I have to do some serious crawling on rocks or dirt or in rubble. A rucksack with a pair of binoculars, food, water and kit, a utility knife in my right boot, and around my neck on a chain, a little talisman from my first Creeper kill: a toe joint that somehow got broken off. Maybe it's dangerous to tempt the enemy by bringing this souvenir along but I don't care. It makes me feel good, knowing I'm going hunting with a war trophy dangling down my chest. In the center of my vest are slings carrying six 50 mm rounds for my Colt M-10 rifle. Each round had been carefully inspected and accounted for before I had left the base, since one round is worth a hundred New Dollars, or about ten weeks pay, so you don't want to lose or waste them.

Then I open a small jar, rub anti-burn and anti-flash cream on my face and neck, and after I clean up, I pull on a pair of anti-burn gloves. Next up is a set of passive night goggles, and a Kevlar helmet. We Recon Rangers laugh at the helmet; about the only thing its good for against a Creeper is to keep your brain matter in one convenient place for pick-up if you get toasted, but regs are regs. I pull goggles over the lip of the helmet. I check my left boot, where a spare set of dog tags rests, inserted in the laces. Usually boots and feet, and not much else, are left behind after a direct hit.

One more thing. I kneel on the dirt floor of the barn and say a couple of prayers. Sometimes it's an "Act of Contrition" or an "Our Father," or sometimes it's the famed astronaut Alan Shepard prayer: "Please God, don't let me fuck up." (Which is kinda ironic, since popular barracks-room night chatter is that one reason the Creepers came here was because they detected the start of our space program.)

This early evening, all I can manage to get out is, "Please, God, let me win," which I repeat a few times. I get off the floor and turn around, to see a small girl with blonde hair and big eyes looking up at me. She has on dirty khaki pants and a Red Sox T-shirt cut and mended to fit her slim body. My mouth is dry. She looks nine. Nine years old.

"Mister?"

"Yeah?"

"You gonna kill the monster?"

I squat down, touch her cheek. "You bet sweetie. I'm gonna kill that monster. Gonna kill him dead."

Her face is serious. She bites her lower lip. There's a smudge of dirt on her forehead. I get up, reach into a cargo pocket of my pants, take out a black and dark green plastic wrapped treat. A Hershey chocolate bar. Her eyes widen at seeing the rare treat. On the back of the chocolate bar in large white letters: PACKAGED UNDER AUTHORIZATION OF DEPARTMENT OF DEFENSE. NOT FOR RESALE OR REDISTRIBUTION.

I pass the candy bar over to her. As one of my drill sergeants had said years ago, rules were sometimes made to be broken. "There you go, hon. Run along now and be with your mom and dad."

She trots away, smiling, holding the precious piece of candy in both of her hands, then she bursts out laughing with glee.

I watch her race up the porch and wait for a minute or two. Thor moves and rubs up against my leg.

"Let's go hunting, pal," I say, and we leave the barn.

With Thor at my side, I go around the barn and past burnt fencing, and the two dead cows. Before me is a slight decline, with trees scorched and tossed aside, trunks snapped in two, their interiors bright white and yellow. I go past a line of boulders and then descend into the woods. The sun is setting off to the west, by the Connecticut River valley. In a patch of blue sky overhead there's another quick line of sparks and flashes as more debris re-enters the earth's atmosphere.

I stay away from the charred path the Creeper made. To blunder in like that usually means a quick and painful death from burns, either from a laser strike or from the flame weapon Creepers use. Instead, I flank the torn up path and move slowly, and when I'm deep into the woods, far away from the farm, I find a rock and sit down.

I pat the side of my leg. Thor comes up, sits down next to me, and I scratch his head. My heart thumps along. So does his tail. I take a deep breath.

"Let's wait, bud," I say. "Plenty of time later for killing."

Then the trembling starts, in my hands and legs. It always happens at the beginning of a hunt, and I'm always glad it happens away from the rest of my squad. I shake and shake, it's hard to breathe, and for a few moments, it's like I'm going to barf up that great lemonade I just drank. Something dark inside of me threatens to crawl out, a horrid temptation to stay here for the rest of the night and just before daybreak, fire off the green flare that indicates nothing was found, to be a coward, a chicken, don't even move. After all, who would know? Nobody, except me, of course . . .

I clasp my arms around me, rock back and forth. Thor rubs his head against my leg. I think about Dad and the photo inside of my vest, and the shakes ease away. I catch my breath and sit still as night descends upon the woods, and I hear birds chirping and peepers crying out.

I keep quiet, not moving, and Thor, a good partner, stays by my side, letting me set the pace. Night settles and I slowly move my head, listening and watching, letting all of my senses adjust to the new night. With my damaged hearing, I could have gone out on disability months ago, but that wasn't going to happen. A desk job would have sucked, I wasn't going to leave my buds and most of all, I wasn't going to abandon the hunt, no matter how butt-hurt scared I get before each Creeper mission.

The Colt M-10 is comforting across my lap. A good weapon, but it's only as good as the soldier holding it. Although he didn't say it, I know the Ell-Tee brought me specifically to the ambush site, hoping I would be the one to find the Creeper.

And kill it.

It's dark now. Wind rustles the branches from the trees about me. My sight, hearing, and sense of smell are now all tuned into the hunt.

Now I freeze.

Wait.

A faint sound.

I wait some more.

I don't dare move.

I can't even hear Thor breathing.

Then it comes again, probably because the wind shifted.

A faint *click-click* sound.

Metal rubbing against metal.

Click-click.

Creeper sign.

I lower the night-vision goggles over my eyes. I get up, Colt M-10 in my hands, and Thor gets up as well, as we go deeper into the woods.

CHAPTER THREE

Before the war, night vision goggles turned night into day for my predecessors. A decade later, the goggles are substantially more low-tech, designed with some form of liquid crystal that works to amplify the ambient light out there. Only one eyepiece has the crystal; the other is left blank so that a sudden burst of light, like from a hidden Creeper, won't overwhelm and blind you. They're not perfect but they work better than nothing, even with the blind spots on either side of my head.

Thor at my side, I hold my Colt M-10 at port-arms and take my time. Right now, I'm in the Recon part of my job description, finding out where the Creeper is and what it's up to.

Click-click.

I take my time, mouth dry, heart thumping merrily along. I move as quiet as I can, moving randomly, here and there. I keep the Creeper sound in range, but I don't blunder straight ahead. I don't move in a pattern, don't move in a predictable way. Doing that means another way of getting torched to a cinder, and Abby doesn't dance with cinders.

With the aid of the goggles, I stalk slowly through the woods and brush. Moving a few yards. Stopping. Moving to the left. To the right.

Thor is right by me.

Thought about his ancestor, the one that went up against bin-Laden. At least his handlers were part of a larger group when they dropped into that village in Pakistan, with the full force and fury of the United States behind them. Here, except for Abby, out there pedaling and my fellow Recon Rangers, up and down this valley, I'm on my own.

Hell of a way to run an interstellar war, but that's all we can do.

I stop.

Click-click.

Sounds louder, but something is wrong.

Something is wrong.

I kneel down, rub at Thor's neck. He's softly panting but he isn't trembling.

Click-click.

In front of me is a rise of land, and I catch a glow of light reflecting off the leaves of an oak tree.

I try to swallow.

No joy.

Thor rustles some.

But he isn't trembling.

Click-click.

I get up and move to the right of the glow of light, and work my way through a low collection of ferns and brush, and the clicking sound gets louder.

What the hell?

The light is coming from a small campfire, and sitting around the blaze are two men. Large canvas bags are nearby, and the man nearest the fire has two pieces of metal in his hands. Every now and then, he strikes one piece with another, making the *click-click* sound.

I shake my head. Idiots.

Easy enough to go around them but I can't do that. Can't have these morons at my rear, screwing things up, doing God knows what.

I clear my throat, call out. "Hello the camp! National Guard, coming in!"

The two men whirl and stand up. I pull my goggles up, letting my eyes adjust to the campfire. I sling my Colt M-10 over my shoulder. They seem to be in their 30s, or maybe in their 50s. Hard to tell in the light, especially since most civilian men, it's hard to guess their age. Going from the twenty-first century to the nineteenth century in the space of a weekend ten years ago can do that to a fellow. Wearing torn, dirty jackets and pants. Old sneakers that look like they're rotting on their feet. Bearded faces and suspicious eyes. Civilian model shotguns up against a fallen tree trunk, within easy grasping range.

"Name's Knox," I say. "With the National Guard. On official duty. What's up, guys?"

The guy on the left with red beard looks to the guy at the right, whose facial hair is black. "We're huntin'," black beard says. "Same as you."

"How's that?"

Red beard holds out the metal pieces. "We know a Creeper was out here the other night. We plan to call 'em over."

I try not to laugh. "And do . . . what? Ask him for a ride?"

Black beard spits into the campfire. "Nope. Gonna capture him." He kicks at the canvas bags. "Got some heavy duty chains here, two fire extinguishers, wool blankets and water. We figure, we get him close, we can keep his weapon claw cold with the extinguishers, wrap 'em in wet blankets, long enough to chain 'em up and keep 'em from moving."

I say, "Why in God's name would you want to try that?"

Black beard says, "Word we heard, the Gates Foundation people, they're lookin' to pay out ten-thousand New Dollars to anyone who can capture a Creeper live. We're lookin' to do that."

"Guys, the Gates Foundation has been offering that reward for about nine years. You know how many civilians have won it? Zip. Zero. None."

Red beard is defiant. "Don't care. We're gonna try. You can't stop us."

"Negative on that, guys," I say. "Since yesterday's Creeper attack this whole county has been declared a military reservation. You don't have authority or permission to be here. So get the hell out and leave it to the Army."

Black beard laughs, spits in the fire. "Leave it to you, a damn kid, hunh?"

It shouldn't, but the insult burns at me; one I've heard many times before, and which still ticks me off. "No, leave it to the Army. Final warning. Put the fire out, get the hell on your way. Otherwise, you're interfering in my mission and I'll be authorized to—"

"The hell with your mission," the red beard says defiantly.

"Insulting my mission won't work," I say. "Look, guys, I'm also trying to save your lives. So how about some consideration?"

Black beard says, "Tell you what, you get the hell goin'. Okay? Woods are big enough for all of us, hunh? You do your thing, we'll do our thing."

I sigh for their benefit, pull out my 9 mm Beretta, cock the hammer. Red beard laughs. "The hell you going to do, pop us?"

"That's right," I say, and I shoot his friend in the leg.

The sound of the report is sudden and loud, followed by black beard crumpling and red beard yelling. I step closer and aim the pistol at one head, and then another, and then back again. "I'm now ordering you to leave this military reservation immediately. Or under the current Martial Law Declaration, I'm authorized to use deadly force against you both."

The guy I shot is rolling side-to-side, hands on his right thigh, moaning, blood seeping through his clenched fingers. His friend red beard is standing still, hands empty. He looks over to the shotguns, looks to me. Thor growls. I guess he's on a steep learning curve, because the guy doesn't move.

I say, "Are we through here, fellas?"

Red beard says, "Yeah, we're through here."

"Outstanding."

Keeping my Beretta trained on him, I reach to the side of MOLLE vest, tug open a quick-release, package dropping it into my hand. I toss it over to the two men. "First aid kit. Get your buddy bandaged up and get the hell out. Do you understand?"

"Yeah."

"Then let's make it more specific. Get the hell out, and if you hesitate, you go for those shotguns, you make any trouble for me at all, I drop you both here. Then I'll complete my mission. Then I'll tell my superior officer where to retrieve your bodies, if it doesn't slip my mind."

The guy with the black beard groans. His friend reaches down, picks up the first aid kit. "Give me a couple of minutes to dress him before I kill the fire?"

I step back, Thor at my side. "I'm a pretty level guy," I say. "Sounds fair to me."

As he works on his friend, I quickly secure both shotguns, unload them both, and toss the shells into the darkness. With Thor I back away and go back in the woods, and looking back a couple of minutes later, the glow from the fire disappears.

Glad to run into a couple of reasonable civilians for a change.

Another hour of going humping through the brush, pausing and waiting, listening and watching.

Nothing. Nothing at all.

Thor stays by me, though sometimes he runs ahead or to the side, sniffling and poking about. The woods thin out some and it looks like we're coming to a stretch of pasture. Open ground. Dangerous, but I'll just poke around a bit.

The woods are gone now, with a stone wall ahead of me. I climb over it and Thor covers it with one easy jump, and it's a field all right, a field of hay. I look around and don't see anything out of the ordinary.

Nothing.

Then I look up at the night sky.

It looks to be on fire.

I take a break, sitting back at the treeline, my back up against a big boulder, taking a healthy sip of cool water. Overhead the night sky is a mess of moving dots of light, and an occasional stream of sparks as something burns through the atmosphere. Time was the night sky was supposedly a peaceful place to look at the stars and planets and moon, and think sweet thoughts about the gentle universe and man's place within it.

For the past ten years, though, it's been a battleground, and normal people hate looking up at the night sky, since looking up there every night tells them the truth, that we are at war, and were losing.

I was only six when the Creepers arrived. From what I've later learned, their arrival was mostly ignored because of other, supposedly more important things that were in the news. Like a mom in the United States accused of murdering her teen daughter, a political scandal in Europe involving underage prostitutes, and a war bubbling in the Middle East between Israel and almost everyone else. The stories of scientists being puzzled by approaching objects that looked like comets but didn't seem to act like comets were put on the back pages, until it was too late.

Looking up, what I see are the result of the Creepers arriving in orbit, when they destroyed every satellite up there, including the International Space Station, whose resident six astronauts (or cosmonauts, I can't remember) were the first casualties of the war. So debris is scattered all around low earth orbit, and that debris field was greatly expanded last month when the Creeper orbital base was blown up by that surprise, last-ditch U.S. Air Force raid.

More debris burns its way down to the ground, leaving a billowing trail of sparks.

Then, off to the far south, something that's definitely not a piece of space garbage. A quick pulsing flash, then a straight line hammers down to the Earth's surface, like a glowing white string stretching up to space. I wait, wondering if I'm going to hear the sound of the impact, but I guess I'm too far away, since I don't hear a thing. But I know what I've seen: one of the Creepers' killer stealth sats, still at work up there in orbit. Even with the Creepers' orbital base gone, the killer stealth sats are still at work, either on automatic or being manned by a Creeper or two, we don't know.

The target? A military unit. A convoy. A city. Somebody foolish enough to take an airplane up in the air.

Who knows. Whatever it was, it's now charred.

But hey, remember, the war is over.

The wind shifts. I catch a scent of something.
I wait.
Sniff again.
Cinnamon.
Creeper sign.
Beside me, Thor whimpers and leans against me.
"Yeah, I smell it too, bud," I say. "Let's roll."
I get off the stone wall and fade into the woods, Thor panting hard at my side. I go in, wait, stand near a birch tree. With the goggles on, I see ghostly shadows of trees, boulders and brush. The scent of cinnamon disappears, then comes back again.

I scratch the back of Thor's head, lean down to him. "Go, boy, hunt!"

He springs out like a rubber band being shot from my finger, and he disappears into the trees. He's a big dog but he knows how to move silently through the woods. I move as well, not going in a straight line, backing up, trying to be unpredictable.

Creepers seem to like predictability, and I'm not going to give this one any advantage.

I move deeper into the woods, the scent of cinnamon even stronger. I lift up my M-10. I know my predecessors, back in the days when they were hunting and killing fellow humans, carried loads of ammo and would often "rock and roll," meaning they could fire their weapons at full automatic, emptying a magazine of thirty or so rounds in a matter of seconds. I don't have that luxury. The other members of my platoon don't have that luxury. And the U.S. Army and associated National Guard units and the Marines don't have that luxury.

What we do have is a single-shot, bolt-action Colt M-10 50 mm rifle, and as I go into the woods, the smell of cinnamon strong in my nostrils, I give up another prayer to one Cynthia Ellis-Kimball of Colt Firearms, once upon a time housed in Hartford, Connecticut. One of the few men and women who thought ten steps ahead when the war began, she was a senior engineer at Colt and managed to disassemble and evacuate lots of vital machinery and tools from their plants before Hartford was slammed.

Thanks to her foresight, me and several thousand others have the only reliable weapon to fight against the Creepers.

Which is currently unloaded.

The land descends into a swampy stretch, and I still move about in random directions, pausing, waiting, and then—

A barking dog.

Off to my right.

"Good boy, Thor," I whisper. "Good job."

I shift my direction, slip out of the swamp, and in a low crouch, jog on up to drier land.

A few minutes later, a light flickers in the distance, and something heavy in my chest goes *thump-lump*. Real close now. The smell of cinnamon is quite strong. Another bark from Thor, telling me where to go. My lips stick together and I try to moisten them with my dry tongue, and it doesn't work.

I work around a stand of trees, see the flickering light grow stronger.

Now.

I quietly drop my assault pack, leaving only my gear harness and bandolier. I get on the ground, start moving among the leaves and branches, taking my time.

Click-click.

Click-click.

Click-click.

The sounds of the Creeper exoskeleton at work, whatever the hell its work happens to be.

I keep crawling low to the ground. Moving a few inches here and there. Another bark from Thor, but he's a smart puppy. He knows his job, just like I know mine. I move up some more. The light grows stronger, as does the smell of cinnamon, now really a stench, and the sound of the exoskeleton.

I pause.

Real close now.

There's good cover where I am, some low brush and ferns.

I slowly raise up my head sideways to keep a low profile.

Look down.

Look down upon Hell.

CHAPTER FOUR

I fight against the urge to pull away, to race back to my assault pack and run all the way back to the dairy farm. This isn't my first Creeper sighting but by God, each one is different and terrifying in its own way.

You'd think you'd get used to after a few years, but you'd be wrong.

I take a deep breath, let it out, take another deep breath, let it out.

My hands tight against the Colt M-10, hoping they don't shake.

The Creeper is below and to the right of me, maybe fifty or so meters away.

It looks . . .

Looks like a . . .

Well, looks like a damn nightmare, it does.

Start by thinking small.

Think of one of those black scorpions that live in the Southwest. Eight legs, long tail with a barb at the end, two claws and tiny head. Remove the long tail, put it where the head belongs. That's the new head, a segmented length almost as large as the body itself. The center arthropod. Reduce the size of the claws. The claws are now tool-based. Sometimes they are pincers. Sometimes they are weapons. No matter what they are, though, they're always dangerous. Instead of a living exoskeleton, the Creeper's exoskeleton is made of a blue-gray metal alloy, said alloy still being studied and analyzed ten years after the war began, any weaknesses still undiscovered.

Inside the exoskeleton is the living creature that's a Creeper, which looks about the same as the exoskeleton, except uglier, if that's possible.

Its flesh is a purplish-gray, it's segmented like a real scorpion, and the braincase and eyestalks are the stuff of nightmares.

Oh. By the way, the exoskeleton is essentially bulletproof, flameproof, and resistant to almost every type of explosive save nuclear.

Got it?

Now take the image of a scorpion, maybe the size of a child's hand, and expand it up to the size of a small school bus.

That's a Creeper.

Close enough to nearly spit at.

This one is busy at its hellish work. Around it are the remains of a cabin, up against a wide stream. Strange but true, Creepers have a fixation with moving water. Don't know why, just is. It has one weapon claw, up in the air, moving about, constantly scanning 360-degrees and evaluating. The center arthropod moves side to side. The other claw is a manipulator, and it's moving bits of lumber and shingles from the cabin it's trampled. This Creeper looks like the Research model. Around the perimeter of the cabin, two pine trees burn merrily along. Off crumpled past the debris are the bodies of a man and a woman. Their clothes have been stripped off, and it looks like the Creeper's done a quick vivisection. My jaw tightens right up. Another reason for the 9 mm at my side is to make sure I don't get captured. Lots of rumors and stories of civilians and military personnel being captured by the Creepers over the years; not one tale of anyone escaping.

Click-click.

Click-click.

Click-click.

I remember a joke from Wolwoski, one of the guys in my squad. "Insect bastards come all this way across interstellar space and they don't have good lubricants? Is that it? Cripes, maybe we could have avoided all of this crap if we had offered them a WD-40 trade deal or something."

I look at the torn bodies of the man and woman again. Hah-hah.

I watch the Creeper, feeling everything else slip away except for me and for it, getting into the zone. And I shake my head in frustration.

I don't have a good shot.

The only weakness Creepers have is a section of the center arthropod, where there's a metallic membrane of some sort that helps them process the Earth's atmosphere and breathe. But the way the Creeper is facing, rooting around in the rubble of the cottage, I can't see it.

I inch backward down the slight slope of land, evaluate my options. My flare gun is digging at my side. Think about taking it out, inserting a yellow cartridge, finding an open spot to shoot it up into the busy night sky. Yellow flare, meaning Creeper in sight. Abby would spot my signal out on the dirt road, would ride furiously to a local telegraph station, signaling for other units to arrive here, set up a perimeter. If I was lucky, the first guys on scene would be other members of my Recon Ranger platoon. They'd fan out as trained and set up an overlapping field of fire.

But that would take time.

Lots of time.

Hissing and clicking sounds from over on the other side of the slope.

One other thing. Hard experience over the years had shown that a one-on-one fight has the best chance of success against a Creeper. For some reason, Creepers either know or sense when there is more than one armed human out there. Lots of squads, platoons and companies of brave soldiers and Marines had died to learn this very important lesson.

A bark.

And they usually ignored dogs.

I climb back up, eyeball the Creeper. About fifty meters away, it's still doing its alien work. If I move to the right, and if it stayed in roughly the same position, and if I'm not detected, I could get a good shot off.

Lots of ifs. Not many choices.

I ease myself down the slope, touch the front of my vest, where my rosary and picture of my family are hidden away.

Take a deep breath, and another.

Finally put my hand to my bandolier, I take out a 50 mm round for my Colt M-10. In the faint light from my goggles, I easily grab the base. It's set on safe. I twist it once to the right. It clicks into place. The round is now set for ten meters. There are two other settings, twenty-five meters and fifty meters. I slide the bolt open, insert the round, close the bolt.

"Rock and roll time, baby," I whisper, getting up.

I move to the right, taking my time, moving through a stand of saplings. Another bark from Thor in the distance. Keeping an eye on the Creeper for me. The ground opens up; I slowly slosh through some mud. Gauge in my mind's eye how far I've gone. Look up to the sky. More chunks of debris, burning into the atmosphere, lighting up this stretch of forest with ghostly shadows.

I clamber up the slope, steeper now, my breathing getting harder, the Colt M-10 firm in my hands. Ten or so meters, I guess. That's how the rounds were designed to work. A lot of research, a lot of experimentation, and a lot of dead soldiers led to this round in my Colt. It's a binary chemical weapon, two types of chemicals contained in one cartridge. When fired, it flies to the pre-selected distance and explodes, the two chemicals blending into one. A cloud envelops the Creeper right around the center arthropod, where the breathing membrane is, and if you had a good shot, and there wasn't much of a breeze, then you end up with one dead Creeper and one relieved, sweaty soldier.

What kind of chemicals? Damned if I know; one of the many things that are on a "need to know" basis, and I didn't have a need to know. Didn't care either; so long as it worked, the chemicals could be salt and sugar. Not technically correct of course, but so what.

Up the slope, getting closer, passing by some rotting wooden fence posts, ground getting steeper, the protective vest tight tight, tight, around my chest, my legs heavy, my arms heavy, the family photo and blessed rosary safe inside and just a few feet more and—

I fall flat on my face.

I can't move. My MOLLE vest and all its pouches, loops, and hooks has caught on old bailing wire that was wrapped around the fence posts. The more I pull forward, the more the wire pulls back—and the more I risk the fence posts springing free, snapping back and giving away my position.

Damn it to hell!

I stop, breathe, then slowly start to pull the wire off each individual snag on my vest and gear, focusing on quietly pulling the wire off, and then holding it so that it slides gently back into place without springing violently—and obviously—back.

A piece of wire snaps back, catching me in the face, surprising me so that I slide back some, my M-10 falling free, and I—.

Roll over. Look up.

Creeper standing right over me.

CHAPTER FIVE

I freeze.

Stay frozen.

Don't move, don't blink, don't breathe. Pretend to be a stone.

The main arthropod is right overhead. The two claws are in motion, rotating, like separate dog heads, sniffing and sniffing for their prey. The faint whir of machinery working inside the Creeper.

I'm a dead man. That's all she wrote.

I have a sudden urge to piss my pants.

Instead I roll, scramble, roll and grab the barrel of my Colt. I keep my head down and instead of running down the slope, I run uphill, whispering "oh God, oh God, oh God" as I push myself underneath the Creeper.

No other choice.

Going the other way means I'll be scorched flesh in a manner of seconds. This way, at least, I have a chance, as small as it is.

I bend over low, run run run, my Kevlar helmet scraping a couple of times on the Creeper's underside, the Colt M-10 in my hands, and I'm out on the other side, breathing through my mouth so I don't pass out from the cinnamon stench.

Just when I think I'm going to make it, I'm slammed in my back and go airborne.

I hit hard on the opposite slope, dirt in my mouth and eyes, left ankle hurting like hell, and I tumble, roll, and fall, landing on my back, the chin strap from my helmet digging so hard into my throat it chokes me.

The clicking noise is louder, accompanied by a harsh buzzing. I sit up, pushing myself with my left hand, seeing the Creeper flick around, knowing one of its rear legs had kicked out and caught me. The two claws are up rotating and a bright flash and hissing sound bursts out from the weapon claw, as a wide-beamed flame zips over head, catching the top of the wrecked cottage and a nearby birch tree, sparks and flames boiling over.

Can't find my Colt.

Can't find my Colt.

I race back as the Creeper is now facing me and damn it, I'm almost close enough for a good firing solution, but I can't find my Colt.

The Creeper crawls down the slope—I pull out my Beretta, useless, but better than sitting and waiting to get scorched. I bring up my pistol and there's a flash of fur and barking, and damn me, it's Thor!

The lunatic dog knows from his training he's not supposed to get close to a Creeper, but he's running right among the Creeper's metal legs, barking and snapping. As the two claws and main arthropod lower, I holster my Beretta, get up and run, then trip and fall, and I see I've fallen over my Colt.

Weapon in cold, shaking hands.

Looking back, gauging the distance.

Not quite there.

Damn!

I trot some more, get behind the wreckage of the destroyed house, more flames erupt overhead, heat baking my back and neck, and the barking stops, and I turn, drop to one knee.

Still not there! The damn alien is low to the ground, and—

Thor races through, the brave little bastard, dodging around the Creeper's legs, and it moves and rises up and the M-10 feels invincible in my hands.

Bring it up and through the iron sights, see the Creeper standing still, rotating its two claws in my direction. I look right up and pull the trigger.

BLAM!

I'm used to the recoil but the punch in my shoulder still makes me gasp, and before I can breathe again, there's a smaller ***POP!*** and a gray-white cloud appears in front of the Creeper, drifts right up against the main arthropod. Training kicks in and I snap the bolt back, ejecting the spent shell, grab another 50 mm round from my bandolier, and the Creeper is still moving.

Still moving right at me.

I push the side of the round against my leg, rotate the base so I can get that first setting, and put the round in and—

Miss the open chamber.

Round drops to the ground.

I stare up and look and feel for the round with my free hand and—

The Creeper stops moving.

The claws shake, tremble, and then sag.

The main arthropod vibrates as well.

I take a deep, satisfying breath, get up, legs woozy.

One of its six legs starts shaking and shaking, like the machinery and electronics inside of the exoskeleton has gone crazy. Something I've seen before and which always fills me with a sharp and fierce feeling of joy. I lower my Colt, kneel down and retrieve the fallen round. Other legs of the Creeper are now shaking, trembling, and the whole main structure is swaying back and forth, then forward and back, and then side-to-side again.

A high-pitched whining noise pops out of the Creeper and then it drops forward, into the dirt and slope, and slides towards me a few yards. A few more quivers of the legs and that's it.

The exoskeleton is still. The Creeper inside is dead.

There's a brief, hard stink of burnt cinnamon. A passing breeze thins it out. Flames and sparks continue to flicker and fly from the burning trees and debris from the destroyed home. I put the dropped round back into my bandolier, stroll up to the dead Creeper. From the light of the burning fires I make out the exoskeleton pretty well, seeing marks and discolorations along the joints and legs that means this one is fairly old, which improves my mood even more. Nice to know I've snuffed out one of their vets. From the mid-section of the main arthropod, some green and brown goo is oozing out. That's the section where the breathing membrane is located.

I whisper, "Nice shooting, Tex," and step closer. Above and below the breathing membrane are articulated joints for the main arthropod. Another Creeper weakness, but one desperately hard to exploit. There's a gap between the joints where a careful, disciplined and very, very skilled sniper could send in a depleted uranium round and kill a Creeper. During the frantic early years of the war, sometimes those snipers were the only ones bringing the war home to the invaders, and I don't think a single one of them has ever bought a drink or meal for him or herself since then.

I met a sniper like that two years back, at the Battle of the Merrimack Valley, where a number of Creepers were moving from a base in Connecticut and where I earned my first Purple Heart. The sniper was a heavy-set guy named Woods with a beard down his chest and wearing blue jeans and a dirty fatigue jacket. He was clearly out of uniform, but no one bothered him. His spotter was his plump wife, who quietly told him range and windage with the aid of a spotting scope and her experience. In the space of an afternoon, he had nailed four of the Creepers. Each time he sent a round downrange, he and his wife would pick up and race to another hiding spot, just in case a Creeper or one of the killer stealth sats was tracking him. All he said to us admirers as he packed up his Model 300 Remington long rifle when the day was done was, "Well, we sure did God's work today, fellas, didn't we."

I walk over to the burning wreckage of the home, shake my head. Looks like a nice little place. Near a stream bank for fishing and fresh water. Lots of ice in the winter to store and trade with some of the farms and local stores. Maybe a field nearby for some crops in the spring. A quiet, peaceful place to hang out and survive.

I call out. "Thor! Come, boy."

The man and woman have been tossed to one side, like broken dolls being thrown away. Their clothes have been stripped away except for their footwear and it looks like the Creeper had performed some type of rudimentary autopsy, using a narrow laser beam from one of its claws. Blood and organs are still oozing out. Hard to tell their exact age, maybe 40's or 50's. In the faint light I can make out wedding rings on their dead-white fingers. I squat down, wipe at my forehead, look at two of my dead fellow Americans.

"Sorry I didn't get here in time," I say. "Honest to God."

I stand up, move back to the dying flames from the shattered house. When I get back to base, I'd report the bodies to Graves Registration, who'll either take care of it themselves or deputize a sheriff's deputy or local cop to do it. At the dead Creeper, more ooze is coming out of the membrane area. Always happens. When a Creeper is killed, there's nothing for its Graves Registration to pick up. The body immediately disintegrates into a soft liquid within seconds of death. Must be hell for morticians back on their home world.

But it also makes it difficult for the white coats on this world to figure out who the hell the Creepers are, why they're here, and how best to hurt them and kill them. Again, "need to know" and Operational Security and all that, but it's easy to figure out that the binary Colt M-10 round I just used to kill this Creeper was developed because extraordinary brave men and women had actually captured some of them alive.

Don't know how they did it. Just glad they did.

It looks like the fires are going to die out on their own. Good. Stories we hear every now and then tell about Creepers raising hell out in the west during drought season, causing huge forest fires. Hell of a thing for those states out there, having to fight both fires and Creepers.

I go up to the dead Creeper. The oozing has slowed down. The cinnamon smell is almost gone. An Intelligence Recovery team would eventually come here and drag it out of the woods, to be probably studied at one of the exiled Harvard or MIT campuses.

I rear back and kick the nearest jointed claw. "Sucks to be you, hunh?"

When I had killed my first few Creepers, I had made it a point to do a victory dance around the dead exoskeleton, calling out the names of my mom and sister, kicking and kicking, sometimes pissing over the cold metal. All that's past now. It's just good enough that I'm alive and it's dead.

Which is fine by me.

I sit down on the nearest, outstretched leg of the dead Creeper, and—

Something grabs my foot.

I scream.

Tug away and start laughing.

"Damn it, Thor!" I say. "Damn crazy dog, I could have taken your head off."

I rub his head. He moves his head against my hand, licks my palm.

Pure joy and love.

From somewhere out there, the tears just roll out. I can't help it. Always happens after a mission. I kneel on the dirt ground, this battleground, and I hug Thor tight, my face buried in his fur, the scent and the feel of the fur so comforting. I sob and sob, my face wet with tears, and smell the fur of my boy, and for a while, I try to think of nothing, nothing at all.

Can't help it.

Some time passes. I let Thor go and wipe at my eyes and face, and find an open space past the dead Creeper. I take out my flare pistol, break open the action, insert a red cartridge, close it up tight and fire it up into the sky, which is graying out as dawn approaches. The flare shoots right up into the air, telling Abby and everybody else in my Recon Ranger squad that we have a dead Creeper and a live trooper.

Nice equation.

CHAPTER SIX

Back in the old Army transport truck once again, except this time, Thor and I are riding up front with Lieutenant May and his driver Schwartz, our reward for having killed the Creeper. Behind us in the truck is the rest of my Recon Ranger squad, and after a successful kill mission like this, there's usually laughing and singing from the rear.

But not during this gray dawn. We're down one trooper. PFC Raymond Ruiz didn't return to muster and neither did his dog. Not sure what happened. Desertion, possible but doubtful. Not from Recon Ranger. Maybe another Creeper attack but Creepers are hard to overlook, so the thought is that a Coastie gang might have nailed him somewhere in the woods. Later today there'll be a search party, and we'll join in after some rest, but we're a subdued crew as we head back to Concord.

Schwartz—who boasts he could convert an old washing machine into a hot tub—drives expertly along this stretch of Route 112, juggling valves and switches to keep the engine running, his black-rimmed glasses with one cracked lens constantly sliding down his nose. Here dead cars from a decade ago have been successfully pushed or dragged over to the sides of the road. We then get onto Interstate 89, and there's even more abandoned vehicles, and we have to do a bit of maneuvering as we approach the state capitol, passing in and out of the lines of dead traffic. Each car or truck has a faded slop of white paint on the windshield, the letter C. Means that after the Creepers deployed their airborne nukes on 10/10 and fried the world's electronics, search teams went through these cars and either led away the living, or pulled out the dead. C stood for Cleared back then.

At one point we pass a chain gang from the state prison, the prisoners in faded orange jumpsuits working on a line of cars, pulling them off to the side of the pavement, using a team of State Highway Department horses with block and tackle, clearing the highway.

Grass and small brush are growing knee-high in cracks in the pavement.

Some clearing.

Some progress.

As we get closer to Concord, I keep a hand on Thor, who's been sniffing and clawing at my assault pack ever since we left the farmhouse over in Montcalm. Thing is, when I emerged from the woods a few hours ago, Gary Parker, the grateful dairy farmer who once lived and worked in a now-dead city, passed over a brown paper package, tied tight with string. "Here you go, soldier," he had said. "A couple of fine steaks for you and your pals. Doubt the County Rationing Board will miss 'em, if you know what I mean."

"Just doing my job," I had said.

He had pressed the steaks in my hand. "You gave my little girl the sweetest treat she's had in months. Didn't have to do it, but you did. So call it a trade, okay?"

So I had said okay, and now I was doing my best to keep Thor from having a huge breakfast in the truck's cab.

Schwartz takes the Clinton Street exit off the Interstate, and after navigating through some side streets, comes to the main gate of Fort St. Paul, formerly known as St. Paul's School, a prep school that's been here since 1856, and which has been a National Guard base for ten of those years. As Schwartz downshifts and slows, we approach a group of protesters outside of the gate. The signs are handmade with paint on wood or large pieces of plastic.

END THIS ENDLESS WAR

ACCOMMODATION, NOT CONFRONTATION

PEACE NOW

END MARTIAL LAW

And a smaller one, at the end of the protest line, its plaintive words being held by an elderly man, in gray slacks and a long tan coat, light blue cap on his head:

GIVE US OUR SCHOOL BACK

Around the grounds of the school deep moats have been dug, one of the few things known to slow down Creepers on the move. Unlike forts in the past, there are no guard towers looking out. Too easy for Creepers or their killer stealth satellites to burn. But there are battlements, there are OPs—Observation Posts—out among the 2,000 acres of the school grounds, and there's lots of net camouflage to cover walkways and pieces of equipment.

The truck slows down and the gate opens up, and the protesters look at us going in, tired and a bit dirty, and it's like they don't have much energy left to protest us.

I crossly say, "Didn't they get the word the war's over?"

Schwartz says a spectacularly foul obscenity and the lieutenant just grunts. "Maybe they don't know what to do if the war really is over."

The truck grumbles onto the grounds of the base, and the gate closes behind us. I still hold onto Thor's collar. "Really over, sir?"

We round a corner. Troops are on the march, doing P.E., and there are horse-drawn wagons hauling gear off to the different buildings, and other personnel on bicycles. In the distance there's a skateboard park and some guys and gals off-duty look like they're having fun, skating up, down and around. Once upon a time the brick buildings here were dormitories, classrooms and administration buildings. Now they are barracks, training centers, and whaddya know, administration buildings.

My boss says, "Just because the orbital station got whacked doesn't mean there's not a lot of fighting left ahead. Last night was just an example, Randy. How many more Creepers are out there in their bases? Or roaming in the wilds of Africa or Siberia or Canada?"

I keep my mouth shut. I'm too tired to think of much of anything, and seeing those protesters pissed me off. I know, I know, First Amendment and right of protest, but last night, when I was that close to getting my head burned off by a Creeper for the benefit of those protesters back there, guaranteed they were sleeping warm and safe, pretty confident they'd wake up in one piece the next morning.

Lieutenant May's mood seems to brighten. "But hey, maybe the President is right. Maybe the war is over. You're still a teenager, Randy. Any idea of what you'll do once you get out of the Guard?"

Thor whines some, as he keeps frantically sniffing at my assault pack.

"Haven't thought that far, sir," I say. "Pretty much all I know is killing Creepers."

Lieutenant says, "Lucky for us."

We get off at the disbursement area before Schwartz takes the truck back to the motor pool. Standing loosely in a group is a tired and worn five-member Recon Ranger squad, weapons slung over our shoulders, dogs on leashes, except for Thor, and Abby standing by herself, yawning, holding her Trek bicycle. Nobody says anything, but we're all painfully aware that one of us is missing, Ruiz, the new guy.

The lieutenant stands before of us. "We did well, Rangers. We got a Creeper report, responded in less than a day, and ended up with one Creeper dead. Good job, team."

I try not to yawn. Earlier on, when I was younger and dumber, I would have been upset that I wasn't being singled out for killing the Creeper. Now it doesn't matter. The lieutenant is right. We were a team last night, and when my flare soared up, they came in my direction, to help me out, provide support, have my back. Any one of us could have been in the barbecue seat last night; it just happened to be my turn.

The lieutenant goes on. "Get your M-10s back to the armory, go to the S-2 shop for debrief, take a rest, and report back to me at 1600 hours. Then we'll saddle up and join the search for Ruiz. Any questions?"

Not a word.

"Make it happen, Rangers. Good job."

I walk over to Abby and she smiles, though she looks as tired as I feel, and we fist bump one more time. I say, "I survived. No crispy critter for you."

Her smile gets wider. "So you did. And I keep my promise. First dance tomorrow night, soldier."

I glance to see if anyone's looking, since what I'm about to do is terribly out of order, but I don't care and kiss her cheek. She giggles and says, "Later," as she wheels her Trek away down one of the paved school paths.

The rest of us disperse and straggle over to the Armory, which used to be a student assembly building. At a long metal counter, one by one, we turn in our M-10s and bandoliers. The armorer, a balding old master sergeant named Thornton with gray hair in his ears, takes my belt and winks. "Nicely done, pal. One missing cartridge, one dead alien. Fair damn trade, eh?"

By now I'm so tired all I can do is murmur, "Yeah, that's it," and then I go out, brushing by other members of my squad—Smith, Millett, Chang and Zane—and Zane catches my elbow as I go through the swinging doors.

"Not following regs, Sergeant, are we? Leaving your dog unleashed?"

During a base tour a couple of years ago, one of our hunting dogs bit the previous governor of New Hampshire, a pompous jerk who deserved it, but as a result all dogs on base need to be leashed. But not Thor. Not ever.

"He's well trained," I say. "Some would say better trained than you, pal."

Zane's hand is still tight on my elbow. "Speaking of training, Sergeant, why did you let Ruiz go out alone? It was his first op. You should have buddied him up."

I pull my arm away from his grasp. "Woulda, coulda, shoulda. The C.O. signed off on his training and experience, and so did I. Got a problem, take it up with him."

He grabs my elbow again. "He looked tough, but he was just a scared kid, Sergeant. Just a kid."

I pull away. "Just like us, Zane. Just like us. You grab my elbow again, you'll be losing it. Do I make myself clear, Private?"

He storms into the armory and I walk out, Thor with me, feeling sour and even more tired.

My next stop should be south, towards the Intel shop.

I go west instead, to the post housing.

The housing once belonged to the teachers and administrators of the school before the war, and now it belongs to the base's senior officers. In the confusing and horrifying first months after 10/10, surviving military units all across the country set up alternate posts after the Creepers had flattened their home bases.

In Concord, the state capitol, the National Guard units withdrew from their main armory and eventually ended up at St. Paul's, where most students and faculty had already fled to whatever safety was supposedly out there. Only a couple of armories across the state were eventually hit, but there's still no rush to get back to the surviving armories. Even with the orbiting Creeper battle station destroyed, the killer stealth sats are still at work—probably, hopefully—on automatic.

As I walk along the paths to the housing, I think of what it must have been like to be here back before the war. To have been one of those privileged and safe students in this wonderful school in rural New Hampshire, where all sorts of classes were taught, from medieval art history to philosophy to the history of Greek plays.

Now survival and the bloody art of war have been added to the curriculum.

I yawn. I'm too tired to feel jealous of my coddled predecessors.

At a small white Colonial house among a row of similar houses, I pound on the front door, using a brass knocker. The paint is peeling and shrubbery about the front and side are overgrown. Grass is growing in cracks on the driveway.

A girl about eight years old answers and looks up at me. She has on a white T-shirt and clean jean overalls. Her black hair is freshly washed and she seems suspicious. "You looking for mom, Randy?"

"I sure am, squirt."

She turns and yells, "Ma! Cousin Randy is here!"

I wince from the loud yell. Heidi has the lungs of a drill sergeant, and she turns and says, "Can I play with Thor?"

"Not right now, hon," I say. "He's tired and so am I."

"Later, maybe?"

I rub the top of her head. "Later, no problem."

My Aunt Corinne shows up, smiling hesitantly, wiping her hands on a towel. She's wearing black slacks and plain gray sweatshirt, and her eyes look tired.

"Randy, good to see you."

I squat down, unzip the side pocket of my assault pack, pull out the wrapped paper package from the dairy farmer. "Here you go. A treat for you guys, if you haven't planned your meal tonight. Fresh steak."

Thor wags his tail and barks, and I scratch his ears, and gently hold him back as he sniffs at the wrapped meat. Corinne gently takes the package. "Randy . . . that's so generous. Would you like to stay for dinner?"

I shake my head, start to turn. "Sorry, Aunt Corinne. Gotta run."

She calls out as I walk up the uneven flagstone path. "You're always welcome to move in and stay with us, Randy! Always!"

As if, I think, as I get back to the war.

In one of the brick classroom buildings, the S-2 shop—the intelligence section for our battalion—is in a couple of rooms on the first floor. I have two debriefers, one an old-timer named Fernandez and the other a new guy named Knowles, both captains.

I sit in front of a wooden desk that no doubt once belonged to a teacher, the two of them sitting across from me. Thor flops himself down on the dirty tile floor, panting, looking around. The officers are using paper and pencil as old-style manual typewriters are being pounded in one corner of the room by some enlisted men. There are plenty of filing cabinets and wall-maps depicting Creeper sightings and killings in New England, and photographs of the nearest Creeper bases: three outside of the suburbs of Boston, one in the western part of Massachusetts near Springfield, one in northern Connecticut and two along the coast of Maine.

None in New Hampshire, though trust me, we've never complained about being overlooked.

There are also large blown-up photos of the three types of Creeper exoskeletons, and one photo, marked Top Secret, that shows a living Creeper, pulled out of a disabled exoskeleton, deep in snow somewhere.

I look away from that horror and Fernandez says, "Care to describe your engagement last night?"

"Not a problem, sir," I say, and spend the next fifteen or so minutes recalling the hunt and the battle, and Knowles raises a hand and interrupts. "Hold on. You say you shot a civilian?"

"I did."

"Was he threatening you?"

I say, "He was threatening the mission."

"But was he threatening you personally, Sergeant?"

Fernandez's face is impassive. Knowles looks angry. I reply. "Sir, he was threatening the mission. When the Creeper was sighted, the county automatically became a military reservation. I had the authority to get him to leave the area. He refused to leave."

"So you shot him," Knowles says.

"I wounded him. In the leg. He and his friend, not only were they jeopardizing the mission, they were jeopardizing me and the other civilians in the area. They were trying to attract a Creeper's attention and planned to capture it by using some chains and a fire extinguisher. They refused to move. I did what I had to do."

"By wounding a civilian," Knowles says.

"By saving him," I reply. "If they had attracted a Creeper, in about ten seconds, they both would have been flamed."

Knowles angrily writes something down and Fernandez quietly speaks up. "Let's move on."

So knowing my face is flushed, I go on and tell them about the hunt, and the kill, but seeing how Knowles is being a dick about the whole matter, I leave out the part about Thor coming to save my young butt. Dogs are trained never to attack a Creeper, and seeing how Knowles is reacting to my mission, I wouldn't put it past him to take Thor away from me for remedial training or something.

Like I'd allow that to happen.

Asshole.

CHAPTER SEVEN

Finally back in my barracks, which used to be a student dormitory, I get to my room and unlock and roll in, Thor behind me. I'm fortunate to have a single and I close the door, make sure there's water and food for Thor—some dried venison—and I unload my gear, put my 9 mm on my small desk, and even though I'm about ready to fall asleep, I spend the necessary time to make the weapon safe and clean it.

When I'm done cleaning I take my family photo and put it back up on the small bookshelf over my bed, and reach behind a row of books and take out a slim leather journal. There's a Bic pen inside the cover and I jot down some sentences about the day. I close the cover, put it back, and flop down on my bunk, look up at my meager collection of possessions. At one end of the shelf is plastic model of what was once called a cell phone. It was a toy I got eleven or twelve years ago. Dad tells me that when I had the toy cell phone, I'd pretend to call Mom and tell her to come home early and make me mac and cheese.

I remember playing with that toy a lot during the first year or two of the war, hoping against hope that my Mom would somehow hear me and find her way to my Dad and me.

I want to stop thinking about that and I close my eyes and fall asleep in a couple of minutes.

Something furry and wet presses against my face. I push it away, it comes back.

I open my eyes.

Thor is by the side of my bunk, panting, looking on with an expectant look on his face.

"Oh, come on up," I say, and Thor seems to grin as he jumps up on the bunk. He rotates twice and then thumps down, wags his tail, and lies down.

"And don't snore," I warn him, but it's too late, as he starts sawing wood.

I wake up with someone knocking at the door. I yawn and toss off my olive drab wool blanket. Thor rolls over with a doggie sigh and I say, "Some damn hunting dog you are," as I step barefoot across the cool tile floor to the door. I unlock and open it up, and in front of me is the oldest man I know. He's in standard fatigues that hang on him like they're a size too large, and he has almost no hair on his freckled pink scalp. His nametag says MANNING and his rank is corporal. He's the "batman" for the barracks.

"Sergeant Knox," he says, "just checkin' to see if you got any laundry."

"Sure, hold on," I say. I duck back into my room and grab a canvas bag, which Manning takes from me with a wrinkled, shaking hand. Nobody knows how old he is, but I did hear him say once that he had served in Korea, which means he's *old*. Like a lot of other vets, he re-upped after the war started. Once upon a time the U.S. Army and the National Guard didn't have batmen for their troops, but now we supposedly experienced fighters aren't supposed to worry about cleaning, laundry and other necessary chores.

Manning says, "Also wanted to let you know that Lieutenant May has canceled your 1600 meeting."

My stomach feels cold. "Dead?"

He sighs. "Yeah. They found Ruiz a couple of hours ago. Shot to death, body stripped. Hell of a thing. Damn Coasties killed his dog as well. Bastards. But at least the morons had the good sense to leave his M-10 behind. No way they could sell or trade that."

"Any leads?"

Manning shrugs. "Not sure. Word is, the State Police and the county sheriff have joined the hunt, plus some militia types. Figure it out, Sarge. You think the locals want the Army folks defending them getting ambushed and robbed?"

I remember the protestors out at the main gate, and say, "You'd think."

Manning starts to walk down the hallway, dragging my canvas laundry sack along with a few others, and I call out, "Mail call come?"

"Yep."

"And . . ."

He turns, thin lips pursed. "So sorry, Sergeant. Nothing for you."

My throat thickens and I close the door. The silence from my dad continues.

I sleep pretty deep for a good chunk of the day, and when I wake up I get a chit for a hot shower later in the day. I bring Thor back to the kennels and then I work out in the gym, lifting weights, working some reps on my legs, biceps and back. It's a weekend so it's relatively quiet. Then I cash in the chit for a ten-minute hot shower, and then head off to the D-Fac, or dining facility, which is pretty much the same school dining hall. I see Abby chatting it up with Dewey, a plump mess officer with short blond hair who had slipped Abby a rare Red Bull the other day.

I nudge Abby as I get in line with a scratched plastic tray and say, "Still trolling for Red Bull?"

Abby nudges me back. "Keep it real, dear sergeant. Keep it real."

Dinner tonight is some sort of chipped-beef slop over stale toast and watered down iced tea, and my stomach grumbles as I think of those thick juicy steaks I had passed over to my aunt earlier this morning.

With dinner quickly and thankfully over, I go over to the kennels and retrieve Thor. Although the PFC on duty is reluctant to let him go—all dogs on post are supposed to be housed overnight in the K9 quarters—I convince him that I'm taking Thor out for a confidential night training mission, which isn't much of a lie.

On the way back to my barracks, I see two flaming chunks of space debris light up the southern night sky, and then it's to bed and lights out.

I'm dreaming about hearing my mother's voice, as we're on a ferry heading out to Edgartown on Martha's Vineyard, when the ship's siren cuts in and starts screaming and screaming and screaming.

I wake up, Thor across my legs, sheets piled up and I realize it's the base warning siren.

Creeper attack.

I kick the blankets off, roll out of bed, fumble for a second with the matches at my nightstand, and light off a candle. Thor is already by the door, tail moving furiously, waiting to get into action. I dress quickly, but take the time to pack my battle-rattle gear, the rosary, family photo and Creeper toe joint; and buckling on my Beretta, I launch myself out the door, as Corporal Manning races down the hallway dousing the gas lamps.

Outside now, the rest of the troopers from my barracks are following me, buildings around us going dark, the only illumination coming from hooded lamps along the walkways and roads. By the time I get to the Armory its double doors are propped open, and there's little talking as Colt M-10s and bandoliers of 50 mm rounds are tossed to us. To keep some sort of order, we yell out our last names as we pick up the gear, as overworked Armory personnel keep the weapons flow going.

"Ouellette! Magsaysay! Gagnon!"

I grab my weapon with one hand, bandolier with the other, shout out: "Knox!" and then run outside, as Thor races along with me, tail wagging, keeping quiet as I run to my attack duty station. All around me are the sounds of boots slapping on the pavement, and the *click-clack* of M-10s being loaded with the anti-Creeper rounds, as my fellow Rangers prepare for an attack.

This isn't like the other night, when I was on my own, hunting for a Creeper. I'm with two other troopers from my platoon, Corporal Joyce Dunlap and Staff Sergeant Hugh Muller. Dunlap and Muller are dressed like me, with a mix of battle rattle and personal clothing; not much time for uniform. But we're all in helmets and protective vests, even though Dunlap is wearing baggy khaki shorts and Muller is wearing light pink shorts that look tight and damn uncomfortable. I'm the only one with a dog, and Thor settles down in one corner of the battlement.

Muller picks up a field telephone, turns the crank a few times, and whispers, "Battle Twelve, up."

He's a year older than me, outranks me, and seems to take delight in reminding me of this most times we're thrown together. He listens for a moment, nods, and whispers, "Battle Twelve, out."

Then he tosses the phone receiver back into its slot. "Listen up. Two civilians separately called in a Creeper sighting. On approach out of woods adjacent to the interstate, then started moving northwest along Clinton Street."

"On the street?" I ask. "You sure they weren't drinking?"

Dunlap laughs and Muller says, "That's what got reported. So here we are."

I pick up my Colt M-10 and peer sideways over the battlement. Turning your head sideways exposes less of your skull, especially if you just expose one eye for a quick scan, then duck back down.

"Ain't that the truth."

It's a hell of an understatement, but the Army had to adjust day to day to a new type of enemy, and one of the lessons learned was not making defensive bunkers. When your opponents had mortars, AK-47s, RPGs—even T-72 tanks—heavily fortified bunkers made sense. When your opponents were nearly impregnable exoskeletons with laser and flame weapons, heavily fortified bunkers were quickly called barbecue pits, and for good reason.

So the defensive perimeter of Fort St. Paul consists of moats, trenches OPs, and battlements like the one were in, scattered along the rim of the moats. Made of concrete blocks and bricks, it's a good place to hide behind while keeping view of the moat, and the cleared areas of fire on the other side. Like the battlefields back in the Great War, early in the last century, before we started numbering them.

The plan, such as it is, is to hope that if a Creeper comes at us, it has to clamber down into the moat, come up, and expose the main arthropod to three troopers with M-10s. If any incoming fire erupts from the Creeper, it's hoped that by ducking behind the brick and concrete, we'd have a chance to survive.

Hope. Chance. Hell of a way to run an interstellar war, especially when we've been on the losing side for most of my life.

I grab a pair of binoculars, scan the field of fire set up in front of us. There's a range card, a simple sketch of our sector that lists exact distances to various terrain features, and highlights both "kill zones" and "blind spots," fastened to the wall in front of me, but I have it memorized. The "mound" is 80 meters away. The "double stump" is 140. A slight depression running north-northwest from the moat is deep enough for a man to crawl through unnoticed, but not for a Creeper. Trees, brush and buildings long ago have been cleared out. Every couple of weeks, convicts from the local state prison come by to cut down the growth. There's a road out there, Jefferson Street, and I note a few homes scattered along the length that I can see.

"Knox."

There's a tone to his voice. I say, "What's up, Sergeant."

"Mind telling me why you have a dog with you tonight? It should be in the K-9 kennels."

"Guess he didn't like the film they were showing in the kennels, Sergeant. I hear it was an old Rin-Tin-Tin movie. Thor thinks Rin-Tin-Tin is way overrated."

Another laugh from Dunlap, which seems to piss off Muller. "Knox, you know the regs. Dogs are only issued for operational reasons. Not as playthings or toys or to be your best buddy."

"Tell the truth, Sergeant, don't like the term 'issued.' Thor isn't a piece of gear, like an M-10 or a canteen."

Muller says, "Don't like your attitude, Knox. Never have. Just because of who you are, doesn't mean that—"

Dunlap says, "Guys, shut up."

Muller turns. "What did you say?"

Her voice tight. "Movement. Movement on the road, heading north."

As one we move to the front of the battlement, and Thor gets up right next to me. I focus the binoculars, say aloud, "Tracking. Good eyes, Dunlap."

Dunlap nods in appreciation, as she raises up her Colt M-10, rests the barrel on top of the battlement, brings her cheek to the butt stock, takes a sight, and scans her sector. I immediately hear her breathing change, become more measured, ready to pull the trigger—slowly—right in between the rise and the fall of her breathing. We all do it. It's second nature now.

About 300 meters out the Creeper scurries from the left side and moves in a straight line, right along the road, its legs moving almost as one, the claws out, the main arthropod sticking straight out. My mouth dries right out. I hear the *whir-whir* of the field telephone behind me, as Muller reports in a harsh whisper: "Battle Twelve, Battle Twelve. Confirmed Creeper sighting. Battle version. Three hundred meters, walking speed, northbound on Jefferson Street."

He listens for confirmation from the Command Post and then says, "Battle Twelve, out."

I keep staring at the Creeper over the sights of my M-10. Don't think I've ever seen one so clear and out in the open like this, going up the road like a damn tourist or something.

I whisper, more to keep the Creeper steady in my sights than because I'm worried about sound, "What's the word, Sergeant?"

He joins us on the edge of the battlement. "Observe and report. That's it. Observe and report."

The Creeper stops. Its two main claws rotate in the air like cobras, seeking a target, seeking a meal. Dunlap finally says, "What's the goddamn point?"

"What do you mean, Dunlap?" I ask.

"A decade ago the damn aliens come across light years to Earth, drown our cities, kill millions, zap aircraft and ships, throw us back to nineteenth-century technology . . . and for what? So they can crawl freely at night in the state capitol?"

Muller says, "Doesn't have to be a reason."

Hating to admit it, I agree with Muller. "Staff sergeant's right, Corporal. They're aliens. There you go. *Aliens.* Whatever they do, however they destroy, it makes sense to them. Doesn't have to make sense to us."

She laughs slightly, but it's a brittle sound. "You'd think after ten years, if they'd wanted us all dead, they could design a virus or plague to kill us all off. Why take all this time just to, what, burn a few cows and a dairy farm like they did the other day?"

Muller's voice is sharp. "Stop thinking so much. Focus. Observe and report, and keep your damn weapon trained on that bug."

I shift my weight slightly, slowly, from one foot to the next. It's cold and damp out. Wish I had put a jacket on underneath my protective vest. "What I'd like to observe and report, Sergeant," I say, "is that I wish we had an Air Force to call in some close air support. Or an Apache gunship. Hell, even a self-propelled howitzer. Sort of even up the odds."

Dunlap eagerly joins in. "How about some M1-A1 tanks, with special Colt-made shells. With laser-resistant armor so that—"

A flash of bright light dazzles my eyes, and a flame blossoms out from one of the houses on the road. The house roars into visibility and the Creeper's claws move in a sweeping motion, as the house explodes and flaming shingles and wood get tossed up in the air in a blossom of smoke, flame and debris.

Muller is quickly on the field telephone, "Urgent, urgent, urgent. This is Battle Twelve. Creeper firing civilian houses on Jefferson Street. Repeat, Creeper firing houses on Jefferson Street."

I say to Dunlap, "We're way out of firing range, Corporal, don't you think?"

"That's right, Sergeant. Way out of range."

Another house explodes. Someone is screaming out there in the flaming darkness.

Our staff sergeant comes back to the battlement. "Are we good to go?" I demand.

Muller says, "Observe and report. That's all."

It seems like two voices are screaming in the distance.

"Sergeant, there are people dying out there," I say. "Me and Dunlap, we can get across the moat, through the open space . . . be there in a minute or two."

Muller's voice is tight. "We're to stay put."

A third house is now a ball of flames. The Creeper is up on four of its eight legs, like it's trying to gain a height advantage over the poor homes in front of it. "Well, did they say if a quick reaction force is going out there? Did they?"

Muller said, "I didn't ask. I'm sure one's gonna be dispatched, Knox, so hold tight."

Right. Hold tight. Any quick reaction force means one of the precious few diesel trucks might be spared—doubtful, even in an attack like this—which means a steam-powered truck has to be lit off, which means long minutes as the firebox gets hot enough to make steam and—

I turn around and say, "Sorry, Sergeant Muller, my bum ear. What did you just say?"

"Knox, I don't care who you're related to, don't you dare move!"

I move past Thor and say, "Come on, Thor, let's roll. The staff sergeant just told us to move!"

I run down the steps of the battlement, Muller yelling after me.

Keeping a journal is against regs, because supposedly it violates OPSEC, Operational Security. Yeah, right, as if the Creepers are going to grab a hand-written diary off a dead sixteen-year-old and use it for intelligence. Not sure if they can read English handwriting; only know that they can detect high energy use—cars, ships, computers, power plants—and blast them all to pieces whenever they feel like it.

Figure a journal like this will be useful once the war is done. If I live, maybe when I'm 25 or 35 or something like that. Books will be written, I'm sure, and the generals and the presidents who said they did all the thinking, fighting and dying, will write most of the books. This way, I can write a book from what it was like to be a grunt, BBQ bait, the ones slogging to kill the Creepers, face to face. Or face to arthropod.

Journals are for stories, memories, or so my English teachers said. So here's a memory. Was in the Boy Scouts, when I was eleven. New Hampshire scout troop, since Dad had dual state citizenship because of a vacation cottage up on Bow Lake. Doing salvage work in some of the homes near the Boston tsunami strike that got soaked but didn't get crushed. My patrol was in a Marblehead neighborhood close to where I had grown up before the war. Times have changed since then, Boy Scouts now make sure scouts don't go to their hometowns, but that rule wasn't in place back then.

Chore's pretty simple. Break into an abandoned house, secure usable clothing, blankets, canned and bottled foods. Even if years have gone by after the stale dates on the food, it's still edible, most cases. Mark the outside of the house with spray paint for pick-up crews to gather up the salvaged stuff. Go to another house. Sometimes you find remains, most often you didn't. This far from Boston most people got out before the waves struck. A very few times you find survivors, folks who managed to hang on and didn't want to leave their homes, even after five years of no power, gas or grocery stores.

Anyway, was working one day, when our troop's Senior Patrol Leader—a real dick named Calhoun—came running up to this ranch house I was working at, out of breath, big smile on his face. Hey, Knox, he said. Didn't you say your older sister, her name was Melissa? I dropped the green plastic trash bag I was carrying. Yeah, I said, Melissa. Calhoun jerked a thumb behind him. Three houses down, real doll living there, said her name was Melissa.

I ran out after Calhoun, legs pumping, lungs burning, got to a two-story Colonial with faded blue paint, door wide open, mind racing, thinking of Melissa, thinking about what I'd tell Dad, maybe she knew where Mom was, oh my God, and—

Inside the house. Dark. No furniture. Rug rolled up. A fireplace and—

On the mantelpiece, a doll, about two feet tall, sitting there, plastic smile, yellow hair, and a scrawled tag attached to her toe.

MELISSA.

Behind me I heard Calhoun and others laughing at me.

Eventually it took three of the other Scouts to get me off Calhoun, but not after I nearly slit his throat with my Scout knife.

Year later, when I was twelve, I left the Scouts and joined the New Hampshire National Guard.

How's that for a story?

CHAPTER EIGHT

Thor and I race down the steep slope of the moat, across the swampy and thicket-filled bottom, and then clamber up the far side. Thor seems happy to be with me, and I know it's stupid, running across an open field like this, but those screams . . . I can't let it go.

The brush and the grass whip against my shins and knees as I get closer to the flames. Three houses are now burning along, and the screaming has finally stopped. My booted feet hit pavement, and breathing hard, I advance up the road.

That's when the stupid part hits home. I'm alone with Thor, with no flare gun at my side, with no back-up waiting to roar in and help me out. It's just me and my dog. I advance up the road, Colt M-10 straight out, hoping that once Staff Sergeant Muller gets over being pissed at me, he'll tell the CP that I'm out here by my lonesome, so that maybe other soldiers can be peeled away from the nearby battlements to join the fun.

The light and the sound of the flames and the stench of things burning are all overwhelming me. Thor keeps stride with me, as I pace up the road, looking, scanning, not seeing any target.

Up ahead. First burning house. Then the second. And the third. They look like small Capes, homes built here during the 1950s after the last real big war, nice homes for the returning veterans, full of piss and vinegar and a G.I. Bill after destroying fascism on both sides of the globe.

At the first house, a body is halfway out of the doorway, collapsed on a brick set of steps. It's charred so badly I can't tell its age or sex. I take a deep breath, move along. At the second home, bodies are scattered on the burnt front lawn. Three small shapes, two larger shapes, smoke wisping up from the blackened corpses.

Mom, dad, and the kids. Killed in view of a military base supposedly dedicated to their protection. Some job we're doing.

I look up. The night sky is its usual chaos of moving dots of light and flares as debris comes back home to earth.

Thor is right next to me. If it weren't for him, I think I'd turn around and run back to the fort.

Third house, burning along. A bearded man with a ponytail is standing on the lawn, staring at the flames roaring up from what was once his home. Two young boys are at either side, holding onto him. They are all barefoot, the boys wearing pajama bottoms, their dad in a patched pair of jeans. The boys have their heads burrowed in dad's side. Dad turns to me, eyes wide.

"It's gone," he says, voice raspy.

I lower my Colt. "Do you know where it went?"

He tries to move but it's hard to do, with his sons holding on so tight to him. He raises an arm and points it to the northern end of the road. "It . . . it hit the Crandall house, then the Johnson's, and then ours . . . me and the boys, we ducked into the woods. My wife . . . Thank Christ she's working the night shift at Concord Hospital. From the woods, I saw the damn thing move fast . . . I mean, real, real fast . . . could be miles away by now."

My legs are quivering and I sling my M-10 over my right shoulder. Thor sits down and he doesn't seem to sense anything alien in the neighborhood. Poor civilian seems right. Creepers can creep right along at the speed of a lazy cockroach, hence the name, but when they want to, those eight legs can move *fast* and they can be over the horizon in a manner of minutes.

I say, "I'm sure the Concord Fire Department and the Red Cross will be along soon, sir. You just take care, okay?"

I rub Thor's head and make to walk back to my duty station, and one really angry staff sergeant, when the man says, "Oh, do you mind?"

I hesitate, wondering what in hell he's going to say to me, especially since he's just seen his neighbors get scorched down, his home and their homes flattened and destroyed. So I'm not really ready for what happens next.

He breaks free from his sons, comes over and offers a hand.

"Thanks for your service."

I make it back to the battlement and Staff Sergeant Muller meets me at the bottom of the stone steps. His face is taut and he says, "That was disobeying direct orders, Knox. Clear as can be."

I tug my helmet off, tap my left ear. "Sorry, staff sergeant. My bum ear. I was certain that you said move. So I did."

He crosses his arms. "Dunlap will back me up when I meet with Lieutenant May. You're going to be in hack so long that when you get out, that damn dog won't even recognize you. What do you think about that?"

I tie my helmet off at my utility belt. "I think Dunlap might think differently."

"Yeah? Why's that?"

I brush past him, to go back up to the top of he battlement. "Because I don't think she—or you—will want me telling the lieutenant how you both ended up in our duty station wearing each other's shorts. Hard to tell the right size and color in the dark, am I right?"

That shuts up Staff Sergeant Muller pretty well as I get back to where I had started out, Dunlap on the other side of the battlement. Thor lays down and stretches out, and across the moat and field of fire, I see additional movement, and bring up my binoculars. A truck from our Quick Response Force is there, and I hear the tingling of bells. Two horse-drawn steam-powered fire pumpers roll in from the Concord Fire Department, red lanterns hanging from the side. Soldiers and dogs start moving up the road, and firefighters get to work, watering down the smoldering homes.

I take my Colt, work the bolt and expel the 50 mm round, twisting the bottom back to safe.

Muller finally comes up and stands in one corner, and it's one quiet post until the field phone rings and sends us home, just as a series of horns blow across the fort, signaling an all clear.

After turning in my Colt and ammunition at the Armory, I trudge back to my barracks, other soldiers from my squad and platoon eddying about me, but I'm too tired to join in the gossip and chatting that goes on, except a quick slap on my butt gives me a jerk.

Corporal Abby Monroe joins me and I toss my left arm around her, give her a quick squeeze. "How was your alert, corporal?"

"Pretty damn routine, glad to say," she says, leaning into me as we walk a few yards, my arm still around her, feeling damn fine. "Went to the CP, trusty Trek at my side, and waited to bike out with dispatches in case the phone lines were cut. They weren't, so I sat on my butt. How about you?"

"Ticked off Staff Sergeant Muller," I say.

"Want to say any more?"

"Not right now," I say. "Try me later."

"'Kay," she says. She moves to break away and I say, "Not so fast, Abby."

We're in a shadowy part of the walkway, which works for me, and I give her another inappropriate kiss—this time to her sweet lips—and she squeezes my hand and heads off to her own barracks.

I unlock the door and go in, Thor right behind me, and I'm not sure what time it is. I light off a candle and there's a rap at the side of the door. It's Corporal Manning, and he smiles at me. His small teeth are yellow and brown.

"Glad to see you made it back, Sergeant."

"Glad to be here," I say, stripping off my gear, putting it carefully back where it belongs. Thor jumps on my unmade bunk, moves in two circles, and then thumps himself down.

"Hear you got in a pissing match with the staff sergeant."

I shake my head. "Jungle drums move quick."

He grins, taps a wrinkled finger at the side of his nose. "Us old-timers, we stick together, we pass little bits of news along. So good for you. Muller's not a bad sergeant but sometimes gets too big for his pants, but you be careful."

"I will," I say.

The corporal leans out, like he's looking up and down the hallway, to make sure he's not being overheard, and then he says, "I know you don't use it, but make sure you never think your family connection will save you if things hit the fan, Sergeant. Number of people out there would like to take you and your family and shove it up your butt at the right time."

I rub at the back of my head. "The only family I think about is my dad . . . if he ever gets my mail."

"True enough. Feel like a cold treat to cool you down?"

I cock my head. "A what?"

From his baggy fatigue pants, he reaches into a side pocket, pulls out an aluminum can, red and white. I stare at it. Coca-Cola. He pops the top open and passes it over. I take a long, satisfying cold and biting swig.

"Holy God," I say, as I lower the can. "Where did you get this?"

"From the colonel's private stock, and don't say any more. But I figured what you did last night, and what you did right now, you deserved it."

I pass the can over to him and he doesn't stand on ceremony. He takes a healthy swig himself and passes it back. I take another cold swallow, feeling the tickling in my mouth and nose from the carbon dioxide. Last time I had a Coke was at the fort's Christmas celebration, about five months ago.

"Ask you question, Corporal?"

"Sure," he says, leaning against the doorjamb.

"Last floor bull session, when you were passing out the clean laundry . . . were you telling the truth about that television show?"

"The one about the housewives?"

"That's the one," I say. "Tell me again."

The old corporal says, "For a few years, just before the war started, one of the television channels, they'd run these hour-long programs about these rich housewives."

"From New York?"

He nods. "That's one of the places. And New Jersey. California. Atlanta. A couple of others."

"An hour long? Really? What was so interesting about these housewives that they could do an hour show about them?"

"I don't know what you mean."

"I mean, were they artists. Or doctors. Scientists. In the military. Were they something like that?"

Manning laughs, though it's more of a cackle. "Hell, no. Most of 'em didn't do a damn thing. They were rich, and they were bored, and they spent a lot of time at parties or restaurants, gossiping about the other wives. Truth be told, a few were kinda pretty to look at, but most of 'em were as dumb as a sack full of hammers."

"So what was the program about?"

Manning says, "Didn't you hear me? The program was about the housewives. Camera crews followed 'em around and later showed their eating, their dressing, their fights and their parties. That was it. That was the program."

I turn the cold Coke can around in my hand. "And people watched that? Honestly?"

"That they did. They were pretty damn popular."

I take one last swig of the cold Coke, pass the rest of it back to the good corporal. "Good try," I say. "I don't believe it. Can't believe anyone would be that dumb to make a program like that, and dumb enough to watch it."

Manning gratefully takes the can from my hand. "Funny thing is they did."

When the corporal leaves I close and lock the door, and push Thor aside to climb into my bunk. A quick check of my watch shows it's three A.M. Later in the day, that evening, to be specific, is the Ranger Ball. A dance where I was promised the first one by Corporal Abby Monroe. At least three hours sleep if I'm lucky, before I have to get up and face the day and hit the books.

Some luck.

Banging on the door wakes me up just before reveille. I don't know how much sleep I got but I know it's not enough. It's never enough in the Army.

I get out of bed and Thor yawns and snuggles himself back in my bedding. I look to him and say, "Some guard dog you are." He yawns again and flops over. So I'm not a happy sergeant when I open the door, and I become even unhappier when I see who's standing there: an MP from the post's Provost Marshal office, about my age. His nametag says SALTIER, and his rank is PFC but he's all attitude, standing there sharply in a clean uniform with the MP patch on his left upper arm. His face is puffy and pimply, but he still carries himself like he's a cop, which he is.

"Sergeant Knox?"

"Yes," I say.

"Sir, you're to report to the Provost Marshal's office at oh nine-hundred."

Oh crap, I think. Staff Sergeant Muller must have decided to go all out against me and not worry too much about the Mystery of the Swapped Shorts.

"I see," I say. "Any idea of what's going on?"

He shakes his head. "Some sort of complaint, sir, that's all I know. And that you're to report at oh nine-hundred. Any questions?"

Lots of questions, but none of which this chubby young MP can answer for me. "No, no questions."

Saltier leans to the left and peers over my shoulder. "Sir, is that a K-9 unit in your bunk?"

I don't bother turning around. "It is."

"Sir, I'm sure you know the regulations about unauthorized K-9 units staying overnight in the barracks."

"An oversight, I'm sure."

Something that looks like it might be a small smile splits the MP's face. "If you'd like, sir, I could help you correct that oversight by returning him to the K-9 barracks."

I feel a bit better towards the cop. "That would be great, private. I'd appreciate that."

I grab a leash, secure Thor, and he gives me a look of sad betrayal, as he and the MP leave the room, leaving me alone and in one hell of a mess.

CHAPTER NINE

A little bit of luck is that I have nearly three hours to get ready, so I scramble around my room and the barracks to do so. In going to see the Provost Marshal, I'll need to look sharp, since she's a tough old broad who used to be a New Hampshire Superior Court justice before the war. I'm lucky my dress shoes still have a pretty good shine, and it's been a long time since I had to wear my formal Army Service Uniform, but luck is with me again. I can actually put my hands on the necktie, and the white shirt is in pretty good shape, except for a sweat stain around the collar.

I trade a Hershey bar for a ten-minute shower chit from a trooper down the hallway, and after a breakfast of stale toast, powdered eggs and venison sausage, I use the chit, and am ticked off when the water comes out rusty and lukewarm. Waste of a good chocolate bar and a shower chit.

But I pull myself together and get dressed in my Army Service Uniform, I walk over to the Provost Marshal's office, crossing near the playing fields. At a paved parking lot that is cracked and which is mowed every Sunday, a new group of recruits are standing still, their front feet smack dab up against a faded yellow line on the old asphalt. First Sergeant Wendy Messier is standing before the dozen or so boys and girls—mostly twelve or thirteen—bawling them out, standing with the help of two metal crutches. Her right leg is off below the knee, and she's been having a hell of a time getting a prosthetic that fits. The kids looked scared, as they should be, staring out at the First Sergeant, and I resist the temptation to give 'em a cheery wave as I walk by.

At the Provost Marshal's office, I get the second big surprise of my early day: in her office is not Master Sergeant Muller, but two civilians, one who is dressed in a ratty gray suit and necktie, and the other who is bearded and has a bandaged leg and is holding wooden crutches in his dirty hands.

It's the civilian I shot the other night.

Captain Gail Allard has short brown hair, a beak of a nose, and is as skinny as a coat rack. She's behind her desk, piled high on each side with papers and file folders. Her office is windowless, with filled bookcases and filing cabinets, and a manual typewriter on a stand in the corner. There's a United States flag, a U.S. Army flag, and the State of New Hampshire flag on small sticks set in a black foam bulb on her desk. The only decoration is framed certificates of her law degree and other achievements, and a formal portrait of the President.

She folds her hands together and leans over the desk. "Have a seat, Sergeant."

"Yes, ma'am."

I sit down across from her. She looks to the two civilians. "This is Attorney Michael Farrell. He's representing Fred Mackey, of Purmort. I take it that you and Mister Mackey are acquainted?"

"Yes, ma'am."

Fred is glowering at me, and I understand why. In this cool and slightly dusty office, it probably seems obscene seem to him and his lawyer that I shot him in the leg the other night.

But I didn't shoot him in this office. I shot him at night, in the woods, within range of a Creeper.

Doesn't sound obscene to me.

Captain Allard goes on, her voice strong and slow. "Mister Mackey is intending to file a complaint against you for what occurred two nights ago."

"Yes, ma'am," I reply, remembering what old Corporal Manning had once told me: never be first, never volunteer, and especially, never volunteer information. So I was going to let Captain Allard take point on wherever the hell this was going. In most people's eyes, I'm not officially an adult, but I like to think I'm also not officially stupid.

"He's represented here by Attorney Farrell," she continues. "You, of course, have every right to have counsel represent you. But in the interest of time and of getting to the bottom of this matter, I was hoping we could proceed with this rather, er, informal gathering. If that's agreeable to you, Sergeant Knox."

There are fellow troopers back in my former dormitory who are barracks lawyers, always nit-picking and debating the finer points of law and regulations, especially when they get into hack, which seems pretty common for them. And even though her face is impassive, I see Captain Allard is showing me a path out of this mess.

"Absolutely, ma'am," I say. "I have no problem with that."

She turns her head to the lawyer, the better-dressed of the two. "Mister Farrell, is it all right with you and your client if I proceed?"

Fred Mackey starts to say something but his lawyer puts his hand on his arm. "Captain, I think we'll go along with that. All we're seeking here is justice for my client, who was brutally and suddenly shot without provocation by this young man here and—"

She raises a hand. "This isn't a courtroom, counselor, so if you could restrain from making speeches, we'll get along that much faster. Fair enough?"

He nods. His hair is carefully combed and his suit is mended here and there, and I wonder how he scrapes along, being a lawyer during war time, and then I realize I don't particularly care.

Captain Allard turns to me, face sharp. "Sergeant Knox."

"Ma'am."

"Please inform me, Attorney Farrell and Mister Mackey your current rank, assignment and duty station."

I do so and then she asks, "Were you drafted or did you volunteer?"

"Volunteered, ma'am."

"At what age did you volunteer?"

"I was twelve, ma'am. At the time, under the President's National State of Emergency Declaration, the enlistment age had been lowered to twelve, with a surviving parent or guardian's approval. My father gave his approval."

The attorney raises his hand. "Captain, I appreciate this background of Sergeant Knox, but I really don't see the relevance of where this is going."

Fred Mackey mutters, "What a waste of friggin' time. Goddamn punk shot me in the leg, he did."

Captain Allard doesn't even blink. "I appreciate the patience of you and your client. This shouldn't take long. Sergeant Knox, for the benefit of our civilian . . . guests, here, please point to the badge on the upper left side of your uniform blouse. The one that looks like a musket with a half wreath about it. What's the name of that badge?"

"That's the Combat Infantryman Badge, ma'am."

"How does one receive the Combat Infantryman Badge?"

"For actual combat in the field against the enemy, ma'am."

"You didn't get that for being a support unit, or doing laundry, or counting boxes in a warehouse."

"No, ma'am."

Captain Allard continues. "The two Purple Hearts? How and where did you receive those?"

I shift in my seat. "I received the first one two years ago, at the Battle of Merrimack Valley."

There's a sudden intake of breath from the attorney. Everybody in New England knows about that battle. Captain Allard says, "Is that where you received that burn injury that damaged your left ear?"

"Yes, ma'am."

"The second Purple Heart?"

"An engagement last year, in Nashua. During an early morning attack on an elementary school. Part of the roof collapsed and I got a piece of broken wood shoved into my leg."

"And what's that star hanging from that ribbon, just below the other line of emblems?"

"Bronze Star, ma'am."

"And the 'V'. What does that indicate?"

"For valor. Ma'am."

"For what were you awarded the Bronze Star, with the 'V' for Valor?"

It's starting to get warm in the room, and I see by the clock that I'm in the middle of missing an important engagement. But I have no interest in speeding the Provost Marshal along. "That was also awarded after the Battle of Merrimack Valley."

Attorney Farrell tries to salvage the morning. "Captain, if we could—"

"Absolutely," she says. "Sergeant Knox, two evenings ago, you were in Montcalm, were you not, assigned to respond to a Creeper attack on a dairy farm?"

"Yes, ma'am."

"In the course of your reconnaissance mission that evening, did you encounter Mister Mackey at any time?"

"Yes, ma'am, I did," I say.

"What were the circumstances of that encounter?"

I took a breath, trying to avoid the death-by-eyeball gaze from Mackey. "Captain, in the course of my mission, I heard a clicking noise, similar to what I've heard before when Creepers are on the move. Further investigation revealed Mister Mackey and a companion, by a campfire, attempting to attract the attention of the Creeper by imitating its distinctive noise."

The captain turns to the two civilians, looking stunned. "Is that true, Mister Mackey?"

He's still defiant. "Why not? Me and my cousin, we heard the Gates Foundation, they wanna pay out ten thousand New Dollars to anybody who can capture a Creeper live. So that's what we was tryin' to do."

"Sergeant," Captain Allard continues, still looking at the bandaged civilian with disbelief. "Do tell us what happened next?"

"I advised Mister Mackey and his companion that they had to leave, that they were in an area that had been declared a Military Reservation due to the Creeper sighting, and that their lives were in danger if they stayed there."

"Did they leave?"

"No, ma'am."

"What then?"

"Captain, I warned them that they had to leave. I told them that their lives were in danger. They became belligerent. They refused to leave. I decided I had no other option. So I shot Mister Mackey."

"In the leg?" she asks.

Mackey shouts, "Of course in the leg, you dumb broad! Can't you see the damn bandage?"

"Sir," she says crossly, "you are on this post as a guest. Counselor, please advise your client to stay quiet unless he's asked a question."

Farrell whispers something into Mackey's ear, and his face is red and he glares at me, but he keeps quiet.

"Sergeant, do go on," she says.

I say, "They refused to leave. There was a Creeper in the area. They were interfering with my mission. I didn't want to shoot him, but I didn't have time to debate or discuss."

"What happened after you shot him?"

He said "ouch," I thought. Aloud I say, "I gave his companion first aid supplies. I departed the scene. Approximately fifteen minutes later I encountered the Creeper. I engaged the Creeper, it was terminated, and then I launched a flare, to inform the nearby combat dispatcher that the scene was secure."

Captain Allard folds her hands again, glances over at the lawyer, lets out a sigh. "Counselor, let's look at the facts, all right? According to the Status of Forces agreement with the state of New Hampshire, any complaint filed against a member of the armed forces on this post will be adjudicated with a panel consisting of two civilians, two members of the military, and the district's state senator."

Farrell leans forward but the captain raises her hand. "Based on Sergeant Knox's extensive service record, decorations, and his participation in the Battle of Merrimack Valley, plus your client's trespassing in a military reservation and his attempt to interfere with the sergeant's mission, do you really think you have a case? Especially when he would have been within his rights to kill your client at the time?"

Mackey says, "Damn right we have a case! He shot me!"

Farrell looks like he'd rather be anyplace but here. He coughs and says, "Well, now that you mention that, it seems that—"

Captain Allard opens the top drawer of her desk, removes a pad of paper. "Tell you what, counselor. I appreciate you coming here and getting this resolved. I'm sure you know from your fellow attorneys what has happened to some people who have made claims against the armed forces that their, um, neighbors have thought were baseless. Very unfortunate, of course."

She takes a pencil, scrawls something on a piece of paper, passes it over. "Here. Before you and your client leave the base, you can have lunch at our dining facility."

Farrell looks ashamed and now I've changed my mind about the poor guy; feeling a touch of sympathy for a grown man trying to make a living in a strange world that has little in common from the place where he went to law school and started his practice. When all most people care about is getting enough to eat and not getting sick, it must be rugged out there for a lawyer to survive. He takes the paper and says, "Very well, Captain."

Mackey turns and says, "You're fired, you shyster. You're fired. I'm outta here."

He gets up and grabs his crutches, thrusts them under his arms, and he and his dismissed attorney get to the office door. Mackey says, "A kid. He's just a goddamn kid!"

Captain Allard softly closes the drawer of her desk. "Whatever his age, he's a non-commissioned officer in the service of his nation. Do remember that the next time you decide to trespass on a military reservation."

When the officer door shuts, the captain rubs at the back of her neck. "Sweet Jesus, Randy, that was a waste of a good chunk of my morning time."

"Sorry, ma'am."

"Sorry doesn't particularly cut it, especially when it comes to civilians." She rubs hard at the back of her neck again. "Especially since the war is over, civilians, can't blame 'em, are going to start feeling itchy. They're going to start wondering why the armed forces are still being treated relatively royally and practically everything they do is either rationed or censored. It's been a long ten years."

"Ma'am, hard to believe the war is over with Creepers still running around out there."

She lets out a deep breath. "Above your pay grade, and definitely above mine. Now, Randy, did you really have to shoot him? Honestly? Or were you just pissed at him and his cousin?"

I'm not sure what she's getting at, so I guess the truth will have to do. "Ma'am, I was angry, there's no doubt, but they were also impeding my mission. I didn't have much time. The Creeper was out there, and I had to find him."

"You could have killed him."

"No, ma'am," I say. "I knew where I shot him."

She eyes me for a moment, and says, "For someone your age, you do have an impressive service record, Randy. But that and an ear that goes deaf at convenient times won't help you forever. Or your family background."

I say crossly, "I've not once used my family, not once, and you know it, ma'am."

She picks up her pencil. "Perhaps, but that's enough for this morning. Is there anything else?"

"Yes, ma'am."

"And what's that?"

I say, "Could you write me a note for Mister Tierney. I'm afraid I've missed today's geometry class."

Captain Allard takes a piece of paper. "Very well, Randy."

"Thank you, ma'am."

CHAPTER TEN

Ah, yes classes. After the dreadful first years of the war, when casualties were so very high, the only way the surviving Congress would allow a change in enlistment laws were to tie them into continued schooling. So even though I enlisted on my twelfth birthday, I still had to go to school at my different postings. Between training, deployments and missions, I still had to find time for geometry, U.S. history, military history, English, Creeper physiology and tactics, and other standard high school courses.

But no driver's ed. Not many running cars left out there.

This afternoon my class in English Composition is over and I get up from the desk, thinking ahead to the Ranger Ball this early evening, when my instructor, Mister Lewis, motions me over to his corner of the classroom. Mister Lewis is an old, wrinkled man with loose flaps of flesh around his cheeks and neck. He is one of a handful of teachers from St. Paul's who stayed behind when the war began and I once saw a black and white photo of him back in the day, when it looked like he weighed nearly three hundred pounds. He lost a lot of weight during the famine years and has never put it back on.

He smiles cheerfully at me. His eyebrows are white and bushy, and look like old brushes that have been working way too long. He says, "Randy, that last essay you wrote, about when you salvaged that house in Rockport when you were in the Boy Scouts, was spectacular."

I feel warm and safe all of a sudden. "Uh, thanks, Professor Lewis."

"No, I mean it," he says. "The descriptions . . . the smell of dried mud, of old seaweed in the yard, of the torn wallpaper. The feeling that you were trespassing as you searched through the cupboards, looking for canned goods . . . and the ending, when you wished that you could go back there someday, when things were better, and apologize to the family that lived there when they moved back. Very moving. Randy, you keep that kind of work up, and you'll be on track for getting an 'A' at the end of this term. If you talk to your fellow classmates and soldiers, you'll know I don't hand out 'A's very often."

My face feels even warmer. "Thanks again, professor," and I make to leave, and he says, "Not so fast, Randy. Pull up a chair."

I sit next to him, look at the clutter on his desk, the dusty books and framed etchings of writers like Shakespeare, Wordsworth and Longfellow, and shoved in one corner, a dead computer terminal. He has on an old suit that's shiny along the sleeves, and a red bowtie that's almost hidden by the folds of skin.

He says, "You've got a real talent for writing, Randy, and I hope you develop it. What were you thinking of doing after you're discharged?"

Now I don't feel so warm and safe. He's asking questions I've been avoiding. "Discharged? What have you heard?"

He shakes his head. "Nothing official, of course, but the President's said the war is over, correct? Eventually the Creepers and their bases here will be destroyed, the killer stealth satellites in orbit will be hunted down and disabled . . . you've been in service for quite some time, have seen plenty of combat. If other wars in the past can be used as an example, I'd say you'll be eligible to return to civilian life at some point. When that blessed day occurs, Randy, instead of going to the Army's War College, I would hope you'd go to one of the universities that are still open. A talent like yours shouldn't go to waste."

I say the first thing that comes to mind.

"Professor, I don't know how to be a civilian."

Back in my room, checking my class assignments for tomorrow, thinking about what Professor Lewis had just said. Go back into civilian life? What the hell was he talking about? My early memories, before the war, are all a jumble of images, tastes and shapes. Riding in a car. Riding in a boat. On my mother's lap, as she shows me a funny cartoon on a laptop computer or tablet. Looking out a window, nice and warm and dry, watching the snow fall, wondering if Santa has gotten my e-mail.

After that, it's even more of a jumble. Dad and Mom looking serious. The television on all the time, mostly showing white static. Phone ringing. Melissa crying in her bedroom. Me and Dad, driving in his Volkswagen. The car dying. No lights. Living in a tent in a high school football field somewhere. Dad silently weeping in the corner of a smelly canvas tent. Eating dandelion greens, old stale cheese, sour apples.

I push all those memories away. Long ago I learned that when a Creeper can attack at any time, memories like that just get in the way of doing your job, and living one more day.

Beside, it's time to get ready for the Ranger Ball.

In my closet I pull out a nice salvaged pair of Levi's, a bit long and floppy around my feet, but looking nearly brand new. I also have pair of Nike sneakers that I only take out for special occasions, and I'm trying to decide if I can get away with a Hawaiian shirt that has a rip on the back, but which has been expertly stitched together, or a plain green T-shirt that's brand new, when there's a knock at the door.

I open it up and Mike Millett comes in, a Specialist in my squad. He's squat, muscular, with tiny eyes under strong wide eyebrows, but he has a booming laugh and an almost uncanny ability to find a Creeper in pitch darkness.

"Sergeant, can you help a brother out?" he asks, his booming voice nearly shy.

Warily, I say, "Depends."

He sits down heavily on my bunk, making the springs squeak. "Thing is, I got a date tonight, for the dance. Doris, who works in the dining facility."

I turn my desk's chair around and sit down, resting my forearms on the back. Doris is a quiet girl, works in the dishwashing area. A contract civilian who walks with a limp, because of a broken foot years ago that never healed quite right. "Good for you, Mike. How can I help?"

He kicks off his shoes, sticks his feet out. Big toes pop out from holes in each olive drab sock. "That's how all of my socks look like. See? Can you lend me a pair?"

I say, "You expecting to show Doris your feet tonight?"

"Don't you remember, last dance?"

"No, I don't," I say. "Didn't go. Pulled guard duty that night."

"Oh," he says. "Well, they were playing some of that 1950's music, real fun stuff and the guy spinning the records, said that back then, dances were called sock hops, so we all had to kick our shoes off. Suppose he does the same thing tonight? I don't want to look ridiculous in front of Doris."

I say, "You promise not to tear them with those big feet of yours?"

"Promise," he says.

"And you'll wash and dry them before you bring them back?"

"Hell, yeah, Sergeant," he says. "You can count on me."

I get up from my chair, go to my bureau and open the top drawer. Pull out a pair of socks, toss them to Mike, who catches them with one hand.

Grinning, he gets up. "Thanks, Sergeant. Owe you one. Hey, how did your provost general meeting go?"

I close the drawer. "Fair enough," I say. "Funny how civilians get ticked off when you shoot them for not listening to reason."

"Ain't that the truth," he says. "Hey, just so you know, services are on for tomorrow for Ruiz. Ten hundred hours."

"Thanks," I say. "Hey, before you leave?"

He's by the door. "Sure, Sergeant."

"About Ruiz . . . I heard some in the squad think I should have intervened. Shouldn't have let him go out on his first Recon Ranger op by himself."

Millett looks solemn, no longer the happy fellow ranger, coming in to cage a pair of clean socks off his sergeant. "Was it Zane?" I ask.

He stays quiet, and then Millett juggles his new pair of socks in one beefy hand. "Thing is, Ruiz had a sister. Celeste. Real cutie. Word I heard, Zane was sweet on her. Was becoming close buds with Ruiz, hoping to make way with Celeste." Mike shrugs. "Not your fault, Sergeant. The Ell-Tee thought he was ready, you thought he was ready . . . we had a job to do."

"I guess so."

"Yeah, well, not sure if you heard the other news."

"What's that?"

Millett opens the door. "County militia tracked down the Coastie gang that ambushed Ruiz and his K-9. Two guys and two girls, from Baltimore. God only knows how in hell they kept alive so long and found their way up here."

"I'll be damned," I say.

"You?" he says. "Maybe so, but those four . . . oh yeah, they're damned. The militia found some of Ruiz's gear on them and they had a quick trial. Boom."

"Shot?"

"No, hung from that covered bridge Ruiz had been dropped off at," Millett says, going down the hallway. "Figured they wanted to save ammunition."

With Mike Millett gone, I decide I'm going to be colorful tonight and choose the Hawaiian shirt, but Professor Lewis's words are still nagging me, because what will I do if I do get discharged? Or would I want to go career? That was one hell of a thought, for like everybody else in my squad, platoon, company, battalion and probably the entire armed forces of the United States, I bitched and moaned about the food, about the officers, about the President and Congress and the war and how the damn civvies are always screwing things up . . .

But with no more war, what could I do?

What would I do?

Another knock on the door. Damn, I thought, must be my night to be commissary for the entire squad.

But when I open the door, it's my platoon leader, Lieutenant David May.

And he doesn't look happy.

"Randy," he says. "You've got a problem."

An Excerpt From the Journal of Randall Knox

Perimeter guard duty last night, made even more fun when I was assigned the newbie in our platoon, sturdy girl named Pittman from the upper reaches of Maine. Complained to the lieutenant about having to babysit a newbie, but the Ell-Tee reminded me of the last two times I was late for P.E., and did I want to babysit newbies for the next quarter in addition, so I shut my mouth and off I went.

Pittman, like all newbies, is eager to get at it, maybe even get a chance to chase a Creeper. Said she was the best shot in her family, always kept the smokehouse filled with venison. Told her to relax, our job was to poop and snoop along the outside perimeter of the fort, keep watch for two-legged marauders, not eight-legged. Cool cloudy night, kept an eye on Pittman. She was nervous but hid it well. Wanted to hear war stories from me and I had to tell her to shut up, to focus on the mission, however routine it seemed.

About a half hour in, at the northwest corner, Pittman found a break in the fence line, saw a wooden pole with some slats nailed to it, used as a ladder. We unslung weapons, moved in slow. Pittman whispered if we should call for back-up, and I told her to quiet it down. Heard noises, got a good idea of what we'd find, but I wanted to see how Pittman reacted. About ten minutes in, came to the Rockford Dining Facility. Told Pittman to back me up. Flashed on light and caught three young kids rummaging around in the waste bins out back. Pittman wanted to get to one of the comm shacks, get word out to the post Provost Marshal to get the kids arrested. Told her to relax. Kids shaking with fear, even though one real young kid—girl or boy, couldn't tell—wouldn't stop chewing on a chicken bone. Tossed them over my night field ration pack, told 'em to get the hell out. They ran like squirrels being chased by Thor, though the youngest one still had a hand on the chewed chicken bone.

Pittman seemed P.O.'d. Asked me why I let them go. Told her I joined up to fight Creepers, not bust kids who are starving.

Rest of tour went quiet, signed out, sent message to Facilities to get fence line fixed. Pittman seemed to learn a good lesson. We'll see.

CHAPTER ELEVEN

"May I come in?" he asks, and I step aside, mind whirling, guts churning, thinking all right, maybe *this* time Staff Sergeant Muller filed a complaint. The lieutenant comes in, sees one chair, and sits on the edge of my bunk.

"Have a seat, Randy," he says.

I take my chair and he sits there, West Point graduate in a nice clean uniform and almost new boots. His hooked prosthetic arm sticks out to one side. "Here's the deal," he says. "The colonel wants to see you."

"Me?" I ask. "What for, sir?"

The lieutenant goes on. "He has something in mind for you. I suggest you listen to him and if you don't like it, refuse."

"Refuse, sir? How can I do that?"

He stares right at me. "You're a smart one, Randy. Skirting the rules. Using your hurt ear for your own advantage. Getting what you want. I think if you want to, you can say no to the colonel without any problem, by using your . . . creative skills. But be careful. Do you get what I'm saying?"

"I think so, sir. I think so."

"Good." He steps up and I ask, "When does he want to see me?"

He glances at the watch on his sole arm. "Just under an hour. At six P.M."

Something heavy and cold sinks in my chest. "But that's when the Ranger Ball starts, boss."

The lieutenant walks to the door. "So ask the colonel to go with you to the dance if you'd like. But don't make him wait."

Almost an hour later, ticked off that I'm out of civvie clothes and back into uniform, I'm walking to the colonel's offices, which used to house the school's headmaster. From the distance and with my good ear, I hear the disk jockey warming up for the dance, playing a rock and roll tune from the Sixties. The damn music nearly tugs me over to the base gym, which has been cleared out for the dance. No wonder the Sixties was such a screwy decade; that music made you want to move, to reach out, to rebel, to do everything differently.

At the headmaster's building, a nice construct of old wood and brick, I trot up the stairs and go to the outer office, where the colonel's administrative aide sits, an older woman named Bouchard who was once in the Air Force and re-upped into the only unit that would take her after the war began. She has a thin face and prominent nose, and while she's now a lieutenant in the Guard, rumor has it that she was a full colonel in the Air Force before retiring.

I stand at attention and announce myself. "Sergeant Randy Knox, reporting to Colonel Malcolm Hunter, ma'am."

She purses her thin lips, makes a notation on a piece of paper with a pencil, and says, "Nice to see you on time, Sergeant, but the colonel has a visitor. You may take a seat."

I look up at the wall clock. Six P.M. The Ranger Ball is starting and Corporal Abby Monroe is stepping out on the dance floor, looking for her promised first date, and here I am, cooling my heels outside the C.O.'s office. Damn. If I had been smarter, I would have sent her a note or something, to explain why I'm not there on time.

Had no time to be smart. At my side are a couple of newspapers. I pick up the latest copy of *Stars & Stripes*, only a week old. Sorry to say for its writers and editors, I skip most of the stories. They are mostly tales of fellow brave soldiers, fighting Creepers, rescuing civilians, and doing good in the community. Lots of heroics. Despite what Captain Allard tried to do a few hours back, I ain't no hero, and don't want to be. Heroes get their charcoaled remains buried and get speeches said over them. That's not for me.

I'm not saying the tales in the newspaper are made-up, it's just that I'm tired of reading them.

Instead I look for the cool nuggets here and there, like the headline *SECDEF PROMISES MORE DETAILS ON ORBITAL RAID*, which is about the entire story, that the current Secretary of Defense promises that one of these days, more information would be revealed about last month's attack on the Creepers' orbiting base. Operational security and all that, and no, he wouldn't say if the Air Force crews involved had seen a certain movie about star wars before launch. I smile at an old memory, from a few years ago, when dad was reading *Stars & Stripes* in our post apartment and he burst out laughing. I asked him what was so funny, and he pointed to a story about how what was left of LucasFilms was filing suit against anyone using the copyrighted term "Death Star" in describing the Creepers' orbital base. Then dad laughed again and said, "Randy, when I was your age, when we worried a lot about the Russians, there was an old joke that after World War III, the only creatures still thriving would be cockroaches and lawyers. Glad to see the joke still works."

Maybe so, but even knowing what I know about the history of Russia, I still admire them since they have a pretty good method of destroying Creeper bases. Once a base has been extensively surveyed and plotted, they send in squads of three men, each one carrying a component of a ten-kiloton nuclear device. The squads move low and slow, sometimes taking a week to cover just a few hundred meters, and once they get up next to a base, they assemble the nuclear device and set it off.

Oh, and they set it off by hand, so as not to be detected by the Creepers, who are experts at detecting and destroying most electronic devices. One of the girls in my platoon, named Lopez, shook her head once at an intelligence briefing describing this kind of attack and said, "Man, that's freakin' hardcore."

Can't argue with that.

I flip through the pages, seeking other nuggets. *SIEGE OF DENVER CONTINUES*. Ouch, those poor folks in the mile-high city. There's been stories of sieges going on at other cities across the world— Brasilia in Brazil, a couple in Africa, Lyons in France, Kiev in Ukraine—but only Denver has gotten the attention of the Creepers here in the States. They set up their exoskeletons around the city and because of the lack of tree cover and other hiding areas, they scorch anything and everything trying to get in or out of Denver. There's a constant pitched battle to thin out the exoskeletons, but their killer stealth satellites do pinpoint strikes on the forces trying to break in, or at least take in food supplies.

Food supplies. I've heard rumors about classified attempts to bring in food, from using old sewage tunnels and even hot-air balloons, but it's hard to feed hundreds of thousands of people with such meager resources. The story is grim and it says the Mile-High Stadium has been closed to further burials.

A turn of the page. *ALASKAN, HAWAIIAN DELEGATIONS ARRIVE TO ADDRESS CONCERNS.* The story is written with vague words of compromise and mutual respect, but I know the real story: after ten years of constant war and near isolation, the states of Hawaii and Alaska aren't particularly happy about being governed by steamship and telegraph by a President who can't even address the nation by radio or television.

One more story, in the back, the tiniest one but the most intriguing: *CONTACT MADE WITH SOME MIDEAST UNITS.* Now that's a story I wish was longer, for it touches on one of the spookiest stories coming out of the Creeper war. Once the war began, communications were cut off, meaning tens of thousands of American troops stationed overseas in Europe, Asia, Africa and the Middle East lost contact with the National Command Authority. Ten years is a long time, and some of the overseas units set themselves up as mini-empires in the country where they were stationed, while others hired themselves out as mercenary units to whatever governments managed to survive, and still others simply collapsed from desertion or death. My Roman history instructor last term, Shapiro, said it was like the ten thousand survivors of the famed Ninth Legion of Rome, defeated in 36 B.C. in Turkey, the prisoners taken east never to be heard from again, except for stories that they worked as mercenaries for the ancient Chinese and intermarried into the local population.

Now with steamships and telegraph stations returning, some of these ghost units have been heard from, and like Alaska and Hawaii, times and circumstances have changed. Do they stay where they are, or do they re-pledge their loyalty to an unelected President most of them have never heard of?

A light flashes on Lieutenant Bouchard's desk. "You can go in, now," she says crisply.

I get up and stroll to a polished wooden door with a painted plaque stating, COL. MALCOM HUNTER, COMMANDANT, FORT ST. PAUL. I knock once, wait, hear a voice from the other side call out, "Enter!"

I open the door, close it behind me, stride in, stand at attention in front of the colonel's desk. I don't salute. My cover is in my hand and salutes are only exchanged when both parties are wearing their hats. I can't tell you how many times I've seen old films during movie night, especially the black and white ones after World War II, that show salutes being tossed around like they were part of some secret lodge or something. You'd think the vets after the last Big One would know better, but they were no doubt busy building houses, getting married and producing babies.

There's a civilian sitting in one of the chairs in front of the desk, but I only note him from the corner of my eye. The colonel is in his fifties, face tired, wrinkles around his forehead and eyes, nearly bald, black hair a rim at the rear of his head. His uniform is clean and neat, as are the piles of papers and folders on his desk. The office is wood paneling, Oriental carpeting, and bay windows that overlook the fort's grounds.

He says, "Sergeant, I'd like you to meet Ezra Manson. Mister Manson is an executive assistant to the governor."

I turn, see the civilian look up at me with distaste, like he hadn't enjoyed his salvaged ten-year-old can of Dinty Moore beef stew for lunch. "Sir," I say, but he doesn't get up, and doesn't offer his hand. He looks to be in his thirties, wearing a dark gray suit that looks pretty good. Perhaps it's even recently made. His hair is dark brown, neatly trimmed, matching a neatly trimmed beard. I look down at his hands. His fingernails are short and clean. I'm sure he's never had to worry about getting a ten-minute chit for a hot shower.

Colonel Hunter says, "Have a seat, Sergeant."

"Sir," I say, and take the chair to the right of Mister Manson.

The colonel leans back in his leather chair. There's a muffled squeak. "I'll get right to it. Mister Manson will be departing the capitol tomorrow as a special courier from the Governor to the President. We've been asked to provide an armed escort. That will be you."

It's like the room is slowly being sent back to December, for I feel chilled. "Me, sir? To see the President?"

The colonel comes forward in his chair. Another muffled squeak. "I'm sure you've heard of him, am I correct?"

I'm embarrassed in front of the civilian. I don't like the feeling. "Yes, sir. I have."

"You'll receive the necessary orders and paperwork from Lieutenant Bouchard before you leave. But in a nutshell, you're going to be Mister Manson's new best friend. You're not to leave his side. You're to ensure that he and his dispatch case reach the capital and the President . . . or at least his Chief of Staff, Tess Conroy. Once he and his dispatch case have arrived in the good company of Miss Conroy, you'll be free to return. Questions?"

About a half-ton or so of questions, but Mister Manson beats me to it. "Him? Colonel? Are you serious? He's just a teenager."

Colonel Hunter frowns. "He's a sergeant in the National Guard, attached to the U.S. Army . . . and nowadays, there's not much difference between the two. Most National Guard units like us use our original designations for pride's sake, and the Army wisely allows us."

"I don't care if he's in the airborne, he's just a kid!"

Colonel Hunter says, "The governor asked for an armed escort. I'm giving you one of my best, no matter his age. Complain all you want. This is the soldier you're getting."

Manson looks trapped and I feel something out of the ordinary: respect for Colonel Hunter. He stands up and says, "Fine. Your call. To give me a boy to ride with me on a vital mission to the capitol. Just make sure he's not late."

"He'll be on time," the colonel says.

Manson leaves, but as he's going through the door, the colonel calls out. "Oh, Mister Manson. If I may."

"Yeah?"

"Just so we're clear, I'm assigning Sergeant Knox to provide you with security on your trip to the capitol. I'm not giving you a damn thing."

Manson slams the door pretty hard on his way out.

CHAPTER TWELVE

The colonel looks at me and I rub my moist hands on my uniform pants.

"Randy."

"Sir."

He lets out a long whoosh of breath, rubs both hands across the front of his head. "Damn governor . . . damn civilians." Then he surprises me by saying, "Ah, forget I said that. They're doing their best, under terrible pressures."

I keep quiet, still trying to figure out what's going on, when the colonel goes on, voice reflective. "Ten years later, most of this planet is back to medieval times, hungry and illiterate people being ruled by kings or warlords. We're one of the few remaining places that still functions . . . as best we can. So I guess civilians here do have their role."

I find my voice, "Sir, why me?"

He lets his hands down on his desk. "Why not you? I'd love to say that I was stretching the truth, but you are one of my best."

"But just one escort? Why not two? Why not a squad?"

The colonel says, "Because you're escorting a messenger. Not the damn governor himself. You'll be fine. Two or more escorts would raise questions. Don't need questions. But don't get cocky. Do your job. You get with Manson at the Concord railway station at oh nine hundred tomorrow and you be his new best friend. Don't leave his side. He goes to the bathroom, you say your bladder is full and you go, too. You stick with him until he's with the President or Miss Conroy. If something . . . untoward happens, make sure his dispatch case ends up with the President or Miss Conroy."

Remembering what Lieutenant May had said earlier, I say, "Do I have to go? Sir?"

His lower lip twitches. "If you want a direct order, consider it done. But truthfully, Randy, I can't see you passing this up. A trip off post. A train ride. A chance to get to the Capitol. I think I know you, Randy."

I snap back, "Don't be so certain. Sir."

He rubs at his forehead again. "Look, the door is shut. It's just you and me, Randy. So you can knock off the yes sirs and no sirs."

I stare at him carefully. "Is that an order? Sir?"

He replies just as carefully. "No, it's not. But . . . it's a request, Randy. I get enough yessirs and nossirs all day that I hear them in my goddamn sleep. So give me a break, all right?"

"All right . . . sir, er, sorry."

The colonel says quietly, "Any word about your dad?"

I try to keep my voice calm. "I think you'd know that already, Uncle Malcolm."

"I don't know the incoming mail status of each soldier on this post."

"I find that hard to believe, sir . . . uncle."

He shrugs. "Don't care if you believe it or not, but it's true. I'm sorry to hear you've not received word from your father. Communications with the West Coast can still be iffy. I'll see what I can do."

I doubt that, is what I think, but I keep my mouth shut. The colonel is a brother to my dead mom, and was a car salesman and a sergeant in the N.H. National Guard when the war started. As Dad told me more than once, a long war and heavy casualties equals quick advancement in the ranks. I guess he's okay as far a commanding officers go, but I don't like him for a good reason: he blames Dad for his sister's death, and has never made a secret of his dislike of my father. He and Dad have clashed lots of times since I've been assigned to Fort St. Paul, and it all comes back to when I was six and during those first confusing weeks after the war began, when mom and my sister were separated during the evacuations. Uncle Malcolm thinks Dad was a coward back then. I doubt that very much, but I've also never had the courage, ask Dad for his side of the story.

"Thanks, I appreciate that," I say.

My uncle looks at his desk clock. "I know you're missing the Ranger Ball. But I want to make sure I can answer any questions you might have."

"Any idea of how long I might be gone?"

"Depending on the train service. One, two days out there, same amount back. A lot depends on the condition of the tracks and the locomotives."

"I appreciate you saying I'm one of your best, Uncle Malcolm. But again, why me?"

"I've made the decision, Randy. Let it be."

I look at my uncle's worn and harsh face. "I think I know why."

His look is impassive. I go on, feeling a bit bold with all this leave out the 'yes sir' and 'no sir' nonsense. "You've just engaged in a bit of payback, that's all. You don't like being bossed around by the governor, don't like having to supply somebody to babysit a courier. So you give them somebody my age, to insult the governor and his executive assistant."

He picks up a pencil, puts it down. "Just like your father. Thinking too much. Any other questions?"

"Weapons?"

"What, you're thinking of bringing a Colt M-10?"

"I was thinking about it," I say.

He shakes his head. "Forget it. You're providing an escort. Not going on a Creeper hunt. You'll be representing the Guard and Fort St. Paul and uniform of the day will be Army Service Uniform, with sidearm. If you do see the President, don't waste his time. He's a very busy man. Plus to be absolutely clear here, this assignment of yours is classified. What you've been told in this room is to stay in this room. Anything else?"

I note the dismissive tone in his voice and say, "No, uncle."

The pencil is again in his hand. "Very well. Dismissed."

I get up and make to leave, and he says, "Randy?"

"Yes?"

"Thanks for the steak. It was delicious. Your aunt Corinne and Heidi enjoyed it. But just so you know . . ."

My hand is on the doorknob. "What's that?"

His voice is harsh. "I know Aunt Corrine has invited you to move in with us. Forget it."

"Already forgotten . . . sir," I say, as I go into the outer office.

Later I make my way to the gymnasium, back in civvies once more, where the Ranger Ball is being held. I'm so very late, but the music is still loud as I go through the doors and onto the dance floor. The music comes from a man named Clayton who used to own a radio station in the state's largest city, Manchester. He wears jeans and T-shirts that have some sort of awful color pattern that's called tie-dum or tie-dye or something like that. His gray beard comes down mid-chest. His gear is more than a half-century old, and because of its age, it survived the opening weeks of the Creeper war, scores of specialized nukes were dropped into the upper atmosphere, the EMP effects catapulting most of the world back to the late 1800s.

Once upon a time, I've learned, guys and gals my age could carry around thousands of pieces of music on a little computer smaller than my hand. Now, the music playing tonight at the Ranger Ball comes from round black discs called records, with lots of pops and static and scratches, and some of them are older than Clayton.

I'm greeted with a slow-moving tune from the "Beatles," and I scan the interior of the gym. The male-to-female ratio is about three to one, so there's a fair number of young men standing by themselves against one wall, where bleachers have been folded back. The dance has been going on for a while and there's the scent of sweat and the sound of laughter and a feeling that maybe, just maybe, this war is really over and that this wouldn't be the last dance for some of us.

Civilian life, I think. What could it possibly be like for someone like me?

I look in particular for one special some of us, and find her doing a slow dance with Dewey, the mess officer, who's plump-looking in khakis and a white T-shirt. Abby looks fine in a short black dress exposing her strong tanned and scarred legs. She spots me looking at her and sticks out her tongue. Maybe she's joking, maybe she's not. I wander off to what's left of the refreshment table. There are two half-empty bowls of punch, a couple of platters of crackers and fruit, mostly scrounged through, and some dirty napkins. The "Beatles" song is still playing. I'm nudged and see it's Clayton, the disc jockey. He raises his voice a bit. "Enjoying the night?"

Not particularly, but he looks eager so I say, "Yes, very much."

He scoops up a handful of crackers and fruit, stuffs them into his bearded mouth. "Love this old music. Funny world, eh? Was a time when I couldn't keep track of the new crap that was coming out every year by some non-talented kids with fair skin and good hair . . . and now they're all gone. Lady Gaga, Sir Gogo, all that crap." He slaps his belly and goes back to his black records. "Just me and my records, real rock and roll, we're all that's left."

Goodie for you, is what I want to say, but I keep my mouth shut.

The slow dance stops and I go out to the gym floor, catch up with Abby, who has a wide smile for Dewey, who still has his heavy hands on her slim body. Then he sees me and drops his hands, like Abby's hips had suddenly burst into flames or something, and shuffles away. To Abby I say, "Sorry I'm late."

Abby shrugs, like it doesn't matter, and I don't like her pissy look. "That's okay. Saved a spot for you for the first three dances, and then I decided not to wait. Something going on?"

I hesitate. "Yeah, but that's all I can say."

"OPSEC?"

"The same."

"Nice excuse."

"It's not an excuse," I say. "Look, I want to—"

The music roars up again, something fast moving from "The Kinks," and Perez, a skinny guy with wide shoulders from our second platoon comes over, and Abby says, "Sorry, Randy. I promised Tio here after Dewey. Later, maybe?"

"Sure, later, maybe," I shoot back, and with the music really roaring along, I go outside. A waste to haul ass out there after seeing my uncle. The night air is cool and crisp, but I note something burning. I go around to the side of the gym and see a flame flickering, beyond some rhododendron bushes, and there's a group of guys from my platoon and the second. A smell of tobacco and someone's smoking a very expensive and forbidden cigarette. There's a small oil lamp on the ground and someone says, "That you, Sergeant Knox?"

"Yeah," I say. "Just taking a breather. Relax."

I can feel them doing just that, since I could have put them in hack for sneaking out of the Ranger Ball and for the cigarette smoking, but I don't have time nor interest in rousting them. Instead I stand there and lean against the brick wall of the gym, listening to them pass the time like most soldiers: either complaining or trying to make sense of things.

Tonight it's the latter, and one guy says, "Creepers don't make sense, and don't nobody else convince me."

"'Course they don't make sense," comes another voice. "They're friggin' aliens."

First guy says, "But they're so damn primitive."

A couple of guys laugh and the second voice says, "C'mon, Harmon, you can't believe that. Damn Creepers arrived here on a friggin' starship of some kind, and in less than a week, they killed off more than half the planet, drowned every major coastal city, and fried so many electronics that my younger brother thinks electricity is something magical."

Then comes the quick reply. "Maybe so, but what did they do next? Hunh? Dispatched those killer stealth sats that kill anything that flies, anything that uses recovered electronics above a certain level, and set up bases where they come out and raise hell. But why? For ten years they parade around in their exoskeletons, killing and burning, and sometimes getting killed in return. What's the point?"

I say, "You sound disappointed, Harmon. Like you wanted them to kill us all off during the first six months of the war."

Harmon says, "Not at all, Sergeant. It just . . . just doesn't make sense."

The music is still thumping from inside the dance hall. I say, "Maybe they're great white hunters."

Somebody else says, "The hell you mean by that, sarge?"

"Back in the mid to late 1800s, rich white hunters would go to Africa and hunt big game," I explain. "It was expensive, they used the latest technology to travel great distances, and sometimes they'd get killed when they got gored by a rhino or trampled by an elephant. Maybe the Creepers are here to hunt humans, just for the fun of it."

The guys keep quiet, and one says quietly, "That's crap, Sergeant. There's no way a technologically advanced civilization like the Creepers would travel all this distance just to kill things. Don't make sense."

I say, "Really? Then look what they're doing. They came across interstellar space and they're doing what, exactly? Killing humans.

Doesn't look like they're making large Creeper settlements, or stealing water or diamonds, or breeding us for steaks, like those old science fiction movies. Maybe it don't make sense, but I'm just reporting what I'm seeing."

Nobody says anything, and I go on. "Look at it this way. You're working in a factory or a farm in England, Victorian age. Barely keeping a roof over your head, a couple of meals away from starvation for you and your family. Each day is one drudge day after another. Then you hear that your rich countrymen are using the most highly advanced steamships of the day to travel great distances to a foreign land to shoot things. What do you think your reaction would be? Does *that* make sense?"

Another pause, and someone says. "Hell of a thing."

"Yeah," another says, "and speaking of hell of a things, you guys hear anything more about possible discharges coming up?"

The talk then turns excited and hopeful, as these young fellow soldiers of mine consider what it might be like, to actually be out of the National Guard, and with that, I head on back to my barracks.

CHAPTER THIRTEEN

Before the war began, there were only four train stations in the entire state of New Hampshire. True story. Now there are at least a dozen, as steam and coal make a comeback under the very non-benevolent attention of the Creepers' killer stealth satellites. Across the country more stations have been built as well, as the government slowly rebuilds the railroads and bridges, as well as rounding up obsolete equipment to fill in the demand created by both the lack of air travel and about ninety-nine percent of vehicle traffic that existed before 10/10.

Concord, the state's capitol, has a train station set up next to the old Boston & Maine railroad tracks that run parallel to the crumbling concrete and asphalt of Interstate 93. From where it's located, it has a good view of the gold dome of the capitol building. The station was slapped together by an Army Corps of Engineers unit a couple of years after the war began, and it's basic concrete and wood. Outside of the entrance is a confusing mess of people and vehicles. There are horse-drawn wagons and buggies, a steam-powered Greyhound bus and two Army Humvees (one of which dropped me off) along with three cars from the late 1950s and early 1960s that weren't impacted by the Creeper attack. Each of those cars has an "A" gasoline ration sticker on its windshield, and when the doors open up, the well-dressed male and female passengers are accompanied by hard-eyed and muscled men who casually keep one hand underneath their jackets.

In addition to the passengers pushing their way into the station, there are a few homeless types outside begging, as well as two guys in ratty Army uniforms sitting in old folding lawn chairs. An empty wheelchair is parked nearby. One is a muscular black guy whose legs are gone just below the knee, and the other is a Hispanic fellow whose face is a mass of burn tissue and whose eye sockets are empty and sunken. There is a professionally-printed sign at their feet with a cardboard box next to it. The sign says, ALL GAVE SOME, SOME GAVE ALL. THANK YOU. And below those words is the official seal from the Department of Veterans Affairs, to let everyone know these guys are legit. Sometimes civilians who get fried by a Creeper try to pass themselves off as vets, and they last maybe a day or two before something bad happens to them.

I drop a pre-war quarter dollar into the box while the black guy eyes me and says, "Stay safe, bro."

"Thanks," I reply. "I'll try."

The blind Hispanic vet moves his head and says, "Smell something fine. Mind if I touch 'em?"

"Not at all," I say, and I lead Thor over, and the Hispanic guy sighs and rubs my dog's head. Thor leans into him. The vet says, "Rubio was my boy, during the day . . . when I got smoked, he stuck with me . . . led the medics to me . . . poor guy got scorched too, didn't make it through the night after I got hit."

The guy rubs Thor's head one more time and turns away. His companion wipes at his eyes.

I go into the train station.

An hour earlier I was in my barracks room, getting ready to depart, still trying to get a handle of what I had to do and where I had to go, when our batman came in and whistled at me. "Looking mighty fine, Sergeant," Corporal Manning says.

"Stuff it," I say, feeling cross. I was still thinking about Abby and last night's disaster of a dance, and I feel out of place, wearing my Army Service Uniform. Stuck in my front pockets are the old photo of my family, my blessed Rosary, and my souvenir from my first Creeper kill.

The old man slowly lowers himself down and sits on my bunk. "You're on a long trip and you're dressed up like you're getting a promotion? Or a court martial?"

"How in hell do you know what I'm doing?"

Manning laughs. "Sign of a good soldier is knowing what his uppers are doing. So why are you dressed like that, Sergeant?"

In my open bag I put in another pair of clean socks and underwear, noting I'm down one set because Specialist Millett hadn't yet returned the borrowed pair. "Orders, what else."

Manning shakes his head. "You should wear your standard fatigues, Sergeant. No matter what anybody says, everything outside of this base is a combat zone. You should dress like that, and carry the right gear."

"What kind of gear?"

"You've been in Recon Ranger this long and can't figure out what kind of weapons to bring?"

"The colonel said Colt M-10 was out of the question."

"Which leaves a lot of other options, don't it."

I look to his old, seasoned and wise face, decide to lighten the subject. "Tell me again about that other television show. Not the one about the housewives. The one about the sisters."

He snorts. "Three pudgy sisters with lots of make-up and expensive dresses who went to a lot of parties, got into fights, got married and divorced, and had camera crews following their every choreographed step. Their mother took pride in whoring them out, and their stepfather had so much facial surgery it looked like his head was made of wax. That was the television show."

"I know that," I say. "But what did they do?"

Manning says, "Just what I told you, Sergeant. That's it. Hell of a thing, watching that collection of idiots, knowing you once went to battle and bled on their eventual behalf."

"Korea?" I ask.

He says not a word, looks like he's thinking. The old corporal doesn't talk much about what's gone on with him, and I think this is a good time to press him. "What was Korea like?"

"Why are you asking?"

"Curious," I say. "Remember? I'm just a kid. We're always curious."

He takes a breath, folds his wrinkled hands across his belly. "Cold. Stark. Like the surface of the moon. Sometimes you could half-convince yourself you weren't even on the Earth. The Chinese . . . they'd attack at night, in huge waves, one right after another, blowing bugles, ringing cymbals. To this day I still can't stand the sound of bugles and cymbals. We fired back, called in artillery strikes, air strikes, and the bastards kept on coming. Had to put wet towels on the machine gun barrels so they wouldn't warp from all the heat. We were outgunned, outnumbered . . . but we pushed them back, by God, we pushed them back . . . not many remember what we did back then, but we did it, when and where it counted."

When he's talking his eyes shift, so he's looking at a far corner of the room, thousands of miles and decades away. His gaze comes back to me. "As bad as it was then, Sergeant Knox, you've got the tougher fight. The Chinese . . . we couldn't understand them either, like the Creepers, but at least they was human. And you . . . I don't care what you been told, you're going into a combat zone. Want my advice, Sergeant?"

"Always," I say.

He gets up, slaps me on my shoulder. "Dress and arm yourself accordingly."

I look to him, start unbuttoning my shirt, knowing I was going to visit the K-9 kennels before leaving. But before he leaves, I call out, "Corporal?"

"Sergeant?"

"If . . . if a letter comes from my dad, you'll make sure to keep it safe, right?"

A solemn nod. "You can count on it, Sergeant."

In the wide hallway of the Concord train station, the benches are hard plastic and are almost full of passengers. A male Amtrak employee wanders the hall, uses a megaphone to announce the next train leaving, heading off to Keene. As the good corporal suggested, I'm wearing standard BDUs and a jacket, denoting my name, rank and unit. Belted around my waist is my 9 mm Beretta, and stuck in my boot is my Army-issue Blackhawk knife. My pack is in one hand, and Thor's leash is in the other. I make my way to a ticket station and present my orders, and the very young lady wearing a well-mended Amtrak uniform that looks two sizes too big for her, does some stamping and writing, and then peers over the counter, sees Thor.

"The dog going with you, too?"

"He sure is," I say.

She glances down at my orders. "I only see authorization for you."

I take my orders from her hand, point to a sub-paragraph. "See that? 'Provide transportation for Sergeant Randy Knox, New Hampshire Army National Guard, as well as accompanying equipment.'"

I show her my assault pack, and then my leash. "This bag and the dog are my equipment, ma'am. Now. Do I get a ticket for him or do I need to contact my commanding officer, so he can talk to your station master?"

She frowns, bites her lip, and does another round of stamping and signing, and passes the cardboard slips over. "There you go. Two round-trip tickets for you and your . . . equipment. Concord to the Capitol, and then back again."

I note the hesitation and awe in her voice in the last sentence. It's not considered polite to say aloud the name of our latest capitol city, like those extremely orthodox Jews who don't say the name of their God aloud or in print. Since the war began, the capitol has moved around the country at least a half-dozen times, before settling in at its current location. It's been there for three years, a record I'm told. The previous times the Creepers found out where the new capitol was located and blasted it from orbit with their killer stealth sats. So even its name isn't mentioned aloud in polite or not-so-polite company.

"Thank you, ma'am," I say, putting the precious cardboard tickets in a side jacket pocket. "I appreciate it."

"Fine," she says, and then dismisses me and calls out, "Next!"

Back in the hallway there are echoes from footsteps and people talking, and a huge clock hangs down from the peaked ceiling. The time matches my own watch and I see there's five minutes to go before oh nine hundred. I take the ticket out, check it. The train departs from Track A in thirty-five minutes. I begin to wonder where my important escortee is.

Some laughter and loud voices, and a squad of about a dozen Marines bustle through, in full battle-rattle, each carrying a Colt M-10, three of them with dogs, German shepherds, on leashes. We all make eye contact and, out of well-oiled habit, give each other the slightest of nods, an immediate acknowledgment of respect, essentially saying "Hey man, been there, done that too. I got your back, you've got mine." Thor is good and doesn't tug at his leash, but one of the German shepherds starts whining and pulling. His Marine handler tugs him back and eyes me. "Sorry 'bout that."

"No problem, marine," I say. "No problem at all."

He takes a gander at my rank and Recon Ranger patch, and says, "Good huntin' now, okay?"

"You too, bro."

The Marines saunter by like they own the joint, and in a way, I guess they do. They call themselves the few, the proud, and although some of my fellow troopers think they're crazy, I've always been happy to have them on my flank in a battle or Creeper search. They have an élan or esprit de corps that some regular National Guard or Army units don't have, and in battle, they're pretty much damn fearless. I heard a rumor once that the Marines were so tough because they only allowed enlistees in who had lost family members during the Creeper war, but that's just stupid talking. Ten years into it, it's hard to find anybody out there who hasn't lost somebody to the Creepers.

As they head out to the tracks, a young girl's voice is at my side: "Excuse me, Sergeant Knox? From the 2nd Recon Rangers?"

I turn and take a pause. She's about my age and is simply the most beautiful girl I've ever seen. She has long blonde hair falling about her slim shoulders, and even though she's wearing a standard U.S. Army dress uniform, she fills it out quite nicely. Her uniform includes a skirt cut just below her knees, and her legs in her flat black dress shoes look mighty fine. Over one shoulder she carries a large black purse. She quietly says, "Sergeant, I'm Specialist Serena Coulson. My brother and I have been assigned to travel with you."

I've been staring at her light blue eyes with such focus that I hadn't even noticed the young man standing next to her and a few steps behind. He looks to be about eleven or twelve, dressed in a light gray suit with white shirt and black necktie. I don't think I've ever seen a guy that young so dressed up.

I look to her and say, "Say again, specialist?"

Now she looks aggravated. "As I said before, my brother and I have been assigned to travel with you to the capitol."

"Says who?" I asked.

"Says your commanding officer, Colonel Malcolm Hunter. He is your commanding officer, is he not? The post commander for Fort St. Paul?"

"That he is, but I'm not buying it. I just got here from the fort. Why don't I know anything about it?"

"How should I know?" I'm admiring how clean and styled her blonde hair is when she adds, "Will this help?"

From a side jacket pocket she pulls out a business-sized envelope, its flap open. The return address is Fort St. Paul, Concord, New Hampshire. I put my assault pack on the cement floor and take out the letter inside. It's on the colonel's stationary, and there's a handwritten note underneath the letterhead:

Randy—

Last minute, I know, but you're to accompany Spec. Coulson and her brother Robert Coulson to the destination previously mentioned. Spec. Coulson's father is a close personal friend of mine and wants the two of them with him on family business. I'm sure you'll be able to perform both missions without fail.

        —Col. M. T. Hunter, Commanding

I want to say something nasty out loud but Coulson's expression and fair skin—was she wearing just a hint of makeup?—make me keep my mouth shut. I hand her the letter back. "Stick around, specialist. I'm going to make a phone call. Just to double-check."

She looks up at the train station's clock. "If I may suggest, sergeant, you should move along. We don't want to miss the train."

Give her credit, she's that close to being insubordinate, but I let it slide and go to a nearby booth for the resurrected New England Bell. There are a number of civilians waiting their turn and I feel a sour tinge of guilt as I push myself to the head of the line.

"Sorry," I say to the farmer who's up next and to the New England Bell worker, a gaunt-looking man with white hair who looks like he hasn't eaten in days, sitting behind a low counter. "I need to make a phone call. Now."

The farmer grumbles and the Bell guy says, "Is it an emergency?"

"No, but it's official business."

He frowns. "Who are you calling?"

"Yeah," the farmer says. "You need to call your girlfriend or somethin'?"

Looking to the Bell guy and making sure the farmer could hear me, I say, "Person to person call from Sergeant Randy Knox, Second Recon

Rangers, to Colonel Malcolm Hunter, base commander, Fort St. Paul."
I write a number on a pad of paper with a stub of a pencil on the
counter, slide it over.

That shuts up the farmer and the Bell guy puts a headset on, presses
a few switches, and says, "Go over there, to booth two. Just pick up the
receiver and you'll be connected."

I thank him and the farmer says glumly, "You know, there was a
time I had a cell phone that could take pictures, surf the Web, and I
could call my brother in London in a matter of seconds. Now, takes
me a half-day to schedule a phone call to call my sister in Indiana."

I say, "Yeah, things are tough all over."

I go to the booth and leave the door open, and Thor sits down as I
lift up the phone receiver. I get a dial tone, hissing with static, and then
it rings once and is picked up. "Colonel Hunter's office, Lieutenant
Bouchard speaking, this is an unsecured line." Usually outside calls go
through the main switchboard but one of the few advantages of being
related to the battalion commander is knowing his private phone
number.

"This is Sergeant Knox," I say. "I need to talk to the colonel."

The lieutenant is not impressed. "You know the chain of command,
sergeant. Talk to your platoon leader, Lieutenant May."

"I would, except I'm on mission directly tasked by the Colonel. And
if I don't talk to him within the next sixty seconds, then I'm hanging
up and heading back to post to discuss the matter with him, face to
face."

I hear her mutter something about somebody being a brat nephew,
and there's a *click*, a pause, and another *click*. "Colonel Hunter," a
familiar voice comes on.

"Sir, Sergeant Knox, at the Concord rail station. I've been contacted
by a Specialist Coulson and—"

"Yes, yes, I saw her this morning and presented her with a note to
give you. Didn't she do that?"

"Yes, she did, sir, but I wanted to ensure that—"

"I've authorized her to do so. What's the problem?"

"Sir, you're asking me to escort the . . ."

"Open line," he cautions, and I continue, ". . . the gentleman in
question, and now you're asking me to escort two more individuals."

"Those other individuals are your age or younger. Are you telling me, sergeant, that you can't handle that?"

"Well, I—"

"And another thing. It appears that a K-9 named Thor is absent without proper authorization. Do you know anything about that?"

Quickly thinking, I whistle and hiss into the receiver. "Sorry, sir, it appears the phone line is breaking up . . . and it looks like the train is coming."

I hang up and smile down at Thor. "Just can't stop getting into trouble, now, can we?"

CHAPTER FOURTEEN

Back out into the main hall of the train station, I meet up with Specialist Coulson, who's standing there with her brother, an irritated expression on her face. "Fine," I say. "You're with me."

"I told you," she says.

"So you did. Do you have your tickets?"

"I do."

I look beside her. "Any luggage?"

"No."

"Really?"

"According to Amtrak, the trip should only take six or seven hours," she says. "We don't need luggage."

"Specialist . . . in a perfect world, the trip should only take six or seven hours. Look around. Are we living in a perfect world?"

She looks up at the clock. "The train should be arriving shortly, sergeant. I don't think we have time for a philosophical discussion."

Again, edging that close to insubordination, but I don't have the energy to fight with her. She was right again, it was almost time for the train. I look around the crowded hall once more and there he is, Mister Ezra Manson, representative to the Governor of New Hampshire, striding our way. He's carrying a soft light brown leather suitcase in one hand, and a dark leather dispatch case in the other, wearing the same suit from the day before. As he gets closer, I see the dispatch case has a chain running from it, up to his wrist. Gee, just like the old films I've seen on movie night.

"Sergeant," Manson says, coming up to me. "Glad to see you're on time." He sees Specialist Coulson and her brother. "Are this boy and girl from your outfit?"

I say, "I don't know where Specialist Coulson is stationed, and it appears her younger brother is not in the service. Beyond that, they are joining us on the trip to the capitol."

"Under whose authority?"

"Colonel Hunter's," I say.

He glances down at Thor. "Is this . . . dog also coming with us?"

"That dog is my battle buddy," I reply, "and yes, he is part of our group."

Manson shakes his head. "Being escorted by a boy and his dog. Not sure if your colonel has a very high regard for you, or a very low regard for me."

I gently tug Thor's leash. "Perhaps it's both, Mister Manson."

And I'm secretly pleased to see a smile on Serena's face. She takes her brother's hand and we walk out to the tracks, quickly passing through a security checkpoint of Amtrak cops and Concord cops.

The train is late, which isn't a surprise. I join the cluster of passengers and I'm pleased to see the squad of Marines I had seen earlier bunching up, like they were going on our train. That's good. I felt naked out in the open without back-up and without my M-10, and I'm glad to be traveling with the few and the proud. Manson is talking to a couple of men his age in suits by a wooden bench, and Serena is standing still with her brother by a concrete pillar holding up the overhead wooden roof, and there's a large framed poster behind them. The poster is in a stylized art deco style, showing drawings of the three different types of Creeper exoskeletons, with lots of red and black. The lettering says:

KNOW YOUR ENEMY

Contact your local police force or military unit if you observe the following:

Unexplained wildfires
Burnt bodies
Burnt structures

Nighttime 'clicking' sounds
Recently made trails in wilderness areas
Strong odor of cinnamon

Creepers Can Only Win If We Let Them!

There's another poster nearby, written and printed in the same style. It shows a stylized city, with a thick orange line coming down from the Creeper's orbital station. The buildings are burning. Underneath, in big black bold letters:

10/10 Never Again!

Maybe so, if the news was right about the Air Force doing their job. But in my corner of the world, the war was still going on.

Wonder if I should complain to anybody.

I go to Serena and say, "So, what's your specialty, Coulson?"

"Special Projects," she says.

"Where are you stationed?"

"Maine," she says.

"Where in Maine?"

"Sorry, sergeant, I can't say."

"OPSEC? Really?"

She nods. "Really."

I look to her brother. "What do you say, pal? Is your sister telling the truth?"

He stares at me with distaste, like I was getting close to spitting on his shiny suit or something. His sister looks at me with an equally distasteful look and says, "Sorry, sergeant. Buddy can't talk."

"Can't or won't?"

"Does it make any difference?"

"I thought his name was Robert."

"Buddy is his nickname. And he's a disabled vet."

I say, "Sorry to hear that. Creeper attack?"

She shakes her head. "No, it was duty-related."

"Oh," I say. "Can you tell me his duty, or is that classified as well?"

She puts a protective hand on his shoulder. "He was in Intel, in the Obs Corps. For two years."

I stare at the young boy, not believing what I had just heard. To serve six months in the Observation Corps was a standard deployment. A year was stretching it . . . Two years? I look at his eyes again, see something I hadn't noted before: they were the eyes of an old man, a man who had suffered and toiled so very much. To be in the Observation Corps means working with a telescope with a motor drive, so you're watching one piece of night sky for long hours, keeping watch on the stars and the floating debris. The point is to track the killer stealth satellites. Even if they're invisible to radar or other means of observation, they can still block—or occult—a star as they move in orbit. What an Observation Corps member does is to keep view on that assigned stretch of the night sky, and call out if he or she sees something pass by a star, making it "wink." Another observer with an accurate timepiece then notes the time and the name of the star that was occulted, and keyed in with other observers, over the years, the orbits and positions of the killer stealth satellites can be tracked.

It's exhausting, grueling, mind-numbing work. No wonder Buddy doesn't talk.

I say, "Can he take care of himself?"

A bit defensively, Serena says, "Yes. He can eat, wash, dress and go to the bathroom. But he doesn't talk. He listens, but . . . look, here's the train."

There's the mournful howl of a train whistle and I look up the tracks. A steam train is moving along stately, smoke and steam trailing behind, and it passes by and then slowly grinds to a halt. The locomotive is old, of course, and there's a yellow and blue sign painted on the side: SPONSORED BY WAL-MART, AS TOGETHER WE REBUILD AMERICA. The passenger cars are a different mix, all painted roughly with the blue and white Amtrak color scheme, but underneath the paint job other names are visible: Conway Scenic Railway, Kennebunkport Trolley Museum, New York MTA. Since the war started there was a scramble to get passenger cars from all across the nation, even if it meant raiding train museums and short-line excursion railways for tourists.

As one the group of passengers moves onto the train. Coulson and Buddy are in front of me, and Manson catches up. "So how did those two get to join us, sergeant?"

"Colonel's orders."

"Why?"

"Ask him, sir, if you'd like to know more."

"Doubtful," he says. I give him a closer look and feel a shock of recognition. His eyes seem almost as tired as young Buddy Coulson's, and I recall what my uncle had said. It was civilians like him that kept things going, so we weren't being ruled by kings or warlords. For the briefest of moments I feel glad to be with him.

But I'm sure the feeling wouldn't last.

A conductor wearing an Amtrak jacket with patches on the elbows directs us to our car, and after putting my assault pack in an overhead bin, and helping Manson with his luggage, we sit down. Manson and Buddy sit on one seat, and Coulson and I sit across from them, Serena putting her large black purse in her lap. Thor sniffs around and rolls and sits down on the wooden floor. Manson frowns and crosses his legs, and Buddy looks down at my dog. For a moment I almost believe he smiles.

We wait some more and I look out the near window. There are only a few people left on the platform, and—

Someone approaches from the inside of the train station, pushing a bicycle at her side.

Corporal Abby Monroe.

She's looking around at the few people left on the platform, looks to the train.

There's a thump and a bellow of steam as we start moving out.

Abby keeps looking.

I fumble with the window.

It won't move.

It's stuck.

I bang at the window with my fist, and Abby's head spins about, looking right at me, and I raise my hand.

She raises a hand, smiles.

Then she blows me a kiss.

I'm torn. I want to throw her a kiss back but I know Coulson and Manson are looking at me.

Then it's too late. The train has left the station, and Abby has faded from view.

I sit back down.

An Excerpt From the Journal of Randall Knox

Date night with Abby. Off to the 89 Café. It took a while to set up a date, with our conflicting training and deployment schedules. Plus we need to be discreet. Dating is forbidden between different rank structures, i.e., enlisted boys or girls can't date NCO's, NCO's can't date officers. It's officially discouraged among platoon members, but again, if one is discreet, the officers tend to look the other way.

Which is why I took Abby to the 89 Café. There are a couple of joints within walking distance of the post but too many of our fellow troopers go to them. So Abby managed to borrow a bike for me from the Motor Pool—saying she was taking it out for a test spin, hah hah hah—and dressed in civvies, we left Ft. St. Paul for a half-hour ride out to the café. A pleasant night, not even dusk yet, and we rode at a steady pace over cracked pavement where we could chat about post gossip, the lousy food in the dining hall, our last Creeper hunt, and the customary chit-chat between soldiers and friends. Under our civvies—we're both wearing windbreakers, slacks and T-shirts, clean but nothing too fancy—are holstered Beretta 9 mm automatics.

We may be off duty, but by God, we're not going to be unarmed.

The 89 Café is in a big farmhouse within walking distance of Interstate 89. Story is, after the NUDETS happened on 10/10, some of the passengers that left their dead cars and trucks on I-89 went to the farmhouse, where the family there welcomed them in. They stayed and started working to earn their way, and refugees stopped by and paid for food and shelter, and ten years later, it's changed some, but it's still there as a tavern and sleeping joint.

Out about the large farmhouse there were a couple of pre-war cars, with their guards sitting on the hoods, shotguns across their laps. Horses were at rest by two hitching posts, and there were about a half-dozen wagons parked out in a nearby field. Music comes out from open doors and windows, and after locking our bikes at a crowded bike rack, I took Abby's hand and we went in.

The admission fee was one new dollar apiece—pretty steep—but worth it to be far away from the post. Inside the music was loud from a live band of guitar, drums and piano, and there's sawdust on the floor, and a long bar and tables, and we got a table in the corner. The place was pretty crowded and it's fun to be out with civvies. We danced some and had lemonade and small cheeseburgers that supposedly come from cows raised nearby, and we laughed and kissed and danced some more, and when the band took a break, it all went south when a sour-looking man in a cheap suit with patches on the knees and elbows came over. He wanted to know how old we were, and when I snapped back, old enough, he showed the both of us a badge and said he was an inspector from the State Liquor Commission. Big deal, I said, and he said, oh yeah, big deal, you're underage, so get the hell out.

I said the hell I will, and I showed him my National Guard ID, and he said, big freaking deal, don't care what uniform you wear, you're still underage. Out you go, or I'll pull this bar's license, and I'll get you in hack with your superior officer.

I said I've got a commanding officer, but nobody's superior to me back at my post, and Abby squeezed my hand and pulled me away from the table. I made sure I paid our waitress and outside I was pretty pissed, and to Abby I said, so much for the thanks of a grateful nation, hunh?

Abby kissed me and said, night's still young. I can sneak you back into my barracks room and show you the thanks of a grateful Abby. I said, what about the night guards? Abby said, you wouldn't believe what they won't see or hear in exchange for an unopened box of ten-year-old Kotex.

I biked back pretty fast to the post, following a laughing Abby, who's much speedier than I am.

CHAPTER FIFTEEN

As we pull out from the station, Serena says, "That was sweet. Girlfriend?"

"Fellow Recon Ranger."

"Violating the rules against fraternization?"

I stare at her. "Is that any of your business, Specialist Coulson?"

She tries to stare right back at me, and then lowers her eyes. "No, Sergeant."

Manson laughs. "God help us."

"What's so funny?" I ask, turning my sharp-eyed look to him.

"Never mind," he says, looking out the window. We're now south of Concord, running parallel to Interstate 93. Sunlight glints off the windshields of the abandoned cars on the highway.

"Mister Manson," I say with exaggerated politeness. "Do go on. I've been accused by some members of my squad of not having a sense of humor. I'd love to learn why the specialist and I made you laugh."

Manson looks at the specialist, and then looks at me. "No offense, Sergeant. But you're sixteen, correct?"

"Yes."

"And Specialist Coulson, would you mind telling me your age?"

"Fifteen."

The train is rattling along now, the old railroad tracks bumpy and making the carriage shudder and shake. Manson raises his voice. "Please don't take offense, but you're teenagers . . . children. When I was your age, I was thinking about getting my driver's license, updating my Facebook page, and trying to get enough money for a new iPhone. Back then, my God, we had a term for parents who were overprotective. We called them helicopter parents, because they hovered over their children for years, making sure they didn't hurt themselves, or fail in school, or get fired from a job. Back then being your age meant being coddled, protected, having everything handed to you."

I say nothing, for this is a tale I've heard many times from my so-called elders over the years. It's like they have a need to apologize to us kids for the state of the world or something. He says, "Now, for the most part we depend on you . . . teenagers to defend us. To carry weapons and fight when you're not old enough to drink, vote or get married. It's a funny thing, that's all. From one generation to the next. From a pampered class to a warrior class."

Coulson looks like she's about to speak, but I beat her to it. "That was never our choice, our decision, was it, Mister Manson? We're defending you because so many adults have died over the years, fighting the Creepers. That's what we do. We fight, we resist, we protect. You, for example, Mister Manson, if you felt so strongly about teenagers defending you, you could resign your position in the state government and join up. I'm sure with your age and background, you'd become an officer in no time."

Manson chooses his words carefully. "I didn't mean to insult."

"Mister Manson, I've served in the New Hampshire National Guard for nearly four years. Since I've put that uniform on, I've never allowed anyone to call me a kid, or boy, or child. Do I make myself clear?"

Serena is smiling widely and Manson steps up from his seat. "Your colonel will know what you've just said, Sergeant."

"Outstanding," I say. "I look forward to the day when we can both tell him about this little talk."

Manson's face colors. "In the meantime, I'm moving to another seat."

I nod. "Mister Manson, go right ahead. But I do ask that you remain in this carriage in my line of sight. I'm under orders to escort you to our destination."

He doesn't say a word, but he steps out into the aisle and finds an empty seat about three rows back. With his seat abandoned, I point to it and say, "Thor, go." I know dogs can't smile but he seems to grin when he gets off the hard floor and jumps up on the empty seat.

Serena says, "Good for you."

"Excuse me?" I ask sharply.

She repeats and adds, "Good for you, Sergeant."

I turn and look out at the passing landscape of trees, nearly deserted roads, and the old brick buildings of Manchester as we move south.

After about a half hour of travel, the train starts to slow down, and through the window, I see a piece of history, parked on an otherwise deserted stretch of highway. When the Creeper war started, nearly every ship at sea lost its engines and steering, and nearly every aircraft in the air lost power. Most of them crashed. Up on the highway rests the remains of a British Airways Boeing 747, coming into approach to Boston. With engines out and Boston no longer there, the pilot and co-pilot managed to wrestle their nearly-dead aircraft to a landing on this piece of interstate.

Pretty fair piece of flying. I wish I could have met them.

The 747 is still there, and I see smoke wisping its way up in the sky from fires built near the wings and fuselage. The way I've heard it, a number of passengers still live in the aircraft, still waiting to go home, wherever their home is.

After about an hour the train rattles again, slows some more. The landscape out there looks familiar, and I'm chilled. We're approaching a river valley, and an Amtrak conductor comes through, holding onto the seats to keep his balance.

The conductor yells out, "Ladies and gents, we're stopping for fifteen minutes to take on wood and water. We should've filled up at Concord but they was low on supplies. Feel free to step out and stretch your legs, if you'd like. But don't go far. The train whistle will blow twice, and then we'll depart."

Good, I think. I'll just stay in my seat.

The train comes to a shuddering halt. Serena looks to her brother Buddy, who's calmly staring out the window. Thor is dozing on his side, all four legs dangling over the edge of the seat. The rear carriage door snaps open and I'm content to stay, but up ahead, Mister Manson gets up and steps off the train.

Damn.

I rub Thor's head. "Come on, pal."

I move around Serena and with a leashed Thor at my side, I step through the aisle and go outside. Thor sniffs the air, raises a leg against a railway track, and lets loose a stream of urine. It's a late cool morning, slightly overcast. To the right and below, a valley descends to the slow-moving Merrimack River. Bordering both sides of the river are the old brick buildings and smokestacks of Lowell, a Massachusetts mill town that's been here for a couple of hundred of years. Most of the brick buildings are shattered and blackened from being blasted a couple of years back.

I take a deep breath. My chest is so tight it's like I'm wearing body armor. Around me on this slope of the valley, the ground has been torn up, disturbed, trees tossed aside, exposed roots dangling, clumps of dirt still hanging onto them. Long lines of trenches remain open in places, with scraps of clothing and broken wood. There's other debris as well. The blasted hull of an Army M1-A1 Abrams tank, rolled on its side, the barrel sticking up into the air. Two school buses, scorched and windows broken, the yellow paint still visible. Rusted cables as thick as my wrist, tangled around in the dirt. Up on a far slope, wreckage of an Air Force fighter jet, maybe an F-15 or an F-22. I can't tell. Lower in the valley, two Creeper exoskeletons on their back, their stiff articulated legs sticking up in the air. Grass and brush have grown over some of the torn up landscape, but the area around the exoskeletons is gray and dead.

I look away from the old battlefield, see Manson standing and sharing a cigarette with a man about his age, also wearing a suit. Manson still has the leather satchel chained to his wrist. I wonder what's in the satchel. I wonder why he's seeing the President. Still wonder why I was picked to be here. Two other men in suits pass by, heading towards Manson and his companion, one man saying to the other, " . . . that Tess Conroy, she still has the President's balls in her make-up box, I mean, how long does she think people are going to sit still . . ."

And a muttered reply, " . . . hard to believe that Kansas governor's got the gonads to run against him this fall . . ."

They walk out of earshot. Politics. Can't stand it. Serena and her brother Buddy come up to me, she holding his hand. She looks down at the valley and says, "Is there where it was? The Battle of Merrimack Valley?"

"It was," I say. I turn and look around some more, remembering those frantic days. Serena says something else and I turn back to her. "Sorry, could you say that again? My left ear is burned. Don't hear that well from that side."

She says, "You were here, weren't you. I can tell by your face."

"Yeah, I was."

"Is that where you got your ear hurt?"

It doesn't make sense but my damaged left ear is throbbing with remembered pain. I say, "Tell me where in Maine you're stationed, and I'll tell you, specialist. Does that sound fair?"

She says, "All right. Fair exchange. Bangor."

"Is that where your dad's from?"

"Yes. And now he's at the Capitol. My brother and I haven't seen him in a few months, which is why I got leave to visit him."

I rub at my ear. Lucky, pretty little girl, knowing where her dad is. Unlike me. "Yeah, this is where I got hurt. During that battle. Lost a chunk of my hearing as well."

"Were you in Recon Rangers then?"

"No," I say. "I had joined up only two years earlier. I was with the regular 157th Field Artillery Unit. But during the Battle of Merrimack Valley, we didn't have much in the way of field artillery. We had some 105-millimeter mortars and some AT-4 anti-tank missiles. It was a mixed bag of what had survived the first few years of the war. We used everything and anything we could get our hands on."

The sounds of the passengers talking amongst themselves, the locomotive releasing steam and smoke, the gurgling of the water being pumped in from a nearby water tower, all these noises recede. The memories come back to me, slowly overtaking everything, like a spring flood overflowing a streambed and lapping at your life.

I say, "The Creepers have a base near the Connecticut border. One night a couple of dozen Creepers popped out and started moving north in a skirmish line, burning and blasting everything in their path. General Ray Spenser, a regular officer, stationed at the Pentagon, was vacationing in Vermont when the war started. By the time of this battle, he was ready, as best as he could be, commanding the blocking forces. Most of the country's front-line units had already been destroyed or hollowed out from the first years of the war. The concern was that the Creepers were going to sweep up through New

Hampshire, and then take out the whole Maine coast and some important installations up there . . . so we were going to stop them. He sent out a mimeographed letter, Order of the Day it said. It quoted a famous French general during the Battle of Verdun, in 1916. His name was Robert Nivelle."

"What did he say?"

"Pretty simple, but it worked. 'They Shall Not Pass.' Got it? They had kicked the crap out of us for years, but this time, we drew a bloody line in the sand, and they weren't going to pass. Even if it meant using trench warfare tactics from the last century, they weren't coming through."

I continue staring out there in the distance. "Back then, we didn't have the Colt M-10 rounds. So we made do with what we could . . . hell, we had a couple of platoons of regular 10th Mountain Division, New Hampshire and Massachusetts National Guard units, and even had members from the 369th Sustainment Brigade. They were from New York City and called themselves the Harlem Hellfighters. They'd been out on training up in New York state when Manhattan got hit. They were tough and mean and did everything they could to fight the Creepers."

Coulson says, "How did we win, then?"

I shrug. "Who says we won? There's still some dispute about the final outcome. But by God, we held them here . . . held them here and pushed them back. "'twas a famous victory,' you know. General Spenser, he had a sense of how and where they moved based on intel he got from dispatchers and runners from across the country. The Creepers tend to follow valleys and moving water, for whatever reason. Even then, he had less than a day to prep the battlefield, and prep he did."

Coulson starts to talk and I interrupt, pointing to the valley. "We still weren't able to destroy the Creepers outright. Still can't figure out why those exoskeletons are so tough. But we could slow them, turn them back, and if lucky, cripple or kill the creatures inside. On this side of the valley, the general buried lengths of cables under the dirt. On the other side of the valley, he hid artillery, best as he could. When the Creepers rolled through here, the cables were dragged up, snagging the Creepers' legs. Slowed them down. Artillery units opened fire, chewing up the landscape, rolling the Creepers over, tangling them.

He even had a couple of M1-A1 and A2 tanks and some Air Force jets in reserve, which he sacrificed . . . poor bastards driving and flying knew they were on a suicide mission, and they went in anyhow. The killer stealth sats in orbit were quick in picking up powered vehicles like jets and tanks, but they were able to do some damage before they got whacked."

My breath is catching. "A couple of long-range snipers were there, too, firing depleted uranium rounds into the Creepers' main arthropod stalk. They were able to knock a few out. Even had sappers that went down and wrapped charges around the legs of the exoskeletons while they were tangled up or on their backs. Hardly any one of those sappers came back."

Coulson says quietly, "Were you near here?"

I shake my head. "A klick or two away. We were dropping harassing and interdiction rounds on the Creepers as they got slowed down by the cables or the sappers."

"How did you get hurt?"

Odd, I know, but I'm starting to hear the sounds of shouts, of outgoing rounds, explosions. My knees are quivering. "A new recruit got separated from my squad. He got fried. I went and rescued him, nearly got my head taken off as well. Dragged him back nearly a klick to our position."

"You were very brave."

"Did my job."

"Bet he was happy to see you."

Melendez, that had been his name. Poor old Melendez. "Maybe. Maybe not. A Creeper laser took off his legs at the knees. He screamed every meter when I dragged him back. He was twelve. Just a kid."

The train whistle blows once, twice, and I look to her and then my bud and say, "Thor, let's go."

CHAPTER SIXTEEN

Inside the train, a surprising moment. Manson motions me over and I step up to him, and he says, "I meant no disrespect back there, Sergeant. My apologies. Sometimes . . . I just let the job get to me, be a wiseguy. You work for the governor, a lot of times you gotta say no. No to a town looking for a new bridge. No to a county looking to increase its food rationing. No to families looking for firewood assistance. You say no a lot, you tend to be a son-of-a-bitch."

His eyes still look like a mirror of Buddy's, so I let it slide. "Very well, Mister Manson. Water under the bridge and all that."

A smile and gentle tap to my shoulder. "We get to the Capitol and my job is done, I'll buy you and your two friends the best meal you've ever had. Promise."

I nod and return to my seat.

The ride west is slow and grinding. The train stops because a section of track is being repaired, or a wagon is stuck at a crossroads, or a tree is down across the right-of-way. Thor is a good boy and rests on the padded seat, and Serena and her brother Buddy stay together, Serena sometimes rubbing his shoulder or the back of his neck. Her brother sits quietly, staring out at the Massachusetts scenery as we rumble our way along.

Manson gets up from his seat and comes back to see me. "Sergeant, it seems to be lunch time."

I check my watch. "It certainly does."

Manson waits, and then says crossly, "Well?"

"Not sure what you mean, Mister Manson."

"Lunch. I'm hungry. I want you to get something for me to eat."

I rub Thor's fur. So much for the reasonable Mister Manson I had talked to earlier. "I'm afraid I can't do that, Mister Manson."

I sense Serena looking at me. He says, "The hell you can't. Your colonel ordered you to—"

"My colonel ordered me to escort you, sir. He didn't order me to fetch your meals or your laundry. If you wish to go back to the dining car, I'll gladly go with you. But when it comes to securing your chow, you're on your own."

Manson looks like he wants to argue, and then a couple of passengers start coming up the aisle behind him, and he snorts and moves out as well. I get up and say to Serena, "Can I get you and your brother anything?"

"I thought you weren't fetching chow."

"Not for him," I say. "For a fellow soldier, that's not a problem."

She blushes. I like the sight. She says, "I'm sorry, Sergeant, I can't say yes. I have no money. Just my ration book."

I say, "I'm on account. I'll take care of it. Keep a view on Thor, all right?"

Then I follow my charge through the rear carriage door.

I go through to another carriage, pass the Marines I had met earlier at the train station, and after two more carriages, I make it to the dining car, a small carriage with a countertop and three overworked and harried Amtrak women employees wearing black checked pants and white jackets. A number of tables are already packed with passengers, including a few Army officers. Manson is talking to one of the dining car workers and I elbow my way up, see a printed menu under glass on the counter: bottled water, meat sandwich, cheese sandwich. Not a bad menu, considering. I order lunch for the three of us and after the coupons get torn out of my ration book, I pay with a new ten-dollar bill, President Reagan's face smiling up at me, and then drop an extra fifty cents for a deposit on the plastic bag once I get my change back. With lunch and receipt in hand, to account for my expenses to Lieutenant Bouchard, I turn around and—

Bump right into an Army captain.

"Oh," I say. "Excuse me, sir."

"No problem, son," he says. "Don't worry about it."

I take in his uniform and feel my hands tingle. His shoulder flashes denote RANGER and SPECIAL FORCES, while Combat Parachutist, Air Assault, and Combat Infantryman Badges are stacked on his left breast. On the right, his nametag says DIAZ. I've never met a Special Forces soldier before, and for good reason: they're legendary, and move in different combat circles than the National Guard. Special Forces perform quite dark and secretive missions. Rumors have it that occasionally they've been able to raid inside Creeper bases, and have sometimes taken alien prisoners. Amazing stories, if true, but damn it, some of them must be true. Otherwise how was our Colt M-10 cartridge developed without having prisoners to test on?

I quickly take in three things from Captain Diaz: he's old and bald, with lots of burn tissue around what's left of his misshapen ears and eyebrows. Atop one of his badges is something I've heard about but have never seen before: the Diamond Eagle, denoting someone who's been on active duty for the past ten years. Understandably, not many of those have been awarded.

And the third thing is that he's looking at my nametag with undisguised interest.

"Knox?" he asks through his scarred mouth. "Sergeant Knox? Any relation to Colonel Henry Knox?"

I drop my bag of food and water, bend over clumsily to pick it up. "Yes, he's my father."

Captain Diaz says, "I'm Captain Ramon Diaz. Your father's a good man. A very good man. I just saw him last week. Sorry for his troubles."

"His troubles? Sir?"

We're jostled some from other passengers pushing into the meal counter. He says, "Later, Sergeant. I've got two buds of mine who are ready to faint if they don't get some food into them. I'll meet up with you later and we'll talk."

The Special Forces captain moves forward and I stand still, shocked and surprised and filled with a mixture of excitement and dread. Someone knows where my dad is, and my dad is alive, and—

He's in trouble.

What kind of trouble?

Don't know, but after I get lunch back into Serena and her brother's hands, I intend to track down Captain Diaz and find out exactly what's going on.

I practically trot back through the carriages, seeing Mister Manson at a distance through the glass windows of the doors. One carriage away from my seat and my two younger charges, there's an explosion, a wailing screech of steam, and the carriage tilts and I slam my back and head against the side wall.

An Excerpt From the Journal of Randall Knox

Lecture today from visiting Air Force officer. Said to be an expert on astrophysics. Short little guy, looked pretty nervous. Not hard to understand; since the war started, AF has taken the heaviest casualties. Started talking about where the Creepers might have come from. Two theories: nearby star system, or part of a culture that's been spaceborne for centuries. Either way, why did they come here? What prompted them?

Current idea is that Earth started announcing its presence through various means: first radio broadcasts in early 1900s, atomic weapons testing in 1945, wide-scale television broadcasting in the 1950s, H-bomb test in 1953. Creepers or anybody with right detection gear would know industrial civilization was present on third planet in our solar system. If our neighbors were mean and paranoid—like European empires in 15th century—they might decide to come over and raise some hell.

AF guy started going through star systems in a huge bubble about our sun, listing various stars that could be home to a Creeper civilization. Pretty dry stuff. Started yawning some and found out I wasn't the only one. When AF guy was done, Professor Falconer went to back row, kicked the legs of Jefferson, large black kid, refugee from Roxbury. Falconer asked him why he was sleeping. Jefferson said it was boring, not worth listening to. Professor said, why's that, Private? Jefferson shrugged: don't care where the buggy bastards came from. Just want to know how to kill 'em better.

Have to admit, I like Jefferson's attitude. He got ten extra days, KP duty at the dining facility, but I guarantee most of the guys and gals in the lecture hall agreed with him.

CHAPTER SEVENTEEN

I'm stunned and bite my tongue, and the lunch bag flies out of my hand. There are screams and shouts from the passengers as the carriage roars off the rails, hitting the ground, rattling and bouncing, the train whistle screeching in one long bone-rattling wail. The carriage tilts and bucks and finally grinds to a halt, on its side, passengers and luggage and papers and sacks tumbling to the right, more thumps and shouts. I jam my ankle into one seat and there's another explosion, and up front, a woman starts screaming, "It's a Creeper! It's a Creeper! We're gonna get burnt!"

More shouts, screams, panic rushing through the tilted-over carriage. Too much of a mess up forward with passengers bunched up against the far door, so I reverse course and push my way through the rear door, stumble to the ground, take in the quickening horror. Up ahead the locomotive with the cheerful Wal-Mart sign is on its side, its boilers broken, steam and smoke billowing up into the overcast sky. The coal car has crashed up into the locomotive, and the carriage cars are a twisted tumble, windows broken, flames roaring along the roof and side. Screams and shouts pierce through the air, passengers stumbling out of the doors or hauling themselves through broken windows.

We're in a shallow valley, the near slope rising up to a line of woods, the far slope being overgrown grass and brush, and as the screaming woman had warned, a Creeper is skylining itself at the crest of the hill. Its two main arms are firing down on us; one arm using its flamer, the other a weaponized laser, firing off short bursts that are burning and killing my fellow passengers as they scramble away from the derailed train. I frantically look around for Captain Diaz, the Special Forces officer who knows my dad, and he's nowhere to be seen.

More shouts. The Marines sprint by me, two dogs keeping pace, led by a sergeant screaming, "Alpha, get up on that ridge!" The tail-end Marine looks at me and says, "Come on, Recon boy, haul ass!"

I pull out my 9 mm, start running, heading to the near carriage. The Marine says, "War's over here, bud!"

"Orders!" I shout back, hating how weak the excuse sounds. "I got orders!"

He replies with a loud obscenity, and joins his squad.

Right then I hate myself, and I hate this job.

I climb through a broken rear door. Flames are dancing overhead from slats torn away from the old roof. More screams, and the harsh *snap/sizzle* of the Creeper's weapons at work. Seats have been ripped away and in the smoky haze, people are stumbling about.

"Thor!" I call out. "Thor, come!"

A bark and my chest feels immediately lighter. Even with the carriage tilted to one side, Thor scrambles across to me, dragging his leash. I unsnap the leash and call out again: "Coulson! Specialist Coulson!"

"Here!" comes a voice. From the smoke Serena emerges, holding her brother's hand, holding her large purse in the other. He has a bloody handkerchief pressed to his forehead, but he's not crying or sobbing. "Out," I say, "we've got to get out."

In the tangle of luggage I see my pack, grab it. "Manson!" I yell. "Mister Manson, are you here?"

Serena tugs at my arm. "He's gone. I saw him run out right after the train derailed. Damn near trampled a kid to do it."

I push her ahead of me, Thor moving along, the pack over my right shoulder, pistol in hand. The air is choking. Outside there's another *snap/sizzle* of the Creeper firing down at us. More screams. On the far slope smoldering bodies are at rest. A young girl, about three or four, is sitting up, holding the hand of a burnt body, crying and tugging at the dead hand of her mother or aunt or older sister, the tan skirt miraculously untouched, the upper torso smoking and sizzling.

Most of the passengers huddle down, trying to hide behind the derailed cars. I push Serena again. "Take your brother and go! Get away from here! Head down the tracks, find shelter."

"Why can't we stay here?"

Most of the carriages are on fire. I say, "If the Marines can't kill that Creeper right away, everyone here is going to be dead in a few minutes."

"Are you staying to fight?"

"No, damn it!" I yell again, my tongue hurting bad from when I had bitten it. "Following orders! Just like you've got to do *now*, Specialist! Keep down and move!"

She turns and grabs Buddy's hand, scrunches down and starts running down the far end of the railway tracks, moving around the passengers and debris from the derailed train. I move forward, to where most of the passengers are, calling out, "Manson! Manson! Mister Manson! I'll get you out!"

Through open areas of where the carriages are tumbled over, I see the Creeper hasn't moved from its elevated point. Its two weapon's arms are still moving, the laser flashing out, dazzling my eyes, the flames streaming out, dancing around the locomotive and carriage cars. The Marines are moving fast, executing a precision example of old Battle Drill 1A: one element provides suppressing fire to pin down the enemy, while the second element attempts a flanking maneuver. While old tactics are generally for old wars—ones fought against other humans—they are executing this tactic here and now and I think it just may work. I stand for a second. But something is wrong. I look down at Thor. He's panting, at my side, looking around.

Looking around.

I move forward, the shouts of the Marines cutting through the other sounds, the steam escaping from the ruined train, the flames now roaring along the carriages, the cries and screams of the other passengers shrieking at my ears. Up on the nearest slope, the woods are burning. There are at least a dozen blackened corpses up there, from people who just a few minutes earlier had been sitting safe in their well-paid seats.

Now they were smoked and charred bones and flesh, flames dancing through their clothing.

Move, I think. Move your ass. Find your Mister Manson.

Colored flares launch up into the sky, as the Marines on the other side of the train wreck signal to whomever might be out there that a Creeper attack is underway. More *snap/snizzle* of the Creepers' weapons firing.

The acrid stench of sweat, smoke and fear are blasting through my nostrils, along with the sweet smell of burning flesh, as I get closer to the locomotive. A lumpy charred body is dangling out of the train cab. I quickly look around.

"Manson! Manson!"

There's a heartening sound of *BLAM!* followed by *PLOP!* and then another series of the same sounds, as the Marines return fire with their M-10s. I can't help myself, and I yell out, "Get some, jarheads! Get some!"

I move ahead, fires warm on my face, and there's Manson.

On the ground, hiding behind a blasted piece of wood, arms stretched out, the leather dispatch case still chained to his wrist. I drop my assault pack, holster my pistol, and go to ground, crawling up to him, Thor mirroring me as well, his belly to the ground. Smart dog. I pull at Manson's shoe. Oil and water and lubricant have soaked the dirt and grass around us.

"Hey, Mister Manson!" I yell. "Let's get out of here."

A man is screaming. I turn my head, through the gap of the wreckage, see a Marine stumbling back, aflame. I clench my jaw, turn back to Manson, grab his foot and give it a good hard tug.

"You damn idiot, we've got to move, now!"

The foot is stiff in my hand. I crawl up further.

His head is gone.

Take a couple of deep breaths, try not to start sobbing in fear and frustration, and then I get back to work. I go through Mister Manson's pockets, find a keychain with six keys on it. Desperately avoiding looking at the burnt stump of his neck, I go to the chain and—

None of the keys fit.

None of the keys fit!

Another shout from the Marines. I snap my head around, see two Marines lying down, in perfect firing position as the suppressing element, M-10s braced against their shoulders, then two shots go downrange, a perfect solution and in a one-two punch, the 50 mm rounds explode right in front of the main arthropod's breathing membrane.

Perfect!

I yell out, "Hooh-AH, jarheads!" and I look to see the Creeper pause, shake and tremble and collapse, as the two rounds do their work.

One arm moves, and then another, *flash/flash* from the lasers, and the Marines are dead.

More *snap/sizzles* from the Creeper, and the bodies of the dead Marines burst into sticky blue flames.

The Creeper is still alive.

It's all wrong.

I chew on my bit tongue, trying to get my mouth moist again, and go back to Manson. Still dead. I tug at the chain, attached a handcuff on his wrist.

Nothing doing.

Orders, I think. Orders.

From my boot, I tug out my Blackhawk knife, and get to work.

Minutes later, Thor at my side, I'm running back down the length of the wrecked train, as passengers look up at me, and one young boy in the arms of his sobbing mom yells out, "Are you gonna kill it, soldier? Are you gonna kill the monster?"

Tears pop up in my eyes as I race past his hopeful face, heading down the railway track, Thor at my side, the precious satchel case tight up against my chest, assault pack thumping on my back. The passengers stare at me in disbelief as I run away. I glance back one more time as I run down the side of the railroad tracks. All of the carriages are now burning merrily along, and the Creeper is still at work. The near woods are burning as well. There are lines of smoke drifting up from the positions the Marines had so bravely taken. One more colored flare pops up but the Marine must be injured or dying, for the flare sputters up at an angle and bounces along the grassland into the woods.

Another move from the Creeper's arms, and the place where the flare was launched from is drenched with flames.

Panting, heart blasting, legs and arms heavy, I'm out of sight of the ambushed train, and yell out, "Coulson! Coulson! Where the hell are you?"

About me civilians are straggling and running along, and I look around again, trying to see Serena, trying to see Captain Diaz, but the only uniform around is mine.

"Coulson!"

"Here!"

Up on the left is a treeline and Serena and Buddy emerge, coming down to see me. Serena is still holding a handkerchief to her brother's head, her other hand holding a bulging plastic bag. His clothes and her uniform are disheveled and stained with smoke and soot. I look back up the length of tracks. We've gone far enough so that I can't hear or see anything, but I still have the stench of burnt things strong in my nostrils.

Serena comes to me and I say, "Back up to the trees. You see anyplace up there to hide out?"

"There's a bunch of boulders deeper in that might work."

"Good," I say. "We're going to lay low for a while."

She says, "Has the Creeper been killed?"

"No," I say.

"What's going on back at the train?"

"Everybody's dead back there," I say. "Come on, let's move."

I push her ahead of me and we get up the tree line and further in, to the rocks, the boulders about the size of a large kennel cage. Thor is right with me and Buddy is at Serena's side. We climb in among the boulders and I look around, my chest hurting from breathing so hard. Looks pretty good. I say to Serena, "You hurt?"

"No, but Buddy's been cut."

"Yeah," I say. "Hold on, I'll take care of it."

I drop my pack, unzip it and take out a first-aid kit. Buddy stands there stoically. "Specialist, will you assist? Is he all right with me touching him?"

She says, "It'll be fine. Do what you have to do."

I take her hand away and use the handkerchief to wipe away the blood. Doesn't look that bad. Forehead and head injuries tend to bleed like hell, even though the wounds aren't necessarily that deep. I wipe the wound clean again, wash it with an anti-bacterial cloth, and then tape on a bandage. Looks good. Throughout it all, Buddy stands there in his suit and tie, just staring ahead, not saying a word.

Looking around, I take stock. We have a nice hiding place here, but of course, if a Creeper were to amble by, we're in an open barbecue pit with the only defense being me, my attitude, Thor and my 9 mm Beretta. But that doesn't concern me at the moment. Some brush and birch saplings hide most of the rocks, and inside there's a good wide spot covered with last year's fall leaves on the ground. I note the plastic bag Coulson's been carrying. "What do you have there?" I ask. "Didn't think you had any baggage when you got on the train."

She says, "Buddy and I, when we were making our way out, we went by the dining car and saw some water bottles and bagged sandwiches sitting on the ground. I picked some up, figured we might need it later."

"Some might call that looting, specialist."

"Some might call that salvaging, sergeant," she shoots back. "If what you said is true, then everybody back at the train is dead and everything's burned."

True enough. "You expert in salvaging?"

"Girl Scouts, Troop 414."

"Where did you work?"

"Portland, mostly. You?"

"Boy Scouts, outside of Boston."

Things seem to lighten up with our shared tales. Buddy's standing quietly, watching his sister, while Thor's on the ground, taking a break, licking his paws. "Specialist, we're going to be here for a while."

She says, "Why's that, Sergeant? A Quick Reaction Force should be coming here in a bit. Those Marines sent up a lot of flares, and the stations down the line are going to see our train is missing. We keep on moving, we'll run into that QRF force."

"Maybe yes, maybe no," I say. "But we're not taking that chance."

"I still think we should get moving. We'll run into friendlies, soon enough."

"No, we stay put," I snap back. "Look, Specialist, when's the last time you heard of a Creeper making a daylight attack?"

She ponders that for a moment. "Not sure."

"Usually they attack at night, though they do carry over into the daylight, when necessary. So this attack was unusual, right?"

"Seems like it, Sergeant."

I gently kick the dispatch case on the ground, chain leading away from the thick handle. "I'm sure you noticed Mister Manson had this chained to his wrist."

"I did," she says. "Is he all right?"

"He's dead," I say. "But my primary job, before my colonel told me to watch you and your brother, was to escort Manson and his bag to the Capitol. So put that together. On a train to the Capitol is an important escort with an important package, and a Creeper ambushes this train in daylight. Don't like that at all."

"You think the Creepers found out something important is going to the Capitol?"

"Maybe so. I just don't like coincidences."

She looks down at the leather case, looks up at me again. I say, "And another thing I didn't like was the Creeper. It was too tough."

"Too tough? Meaning what?"

"Meaning I saw two Marines with M-10s set up a perfect firing solution, and they fired two rounds at the Creeper. The rounds went in and exploded, right in front of the Creeper's breathing membrane. One exploding round should have killed it right off hand. Two rounds should have knocked it into next Wednesday. But the Creeper shrugged it off, kept firing."

Her face is pale under the soot on her cheeks and chin. "The Creepers have found a way to get around the M-10."

"Sure looks like it," I say.

"We need to get word to your C.O. or any other Army unit, Sergeant."

Another nudge of my foot to the satchel case. "Eventually."

"Eventually? What the hell do you mean by that?

"It means I'm following my orders, Specialist," I say. "I was tasked to escort Manson, his satchel, and you two to the Capitol. Mister Manson is dead, but I still have orders to follow. We're going to rest up here, have something to eat, and then make our way to the Capitol on our own. There was an intelligence leak somewhere, leading to that Creeper being there to ambush us."

"Sergeant, look—"

"Not open for discussion, Specialist."

She looks grim and looks to her brother, back to me. "Very well. Sergeant."

"Glad to hear it," I say.

"What can I do, Sergeant?"

Thor looks up at me, goes back to licking his paws. "Gather some firewood. Anything old and dry. While you're doing that, I'll clean out some of the leaves and debris here so we don't burn the place up."

"So we're spending the night, then?"

"Yes."

"And what about tomorrow?"

"I'll handle tomorrow when the time comes."

She looks down at the dispatch case. "Do you know what's in there?"

"Nope," I say. "But it's from the governor of New Hampshire, and it's supposed to end up in the Capitol. So it has to be something important."

With the toe of her shoe, she moves the chain leading away from the case, ending in the closed bloody handcuff. "It must have been something, getting the chain off Mister Manson's hand. Did you find a key?"

"No."

"Did you pick the lock?"

"No."

"Then how did you get the handcuff off his hand?"

I turn and go back to my assault pack. "Using my Blackhawk knife."

Her words seem strained. "Your knife . . ."

"Yeah," I say, looking calmly right at her. "I cut his hand off."

CHAPTER EIGHTEEN

Later that afternoon, we have a small pile of firewood in one corner of our cleared area, which is about four meters to a side. Tight and cozy, but it'll do. While Serena was out getting the wood, her brother joining her, I dumped out as much of the leaves and old branches as I could, so our fire tonight won't spread out and torch us in the process. Bad enough Creepers want to do that on purpose, it'd be a hell of a thing to do it by accident. By now it's quiet, and I haven't heard any more noises, meaning the Creeper was on the attack or at work. No *click-click* sound, no smell of cinnamon, and even the smell of things burning has lessened.

Shadows are lengthening and we're all enclosed in our little stone encampment. Thor has gone out and has done his business, and in one corner of our camp, I've set the fire. Serena says, "Why against the rock? Why not put it in the middle?"

"Because the heat will reflect off the rock and do a better job of warming us," I say. "Plus the stone will absorb some of the heat so when the fire dies down later, it'll still put out some warmth."

"Oh," she says.

Our dinner is the sandwiches and water Coulson salvaged from the diner car, and I take one called meat and another called cheese. I eat half of them and give the other half to Thor, who licks my hand in between his bites. I also take out a collapsible water dish from my assault pack, fill it with water and listen with contentment as Thor drinks his fill, lapping and lapping. Coulson sees me and says, "Ask you a question, Sergeant?"

"Absolutely, Specialist."

"You did something . . . funny when you went into the train car after the Creeper hit us. Do you remember?"

"Not really, but I'm sure you'll enlighten me."

She chews some, swallows. "First time I heard your voice . . . you called out for your dog. For Thor. Not for me, or for Mister Manson. Why's that? Why did you call out for your dog first, instead of one of us?"

I take a swig of water. "I've known him longer."

As it gets darker, I grab my assault pack and see Serena and Buddy huddling together, getting as close as they can to the flames. I say, "I hope you take this as a lesson in proper planning, Specialist. You went on a train ride, expecting and hoping it would end in just a few hours. Now you and your brother are freezing your asses off in western Massachusetts. You know what they say, fail to plan, plan to fail."

She's hugging herself tight with her arms, but Buddy seems complacent, just taking everything in. He ate a meat sandwich and drank from the water bottle, but again, didn't say a word. Looked at me, looked at his sister, looked at my dog. Then repeated.

"Thanks for the reminder, Sergeant."

I sigh and take pity on them. From my pack I take out a folded reflective space blanket, lightweight, but good enough to keep them warm as it gets cooler. I toss it over to Serena and say, "This'll keep you and your brother warm tonight, Specialist."

"Thank you, Sergeant," she says, catching the blanket and carefully unfolding it, draping it over herself and her brother. "But what about you?"

I say, "I'm a tough old sergeant. I'll make do. But remember one thing."

"What's that?"

I nod to the space blanket. "That blanket's probably as old as you are. Don't tear it, don't burn it, and for God's sake, don't lose it."

"I won't."

"Good," I say, scratching Thor's head. "Don't be offended, but it'd be a heck of a lot easier to replace you than that blanket."

She doesn't say a word, just eyes me oddly as she pulls the blanket up around her pretty chin.

⊕ ⊕ ⊕

I take Thor out to do his late evening business, then look back to check our hiding place, such as it is. Firelight is flickering through the large open areas among the boulders, but I'm not that concerned. We're not an apparent target for any Creeper roaming around in these woods, and my only concern is to run into a random Coastie gang who might notice our camp, but they'd be coming up against me, Thor, and Italy's finest gun manufacturer.

Course, not sure what—if anything—Italy is manufacturing nowadays.

I spare a glance up at the night sky, seeing the random bursts of light and flares as space debris continues its orbiting, hitting each other, burning into the atmosphere. I think about silent Buddy and his job in the Observation Corps. Tremendous patience and skill, standing night after night in front of a telescope, week after week, month after month, for more than a year . . .

I think I'd draw back and keep my mouth shut, too, after enduring something like that.

"Knox coming back in," I call out, and Thor and I get back in among the boulders. Thor finds an open spot and flops himself down, starting to lick his paws. I scratch at his head and shoulders and he wiggles under my touch. It's toasty warm and Buddy is sleeping, and his sister has the space blanket up around her chest, and she's rummaging around in her large black purse. I wonder what she's looking for and I'm surprised when she pulls out a glossy magazine.

A magazine!

I say, "Where did you get that antique?"

She gingerly turns one page, and then another. "From my older sister. She had a subscription before the war started."

"What's it called?"

She shows me the cover. In the firelight I make out the letters— *Seventeen*—and a photograph of a young woman model, impossibly dressed, impossibly well-groomed, and so beautiful it almost hurts to look at her.

"Over ten years old," I say. "Why are you reading it?"

"Re-reading," she corrects. "I just like to look at it, see what I'm missing."

"That's pretty funny," I say.

Her voice cuts at me. "I don't find it funny at all, Sergeant."

"Sorry," I say. "Don't think I understand."

She flips another page. "I'm fifteen. Get that? Fifteen. Before the war started, girls my age had everything. Everything! They were safe, they had plenty to eat, plenty of clothes . . . and my God, the luxuries, stuff we can only dream about. Tiny computers you could carry around that you could make phone calls, take photos, go to the Internet and get any kind of information you wanted. Do you know you could type a message on those phones, and your sister or boyfriend halfway across the world, they'd get the message, instantly? Can you imagine that? Instantly! I got a letter from my mom just the other day. Took almost a month to get across the country."

Another furious flip of the page. "Girls could go to school, go to any school they wanted, and what did they worry about? Boyfriends. Being popular. Being thin and pretty and having the right clothes. And, oh yes, thinking about getting a driver's license. That's it! Didn't have to worry about starving, about getting scorched, about your friends or family being scorched . . ."

I didn't care to hear any more. "That's the way of the world, Specialist."

"Maybe so, but doesn't mean I have to like it. I hate the damn Army. No offense, Sergeant."

"So why did you enlist?" I ask. "You could have stuck it out, see what your draft board said when you turned eighteen."

She snorts. "Sure. Stuck it out. Doing what? Going to school and doing mandatory volunteer work at a local farm, worrying about your clothing rations, food rations, all that. At least the Army you get better fed, for whatever's that worth."

"Then what do you want, Specialist."

Surprisingly enough, it looks like there's tears in those pretty blue eyes. "Tell you what I want," she says, her voice soft and strong at the same time. "I want what was taken away from me and everybody else. I want a sweet soft life. I want out of the Army. I want to be a girl, not a soldier."

"See what you mean."

She says, "Really, Sergeant? Do you? How long you've been in service?"

"Since I was twelve."

"Four long years. Don't you want out as well?"

The thought makes me pause. Become a . . . boy? A teen? Not a soldier? I say, "Don't know what I want. Right now, just following orders, killing Creepers. That's enough for me."

Okay, maybe a lie. But I wasn't going to talk to her about my English teacher and my writing and the terror that awaits me in civilian life. Thor yawns and glances up at me, like he wishes we humans would shut the bleep up so he could get to sleep. I add, "You'll probably be out of the Army soon enough, Specialist. President said last month the war was over. Remember?"

She shoots me a look. "Sure as hell didn't look like the war was over at the train today, did it."

I don't argue the point.

I load up the fire for the night with a couple of thick chunks of tree branch, and Coulson puts her old magazine back into her black purse. She turns and pulls the space blanket over her and her brother. I move around, get as comfortable as I can, and Thor snuffles some and gives me room. Some remaining leaves rustle as I move about. From my assault pack I remove my journal, make a quick scribble of the day's events, and then put it back in. Next out is an extra fatigue jacket and I drape it over my torso, stare at the orange coals, try not to think of all the times I've seen things burning over the years, my ear throbbing at some memories that want to come out to play, and I think instead of the train and the ambush and before that, the Special Forces captain, Diaz.

My dad. He saw my dad just a few a weeks ago, and was sorry for his troubles.

What kind of troubles?

And where the hell is Dad?

I close my eyes.

Thor moves in closer, and I enjoy the smell of his fur and the body heat rising up from his body. It helps relax me, eases the thoughts in my mind. So many times before, Thor and I have been out on a mission, and on those occasions, after some dark deeds have gone on, his presence has been a comfort when I've tried to go to sleep.

My boy doesn't disappoint me tonight, and I soon drift off.

⊕ ⊕ ⊕

Something touches me and instead of jerking to full attention, I
bring my right hand down to my Bianchi combat holster, grip my 9
mm Beretta. I open my eyes. Only a few coals are still glowing there,
at the other side of our stone hidey-hole. I don't move my head. Just
move my eyes. Thor is snoring softly. Buddy is curled up, also asleep.

But no Serena.

Where's Serena?

Another touch, and I know where she is. I raise my head and she's
near me, whispers, "Sorry, didn't mean to wake you."

"What's up?"

"Buddy's sleeping lousy. He's kicking and squirming, waking me
up. And I'm cold."

I whisper back. "Roll over then."

She rolls over and I put my hands on her shoulders and say,
"Squirm over there, next to Thor."

Serena moves and I cuddle up next to her, drape my coat over the
two of us. I say, "Body heat should help out." I think and say,
"Specialist, I'm not being forward here, but I'm going to put an arm
around you. It'll help."

She says, "If it warms me up, do it, Sergeant."

I put my free arm around her, pull myself tight against her, my coat
over the two of us. She moves around a bit and whispers, "Thank you."

"Not a problem."

We lay there, still and quiet, and I clear my throat. "The name is
Randy."

"Sergeant?"

"We're out on a mission, don't need to be so damn formal. So call
me Randy. Until we get hooked up with an Army unit or post and have
to act official again. Deal?"

"Deal," she says. "So call me Serena."

"Get to sleep, Serena."

"All right, then."

In a few minutes it seems like she's fallen asleep. I wish I could say
the same. Still thinking about the train. Captain Diaz. My dad, in
trouble. The ambush. The Creeper attack. The Marines dying by the
train.

So much wrong.

So much wrong.

Serena shifts and I stay with her. A couple of strands of her fine blonde hair tickle my nose. Her body is warm against mine. I'm positive I can smell perfume on her. Perfume! Only once in my discreet dates with Abby had she ever worn perfume, a night I managed to get a reservation at a McDonald's in Concord and dropped a week's pay for our meal. I had on my clean Levi's and a striped shirt that was worn at the elbows, while Abby had on a simple black dress that had been repaired with stitchwork on the back. Before we ate I smelled something nice and Abby shyly admitted she was wearing a bit of perfume that had been left to her by her mother. I said she smelled fine all the time, even after bicycling all night on a long op, and that got me a long, sweet good-night kiss back at the post.

But Serena smells just as fine, and I'm quite conscious of her slim body against mine. Feels pretty damn good.

I don't consider I'm cheating on Abby.

But I don't think I'll tell Abby later, just the same.

In the morning we all do our business in the nearby woods, and for a couple of minutes I'm alone with Buddy. He looks at me with a bland expression, and I say, "I want to take a look at your forehead. Is that okay?"

No change in his expression. I go over and check the bandage. Looks fine. Buddy doesn't move. I go back. "Observation Corps . . . tough gig. Can't think of how tough that must have been."

Buddy just sits there. I say, "Your sister. She seeing anyone?"

Still nothing.

Which is fine. No answer means there's still a fifty-fifty chance she's available.

Not that it means anything at all. Just gathering information.

The night before I had a meat sandwich and a cheese sandwich, and for breakfast, I decided to do things differently, so I had a cheese sandwich and then a meat sandwich. Not sure what's in the meat sandwich—beef, pork, horse, chicken—but Thor eats his portion with enthusiasm. Serena feeds her brother and then herself, and after we police the area, she says, "Sergeant . . . Randy, what's on for the day?"

"We follow the railroad tracks back until it crosses a road. Take the road, find a town, go on from there. We're pretty close to the New York border. I'm hoping it won't take too much effort to get transportation to the Capitol."

"All right, Randy." But there's something about her voice that isn't right. It's like she's almost . . . disappointed to be on the move. Waiting for rescue? Waiting for someone to show up?

I'm stiff and chilled from sleeping on the ground, and it's good to be moving again. We go down the slope and start following the railroad tracks. Thor bounds ahead, sniffing and poking his nose around, lifting a leg here and there to mark his territory. He seems to be enjoying the morning as just a dog, and not as a member of the Army's K-9 Corps.

Looks like fun, forgetting you're in the Army.

As we walk I keep watch, seeing ahead and behind us, on either flanks, but it's a quiet morning. Along the side of the railroad ties are bits of trash and debris from passengers who had made it out alive yesterday. A shoe. An empty shopping bag. A baby doll. The air is crisp and cold. Pine trees and low brush are on either side of the tracks, with an occasional white birch tree reaching up, trying to add some color to the woods.

Buddy walks well with his sister. Even after sleeping on the ground, face and hands soiled, his sister still looks pretty good. Her purse is over one shoulder and she holds the hand of Buddy as they go forward. My assault pack is on my shoulders and I'm carrying the dispatch case that ended up killing Mister Manson. I hope it's going to be worth it. The chain and empty bloodstained handcuff dangles by my side.

I say, "Tell me again why you're going to the Capitol."

"To see my dad."

"Why's he there?"

She smiles, "OPSEC, Randy."

"Oh, I see. How long has he been there?"

"OPSEC."

The trees thin out. Thor is ahead of us, head low to the ground. I say, "Is it hard, working for him?"

"I—good job, Randy. OPSEC again."

"Maybe so," I say. "But how's his job, at Jackson Labs? Lots of long hours?"

She stops, jerks as Buddy keeps on walking, holding her hand. Her face is red. She starts, halts once more, and says again, "OPSEC."

I shake my head. "You're going to have do better than that, Serena. I told you about Manson and this package." I hold up the leather satchel. "And I had to do something bloody and awful to get it. Could have kept my mouth shut about everything but I let you in. So here's the deal. My overall goal is to get the dispatch case to the Capitol. Second goal is to tell someone in authority about the Creeper attack yesterday, how the M-10 didn't seem to work. Sorry to say, Serena, you and your brother, you're my third goal."

"But your colonel—"

I interrupt. "My colonel is a state away. I'm here on the ground, making decisions based on the current situation, which tells me there's been an intelligence failure somewhere. You and your brother . . . you could quickly become a distraction. Meaning I leave you behind when we reach a town."

She stops and Buddy tugs his hand away. Her brother goes a few steps further and stops as well. His face is still disinterested. His sister says, "That's a shitty thing to say."

"Being in the Army, Serena, I think you'd be well acquainted with shitty things happening because of the mission. Depending, of course, on your experience. Jackson Labs. They treat you and your dad fine up there?"

Her voice is just above a whisper. "How did you know?"

"Educated guess," I say. "Which you've just confirmed."

"How?"

I say, "Remember back in Lowell, when the train stopped for refueling? When we talked about the Battle of Merrimack Valley? Me and the others, we got an intelligence briefing, of the important places and installations that the Creepers may be heading towards. A place like the shipyard in Portsmouth. The new Navy base up in Falmouth. And Bangor. That's where you said you and your brother was from. What's in Bangor? Used to be a famous writer named King lived there. But Bangor's also the home of Jackson Labs. Lots of hush-hush black work going on up there, stuff that never makes the newspapers. Your dad?"

She walks some and says, "Research scientist."

"What kind?"

"Not sure. To do with the Creepers . . . everything is for the Creepers, Randy, from Jackson Labs to the Centers for Disease Control to whatever's left of John Hopkins."

"And you?"

"His assistant."

"Doing what?"

She shakes her head with a show of exhaustion. "Reading. Research."

"Sounds interesting."

"It was pure boredom. Wish I were doing dishes instead. You want to know why?"

Thor has stopped, looking back at us. He doesn't seem concerned. He goes back to sniffing at the ground.

"Of course."

She looks over at Buddy. "Going through old magazines, books, newspaper clippings, microfilm . . . the smell of mold and dust and mildew. Poking and reading, trying to find one little obscure fact, one little line of text, one formula that might help my dad and the others. Eyes hurting, nose dripping from the dust, back aching . . . and what really sucked was knowing what a waste of time it was. Ten years earlier . . . what I learned in a month I could have found out in an hour on that Internet."

"So?"

"What the hell do you mean, so?" she says, her voice sharp.

"Big deal. You had to go through libraries, books, magazines to find information. So what. Used to be it'd take several hours or so to get from the east coast to the west coast. Now it can take several weeks. We used to be the finest fighting force in the world. Now we're fighting like we're the Polish cavalry against Nazi tanks in World War II. Soldiers who get wounded are dying because the medics don't have the drugs or equipment they had ten years ago, or even five years ago. So excuse me if I don't get all concerned about your aching back."

We look at each other, and she says, "Enough, all right?"

"Works for me."

She steps forward, takes Buddy's hand, and I go on as well, knowing a bit more than before, but still not feeling right.

Something is wrong, something that's still nagging at me.

We walk in silence for a few more minutes, and then the track curves right and goes over a paved road via a concrete overpass.

The four of us go down to the road, and a few more minutes after that, I turn at the sound of an approaching pair of horses, pulling a carriage.

An Excerpt From the Journal of Randall Knox

Three months without a letter from Dad. Had a dream about him last night. Not much of a dream. Just him sitting at our kitchen table, little smile on his face, buttering a slice of toast for me. Lying that he already had breakfast; by then I knew his tricks pretty well, how he often passed his rations to me. Wearing a threadbare UMass-Boston sweatshirt, hair all gray and white, black-rimmed glasses with one stem repaired with a piece of white tape, sagging face clean-shaven. This was when we were in our old quarters, just before I moved out. Those quarters were tight, leaking roof, mice in the cabinets, had to share a bedroom with him. Got bumped there by post commander—my uncle and Dad's brother-in-law—during a round of promotions that led to a shortage of officers' quarters.

Woke up after this dream, in bed, in my barracks room. Feeling blue. Remembered why I had left Dad. I had gotten a lot of grief from my squad and platoon members that I was still Daddy's boy, living at home. So I requested a transfer. Dad was shook up at the time but put a brave smile on it. Said, yeah, it was probably time for me to be out on my own. Hated to admit it, but did like being out on my own, with own room, dining with my buds and gals. Didn't think of how dad felt with me gone, where he went out to eat without me.

Dad went out on intelligence assignments, here and there. Rhode Island. Maine. Pennsylvania. If he was deployed for a while, always managed to drop me a letter.

Three months now. If he was dead or injured, I would have gotten an official telegram.

Hard to get back to sleep after the dream. Still feel blue about leaving him all alone. But Dad never complained. Never.

CHAPTER NINETEEN

The carriage is a four-passenger coach, colored shiny black, and has a small blue Ford logo on the side. A pair of Morgan horses is leading the wagon, with plastic shoes covering their hooves, and a well-dressed man with a thick black beard is holding the reins, a pump-action 12-gauge shotgun hanging from a harness at the side of his carriage. He's dressed in clean jean pants and a light yellow barn coat, and his hands are large and hairy. He brings his Morgan pair to a halt and says, "Offer you a ride, soldiers?"

"That'd be great," I say. "Where's the nearest town?"

"That'd be Adams, but my farm's closer." He peers down from the coach. "How did you end up here, soldiers?"

Serena says, "Train wreck yesterday, a few miles back. Creeper attack."

The wagon driver shakes his head. "Heard about that in town. Bad business. Any one of you need a doctor?"

"No," I say. "Excuse me, but—"

"Looks like you folks could use a ride, a bath and a good meal. Interested?"

Serena speaks up, "Sir, thank you . . . thank you very much."

I keep my mouth shut.

He smiles, gestures with one hand. "Climb up then, and your dog, too. Love dogs."

In a matter of moments we make the necessary introductions, and the farmer is Eddie Carlson, who owns a farm on the outskirts of Adams, a city on the western end of Massachusetts. I settle in at the rear of the carriage with Buddy and Serena sitting across from me, Thor sitting next to me, tongue hanging out, enjoying the ride, looking out at the scenery. I rub his furry neck. The seats are comfortable, cushioned leather. Even Buddy seems to be enjoying himself, though it's hard to tell from the look on his young face.

Eddie turns and says, "Pretty smooth ride, isn't it."

"Sure is," Serena says.

"Should be, paid enough for it, even with new dollars," Carlson says. "Latest Ford production model, called the Henry. Took six weeks for it to be delivered from Michigan, but it was worth the wait."

I keep quiet as our host maneuvers his wagon to the right, onto a wide dirt driveway by a mailbox marked CARLSON, and he says, "Home mail delivery started last month. Pretty good sign of progress, don't you think?"

"Sure is," I say, but I don't really mean it. Even with the comfortable ride I'm feeling grumpy, and it's Serena's fault. I crook my finger at her and she leans to me, just inches away.

"Specialist," I say, keeping my voice low.

She tries to smile it away. "You mean Serena."

I give her my best ticked-off-sergeant look. "Specialist, you should have known better, back there. No reason to tell him how we ended up here."

"You don't think he could figure it out?"

I say, "Enough. I don't want word getting around about us being survivors from that Creeper attack."

She leans back. "You're being paranoid."

"Doing my job. You should do the same."

Up on the dirt road, the farmhouse comes into sight. It's a comfortable-looking two-story home, painted white, with a wraparound porch. There are fenced-in pastures on both sides of the farmhouse, and a barn and another outbuilding towards the rear. A silo and a windmill are nearby. In the pastures are horses and cows. Out beyond the buildings are fields with crops, looking like corn and low vegetables, maybe potatoes. By the barn is a huge oak tree, and there's a tiny white picket fence there, surrounding a stone.

In a few moments Carlson has unhooked his team and says, "My boys are out in the fields, getting the morning weeding done. But if you'd like, give me a few minutes, I'll bring you into the house. How does a hot bath and lunch sound? My wife Beth puts on a good feed."

Serena makes to speak and I say, "We really don't want to impose, Mister Carlson. What we want is to get to Adams as soon as possible."

Carlson grins, scratches at the back of his head. "Tell you what. You let me and the missus take care of you, and then I'll have my boy Edgar take you to Adams, just as soon as you finish eating. How does that sound?"

I reluctantly nod. We really should be getting on our way—between the dispatch bag and passing on the news of the Creeper surviving the ambush, there's a lot to be done—but a meal and a hot bath sounds wonderful.

"All right, Mister Carlson," I say. "You've got a deal."

"Great."

Later we're in the front parlor of the house, meeting Beth Carlson, a pleasant but tired-looking, heavy-set woman with white hair and horn-rimmed eyeglasses, wearing baggy jeans with patched knees and a flannel shirt with sleeves rolled up, revealing thick and muscular forearms. I let Serena and Buddy go before me to the bath, and Beth comes out, their clothes in her hands. "When you take your bath, dump your clothes out in the hallway. I'll do laundry and have your clothes dry before you leave."

She goes off and I gingerly sit on the edge of a couch. There are three chairs, a coffee table, two bookshelves and a dead big-screen television in a wooden console in one corner, being used as a shelf for some plants. On one of the bookcases are a number of photographs. I recognize a younger Eddie and Beth Carlson standing in front of the Eiffel Tower in Paris, with big grins on their faces, holding the hands of two little boys. There are other family portraits as well, including a black-and-white photo of a little girl, sitting on an older Beth Carlson's lap. The photo looks like it was taken on the front porch, and not that long ago.

The room is still. I think I hear Serena talking to her brother. I wait some more, the dispatch case and my assault pack at my feet. I'm tired, my tongue is still sore from me biting it yesterday, and my back aches from sleeping on the ground.

Thor is being a good boy, lying down on the carpet, taking a snooze. I envy him. I close my eyes and lean back against the couch. Time passes. I jerk awake and Thor is still sleeping, and I see why.

It's warm, safe, and comfortable. There are no weapons, no battlements, no moats, no netting to hide weapons and vehicles from the killer stealth satellites. This is just a quiet farmhouse in a rural county in New England. Outside there are horses and cows, quietly grazing and meandering in the fenced-in pastures. This clean house smells of soap, of baked bread, of a quiet life. The rooms back at my barracks smell of sweat, gun oil, and through it all, the dull cold scent of fear. So this is what civilian life could be.

Serena is laughing from another room. I like the sound. She comes into the parlor, rubbing her blonde hair with a towel. Her brother is walking in with her. Buddy is wearing gray slacks and a faded New York Yankees T-shirt, and he still has the bandage on his forehead. But I look at Buddy for barely a second. I'm staring at Serena. She has on sandals and her bare feet have painted toenails. Painted toenails! She has on a khaki skirt that's cut high above her knees—one of the shortest skirts I've ever seen on a girl or a woman—and a yellow knit blouse that's snug about her chest and a bit low cut. I move my head away. I shouldn't stare.

But Serena says, "Guess I clean up well, eh, Randy?"

I clear my throat. "Very impressive, Specialist."

"Serena, Randy. Still Serena."

"Where did you get those clothes?"

Beth comes in, wiping her hand on a towel, grinning. "My fault, young man. I could fit this boy with some clothes from Roger, my youngest. But for Serena here . . . well, I dug deep into my closet, for clothes I had years back, when I was in college."

She touches Serena's shoulder, adjusting the yellow knit top, like she's trying to get back memories of when she was so young and slim. Beth says, "God, I miss those days . . . I was at Northeastern University, in Boston, studying computer science."

Beth pauses. I see she's trying to gather herself. She takes a breath, smiles tightly, and says, "So here I am. No more Northeastern, no more Boston, no more computers."

In the bathroom I strip off my clothes and gingerly open the door, and then place my clothing on the hallway floor. Back in the bathroom I still have my 9 mm Beretta and the dispatch case with a chain and handcuff at the end. One of the lessons from a drill sergeant who worked from a wheelchair back when I entered service at twelve years of age: trust but verify. I'm trusting Eddie and Beth Carlson of Adams, Massachusetts, but there's always a need to verify that trust. Some of the older vets have told me chilling tales from the beginning of the war, when some civilians—crazed by the relentless attacks from the Creepers and convinced all was lost—turned on the military when they could, stealing their clothing, their equipment, their food, their lives.

That wasn't going to happen to me, even now, with the war over. There's a straight-back chair in a corner by a small window. I pull it over and shove the back under the doorknob. I put my pistol and the dispatch case on the chair, and go to the tub, surprised to see it empty. I had expected to use gray water, but Eddie must be doing well indeed. I draw a bath and sink in, the hot water causing me to take a sharp breath, and then I relax, the steam and water soaking my aching muscles. I lie back, look at my skin, see the old scars, the bruises, the scratches. I stretch some and wiggle my toes, the nails black and broken. I sit and listen and remember earlier this day, when I had gotten up before Buddy and his sister and even Thor. Knowing it was still wrong, I did it anyway, going into her purse, taking out that old copy of *Seventeen*. I slowly flipped through the pages in the early morning light, looking at the artifact from another age.

I ignored the words, had looked at the photos, of the beautiful young girls and the handsome young men. Both photos had fascinated me, of young women who were well-fed, dressed and always smiling. The young men looked happy as well, their smiles and skin perfect. They had tasty food and sweet drinks any time they wanted, electronics that gave them music and books and movies in an instant from anywhere in the world, and medical care that was so expansive it could waste resources on straightening their teeth or noses.

I hated and envied them at the same time, and when Serena had stirred some under my jacket back among the rocks, I quickly put the magazine back into her purse.

A knock on the door. "Yes?" I call out.

From behind the door Beth says, "There are clean clothes on the floor, belonging to my boy Edgar. When you get dressed, lunch will be ready. And my word, what a sweet dog you have."

I'm not as well dressed as Buddy and Serena. The blue cotton shirt is so tight that it's hard to button, and the pant legs are so long, I have to fold up the ends so they don't drag across the floor. Eddie and Serena smile as I go into the dining room, but I ignore them as lunch is served. I put my pistol and the dispatch case under my chair. We're in a formal-looking dining room with a hutch on one end, and we eat well, me and Serena and her brother, and our two hosts. Eddie explains, "My boys Edgar and Roger are out in the fields, but they'll be back in a bit. They have to bag their own lunches. I'll have Edgar ride you into town."

I say, "In Adams, is there transportation out west, to New York state?"

Eddie says, "Sure is. Greyhound has a pretty good bus service, leaves on the hour."

I want to ask more but Beth comes in and we simply have the finest meal I've had in a very long time: chicken stew with fresh salad, an oil dressing, and freshly baked bread with sweet butter, all washed down by cold milk that's so thick and delicious it's practically a meal in itself. Thor is at my feet and when I think no one is looking, I slip him pieces of chicken and bread.

When we're nearly done, Eddie looks at me and says, "Suppose you can't tell me why you need to go to New York."

"That's right," I say.

"But a smart fella like me would think you're probably heading to one of the new bases. Maybe even the Capitol."

I catch Serena's eye and I'm pleased she keeps her mouth shut. Her brother is deftly taking a piece of bread and wiping the soup bowl clean. Thor puts his head on my lap. I scratch his muzzle.

Eddie senses he's gone too far and says, "Never you mind. Beth'll tell you that I don't know when to keep my damn mouth shut, that's for sure. You ought to hear what they call me at town meeting every March. But I hope things will change for the better for you and everyone else your age. Heck, from what we've heard, looks like the war is finally over, with their orbital station being destroyed. At least that's what the President says . . . though truth be told, that bitch on wheels that works for him, Tess Conroy, she's the one who really speaks for him. But still, good news . . . but if I can speak cleanly and plainly, most days, for me it was a good thing we got attacked back on 10/10."

Serena drops her spoon. Buddy slowly turns his head. Beth is quiet as she comes in and clears out our dishes. I try to speak, can't find the right words, and Eddie says, "Heresy, I know. But the truth is the truth. Before 10/10, I was an assistant manager at Aubuchon Hardware in North Adams. Had this old beat-up farm, lots of land, and property taxes you wouldn't believe. Now . . . I'm working all of this land, and some land belonging to my neighbors that I've leased. I own that Aubuchon store I once worked at. We farmers are the Googles and Intel of this generation, kids. This is one of the richest farms in the valley. Look at my Ford carriage if you don't believe me."

I try to keep my temper in check. "Good for you. Billions of others weren't so fortunate."

Eddie shrugs. "The price of change, the price of progress. What kind of world were we before the Creepers came? Too many people, too little food and water. Famines. Wars. Refugees. Climate change. Terrorist attacks where people were killed because of their religion. Even in the so-called civilized world, what kind of people were we? Nobody lived life anymore. It was all Twitter, Facebook, e-mails, iPods and texting. Kids rode in cars that had movie theaters in the back so their parents could ignore them. Nobody cared about the land anymore, or their neighbors, or even their country. We were spoiled children. Like it or not, the Creepers took us back to a place that Jefferson had dreamed about: an America of simple farmers and merchants. Minding our own business. Staying out of foreign affairs, foreign wars."

Serena whispers, "So many dead."

"True," Eddie says, turning to her. "So very many dead. After the 10/10 attacks, I lost family, friends and neighbors, too. We're mourning. Of course. But take the long view. Who mourns the millions dead from World War II. Or World War I? Or the ravages of Genghis Khan or Alexander the Great? True, we're struggling now, but if we've truly won the war against the Creepers, like the President says, then ten or twenty or thirty years down the road, it'll work out. People will adjust, will love their new lives. Heck, boy, you're young and strong. If you weren't in the Army, you could start working here tomorrow for me. If you ask me, having the Creepers invade was the best thing that could have happened to this unhappy world."

I rub the top of Thor's head. I'm tempted to tell my boy to tear out Eddie's throat. Serena looks pale. Even Buddy seems out of sorts from what our host has said.

"Then excuse me if I don't ask you," I say.

By the time we're outside on the wide wrap-around porch, I've changed back into my freshly-washed fatigues, but Serena is still wearing the civilian clothes given to her by Beth Carlson. She's carrying her uniform in her hands and says, "Room in your pack for this?"

"Out of uniform, aren't you . . . Serena?"

She says, "I haven't worn anything this nice for such a long time, Randy. Beth insisted that I take her clothes with me. Said she'd never be able to fit in them, and it was a sin to let them go to waste. Look, I'll be in uniform when we get to the Capitol. Promise."

I can't help but smile and I zip open my assault pack, gently fold and put her uniform away. It's an Army uniform, but it's also tailored and cut for a woman, and I like the feel of the fabric. I zip the pack shut, look around. Buddy is standing by us, and Thor is at his feet. I wonder what Thor thinks of our silent companion. Eddie is out by the barn with a young man that I expect to be his son, Edgar. They're hitching up a pair of black Morgan horses to the Ford carriage.

A door slams and Beth Carlson walks out, wiping her hands on a light yellow dish towel. Her face is like stone. She comes up next to me. "You seem like a bright boy."

"Some in my squad would disagree."

She says, "You might not believe this, but you're a hell of a lot brighter than my idiot husband."

"Excuse me?"

"You heard me." In the space of a few words, her voice becomes sharp, bitter. "All that bold talk of a new life, of being a rich farmer instead of an assistant store manager, going back to the life of Jefferson. A simpler and better America. Crap. All crap. He's not in the kitchen every day, struggling to make meals without an electric stove, refrigerator, or microwave."

Her voice suddenly catches. "Look over there, by that oak tree. See it?"

I see it. I had noticed it when we had ridden up to the house. There's a tiny white picket fence surrounding a stone. She takes a choked breath. "That's where my Amber is buried. She was born two years after 10/10. Sweetest little girl . . . I gave birth in our bedroom back there, with the help of a midwife. No drugs. No anesthesia. No spinal block. She was a tough birth but worth it . . . God, she was so sweet, so beautiful. Blonde hair like corn silk. And then . . . two years later . . . there was a measles outbreak in the county."

The horses are now hitched up to the wagon. Beth says, "Measles. Goddamn measles. With no vaccines, no drugs . . . she died in a week. My girl. If it weren't for those goddamn aliens, she'd be alive today. I'd be using my degree and computer skills. And Eddie would still be an assistant manager at a hardware store, dreaming of his precious Jefferson."

She spits on the porch. "Damn fool."

For the second time that day we clamber into a carriage, and Edgar is a younger and clean-shaven double of his father, wearing jeans stained with dirt and a simple light blue farmer's jacket. While getting ready to get into the Ford-made carriage, Edgar is staring at Serena. I make sure she sits right behind Edgar, so he couldn't see her legs by glancing back as he drove the horses. Of course, by doing so, I get to see Serena and her legs, a fair exchange. Buddy sits next to his sister, and Thor climbs up on the leather seat next to me, breathing happy.

He swivels in the bench, a single-shot 12-gauge shotgun at his side, and says, "You folks all set back there?"

"We are."

"What's your dog's name?"

"Thor," I say.

"Does he hunt aliens?"

"Best in the world," I say.

He laughs. "Glad to hear it."

Edgar makes a *cluck-cluck* sound and we're off. Behind us in the wide dirty driveway, Eddie waves at our departure, and he puts his right arm around his wife. She stands as still as a statue. I look one more time at the little white picket fence and simple stone, and then we're down the dirt driveway, on our way.

CHAPTER TWENTY

Out on the town road, the asphalt is still smooth, though weeds and brush are growing through some wide cracks. Telephone poles are one side of the road, the old phone and power lines sagging and broken, dangling down like thin vines. We pass an occasional driveway, some still paved, others made with dirt. There are only a few abandoned cars dumped on the road, and Edgar expertly moves the team and carriage around them.

I say to Serena, "What's up with the toenails?"

She giggles, crosses her arms. "It was Beth's idea. After she got me dressed in her clothes, she said we should go all out. So while Buddy was taking his bath, we went into their bedroom and she did my nails. The local gals have a recipe for making nail polish."

Serena sticks her feet out. "What do you think?"

Her legs are smooth and fine and unblemished, and one would think that painted toenails were definitely a wartime extravagance, but I find her feet adorable. I have this quiet little urge to give them a rub, but with a sense of shame, I suddenly recall Abby's legs: strong, muscular, scarred from tumbles off her combat dispatch bike and once from a flying piece of shrapnel when she rode too close to a skirmish line during a Creeper hunt. I think if someone offered to paint her toenails, she'd counter-offer with a kick to the shins.

"I think . . . I think they're pretty," I say, feeling the words are kind of lame.

She wiggles her toes. She seems to like my words, no matter how lame they are. "So what do we do when we get to Adams?"

"Eddie said Greyhound leaves on the hour, every hour. We just get transport to . . . our destination, and if all goes well, we should be there before nightfall.

"Serena says, "Wow . . . to see Dad, after all this time. Can't believe it." She taps the dispatch case on the carriage floor with her foot. "And you . . . you'll be able to finally complete your mission. What do you think is in there, anyway?"

My turn. "Sorry, Serena. OPSEC."

She takes that in good spirits. "You know, that handcuff on the end of the chain. Bet you could still put it on your wrist. Must be a key waiting for you at the other end."

I shake my head. "Not going to give somebody else a chance to hack off my hand, even if I'm dead."

She smiles. "I can see why."

We ride along and the road narrows, and we no longer see driveways or farmhouses up on the overgrown pasturelands. Even with the narrow road, we still have a view of the sky, and Edgar shouts out, "Cripes, look at that!"

The sky is partially overcast but a fairly large chunk of space debris is re-entering, as big as I've ever seen over the years, bright as a large star, sparkling streamers of light following as it speeds overhead. It disappears behind the clouds but there's still a glow of light as it descends into the atmosphere, and then the near trees block the view.

Edgar says, "Pretty big piece. Whaddya think? Part of their orbital station?"

"Could be," I say. "Lord knows the Air Force blew it into enough pieces."

"It'd be nice if that piece lands on one of their bases, don't you think?"

"That'd be something to see," I say, and Edgar returns to his horsemanship, and Serena says, "My dad says it was a mistake to destroy the orbital station."

Surprised I say, "What's that?"

"You heard me," she says with confidence. "My dad says it was a mistake to destroy the orbital station."

"What, we should have sent flowers?" I ask. "The orbital station was a big as a small moon, built from their star craft. Probably contained thousands of Creepers. It controlled the killer stealth satellites, and it built and sent out the bases that landed on Earth. We knew it communicated with the Creepers on the ground. It was the damn head of their invasion and occupation. Cut off the head, it's easier to destroy the rest."

She says, "That's the popular opinion, but my dad's always taught me not to trust popular opinion."

"So what's the unpopular opinion?"

The road narrows even more, and the trees branches are crowding overhead. Shadows have fallen across the cracked asphalt and it's gotten cooler. Serena looks to her brother, rearranges a strand of hair on his head. Buddy's bandage from yesterday is still in place. Serena says, "My dad thinks we should have captured it. Said it obviously it took years to come up with a plan to destroy it. Why not take a couple of more years and capture it? Think of what we could have learned! The Creepers . . . they're evil, they've killed billions of us, drowned and destroyed scores of cities, but star travel. They know how to travel between the stars. My dad thinks it would have been worth capturing the orbital station, to get that knowledge."

I ponder that, and look at Serena's pretty face. I think of Abby and her brown skin and thick eyebrows, and the scratches and blemishes on her face, and look again at Serena.

"Well?" she asks.

"You know, I hadn't really thought about it that much, but your dad does make sense."

She seems proud. "Really?"

"Really," I say. "Maybe we should have captured the orbital base. Finding the secret of star travel would have been worth it, if only for one thing."

"Which is?"

I scratch Thor's back. "To build our own star craft, to travel to their home world and turn it into glass that glows in the dark."

Some time later the carriage hits a bump as we go around a tight curve, and the dispatch case slides across the floor. I bend down to retrieve it and my pistol tumbles out of my holster. My face warms right up from embarrassment; nothing like losing your weapon to get you into serious hack. I pick up the pistol, sit back up, and the road is blocked by two wooden sawhorses across the road with three soldiers standing next to it. A few meters ahead of the sawhorses is an old-style Humvee, parked to the right. Weapons are slung over their shoulders. A painted sign hangs below one of the sawhorses. STOP FOR ARMY INSPECTION. Edgar pulls the horses to a halt and Serena turns to see what's going on. Her brother stares ahead. Thor sits up, ears at attention.

One of the soldiers ambles over to Edgar. He looks to be about twenty, slim, wearing muddy boots, fatigues and he unslings his weapon, an M-4 automatic rifle. On his head is a soft cap, a size too large. His name tag says MULLEN and his rank is lieutenant. His nose is small and his face is pudgy and worn. His two companions fan out and come at us, from either side of the road. I can't make out their name tags. They both appear to be sergeants, and one has a shoulder flash for the 45th Infantry Division, and the other is from the 26th Division. A sergeant with a wide smile and good teeth goes to the pair of horses up forward and holds their bridles. The other one, who has a shadow of a beard and carries a pump-action shotgun, comes to the opposite side of the carriage. He stares at Serena's legs and he starts smiling as well.

Mullen says, "Afternoon, folks. Just a routine traffic stop."

Edgar says, "Just going into Adams. That's all."

Mullen looks to me. "And you?"

"Going to Adams, sir, looking for transportation," I say.

"And your friends?"

Serena looks to me, face pale. Buddy is still, hands in his lap. The sergeant up forward by the horses comes around and quickly takes Edgar's shotgun. Edgar says, "Hey," and I quickly say, "Sir, if I may, what's the word for the week?"

The sergeant looking at Serena's legs, laughs. Mullen says, "What did you say, kid?"

"The word for the week. Code and counterword. Procedure for encountering troops from other units out in the countryside."

Mullen rubs at his nose. "Code word I got this week was Zulu."

"Oh," I say, and I slap Thor on his back and yell, "Thor, strike!" and I pull out my Beretta and shoot Mullen in the chest.

After the loud *boom!* Serena screams and I yell, "Down, get down!"

and I roll out and follow Thor to the asphalt, landing on my shoulder and side, as my partner leaps out and nails the nearest man in his throat with his jaw. He falls back, screaming and gurgling, as Thor growls and works his strong jaw into the soft throat tissues. The sergeant up forward should move to the left, to get the carriage between us, but he's either too eager or too stupid, and comes at me from the right. From my vantage point on the asphalt, I shoot him twice in the legs, dropping him to the ground. The horses back and whinny, as Edgar swears and tries to control the frightened horses. I scramble up, go to the guy on the ground with the wounded legs, who's trying to grab his rifle—a .22 Remington—and I nail him in the chest with another shot. He stops moving.

The guy with Thor on his throat is screaming, and I yell, "Thor, off!" and my bud instantly backs away. The guy moans some more but I roll and duck as a burst of automatic rifle fire zips overhead. Damn it, I knew I shot Mullen in the chest!

Behind me now, Serena is on top of her brother in the carriage, and Mullen is peeking from around its end, and he takes off, M-4 in hands. I run off after him, and in a few seconds he's deep in the woods, out of sight. Serena yells out, "Leave him be!"

"Not on your life!" I yell back.

I splash through a drainage ditch, stop, catch my breath. Trees are spread out before me, a mix of pines and hardwoods. I take stock, slowly watch and evaluate, recall my basic training. If danger is afoot, there's no need to rush in, because more likely than not, you'll be dragged out by your ankles, ambushed and dead.

To the left. A low oak tree branch is bent funny. I slowly move, looking down.

Drops of blood. I kneel down, giving it a good look. The blood is frothy. Lung shot.

Serena is still calling out. I ignore her.

I slowly move ahead, scanning left and right and above.

More drops of blood. Larger and closer together.

I take my time. I don't think Mullen is going far, but he's got an automatic rifle and I have a pistol.

I whisper, "Always outmanned, but never outgunned."

I move a couple of more meters, see a splash of vomit, and more blood.

Getting damn close. I try to ease my breathing.

Up ahead. Mottled green. I circle around, still taking my time.

A choking cough.

There's an opening in the trees.

I step through. Mullen is sitting up against a white oak, legs splayed out. His M-4 is on his lap. He looks up at me and his hands start working at the automatic rifle, and I kick it free.

"Bastard," he whispers.

"Doubtful," I say. "I've seen my birth certificate."

He doesn't reply. He's bleeding from his chest. Curious, I reach down, tear open his fatigue shirt. Underneath he's wearing an old Kevlar bulletproof vest, but it's old, with previous pockmarks from earlier gunshots, and my round must have torn open the vest by going through a weak part. Lucky for me, unlucky for him.

"Where you from?" I ask.

Blood is dribbling down his chin. "Jersey City."

"Far from home."

"Yeah. But damned if I was going to stay in a refugee camp, rest of my life, starving every day . . ."

"So being a Coastie, robbing and killing, that was a better choice?"

He doesn't say anything for a moment, his head lolling some. His eyes are glassy and unfocused. More blood down his chin. He coughs again. "Gotta tell me, man, what's the code word for the week . . ."

I shrug. "Damned if I know."

I wait to see if he's going to say anything more, but there's a loud, rattling noise from his chest, and his head lolls once again and he doesn't move or say a damn thing.

Out on the road, I walk slowly, Mullen's M-4 slung over my shoulder, two extra magazines stripped from him now hanging from my utility belt. Serena calls out and once again, I don't pay her any mind. I'm curious about the Humvee. I go around to the front and spot a tow bar set below the grill. Interesting. I pop open the hood and there's a large empty spot where the engine used to be. In the nearby woods is a trail. The M-4 is in my hands as I slowly walk up the trail, filled with curiosity.

Which is satisfied rather quickly. The trail opens up to a patch of grassland, and two heavy horses—Belgians, it looks like—are quietly grazing in patch of grass, ropes from their bridles tied to some brush.

A snap of a branch and I whirl around. Edgar is there, holding his shotgun, the weapon trembling in his hands.

"What's up?" he asks.

"They were a Coastie gang," I say. "Had a sweet little gig, it looks like. They had an old Humvee, stripped the engine to lighten it up, and used a team of horses to drag it around. Set up a checkpoint and rob and rape and kill at their pleasure."

"The one that ran away?"

"Dead over there," I say. "I'll show you."

He shudders. "I'd rather not."

I say, "Don't be stupid. You and your family, you hit the jackpot."

He lowers his shotgun. "What the hell do you mean by that?"

"In New Hampshire, a homeowner gets a reward for killing Coasties. Imagine Massachusetts has the same law on its books."

"But you . . . you took care of them!"

I shoulder the M-4. "Yeah, but there's a crapload of paperwork to fill out, and I don't have the time. Plus, you get salvage rights on those two horses. Bet you and your folks can use them back at the farm."

That's gotten his attention, and his eyes lighten up. "That doesn't sound bad at all. Hell, let's get going on."

"Yeah, let's," I say.

Back at the carriage Edgar helps me dismantle the sawhorses and the sign, while Serena is sitting in the carriage, gingerly washing Thor's mouth and paws. He's panting in contentment. Buddy is sitting up once more, but the bandage on his forehead has slipped. Something to fix before we leave. Serena ignores me as she works on my dog. I hand the pump-action shotgun and .22 rifle to Edgar, who puts them on his seat. He and I drag the bodies of the other two men to the side of the road. One dead by me, the other by my dog. We're still a damn fine team. Edgar says, "Pity their boots aren't in better shape."

"Yeah, well, you take what you can get."

He cocks his head at me. "How did you know? I mean, I really didn't get suspicious until that one in the middle grabbed my shotgun."

"Too sloppy," I say.

"The way they looked, then?"

"The way they looked, the way they acted. Their patches were from different units. Nothing out of the ordinary in a large-scale operation, but damn suspicious for a three-man squad. Their weapons weren't right, either. It was a mix. In a squad, everyone should have the same caliber of weapon. That way, in a firefight, you can share ammo. Their tactics sucked, too. All three came up to the carriage. One should have stayed behind, in cover, to support in case there was trouble."

"So when did you decide to start shooting?" he asks.

"At the right time, I'd say."

In the carriage I fix Buddy's bandage and rub the back of Thor's head. "Good boy," I say. Serena stares at me for fifty meters or so as we resume our trip to Adams. Finally she says, "I guess I should thank you."

"If you'd like," I say.

"But you could have warned me. I could have helped."

"I didn't have time," I say. "And forgive me for saying this, Specialist, I don't think I needed your help."

That's good for a score of meters or so, and she says, "Last winter, back at Jackson Labs, a scheduled convoy of potato trucks from Aroostook County never showed up in Bangor. There were food riots. The cops and state police couldn't control it. Then they were rumors that food was being stored at warehouses at the labs. The mob was coming through the main gate. We were all given weapons. I shot at least two, maybe three trying to come over the fence. Two men and a girl about my age."

I keep quiet. All I hear are the *clop-clop* of the horse's hooves on the cracked pavement. She says, "So I know how and when to fight. I'm a soldier, Sergeant, don't forget it."

"I won't."

Then she seems to relax. "You can also stop staring at my legs."

"Not sure if I can do that."

We reach the center of Adams about an hour later, and Edgar says he'll report our firefight to the Adams police, which is fine by me, because too much time has already passed and I don't want to waste hours answering questions. Edgar leads his carriage and horses down Commercial Street, past the post office, where since it's the first

Tuesday of the month, Social Security payments are being distributed. A number of elderly men and women are gingerly stepping out of the post office, carrying bags of cheese, rice and beans. Two Adams police officers are on hand to make sure they're not robbed.

The street has a few steam-powered cars and trucks thumping by, and other horse drawn carriages as well. Mounds of manure are piled up on the old pavement. There's also a constant stream of bicyclists, and something stirs inside of me, thinking of Abby, my favorite bicyclist. I still feel bad about not having waved at her back at the Concord train station. It's now overcast and a fine drizzle has started to fall. We go beyond the City Hall and there's a building on the right that has a faded sign stating Adams Cooperative Bank. A newer sign states CALLAGHAN ENTERPRISES and underneath that sign, a Greyhound bus logo is dangling from two cords. A number of other wagons and carriages are in the parking lot, and Edgar halts his team.

Edgar says, "In there is Dell Callaghan. Dad told me that before the war, he owned a couple hundred acres down by the Housatonic River, lived in a trailer, and was on welfare. Now, he's the richest man in the western part of the state. Owns most everything in town, including the Greyhound franchise. He's sharp but fair, just so you know."

"Thanks," I say, grabbing my assault pack, the dispatch case, and with the M-4 slung over my shoulder. I help Serena down, and she in turn helps Buddy. Thor jumps out, sniffs about the carriage wheels, comes over to me. I rub the back of his sweet head, my killer bud. Edgar says, "Thought maybe that M-4 would be part of the salvage."

"You got the .22 and the shotgun, plus the horses," I say. "Don't be greedy."

He smiles. "Had to try. Good luck on your trip."

"Thanks," and as he guides his horses out to the road, we walk to the old bank building.

There's a table outside and a sign stating NO WEAPONS INSIDE with a hand-scrawled message underneath that says, *This means you!* A grandmotherly-type woman is sitting in a leather chair behind the table, wearing eyeglasses with a thin chain around her neck and a multi-colored cardigan sweater. On the table are enough pistols, shotguns and long rifles to equip a platoon. As I approach she smiles sweetly at me and says, "Planning on going inside?"

"I am," I reply.

She holds a clipboard with a pencil slid in. "Then sign over your weapons before you go inside, son."

I hesitate and Serena says, "Randy, you can leave everything with me. Buddy and I can stay outside and wait."

I unsling the M-4 and remove my 9 mm, pass them over to Serena. The automatic rifle over her shoulder seems to overwhelm her. I drop my assault pack and keep the dispatch case in hand. "Sounds good, Serena."

To the older woman I say, "We okay, then?"

She motions to my right hand. "What's in the bag, soldier?"

"Documents."

"Can I look inside?"

"Sorry, you can't," I reply. "It's locked, and I don't have the key."

She smiles again. "Then go in, sonny, but just one thing."

"What's that?"

The grandmotherly smile is still on her face. "If you're trying to smuggle a weapon in there, the cops won't be called. The hard boys inside will just put a cap in your ass."

She pauses. "I think that's the phrase. Am I right?"

I walk past her. "Close enough."

An Excerpt From the Journal of Randall Knox

Movie night last week. Usually we get black-and-white films from the 1940s and 1950s. Up to speed on Bogart films, Casablanca *being a favorite. Somehow post Quartermaster got a hold of a color film, called* Independence Day. *About alien invasion of Earth, made way before I was born. Kinda spooky at first, seeing the big-ass ships come in and set up in Earth orbit. Then alien ships descend over major cities. Giggles start breaking out. Can't believe screenwriters were so stupid. All these aliens hovering over cities and military doesn't start lobbing nukes at them? President of the U.S., played by a soft-looking guy with good hair, wants to play nice. After a scene of him in Oval Office, somebody in back of gym yelled out, "Whaddya think, Mister President, they came all this way for bread and milk?"*

Loud laughs and shouts. Laughs dribbled out when alien craft started blasting Earth cities, then more giggles eventually returned as a black actor punches out an ugly alien that could be a relative of a Creeper and said, "Welcome to Earth." Then laughter really returned when President meets up with an alien at a secret military base. Even after millions have been killed, cities destroyed, President wants to be friends with the aliens. Laughter so loud it drowns the out film dialogue, laughter continues until some male soldier stood on a chair and started screaming: "Not funny! What's so damn funny? Why are you all laughing? My mom and dad and sisters are all dead! What's so damn funny?"

That's how movie night ended last week.

Tonight they're showing Road to Morocco *with Bing Crosby and Bob Hope.*

CHAPTER TWENTY-ONE

Inside I stand shocked. Electric lights. The place has electric lights! I can't remember the last time I've seen such luxury. The interior still has the outlines of a bank, with teller stations and wide counter in front of me in a large lobby, and open offices off to the right. There are people milling about, some in fine clothes, others in farmer styles or hand-made clothing. Manual typewriters are being hammered and in the near corner of the lobby, there's a small desk with a cardboard Greyhound bus sign. A boy about my age wearing a too-big white shirt and a long blue necktie is sitting at the desk. His black hair is thick and combed over one side. I take a chair across from him and he says, "What can I do for you, soldier?"

"Need three tickets to the Capitol," I say. I hand over my orders and he gives them a glance, and starts flipping through a ticket book, checking the schedule.

I take in the electric lights. "Impressive. How do you pull it off?"

The boy says, "Small hydro station on the river. Charges up batteries that we bring to the building, helps light up the place. Even runs a refrigerator and stove. Pretty cool, hunh?"

"Damn cool," I say.

He looks to my orders again and says, "Can only write one ticket based on these, soldier."

"I've got two other soldiers outside," I say, thinking quickly. "We were on a train yesterday, got attacked by a Creeper. Their orders were lost."

He takes my papers, taps them against his chin, and says, "Sure, I heard about that blow-up. Train track still needs to be cleared. Sucks, don't it. Aw, hell, what do I care. Hold on. So. The Capitol. Ugh. Couldn't pay me to go there."

"Why's that?"

He starts writing laboriously with his pencil. "It's a damn big target, that's why. Look at all the other places that were the Capitol after the war started. Philadelphia, Harrisburg, Cincinnati . . . all eventually got whacked by the killer sats."

"It's been there safe for nearly three years," I say.

"Then it's overdue," he says. He tears off three tickets and passes them over. "There you go, soldier. Three tickets for the Capitol. Leaves in two hours."

"Two hours?" I ask, looking at the tickets. "I heard buses leave here on the hour, every hour."

"Yeah, but there's a bridge out, up by North Adams. And another bus is stuck in Greenfield with a burst boiler. So we're doing what we can."

I take the tickets and an older man strolls by. He's wearing a white shirt that's better fitting than the young boy's, with a clean blue necktie, and his steel gray hair is cut high and tight. His skin is leathery and wrinkled, and he says, "A problem?"

The boy says, "Not really, uncle. Sergeant Knox here, he was hoping to catch an earlier bus. I told him the next one won't be by for two hours."

The older man holds out a hand. "Dell Callaghan," he says. "Sorry for the delay, but sometimes it can't be helped."

I shake his hand, which is callused and worn. "I understand. Just not sure what we're going to do for the next two hours."

"That can be fixed," he says. He fishes around in his pants pocket, takes out a roll of orange tickets. "How many in your party?"

"Three," I say. "Four, if you include my K-9."

He tears off three tickets. "Here's three chits, coffee and doughnuts in the rear. And the coffee is real, not diluted."

I take the tickets. "Thanks, Mister Callaghan. Appreciate it."

"No problem," he says, and his voice thickens. "Always glad to help out a soldier. You see, my brother Craig, he was stationed with the 101st in Afghanistan, just before the Creepers attacked. Haven't heard from him since. Always figured if God sees me helping out somebody in uniform, maybe somebody on the other side of the world will do the same for Craig."

Callaghan walks two steps, turns, and says, "Course, all depends on you believing in God. For me, it depends on what day it is."

After we take a coffee break in the rear of the store—and Serena and I savor the hot, strong liquid, though Buddy turns away at being offered a sip—I let Thor have a couple of doughnut chunks and we go outside to wait for our bus. I take a few minutes to clean and inspect my weapons on a park bench underneath a sheet metal overhang. The rain is starting to come down. Serena looks at me with irritation and I say, "I may be your escort, and I may be delivering important documents to the Capitol, Serena, but I'm a soldier first. One of the first things you learn in basic is to take care of your weapons, so they can take care of you."

From my assault pack I take out my cleaning kit, and disassemble and clean the M-4 I took off the dead Coastie, and I'm surprised to see the barrel is pretty decent looking, all things considered. By now there's a steady light rain, and Serena stands by as I run a cleaning rod through the M-4 barrel, settling down with the old scent of gun oil. It soothes and comforts me. Odd, I know, but routine is good and relaxing. When I reassemble the M-4, I check the two spare magazines. Some skill here as well, for the magazines have a 30-round capacity, but the dead Coastie had only loaded 28 rounds; a good way to save wear and tear on the magazine spring and prevent jamming.

My 9 mm doesn't take as long and by now, near the entrance to Callaghan Enterprises, a small crowd of people has joined us under the overhang, as the rain comes down harder. A blackboard has a white chalk marking saying BUS NINETEEN and APPROX SIX PM. A farmer with a wooden crate jammed with chickens snorts. "Why don't they just say whenever it gets here? Damn aggravating, that's what it is."

Serena has one of my jackets on and she shivers, standing next to me. "If you want, you could borrow a pair of pants."

She shakes her head. "No."

"You like being cold?"

"I like the way I look."

A bell is ringing down the sidewalk, and a bearded man shambles up, wearing a ratty terrycloth bathrobe that used to be white and sandals made from rubber tires. Next to him is a boy of about nine or ten, ringing a brass bell, dressed just the same, only in miniature. The man stops before us and starts preaching, and as one, we either turn away or stare at our feet, willing the pair to just go away. The man has a bellowing voice, full of vim and vigor, whatever the hell vim is.

"We are sinners, all of us!" he calls out, with the boy ringing the bell after each sentence. "God has told me so, for God speaks to me daily! The Creepers were sent here by God to punish the wicked, punish the arrogant, punish us for all we have done to the peoples of the world! For what we did to Baghdad and Bagram and Kabul, it was paid back to us in New York and Seattle and Los Angeles! For the people of Iraq and Afghanistan and Yemen that we burned and destroyed, our own people were destroyed in Kansas and Kentucky and Oregon! For polluting the airwaves with pornography and violence and the cable television, the Creepers silenced us, to keep us from further corrupting the other peoples of the world! And if we do not repent, if we do not recognize our sins, tenfold upon tenfold of the Creepers will continue to make war upon us all!"

He stands there, silent, rain making his beard soggy and flat against his chest. The boy with the bell comes before us, holding out a Tupperware plastic bowl. A few coins are dropped in, and then, ringing the bell, the preacher moves along, calling out, "Repent, sinners, repent! Repent!"

One farmer says crossly to her wife, "Why in hell did you give him a quarter?"

"Just in case," she says stubbornly, one hand holding a sack of potatoes.

"Hunh?"

She shifts the bag from one hand to the other. "Just in case he really does talk to God."

Then there's a hissing sound of steam and the scent of smoke, as the Greyhound bus finally appears.

The driver steps out, a man with a thick moustache, dirty gray slacks, and a soiled Greyhound jacket that has sewn patches on the sleeves. He also wears a Greyhound cap on his head. Around his waist he has a holstered Colt .45 pistol. He goes to the middle of the bus, opens up the cargo doors for luggage, and he turns.

"If I can say, folks, let's move it along," he says in a high-pitched voice. "Already behind schedule, want to see if we can make up some time along the way. All big pieces of luggage, let's put them in, please."

The crowd moves forward and eventually I get my assault pack stored underneath, and the driver says, "You want to bring that weapon aboard, soldier, you've got to unload it and make it safe. Sorry, company rules."

"Not a problem," I say. "How long before we can get to the Capitol?"

The bus driver shrugs. "Depends. Three hours. Maybe four or five. We'll have to see what the roads are like. Just one damn flood can take out a bridge or two."

"Fair enough."

I release the magazine from my M-4, work the action to make sure the chamber is clear, and then put the rifle in safe. I stow the magazine on my utility belt, and with Serena, Buddy and Thor in tow, climb into the bus.

Inside it's dark, damp and crowded. We push our way back until I locate two rows of seats, side by side. Buddy goes to the right and grabs the window seat, and I'm surprised to see Thor jump up and join him. Behind me in the narrow aisle Serena laughs and says, "Looks like your best friend is cheating on you."

"He's his own man," I say.

"You forget he's a dog."

"He's what he thinks he is, and that's what counts."

Buddy raises his hand, starts rubbing the back of Thor's head. Thor grins and pants in contentment.

I move past the empty row, point to the seats. "After you, madam."

She smiles, curtsies, and then goes in and sits down. I sit next to her and the seat is old and smells musty, but it feels comfortable. I stretch out my legs and take in the rest of the passengers. A mix of men and women, some farmers, maybe a couple of businessmen in repaired suits, with serious looks and battered briefcases in their hands. The bus smells of sweat, smoke and grease. A little girl comes by, escorted by an older man and woman who could be her grandparents, and she pauses to stroke Thor's back.

The little girl looks over at me. "Is this dog a monster hunter?"

"He sure is," I say with pride in my voice. "The very best."

She looks up at her escort. "See grannie and grampie? We don't have to worry. This dog and soldier will protect us."

Below us the cargo doors slam shut and the bus driver comes back up, and slowly comes up the aisle, collecting our tickets. He then comes back down the aisle, sits in his chair, and adjusts some levers and valves, and with a belch and thump, we're on our way.

The warmth of the bus's interior and the motion of the wheels make me sleepy, and I ease my head back. I think of my dad and my mom and sister, and the Creepers, and dead Mister Manson and the dispatch case at my feet, and I fall asleep. I can't remember my dreams but I wake up with a start, with whimpering in my ears.

Serena is cuddled up against me. The inside of the bus is dark. She cries softly again and I put my arm around her, and she wiggles some, working her way into me. Her hair is freshly washed and is against my face and nose. I take a deep breath. I feel slightly drunk, like the time Dad let me drink beer at his birthday party last year. Serena opens her eyes and says, "I had a bad dream."

"Don't we all."

Her eyes are wide and inviting, keeping me frozen. There's nothing else, no bus, no war, no Creepers. Just the fair skin and fine hair and blue eyes, and I lean down to kiss her. She doesn't move, doesn't protest, so I kiss her again. And again. She sighs and purrs with pleasure. Serena presses her lips up against mine, and we kiss again and again, my arm tightening around her shoulder, her free hand stroking my hair, and I think of Abby and think of her dancing with that mess officer back at Ft. St. Paul, and I kiss Serena again.

So a pleasing several minutes passes.

Eventually we're just holding hands, my head spinning from the sensations and tastes and memories, and Serena's head is on my shoulder and she says softly, "Back at the checkpoint, afterwards, when I gave you hell about me being a soldier . . . I meant it, but I didn't really mean it."

"Sorry, I don't know what you're saying."

"Then listen better," she says. "What I'm trying to say is thank you. You saved my life, Buddy's life, even Thor and Edgar. You saw the threat and responded. Me, I froze. I'm a soldier, but I didn't do anything except to hit the bottom of the carriage with Buddy. So I owe you, Sergeant."

"Don't owe me a damn thing," I say, but decide it's time for another round of kissing and caressing. When there's another pause, she says, "Word I hear, with the war over, discharges are going to start in about six months or so."

"We'll see," I say.

"What will you do when you get discharged?"

"Not sure," I say. "My English teacher, back at Ft. St. Paul, he thinks I should go to college. Says I have a talent for writing."

"What kind of writing?"

"Anything, I guess." I think for a moment and say, "Maybe I could write a history of the Creeper war. If it's really over."

"It'll be a hell of a long book."

"Somebody's got to do it. Why not me?"

She softly laughs. "That's a winning attitude, Randy."

I think for a moment, and then decide to trust her. A good decision? Who knows. I still have the taste of her on my lips. "Thing is, for the past couple of years, I've been breaking regs."

"How? Smuggling rations to civilians? Speaking ill of your commanding officer? Not polishing your shoes?"

"Keeping a journal."

She says, "Really?"

"Truly."

"I'd like to read it some day."

"We'll see," I say, secretly pleased that somebody would like to read my writings.

She moves in closer against me, if that's possible. The bus drones along, the headlights on, illuminating the bumpy state road, the old highway signs still in place, though they're faded and streaked with bird droppings.

Serena says, "School. I want to go to a real school, with no uniforms, no reveille, no salutes."

"Sounds nice," I whisper back, my right hand stroking her fine, shampooed hair. "What do you want to study?"

"Computers."

I can't help it. I laugh. "Silly girl, there's no more computers."

"Maybe so, but you know the rumors. That some of the deep

military bunkers that weren't hit when the war started still have some computers. Or even some remote mines or storage facilities for company records. That there are enough computers out there to use them as models to start assembly lines."

"It'll take a while," I say cautiously.

"Silly boy," she retorts. "I know that. But if I can get some education in school, and when the killer sats are destroyed and the last of the Creepers and their bases are hit too . . . then they'll start making computers again. We have the book knowledge. It's not all gone. It can happen fairly quickly, Randy. You just have to believe."

"Sometimes all I believe in is the Army, Serena. That's it."

"You're being narrow-minded."

"No," I say, kissing her nose. "I'm being realistic."

And I get a kiss in return.

I fall asleep with Serena in my arms, and I wake up when the bus comes to a halt, brakes squealing, steam hissing. The armed driver gets up from his seat and announces, "Fuel stop, folks. We'll be here for thirty minutes, no longer. There's a diner if you'd like to grab a quick bite. I'll blast the horn for a five-minute warning."

Serena leans back and yawns, and in the faint light from the bus's interior bulbs, I like the view. I say, "I'm going out with Thor, give him a bathroom break."

"Sounds like fun."

"I'm also going to see what the diner has to offer. Can I bring you back something?"

She nods. "That'd be great, Randy. Thanks."

She smiles and I kiss her, and then I unfold myself from the seat, reach down and pick up the dispatch case. Thor jumps down into the narrow aisle, and we go out with some other passengers, and in a matter of minutes, it all goes to hell.

An Excerpt From the Journal of Randall Knox

Field trip today for my Current Military Events class. Three squads from our platoon bundled into an old school bus. Yellow paint faded nearly white, black letters stating FIRST STUDENT. *Long time since regular students got to ride in a bus like this. Drove down Interstate 89 through Connecticut, then to a state road that's all cracked and bumpy. Came to a roadblock, we filed out, stood in a row outside the bus. Got a lecture from a Connecticut National Guard captain with no legs in a wheelchair. Told us what to do, what to expect. Field glasses handed out, captain crossly told us that they better all come back in one piece.*

Moved out in a single file, up a packed earth path on a hill, brush and burnt trees, on both sides. Dispersed to left and right as we approached the crest of hill. Local National Guardsmen escorted us. Flattened down on stomachs. Crawled up to top of hill, peered down. Saw the Creeper base, about two klicks away. Dome in the middle of a housing development. Homes all burnt to timbers over cracked concrete foundations. Some rusting cars still in driveways on flat tires. Couple of twisted piles of wreckage, looked like Apache helicopters. Dome the color of Creeper exoskeleton, blue-gray. No openings. No symbols.

Behind us a lecture started from a National Guard captain. Creeper bases located all over world. Apparently dropped from LEO, from main orbital battle station, able to set up within seconds upon landing. Creeper exoskeletons come out when side of dome suddenly dilates open. Bases under constant surveillance, but sometimes killer stealth satellites zap nearby military units whenever they feel like it. Rare occasions we get lucky when we have adjacent attack units on standby when dome opens up, and outgoing fire goes into dome. Not sure how much damage that causes, but sure screws up their day.

Somebody in platoon said, hey, what about stories about Special Forces being able to go in on raids when opening pops out, get prisoners and intel. Silence from our lecturer. Then he said, looking at his watch, time for our daily love-tap.

Couple of minutes later, hear whistling of incoming round from a 155 mm howitzer. Impact on side of dome. Smoke rose up and drifted away. I focused in with borrowed field glasses. Not even a scratch, it looked like. Another question: what are we doing with this kind of attack? Are we hurting the Creepers?

A sigh. Doubtful. But hey, we're fighting, so that's something, right? Nobody answered.

CHAPTER TWENTY-TWO

In the night by the idling bus, a light rain is falling. The diner is called the Bel-Aire, and it's lit by gas lamps and torches. The nearby parking lot has a couple of dozen cars that have been here for ten years, resting on flat tires, the windshields cloudy. A hitching post holds five horses at bay, and there are a number of carriages and wagons parked on the side. Thor comes by me, lifts up his leg and does his business by a low bit of shrubbery.

I scratch at the base of his tail. "Stay classy, pal, stay classy."

Other passengers are going up the crushed stone walkway, and the doors are held open by two young diner boys dressed in black slacks and white shirts, who are smiling and waving their hands, inviting us in.

As I go up to the warm-looking interior of the diner, I feel like I've had twelve hours of sleep and a hot, long shower. I ignore the cold, the rain and the wind. The touch, the scent, the sounds of Serena rattle around in my mind. I think about the next few hours, of getting rid of this dispatch case, seeing if I can track down that Special Forces captain to see what he knows about my dad, but most of all, to see Serena again once she meets up with her own father. Maybe she'll need an escort back to Concord. Maybe we could get a real meal together somewhere. Maybe tour the Capitol. So many possibilities, so many choices. I'm almost dizzy in anticipation of what's ahead.

I get to the diner's door and realize my money and ration book are back in my assault pack, stored under the bus. Damn. I turn around and Thor looks up at me. My best boy smells things cooking and no doubt wonders why I'm turning around, with the possibility of good treats ahead.

"Gotta get the right papers, bud," I say. "Money and ration book. You know how it is."

I walk back to the bus, sloshing through a puddle, but before going to the luggage area where my assault pack is located, I think back for a moment. Serena didn't tell me what she wanted from the diner. The options at the Bel-Aire were probably limited but it wouldn't hurt to ask. I go through the open door of the bus, up the steps and look down the aisle.

No Serena.

No Buddy.

I walk down the aisle, see some of the passengers sitting still, realizing these folks didn't have money to spend at the diner. They look up at me—old, young, male, female—with a slight sense of shame.

But still. No Serena, no Buddy.

I step out and see the driver talking to a guy dressed like a mechanic, dirty overalls, work boots, wiping his hands on a white rag. I catch the driver's eye and say, "I'm looking for a girl, about fifteen, and her younger brother. He's well-dressed, with a bandage on his forehead."

The driver scratches at his moustache. "Yeah. Sure. Left the bus a couple of minutes ago. I reminded her we didn't have much time."

"Where did they go?"

"Over there," he says, pointing to the front of the bus. From the still-lit headlights all I see is the falling rain and trees.

"What the hell is over there?" I ask.

"There's a short trail. Leads to a lean-to, holds some of the wood we use for the bus."

Damn, I think. What the hell is going on? I nod in thanks and go around to the front of the bus, get to the woods and see a wide trail before me. From the light of the bus a wooden structure comes into view. The rain is falling harder. Thor is beside me and I sense his unease. This isn't right.

As I get closer to the building I slow my pace. It's an open lean-to and I hear Serena talking to someone.

I stop. Take it all in. I should just go around the front of the building and see Serena and ask her what's going on with her and her brother, and bring them back to the bus and get on with it.

I don't like it.

I move closer. The side of the building is rough wooden planks, and through gaps in the side I peer through. Buddy is sitting carefully on a pile of cut logs. Serena is kneeling in front of him. A candle's been lit. Serena is holding Buddy's right hand. She's speaking low but forcefully.

"Buddy, please, we're going to be at the Capitol in just a couple of hours. You've got to be ready for daddy. All right? Are you ready? Are you?"

Buddy stares at his sister with a slight smile. Rain is dripping down my neck. Serena takes his other hand. "Buddy, let's go, okay? Let's try it. Okay?"

Not quite believing it, I watch as Buddy lowers his head slightly and nods at his sister. Serena exhales loudly in what looks to be relief.

"Here we go," she says. "Authentication Tango Bravo Bravo X-Ray Hotel. Report message synopsis. Repeat, authentication Tango Bravo Bravo X-Ray Hotel. Report message synopsis."

Buddy nods. Starts speaking in a low, deep voice, not the voice of a boy. It's the voice of a weary old man. The back of my hands and the rear of my neck start to tingle.

"From Task Force Jackson Labs to Major Thomas Coulson. Message synopsis follows."

He pauses, continues looking at his sister. Begins again. *"Interview with captured alien fighter successfully concluded on this post five days ago. Note Appendix A for list and qualifications of interrogation team, including lead interrogator. Alien fighter was captured three months ago near alien base located near Portland, Maine, by Special Forces Group Four. Nearest translation of alien's name is 'She-Loves-Scent-of-Sacrifices.' She has been deployed on Earth since initial attacks ten years ago. Her position with the Creeper force can be roughly translated as legate. She claims she is not in a position to negotiate on behalf of invasion force, but she does have knowledge of Creeper tactics, strategy and ultimate invasion goals. Her outlining of Creeper invasion goals matches those secured from interrogation two months ago near Denver of alien named 'She-With-Sharp-Tooth-And-Claw.' Interrogation team spent nearly a month with alien fighter, using coercive interview techniques to secure intelligence information. Note Appendix B for copy of Presidential Directive authorizing such techniques. End of synopsis. End of message."*

Then Buddy looks up, his face blank again, and Serena squeezes both of his hands, and then snuffs out the candle. I slide away, Thor obediently trotting next to me.

In the diner I'm trying to keep my thoughts straight and clear. I feel cold and vulnerable and very, very exposed. Just like the first time I went up against a Creeper, all by myself, with a new and fairly untested M-10 in my hands. The diner is crowded and there's a waitress of about twelve or thirteen, in a too-large pink dress, going by me, carrying a notepad in her hands.

"Excuse me," I say. "I need to see your manager, right away."

"All right, soldier, I'll see what I can do." She looks beside me, smiles. "Cute dog."

"That he is."

The manager comes over, a harried-looking guy in his fifties, wearing the same type of black slacks and white shirt of his younger help. His face is sweating and he needs a shave. "What's up, Sergeant?"

"Need an empty room or office, and a tool box."

He takes a white towel from his belt, wipes his face. "You got it. Want something to eat?"

About ten minutes ago, yeah, but not now, I think. "Got any scraps you can spare for my partner?

He shrugs. "Sure. Give me a few seconds."

I stand still and watch the hustle and bustle of the young waitresses moving around on the tile floor, past the stools and booths. There's a low hum of conversation from the diners and by the door, there's a poster for a Red Cross blood drive, a notice seeking a refugee family called Simpson, and another poster listing the three kinds of Creepers. That poster is old and faded.

The manager comes by, leads me to a back room. There's a desk, chair, boxes and a bowl on the ground that Thor dives into, biting and chewing some meat and bone pieces. On the floor by the desk is a toolbox, and when the manager leaves, I go to it. I poke around and find what I'm looking for: an awl and a long, thin flathead screwdriver.

I put the dispatch case on the desk, on top of some time cards and invoices and carbon slips. The chain and bloodstained handcuff are still attached, and there's a leather clasp and lock in the center of the case.

Take a deep breath. There's doing a mission and keeping your nose clean and embracing the suck, and then there's going rogue, going off the reservation, disobeying orders. Door number one or door number two. And instead of going through a certain door, I was thinking about blasting it wide open.

Awl in one hand, screwdriver in the other, I look down at the lock, hesitate. There's a thin bright blue plastic line wrapped around the lock. If I were to break into the lock, I'd snap the plastic line, letting the intended recipients know that it had been broken into.

Orders.

Damnable orders.

I put the awl and screwdriver away into my pack.

From outside comes a blast of a horn. Five minutes to go.

Thor licking the bowl clean nearby.

Thor looks up at me, wags his tale. I scratch his ears.

"Thanks for the reminder, pal," I say, and I go out into the diner, following the passengers out back to the bus.

Inside the bus Buddy is sitting in his seat, and Thor bounds up and joins him. Serena is sitting like she had never left the bus, and she frowns at me as I come up.

"Well?" she asks. "No food? Or water?"

I sit down heavily, put the dispatch case between my feet. "Sorry. Got crowded in the diner and when it was my turn, forgot that my money and ration book were in my assault pack. Then the horn blew. Didn't want to miss the bus."

She says crossly, "And you didn't think of that before leaving?"

A sharp bite of guilt, of thinking about Abby. Once we were on a recon mission that came up blank. As usual, rain started up in the afternoon, and we took shelter underneath an oak tree, waiting for our pick-up, me with Thor, she with her trusty bike. Neither of us had any rations left but it was okay; we scrounged around and found some fiddlehead ferns, whose roots we washed and ate raw, and for dessert, I went to a nearby abandoned orchard and salvaged a handful of dried McIntosh apples. In the driving rain we ate our meager meal, rain dripping down on us, Abby's strong and scarred legs stretching out before her. We had shared laughs, stories about previous recons, and despite the rain and cold and rough meal, it had been a special day.

I spare a glance at Serena's legs and the short skirt she's wearing. Only a few short minutes ago, I had found her and her legs appealing and oh so sexy. Now, in the smelly and smoky interior of the wood-fired Greyhound bus, heading towards a wartime Capitol, she looks ridiculous.

"So?" Serena demands, repeating herself. "You didn't think of that before leaving?"

The driver gets in, shuts the door behind him, and gets into his seat.

"Apparently not," I reply.

She snorts and says, "Whatever."

Sure, I think. Whatever. I look over at Thor, who's sitting calmly with Serena's brother. Buddy looks at me and I feel a flash of fear. He looks impassive and quiet and so very dangerous, with a power and talent I don't understand.

Serena sighs loudly again and settles herself in her seat, and I feel alone and vulnerable, a feeling I don't like. It's going to be a couple more hours before we get to the Capitol, and I'm wondering what to do and what to say when I get there, and in less than a half hour, that decision is thankfully taken away from me.

Serena and Buddy and even Thor are dozing when the Greyhound bus makes a sudden stop, sliding over to the right. Through the windows I make out torchlights and even an electric flashlight or two. I get up and through the windshield, I see we've come to a checkpoint. Recalling what we had encountered earlier in the day, I take my Beretta pistol from my holster.

Serena wakes up. "What's going on?"

"Don't know," I say. "Looks like we've been stopped by cops or something."

"Well, why don't you find out, Randy?" she asks.

"Why don't you shut up, Specialist?" I snap back.

The door opens up and Serena sits up, angry, and the driver steps out, and then comes back with an older woman, wearing an orange rain slicker and a round-brimmed uniform hat. Her face is drawn and her gray hair is matted from the rain. Water drips from her slicker, and in one hand, she's holding a luxury, a flashlight.

"Folks, Lynn Hanratty, of the Albany County Sheriff's Department," she says in a strong voice, despite the exhaustion about her eyes. "We've got a situation here tonight, was looking for some help. Are there any active duty military here?"

I call out, "Right here, ma'am."

She looks slightly relieved. "Oh. Son . . . I mean, Sergeant, that's good. Can you join us for a moment?"

"Absolutely," I say. I reach up to the luggage rack and take down my unloaded M-4 automatic rifle. I sling it over my shoulder and go down the aisle of the bus, Serena behind me, Thor coming along, but I tell him to stay with Buddy. The deputy sheriff steps out and I follow her. There's a roadblock and gas lanterns are hung on the barricade and nearby tree limbs. She leads me to a tarp stretched from a decaying billboard advertising a nearby Dunkin' Donuts, and there's a fire and table and maps and other police officers and a couple of men with long rifles hanging off their shoulders. The Greyhound bus is still, steam and smoke rising up from the rear. By the tarp a few horses are hitched, and there's an old dented, brown police cruiser with a cracked windshield.

I duck underneath the tarp and the deputy sheriff takes off her hat, shakes off some of the raindrops and wipes at her eyes. "This is what we got, Sergeant. We got a Creeper on the attack, less than a half mile away."

She points down to a creased and stained topographical map that's spread out on the table. I ask, "What do you have for a fighting force?"

A harsh laugh. "What you see here, and a few hardy boys, out there in the woods, laying down some harassing fire without getting scorched or their heads burned off."

"Military?"

Another cop speaks up. "So far, you. We can't send up signaling flares with this damn rain, and the telegraph line's down. We've sent out couriers, but it's gonna be a while for help to come."

I look at the map again. "Maybe I'm dense, but what's the problem? Just get out of the Creeper's path until a QRF shows up."

Sheriff Hanratty shakes her head. "That sounds good, Sergeant, but unfortunately, the damn Creeper, while he's moving slow, he's heading straight to a relocation camp. Brooklyn North. Got a few hundred elderly, disabled and children in those tents. Middle of the night like this, we can't get 'em all out in time."

The map is a fine piece of work, at least ten years old, of course. I feel everyone's eyes on me, including Serena, who's touching my elbow. She's whispering, "Randy, look, Randy . . ."

I say, "Best we can do is to slow it down, then. Until reinforcements arrive."

"That's right," the deputy sheriff says.

Crazy and odd and no doubt strange, but at this moment, I almost feel relieved, at peace. The way forward for me is clear. The time for being in the shadows and facing uncertainty and secrets and coded messages and mistrust is over.

It's time to do what I know best.

I look at everyone for just a moment, making sure all are paying attention to me.

"Then under the current National Emergency and Martial Law act, I'm taking command of this situation," I say.

CHAPTER TWENTY-THREE

There's a sudden intake of breath and Serena whispers, "Randy, you can't be serious," and one of the civilian men with a long rifle on his back says, "Hell you say, you're just a kid."

"Kenny, shut up," the deputy sheriff snaps. Glancing at my nametag, she says, "Sergeant Knox is correct. He's the senior military official on site, and it's his . . . responsibility. And duty. No matter his age. What now, sergeant?"

A very good question, I think. A little needling voice inside says, all right, Randy, you hot shot, what now? These good and scared folks are waiting for you to do something.

So do something.

"All right, I need to get back to the bus, get some gear. I'll be back here in about five minutes, and I'll look for the latest situation report. Deal?"

The deputy sheriff nods. "It's a deal, Sergeant."

I turn around and go back to the bus, and Serena is tagging along, trying to get my attention, and I ignore her and as I get closer, I say to the driver, "Need you to open up the middle baggage compartment."

He nods and gets to work and snaps open the side door. I tug out my pack, open it up in the rain, start getting some of my gear out. Thor prances out of the open bus door, sits at my feet, and then gets up, sniffing the air. He starts whining, tail wagging. Serena's hand is on my arm again, desperately saying, "Randy, what the hell are you doing?"

"Getting ready to go into battle, Specialist," I say. I unzip some of the side pockets, take out my family pic, my set of rosary beads and my souvenir from my first Creeper kill. They go into my coat pockets. I also take out Serena's carefully folded uniform and place it in her hands.

"But Randy, you're supposed to escort me and my brother to the Capitol."

I gesture to the bus. "You're probably less than an hour away. You'll be just fine."

"How can you be sure?"

"A gamble we're going to have to take," I say. "We've got a Creeper out there, raising hell and threatening a couple hundred refugees. I'm not going to get back on the bus and be a good little passenger to the Capitol. I've got more important things to do than be a tour guide."

In the rain her hair is sticking to her angry face. I go through my pack again. No body armor, of course, or anti-burn cream. Damn. As somebody once famous said—something I should have remembered from one of my military history classes—you go to war with the army you have, not the army you want.

"Why are you doing this?" she demands.

"It's my duty, that's why."

She steps closer to me. "No, there's something else going on. You've been cold and pissy ever since we left the diner. What's up, Randy?"

I adjust my belt, take one of the magazines and insert it into the M-4 and work the action, then put the automatic rifle in safe, put it back over my shoulder. "What's up, Specialist, is that my mission has changed. My original mission was to escort Mister Manson and you and your brother to the Capitol. Mister Manson is dead. You and your brother can go on your own."

"But—"

I interrupt. "The dispatch case I'm putting in your hands. If you and I don't meet again later on, then you'll see that the case reaches its destination. When you get to the Capitol, look up Tess Conroy, the President's Chief of Staff. Present her the dispatch case with my compliments and tell her how Mister Manson of the New Hampshire governor's office met his end."

"You can't do this!"

"I am, and will," I say. "I was supposed to escort you and your silent brother to the Capitol, to meet up with your father. Fair enough. But I don't know who you really are, except I know you've been lying to me all along."

"Lying? How in hell was I lying?"

I find a small notebook in a side pocket. There you go. I stare at her and say, "'From Task Force Jackson Labs to Major Thomas Coulson. Message synopsis follows.' Sound familiar, specialist? Or was I hearing things?"

She stares right back at me, then tugs some of her wet hair away from her face. "Randy, sorry, OPSEC and—"

"Specialist, I'd like to tell you what to do with your OPSEC, but I don't have time. I've got to get ready for an upcoming firefight. You go on your little secret mission. You don't need me. You get to the Capitol and meet up with your dad. You're one lucky gal, getting to see your father. I haven't seen my dad in months. Not sure where the hell he is. I'm about to go toe-to-toe with a Creeper, while you're getting ready for a comfortable ride to the Capitol. And you know what? I'm fine with that. I'll take a straightforward mission any night than to lurk around in the shadows like you're doing."

The rain seems to fall harder and colder. I go on. "I should have known something was wrong, back when the train was ambushed. Because that wasn't a Creeper that attacked us."

"What the hell do you mean that wasn't a Creeper? What was it, our imagination?"

Thor whines some more, going around in a tight circle. "See what Thor is doing right now? He's responding to the scent of a Creeper. He knows there's one in the area. Back at the train attack? He didn't react like that. Oh, there was an exoskeleton up on that hill, firing at us. But there wasn't a Creeper alien inside. It was either on automatic or there was a human inside. That's why when the Marines attacked with their M-10s, nothing happened. Meaning the train was deliberately attacked by humans, either to get your brother or Mister Manson."

"You've got to be kidding."

"Wish I was. Why was that train attacked? For me? The other passengers? Or two couriers, one operating out in the open, the other in the shadows? Whatever it was, I don't care anymore. I'm just a soldier. I'm good at a fair and open fight. I don't want to fight in your world of secrets and betrayals. Not going to happen."

I take my small notebook and put it in her hands. "There's my journal. Hope you have a chance to read it. It's going to be in your care, along with the dispatch case, my assault pack and Thor."

"Thor? You're leaving your dog with me?"

I take a leash from my assault pack, snap it to Thor's collar. He whines some more and tugs at the leash. He doesn't like being on a leash, which is fair, because I don't like it either. "That I am. Where I'm going . . . I'm not going to be alone. There'll be other fighters out there, giving me info about the Creeper. I don't want Thor underfoot, have him get shot by mistake. There'll be a lot of scared civilians out in the woods, ready to shoot at anything that moves." My throat is tight, and I have to force the next words out. "You're going to take care of my boy, Specialist, and you're not going to fail me."

I pass the leash over to Serena and she takes it. Her face darkens. "Damn you, you're going on a suicide mission, aren't you."

"No, I'm not."

She says, "You're giving me your journal, you're sending me to the Capitol on my own, and you're leaving your dog with me. Sure sounds like a one-way mission to me."

Thor's really whining now and I catch the scent of cinnamon. Not much time left. "Not in the mood for a discussion, Specialist. You have your orders. Now get back on that bus."

She tightens her hand on Thor's leash. "Randy, I—"

I shake my head, gently push her shoulder. "That time's past, Specialist. It's Sergeant Knox. Now get the hell out of here."

Serena starts to the bus door, Thor dragging along, looking back at me. I can't look at my dog and instead call out to Serena.

"Specialist!"

She stops and glances back at me. "Sergeant?"

I point to her. "You're out of uniform. Make sure you take care of that before you get to the Capitol."

Her voice is meek. "Yes, Sergeant."

She ducks into the bus, Thor following her. The windows are rain streaked and dark but still, I can see the passengers in there, looking down at me. A few seem to wave, and I wave back, and then the bus lurches into life, and I watch it head down the road. When the steam and smoke and taillights disappear, I pick up my pack and get to work, my eyes watering and burning, no doubt from the smoke.

CHAPTER TWENTY-FOUR

Back under the tarp, I say, "Deputy, anything new?"

She moves a reddened finger along the map. "The Creeper is still moving along, heading right to Brooklyn North. It'll get there in about twenty minutes. By then, only half of the refugee camp will be evacuated."

"Your forces?"

"About a half dozen deputy sheriffs and local cops, firing where they can. The Creeper seems to be ignoring them. It's traveling adjacent to this streambed—" and she traces a faint line of blue on the map "—and it's not a Battle Creeper. It's Transport."

I nod. "A bit of luck. That means it's bulky and moving relatively slow."

I look down at the map, watching that thin blue line. I put my finger at a point on the map and say, "Is there a bridge here, at this point?"

Deputy Hanratty asks, "Kenny? You know that area better than me. What do you think?"

Kenny's the one who made the stunning observation that I was young, but he steps forward and glances at the map and nods. "Yeah. There's a bridge there. I'd say the Creeper's about ten minutes away from it."

"What's the bridge made of?"

"Dunno. Stone and concrete, I guess."

What a fine map. Wonder if those nice mapmakers from the long-gone U.S. Geological Survey ever thought these carefully designed maps would be used in a war on American soil. I say, "What's the land like around the bridge?"

Kenny says, "Map don't show it, but the stream widens some as it approaches the bridge. Up some from the bridge, to the west, there's another stream that feeds in, coming out of a narrow swampy area."

Good, I think. *Very good.*

Deputy Hanratty says, "Sergeant . . . what do you have in mind? Because there's not much time left. Those refugees . . ."

I tap a finger on the creased paper. "All the men with guns that you have . . . line them up on and around the bridge. Also place some guns over here, to the east of the bridge. Take the best cover you can. The stone and concrete from the bridge should help. When the Creeper shows up, hit the bastard with everything you've got."

There's silence, and I know what Deputy Sheriff Hanratty and the others are thinking. Easy enough to be here and look at a map and issue orders, but I was telling them where to put friends, relatives and neighbors in danger, with a good chance that within the hour, some would be horribly burnt or killed.

Kenny says sourly, "And where will you be . . . Sergeant?"

I wait for just a second, to milk the moment, and then I say, "I'll be here. In this swampy area. Your gunfire, if we're lucky, will push the Creeper up to that other stream, and to the swamp. There, I'll be waiting."

"With what?" one of the men asks. "All you got is that M-4, like the old M-16. That ain't no M-10 you've got."

"Trust me, I know."

"So what will you do?"

"I'm going to kill it," I say.

The rain is coming down steadily, as I work my way up the stream leading to the promised swampland, I'm trying to think if there was ever a time where it didn't rain at least three or four times a week. I quickly give up, recalling that even ten years later, there's a lot of moisture in the atmosphere after a few dozen aimed asteroids from the Creepers flooded all those coastal cities.

A few minutes earlier men were working to set up firing positions on the stone bridge, some of them dragging in logs or boulders to give them more protection from the approaching Creeper. There were a couple of flashes that scared me but it turned out to be an old stumpy guy with bad teeth and a gray beard who said he was a reporter from the local newspaper, the *Times-Union*, who had an old-fashioned camera that used film. Even in the rain, the smell of cinnamon was getting stronger, and to the north was a glow where fires were burning following the Creeper's approach.

Right after the guy took the pictures, a line of refugees came by from Brooklyn North, escorted by a two local cops on horseback. I try to focus on the upcoming mission, but seeing the old men and women riding in the back of wagons, the boys and girls walking along, some of the younger ones, holding hands, strikes at me. There was another flash of light from the newspaper guy and one little girl stares and stares at me. She has the look of someone who has spent her whole life trusting the older ones to protect her, and who has always been disappointed.

Melissa, I think, my poor older sis.

Now I'm soaked through, my feet wet, and with my knife, pistol and M-4, I'm woefully underarmed. Out there is a Quick Reaction Force, riding to the proverbial rescue, but they could be a minute or an hour away. In the meantime, it was up to me, sixteen year old Randy Knox, who—in another life or another timeline—would be worrying about getting his driver's license, or a prom date, or math homework. Not being in charge of a rabble in arms, doing their best to slow down an alien horror that was minutes away from slaughtering scared and shivering refugees from the remnants of one of the most powerful cities in the world.

I slosh along, M-4 in my hands, glancing behind me. I'm starting to hear the hiss of flames, and the glow of flames is getting stronger. Around me are birch trees and pines, blueberry bushes and other low growth, and my mouth is dry and my chest is pounding along something awful. I recall my earlier fib to Serena, about why I wanted Thor away from this battle site, and when I come across a slightly drier piece of ground, I kneel down and try to think of a prayer.

Nothing comes to me. That's scary, almost as scary as the thought of that approaching Creeper. Other things are scary, too, crowding my thoughts. The Creeper at the train ambush site. No alien was inside that exoskeleton, burning the train and its passengers and the defending Marine force. The ambush had been a set-up by my fellow humans, so that either Mister Manson or Serena and Buddy—or maybe all of them—would be killed in a Creeper attack, no questions asked.

Then there's my dad, in trouble somewhere. And my uncle. Did he send me along with Mister Manson because I was the best, as he claimed, or was I sent along so that I'd be killed, thereby avenging his sister's death?

I get up, cross myself, knees soaked through. Too many thoughts bouncing around in my head, so I try to focus and clear my mind for the upcoming mission. Otherwise, I'll be a crispy-critter before even having a chance to fire off a round.

So I return to my sloshing.

In the rain and ambient light from the burning things in the distance, I luck out and find a piece of land in the center of the swampy area that has a couple of big granite boulders and a maple tree growing nearby. On either sides of this rocky outcropping the land is swampy and muddy, rising up to sharp tree-covered slopes.

I check my M-4 and get the spare magazines ready for easy access, ready for combat. I lick my lips. Still dry. I jerk when I hear the sound of gunfire nearby, from the men and a few women by the bridge. The gunfire continues at a fair pace, and then dribbles away. Two explanations: either the Creeper is doing what I hope and want, heading in my direction, or the Creeper ignored the gunfire from the cops and civilians and plowed right through them, lasing and burning them all.

I wipe my face. My first solo command, and there was a good chance that they were now smoldering lumps of charcoal.

Guess I'll know, soon enough.

The glow gets brighter, stronger.

The cinnamon smell is almost overwhelming.

Snap/snizzle of a laser being fired. And then a burst of flame, as birch trees a hundred or so meters away explode into balls of fire. The *click-click* sound of it moving along. Lips are still dry. Cinnamon scent gets stronger. All alone. More *click-click* sounds. From my school lessons, I recall other lonely men out there, doing what they had to do in the oncoming rush of danger. Sergeant Alvin York in 1918, facing down a line of German machine gun nests, killing and capturing more than a hundred soldiers. The pilots of Torpedo Eight off the *USS Hornet* in 1942 during the Battle of Midway, flying into oblivion in obsolete aircraft; and all but one dying against the might of the

Japanese Navy without striking a single ship. Sergeant Paul Ray Smith at the Baghdad International Airport in 2003, fighting off scores of Iraqi soldiers while preventing a casualty station from being overrun, for which he was posthumously awarded the Medal of Honor.

The Creeper comes into sight, moving at a good clip, water splashing up from its moving legs.

My chest hurts, my hands and feet grow colder. This Creeper is larger than the one I had killed the other day at that dairy farm. This one is a Transport Creeper, with the same amount of legs, two weapons claws, and center arthropod. But the rear section is wider and deeper where there's a rectangular opening, where objects get dumped in to be brought back to one of their land bases, such as pieces of machinery, trees, vegetation and sometimes people, either dead or injured.

For what reason? Who the hell knows. They're aliens, and we know next to nothing about them—

Which is no longer true.

I raise up my M-4. Somebody's been interrogating captured Creepers, somebody knows their invasion plans and goals, somebody—

Shut up, I think. Whoever that somebody is, isn't here to provide supporting fire.

"Come on, you creepy bastard, come on," I whisper, keeping still behind the granite boulders. I watch and watch and hope and hope—

The Creeper gets into the swampy area, and it slows down, as its legs sink into the mud and muck, and I whisper again, "Sorry, bitch, you've traveled all this way to get caught up in good ol' Earth mud."

I open fire, setting off two or three bursts of fire at the main arthropod, and I roll down and to the right, as the Creeper returns fire, sending a burst of flame overhead to the maple tree, instantly setting it ablaze. Pieces of burning leaves and branches fall down, and I fire off another couple of rounds, aiming right again at the center of the Creeper. I don't have an M-10 with the chemical rounds, I don't have a good sighting system, and I don't have depleted uranium rounds, but I'm still shooting, hoping for that golden BB to penetrate the breathing membrane and either kill or injure the alien bastard.

More return fire from the Creeper, the *snap/snizzle* of the laser firing this time, and I burrow into the mud, holding my breath, feeling heat scorch the back of my neck. I flounder back some, hitting my elbow against a rock, and I spare a glance. The mud slows down the Transport Creeper but she's still coming straight at me. I fire off one more long burst and my magazine is empty.

I clamber quickly up onto the small spit of land, underneath the burning maple tree. I pop out the empty magazine, pop in a new one, snap the action lever free and another three-round burst is sent down range.

Moving, ducking, shooting. Trying not to think. Trying not to wonder where the Quick Reaction Force is. Trying not to wonder if any of the cops and civilians back at the bridge might be coming my way.

Trying to stay alive.

Trees all around me are now burning. The heat is fierce on my hands and face. I fire again and again and the M-4 is hot in my hands.

Another magazine is empty. The Creeper is slogging through and closer and closer, the cinnamon scent making me want to puke, and I slam another magazine into my M-4 and the action snaps back again.

A *snap/snizzle* of the laser and I scream as something sears my left shoulder. I fall to my knees, nearly waist-deep in water, and I fire one more time and the M-4 jams.

Jams.

I work the action and it's still jammed. Nothing happens.

Damn stolen rifle!

I toss it away, crawl along in the mud and water, left shoulder hurting like hell, soaked all the way through, my hands and the back of my neck tingling from the heat. I unsnap my holster, pull out my 9 mm, and I'm slammed in the side of my head as a Creeper leg strikes me.

The pistol flies out of my hand, plops into the mud. I scramble some more. Flames and smoke all around me and rain is falling. I think I hear other gunshots. I think I hear people. I think I hear a dog barking.

The Creeper is over me. I'm unarmed. Not much I can do.

Then I swear at her, climb up on the rocks and a Creeper leg snaps out, nearly cutting me in two, and I jump at her.

Jump onto the Creeper. I'm on the back of the arthropod, holding my breath from the stench of the Creeper, my hands slipping along the jointed metal, until I grasp a handhold, from some horn or antenna sticking out, and the Creeper moves around, and I'm so close I can hear machinery or fans or something inside whirring along. A weapons claw comes by, trying to pry me off, and I duck.

Nearly fall.

Shouts. Dog barking. Flashes of light. Gunfire.

I'm holding onto a jointed piece of exoskeleton with one hand, flailing around, trying to gain a toehold with my feet, my boots and—

My boots.

I raise up my right leg, lower my hand, grab my knife, tug it free. The light is pretty good from the fires and I see I'm just below the breathing membrane, and I reach up and stab.

Stab.

Stab.

The blade penetrates the membrane. The Creeper shudders. I hear a bellow, or a scream, or a pant.

I stab.

Dog barking.

I look down. Damn me, I don't believe it!

Thor is underneath me, joyous and fierce in the mud, snapping up at the Creeper's legs, and I call down, "Thor, break! Go away!"

Thor looks up, barking and growling, and I don't see him again, as a Creeper leg raises up and falls down, crushing him into the mud as my bud howls in pain.

CHAPTER TWENTY-FIVE

I yell out, "Thor!" and the Creeper's main arthropod twists and falls, and I fly though the air, hoping to land in the mud and water, but instead landing on hard rock and dirt, and I fade and cry out some more.

I wake up groggily, nearly every part of me hurting. Flames are still dropping down from the burning maple tree. My hands and face are scorched. I try to call for Thor but my mouth is full of something. Everything around me is a confusing mix of rain, shadows, smoke and fire. My jacket is torn. I look over and on the ground is the old photo of my family, taken so many years and lifetimes ago. I fade in and out, and then a burning branch falls on the photo, and it curls up and blackens and it's gone.

I close my eyes.

Voices wake me, two men approaching, holding lanterns. I try to sit up and I moan, and the nearest man says, "Kid, that's the damnest thing I've ever seen. How are you doing?"

My mouth is full of something and I spit it out. It's gritty and tastes like dirt. Swamp mud. I try to catch my voice and fail.

The second man says, "I saw it and I still don't believe it. Can't believe it! You took that monster out with a goddamn knife!"

I spit again and say, "Over there . . . my dog . . . find my dog . . ."

I rub my right hand across my eyes and things come into view. The Transport Creeper has slumped down, unmoving, curious men and women moving about with lanterns and at least one flashlight. The surrounding trees are still burning, but the rain is keeping things in check. Some more flashes of light. An approaching thunderstorm? Thor. Damn it to hell, Serena, I asked you to keep him safe . . . keep him with you . . . how in hell did you screw up something so simple?

The first man says, "Sorry, soldier, I didn't see no dog out there . . . look, we better get you to a hospital, report what happened to the authorities. You killed that bastard single-handed!"

"That's right, pal," his companion says. "We got a first-aid team getting here as quick as possible, take care of you. Might take a while, though, we took some heavy hits back at the bridge."

The man is holding up an oil lantern and I see he's about twice my age, wearing a creased leather jacket, dirty jean pants, and workboots. His hair is black and is tied back in a thick ponytail, and he's got a trimmed goatee. He's got a belt and holster around his coat and it looks like he's carrying a revolver. I motion him to come closer with my good hand and he kneels down, and I snap up and tug his revolver from his holster.

"Hey, hey, hey!" he calls out, standing up, and I almost drop the revolver but manage to get it up in my hand. Seems like a .357 stainless steel, maybe a Ruger, good enough to blow a pretty good-sized hole into him.

I cock the hammer back. "Move without hearing me out and I'll drop you right here and now. Okay? And if your friend over there moves, I'll drop you both. Have I got your damn attention?"

The guy slowly nods, as does his friend, and I spit out some more mud. "Here's the deal. Out there in the swamp is my best friend. He's a good-sized dog, named Thor. A Belgian Malinois. He's been hurt. He's by the legs of that damn Creeper. You or your friend, you go there and find him and come back to me. Got it?"

The guy with the goatee looks up to his friend, who I can't make out clearly, and he says, "Sam, do us both a favor and see if you can find the man's dog?"

The second guy's voice is gravely. "If you say so, Carlos."

He sloshes off and Carlos says, "You must like that dog a hell of a lot."

I cough. "You could say that. Where's Deputy Hanratty?"

Carlos says, "She's dead. Creeper cut her in pieces with a laser back up on the bridge."

The second guy called Sam sloshes back, quicker, and says, "Yeah, Carlos, found the mutt. But he's in pretty bad shape. Looks like the Creeper stomped him some."

My right hand is shaking and I bring up my other hand to steady the revolver. "Tell you what, Sam. You said a first-aid crew is coming in for me. You get that crew to take my dog out. I see that crew take my dog out and then I'll give Carlos here back his revolver. Then Carlos can punch me or kick me or do whatever he wants. So long as my dog gets treated. But if my dog doesn't get treated, if he gets dumped where I can't see it, or if somebody cuts his throat and says he died on the way to the vet, then I'll track you down and kill you both."

Carlos sits back on a rock, manages a smile. "Wouldn't hurt a guy like you, even for pulling my own gun on me. Like I said earlier, must be a hell of a dog."

"Some day I'll tell you all about it," I say.

More torchlights approach and Sam directs the stretcher crew out to the swamp. There's some shouting and arguing, but my eyes fill up when I hear a long plaintive howl, as my Thor is put onto a stretcher. I can see shadows moving around and then Sam comes over and says, "You see that? Your doggie just got picked up. He'll get treated best we can . . . maybe we can get him to one of the bigger vet clinics at the Capitol."

I let out a breath, cough, ribs and back and damn near everything else hurting, especially the burning in my left shoulder. I use both hands to lower the hammer back down on the .357 Ruger, and hand it butt-end back to Carlos.

"You kept your word, and so do I," I say.

"Fair enough," he says, twirling the Ruger once before returning it to his holster. He holds out a thick hand. "Carlos Menendez, at your service."

I shake his hand, weakly I know, and I try to get up and grimace and fall back. "Sergeant Randy Knox, New Hampshire National Guard," I say. "Thanks for your help."

"Long way from home, New Hampshire soldier."

I try to see into the darkness, to see where Thor has been taken.

"Aren't we all."

Sam comes back, offers me a canteen, and I take a couple of deep swallows. "Hell of a thing, what you did."

"Did what I had to do."

"True," he says, taking a swig from the canteen. Carlos says, "Know what they found in that Transport Creeper? Old bones."

"Bones? What kind of bones?"

"Old bones, mixed up in rotting caskets. Looks like the damn thing was robbing a graveyard. All this fighting, all this burning and dead folks . . . all over bones." He spits on the ground. "Goddamn Creeper. But at least you got 'em, got 'em dead."

I shake my head. "A team effort. You shooters at the bridge got the Creeper going in my direction. I was able to finish him off."

More sloshing in the mud and a stretcher crew comes in, four guys, exhausted, wearing turnout gear from the local volunteer fire department, carrying a metal Stokes litter between them. They work almost as one, getting me into the Stokes litter, strapping me in, putting a couple of wool blankets over me, and then they take me away, Carlos patting me on the shoulder, me looking at the dead Creeper Transport just a score of meters away.

The firefighters are doing their best, but they're tired and stumble a lot as they bring me through the swamp, making me moan or cry out as the litter bounces around. The first time I get a muttered apology, but by the fifth or sixth time, I think they're too tired to say anything. They bring me back to the bridge, where a clearing station for the wounded has been set up. A large tarp has been stretched from two dead telephone poles, staked to the ground. I'm brought in and dropped off on a set of planks balanced on sawhorses, and a woman comes over to me, a stethoscope hanging around her neck, dressed in faded scrubs. Her red hair is cut short and she briskly looks at my shoulder, my hands, face and feels along my ribs. I wince a couple of times. Further into the station there are at least six men and one woman being examined and treated. Two sheet-covered figures are on the pavement. A woman is by herself on a canvas stretcher, lying some distance away. Her hair has been scorched away, and she holds up her burnt arms up in the air. One man suddenly starts screaming, "Sweet

Jesus, it hurts! Give me something, for the love of God, please, give me something! I don't have any hands left! Help me, please!"

She says to me, "Sorry, you'll have to wait."

Triage, of course. Lightly wounded get looked at later. Those who can be saved by immediate treatment are brought to the head of the line. And those who have no chance, like the woman with no hair, are left to die.

"I understand," I say.

She says, "You're the soldier that eventually killed the Creeper, right? The one with the dog?"

"That's right."

She shakes her head in disgust. "Yeah, you're the one who pulled the pistol on Carlos and Sam, made them take care of your dog. Delayed a recovery team who should have brought back a fighter, not a damn mutt. We lose any more tonight, it's because of you trying to save your damn dog."

I call out to her as she walks away. "Ma'am, you're wrong."

She whirls around. "How?"

"It wasn't a pistol," I say. "It was a revolver."

Some of my clothes are eventually snipped away and my face and hands are dressed with burn cream, and my left shoulder is temporarily dressed and I get a shot of something that makes me warm and foggy. The doctor with the short red hair comes back and writes something on a large cardboard tag, which is looped around my wrist. I don't say anything to her and she returns the favor, going back to the other injured. The guy who was shouting earlier has quieted down.

Morning is starting to break when I'm taken to an old workhorse, a faded white Cadillac ambulance from the early 1960's that's still running. I'm put in the back with another kid about my age, who's doped up from whatever they've given him. Like me, he's covered with a gray wool blanket, but his blanket slumps down just below his knees.

I doze for most of the ride to the hospital. The siren either doesn't work or the driver decides it wouldn't make any difference.

I'm still groggy when we get to the hospital, and I'm processed, poked and prodded, told that I'm at a V.A. institution and I get another shot. When I wake up later I have to piss in the worst way, and I find myself in a ward with five other beds, all of us crowded together. There's no bell or call button or anything nearby, just a dirty white nightstand that has a cracked ceramic jug on top, next to a pitcher of water and a glass. I swing around my legs and do my business, and put the jug on the floor, and then roll back to look at my fellow patients. Five guys, various ages and shapes, and I see bandages, stumps, and lots of burn tissue. The guy nearest to me has bandages wrapped around his hands and most of his head and he says, "Welcome to the Sixth Ward, kid."

"Thanks," I say. "What V.A hospital is this?"

"Stratton V.A. Hospital," he replies. "Welcome to the Capitol."

I pull a blanket over me, wincing some. "You're a welcoming guy."

His laugh is muffled. "Not much else I can do. What unit?"

"Second Ranger Recon," I say. "New Hampshire National Guard. Name is Knox, Randy Knox."

"Good to meet you, Randy," he says. "Slim Easton, First Combined Strike Force, Tenth Mountain. Looks like you tangled with a Creeper."

I gaze around the room. "Looks like everybody here's tangled with a Creeper."

"Yeah," Slim says. "Lucky for us, the war's over, hunh?"

I can't help but laugh, and so does he, and so do a couple of the other guys.

A woman doctor comes by with two nurses who seem about the age of Serena—who should be somewhere out there in the Capitol with her mysterious brother, hooking up with her father—and I'm told I have scattered second degree burns on my hands, face and the back of my neck, along with a couple of cracked ribs and laser burn on my left shoulder, along with a slight concussion. I have a new burn coating on my exposed skin and a firm dressing on my left shoulder.

The doctor pats me on my uninjured shoulder and says, "Count yourself lucky, Sergeant. Could have been worse."

"I've heard that before," I say. "Quick question?"

"Sure," she says, making notation on a clipboard and passing it over to one of the nurses. "But make it quick. I've got a whole floor to go through before lunch."

"I need to check the local vet clinics," I say. "My dog's been hurt and—"

The doctor mutters something and leaves the room, trailed by her nurses, and I sit back, and Slim says, "K-9 partner?"

"Yep," I say.

"Civilians just don't understand, do they. Even if they do work at a V.A. hospital."

"Seems that way," I say.

My stomach is grumbling something awful and I smell cooked food out there in the hallway, along with the clattering of dinner dishes, and an orderly comes in, carrying a tray. He works pretty efficiently and soon enough, we all have lunch trays placed before us. Our meal is clear chicken broth and two slices of dark bread, with some sort of margarine spread and a mug of cold water. I eat all right but my neighbor Slim is having a problem maneuvering his spoon around his bandaged mouth.

I push my tray away and sit on Slim's bed, taking the spoon from his injured hand.

"Thanks, pal," he says. "Appreciate it."

I help feed him and wipe his lips with a rough brown paper napkin as he eats. He smells of sweat and old clothes and burn cream. When he's done he lies back with a sigh and says, "Man, what I wouldn't do for some Ben and Jerry's."

"Ben and who?"

Through the bandages I sense a smile. "Type of ice cream. Very pricey, very fattening. My dad hated it when mom bought it, but she knew her best boy had a sweet tooth and always made sure there was a couple of pints in the freezer. Made in Vermont by a couple of hippie types."

"What's a hippie?"

Slim raises a hand. "Never mind. So, let me ask you then, how did a kid like you from New Hampshire end up in the Capitol?"

"Took the long way around," I say. "Ended up on a train that got ambushed, then took a Greyhound bus and got roped into responding to a Creeper attack near a refugee camp, Brooklyn North. And you?"

He motioned to the other patients in the ward, most of whom are dozing or who are trying to read tattered paperbacks with no covers. "Part of my platoon, taking on two Creepers up by the old Plattsburg

Air Force Base. Mission accomplished, but Christ, we took a burning. You know, maybe I was joking earlier, about the war being over, but what the hell. How much more of the fighting are we gonna have to take?"

I make my way back to my own bed. "Beats me. I'm just a soldier."

"Bah," Slim says. "Hell with that, we're citizens, you and me and everybody else here. President says the war's over, since the flyboys smoked their orbital battle station. Okay, I get that. We cut off the head of the snake, that sort of thing. But we still got Creepers roaming around and those killer stealth sats are still burning or blasting targets on the ground."

"Word I heard," I say, pulling my sheet and blanket up over me, "is that we're doing what's called mopping up. Main force got killed last month up in orbit. Now we're picking off the surviving Creepers on the ground while the Air Force works on killing off the sats. After a while . . . well, that's the theory."

"Hell of a theory," Slim says, gingerly placing his burnt arms over his own blankets. "Want to hear my theory?"

"Sure," I say.

He moves his head back and forth, like he's trying to see who might be listening, and he whispers, "The aliens ain't aliens."

"Sorry, you lost me there."

"You heard me. The aliens ain't aliens. You ever see an alien from inside one of those Creepers?"

"No, but I've seen lots of pics."

He snorts. "Pics can be faked. Easy enough to do. And did you ever see that orbital battle station?"

"Saw it in orbit."

"Yeah, you saw a chunk of light. That's all."

"Sorry, Slim, I don't know what you're driving at."

His voice sharpens. "What I'm driving at, kid, is that these aliens don't have any special powers, do they? Laser beams, flame weapons, really tough metal. Big deal. Some corporations in the world could have put it all together. I mean, real aliens, they'd kill us all off in a day if they were from outer space, right? Or they could beam themselves up and down with no problems. Or they'd come with more than one big-ass spaceship . . . nope, these aliens ain't aliens. I bet they come from someplace on Earth . . . that way, they can kill anybody they want, and everybody's out looking to the stars for the enemy, when the real enemy is right here among us."

"But the proof—"

"And another thing," he says, going on desperately. "There's renegades and traitors out there, you know. Folks who are spies for the Creepers, whatever they are. Give 'em info and support in exchange for not being burned. Some cities and even countries have gone over to the Creepers. That's what I heard about France, some countries in Africa, North Korea . . ."

I'm not sure what to say when another bandaged patient down the way calls out and says, "Sergeant, don't mind old Slim. His real injury happened a long time ago."

Slim says, "Yeah, when was that, Porter?"

The man called Porter—who's missing an arm and a leg—says with a laugh, "That's when your mom's doc dropped you on your head when you was born."

I doze some during the afternoon, dreaming some of Thor, and in a half-awake daze I try to think of a way to track him down, when it seems like supper is approaching. There's another round of dishes moving around out there and an orderly comes in, but this time, he's not carrying a meal tray. He's pushing a wheelchair in front of him, and he's a beefy-guy wearing light green scrubs and whose thick head is shaved. He calls out, "Knox? Sergeant Knox?"

"Here," I say.

He wheels the chair up and says, "Let's go. You're out of here."

"What do you mean?"

He tugs my blankets off, and then says, "Sergeant, just don't know. Just doing what I'm told."

"Am I being discharged?"

A shake of the head. "Nope. Transfer. C'mon, do you mind?"

Slim says, "Good luck, kid," and I say the same to him, and I ease myself into the chair. Out in the hallway I'm wheeled past the nurse's station, and past other rooms and wards, and after going through a couple of sets of double-swinging doors, I come to the first big surprise of the day.

A private room.

I turn and look up at the orderly. "You sure?"

He helps me out. "Sergeant, when I'm home or out raising hell, I'm never quite sure what trouble I might get into. But by God, I know well enough to take a patient from Ward Six to Room Six-Oh-One. So here you go."

I get up from the chair, weave once or twice, and climb into my new bed. The sheets are crisp and smell clean, and the private room is about a third of the size of the ward, but it's all mine. I don't understand and tell the orderly there must be some sort of mistake.

He shrugs, starts out while pushing the chair. "Not my department. Sorry, sergeant."

All alone now, I look around the room again, settle in among the clean sheets and blankets. It doesn't make sense. Nothing makes sense.

A knock at the door. A nurse just a few years older than me come in, shyly, smiling, and is carrying a meal tray. She sets it down on a nearby table and takes off the cover. I stare at my meal. White bread, butter, mashed potatoes, string beans and some slices of roast beef.

I look up. "This is for me?"

She smiles. Her nametag says her name is Doris. "That's right, Sergeant . . . and can I ask you a favor?"

"A favor? Sure, I guess so."

She races out of the room and I pick up the knife and fork, start digging in. The meal is so good that I have to slow down so that I don't get sick. It's as good as the meal I had back at the farm in Adams, fresh and hot, not freeze-dried or salvaged.

Doris comes back in, a newspaper in her young hands. She's grinning widely and unfolds it, holds out a pen. "Would you autograph this for me?"

The newspaper is the *Times-Union*, the Capitol's daily, and I look at the front page for a long few seconds, not believing what I'm seeing, hoping that this is some elaborate joke, but it's not. It can't be.

The front page has stories about the meat ration being expanded, a proposed bond issue to build an aqueduct from the Catskills, and a telegraph story about the young King of England, slightly injured while leading a Coldstream Guards unit against a Creeper attack outside of Canterbury.

But I can only spare those stories a glance, as my eyes are drawn to the lead story and a blurry black-and-white photograph, though while blurred, is clear enough: it shows a Transport Creeper, rearing up, while a young soldier is hanging off the main arthropod, holding a knife in his hand.

Me.

The headline states YOUNG HERO WINS IN HAND-TO-HAND FIGHT WITH ALIEN.

Holy crap. The fine meal and the finer room now all make sense.

I hand the newspaper back

"Can I finish my dinner first?" I ask.

"Of course," she says, and stands there, staring at me, and then she blushes and races out.

I go back to my dinner. I suppose the noble thing would be to say that I had lost my appetite after seeing the newspaper and photograph, but truth is, I'm hungry and finish it all, wiping the plate clean with the last of the white bread.

CHAPTER TWENTY-SIX

After three days of having my own room and eating good meals, I'm feeling a hell of a lot better. I slowly limp up and down the corridors, sometimes stopping in to see Slim, making sure I'm bringing some of my own better food to share. Doris and a couple of other nurses hang out with me, like I'm some damn hero or something, and I hate to admit it, but I use all of their attention for my own benefit. I ask them all to see if they can locate Thor, and one very young nurse named Carrie—maybe twelve or thirteen—who lives on a nearby farm, comes to me and says, "Found him. He's at a K-9 station outside of the Capitol, called Hero Kennels."

I suddenly feel quite warm. "How is he?"

She bites her lower lip, pleased to be passing on good news. "Beat up but getting better."

I can't help myself. I kiss her on the cheek and she giggles and says, "I'm so happy for you, Randy."

"Me, too," I say, feeling that this is one of the best days ever, and that's true for just a few more hours.

That afternoon, I'm reading the *Times-Union* newspaper, thankfully without my photo in it, when an Army officer knocks on the door and strolls in. He's thin, wearing standard fatigues with the rank of captain and the name CLOUTIER, carrying a soft leather briefcase in his right hand. His left hand is an old-style prosthetic. His brown hair is cut short, and there are old acne scars on his cheeks.

The captain sits down. "Sergeant Knox."

"Sir."

He puts the briefcase on his lap, unzips it with his prosthetic hand. "Captain Thomas Cloutier, with the Army Chief of Staff's office." He pulls some papers out and says, "You're far from home, Sergeant."

"Yes, sir."

"According to information received from your commanding officer, Colonel Malcolm Hunter, you were tasked to escort Mister Ezra Manson, an adviser to your state's governor to this location. What happened?"

"We were on a train from Concord, heading to the Capitol. We were ambushed by a Creeper outside of Adams, in Massachusetts. Mister Manson was killed, sir."

The captain peers at a sheet of paper. "Mister Manson was carrying a dispatch case that was to be delivered either to the President or his Chief of Staff. Did you remove the case from Mister Manson after he was killed?"

"I did, sir."

"Where did you go after that?"

"I took shelter and then went to Adams, with the other members of my party. Specialist Serena Coulson and her brother."

"Why didn't you wait until the Quick Reaction Force arrived?"

"I thought it made more sense to leave the ambush site, sir."

Another sheet of paper. "Where's the dispatch case now?"

"The case is with Specialist Coulson, sir."

The captain's eyes narrowed. "Why does she have it?"

"Outside of the Capitol we split up, sir. I was responding to a Creeper attack in the vicinity. She was going on to the Capitol and I put the case in her custody. I ordered her to deliver it as requested, sir."

"But it was your responsibility to personally see that case delivered."

"Yes, sir, it was. But I was faced with a situation where a Creeper was threatening a nearby relocation camp. I had no choice. Sir."

"You could have gone on."

"I didn't. Sir."

"Well, that's a problem, Sergeant."

"Sir?"

"Specialist Coulson and her brother are missing."

⊕ ⊕ ⊕

I try to keep my expression cool and calm, a hell of a challenge.

"What do you mean, missing?"

"She and her brother were on that Greyhound bus that arrived from Adams. They both exited the bus station. From then, she hasn't been seen. She hasn't reported into the Army liaison office in the Capitol. She's . . . gone. Apparently with that very important dispatch case."

Captain Cloutier looks at me and there's something in his eyes I can't quite understand. I don't say anything and he just keeps on looking at me, and then he clears his throat. "If you have any information on why she was here in the Capitol, feel free to share. But only if you're certain that it can be of value. Of course, it's up to you, Sergeant."

This is odd. Why doesn't he just come straight out and order me to tell him why Serena was coming to the Capitol? I know what Serena had told me; that she was coming here to visit her father. But what about her brother? He was coming here with an encrypted message about an interrogation of a live Creeper up in Maine.

So what kind of game is the captain playing?

I don't know.

But I'm sure I don't want to play with him.

"Sorry, sir," I say. "I'm afraid I can't help you."

He almost looks relieved, and then goes back to his papers. "Fair enough. Just a couple of more things and then we'll be done. I know you had nothing to do with that silly newspaper article, but still, what's right is right."

From inside his soft leather briefcase he takes out a small blue case, bordered with gold. He snaps the case open and removes a Purple Heart, which he pins to my pillow. "You'll get the official paperwork later. That was a hell of a thing you did there, son. I'm pretty sure that's the first case, at least in this country, where a Creeper was killed in a hand-to-hand fight."

I don't bother looking at the medal. "I was pretty damn lucky, sir."

He shakes his head. "Good soldiers make their own luck. And if I can say so, you are going to have to count on that luck over the next few days."

"Sir?"

He shakes his head again, goes back to his briefcase. "You're going to get a visitor here in a little while. Be polite, be open, but try not to promise anything you don't feel comfortable about doing."

"But I'm ready to be discharged, sir," I say. "I want to get back to Fort St. Paul."

"Not happening, Sergeant," he replies. "There are other plans for you, so be careful. And one more thing. Your assault pack was recovered and should be here shortly. But here's something of yours that was left back at the swamp."

His good hand ducks back into the briefcase, comes out with a holster, holding my 9 mm Beretta. Both the holster and the pistol have been cleaned. He passes it over to me and I'm scared now, almost as scared as when I saw that Creeper Transport coming at me back by the bridge.

"Sir?"

"You're a soldier, and a soldier should be armed. Good luck, Sergeant."

He leaves and I look at my Beretta, not sure what to do next. What the hell was I going to do with this in a hospital room?

I open up the nearby nightstand drawer, slide it in, and close the drawer. I pick up the newspaper and then toss it across the room.

I get up, a bit woozy, but it's time to get out of here. What the captain had said just reminded me of Corporal Manning, back at my barracks. Dress and arm yourself accordingly. All right, I'm armed and it's time to get dressed. I don't know what's supposedly planned for me, but I don't plan to stick around and find out.

Plan? Find some clothes, get out of the hospital and find a way to a local USO office. Show them my Purple Heart and the front page with my photo, and get a transportation chit back to Fort St. Paul. Put all of this behind me, and get back to work and see if I can find out where the hell my dad is.

I get to the door and find it blocked by two large and well-dressed men, looking at me like I was some sort of patient at a mental clinic, and not a V.A. hospital. They're bulky, well-fed, and have short military-style haircuts. On the left lapel of each man there's a round little gold pin with a red E inside.

The closer one says, "Sergeant Knox?"

"That's right," I say, noticing the tell-tale bulges under their arms.

He says with a smile. "I'm going to have to ask you to wait for a bit. There's someone important coming who wants to see you."

"Who's that?" I ask.

He's still smiling and walks into my room, as his companion stands outside by the hallway. He doesn't touch me or force me, but his bulk and presence pushes me back in. I don't like it. I go to my bed and go past it, taking the only chair in the room. The man stands there, hands clasped in front of him, still smiling.

Some sort of bustle out in the hallway, a woman's laugh, and then a woman strolls in, about fifty or so years old. She's sharply dressed, with a dark blue skirt that's cut just about her knees, with a matching short jacket and white blouse with some sort of gold necklace around her neck. Her blonde hair is coiffed so that it's puffy, and she wears what looks to be diamond earrings. She's also wearing black-rimmed reading glasses that are tilted at the end of her prominent nose, and I spot some kind of make-up on her cheeks and eyelids.

She has a polished black briefcase dangling from one hand, and her other hand is held out. "Sergeant Knox?"

Remembering my manners from my dad, I get up and shake her hand. The skin is smooth, cool and soft. I doubt if she's ever held a weapon or a tool in her life.

"Yes, ma'am," I say. "That I am."

"Mind if I have a few minutes of your time?"

The near bulky guy is looking at me, still smiling, but the smile has an edge to it, like he's daring me to tell his boss that I'd rather take a nap or get a sponge bath or anything else. Still trying to be polite, I say, "Not a problem, ma'am."

She seems pleased, but I get the feeling it's the kind of pleasure she'd express if I were a new puppy, and had just learned not to soil her living room floor. She turns to her man and says, "Riley, if you'd leave us be, that'd be quite nice."

He gives a practiced nod. "As you wish, ma'am."

After he steps out he shuts the door, leaving me alone with the woman. I look back to my chair and my bed, and still with my dad in my mind, I say, "Please take the chair, will you? I'll sit on my bed."

She smiles and her teeth are perfect, white, and look very, very sharp. She sits down and balances the briefcase on her lap, snaps the cover open. I start to ask her a question and she says, "Sergeant Knox,

I've gone over your service record and I must say, I'm quite impressed . . . save for a few disciplinary issues over the years . . . but that's to be expected for a young man like yourself."

I smile at her and keep my mouth shut. She looks at me and I look back, and I say, "Ma'am, excuse me, I didn't catch your name. That is, if you said it."

She laughs for a quick moment, and it's a laugh with no humor or delight behind it. I suddenly feel quite alone, like the first time out on patrol, no back-up, going out by myself against the enemy

"Sorry, young man," she says, her voice full of power and confidence. "I'm Tess Conroy, the President's Chief of Staff."

Now it all makes sense, and it feels like a harsh spotlight has just been splayed over me. I'm quite conscious I'm sitting on the edge of my unmade bed, with fuzzy slippers, hospital pants and pajama top, unshowered and with hair unwashed, burns and scrapes and a thick bandage on my left shoulder.

"It's . . . a pleasure to meet you, ma'am."

Her smile doesn't waver. "If you're telling the truth, then you're one of the few people who's ever said that to my face."

I'm not sure what to say next, and she steps in. "Shall we go on?"

I nod.

She says, "I want to discuss your mission to the Capitol. To escort Mister Manson and his dispatch case. I understand that after a Creeper attack on your train and the subsequent death of Mister Manson, you and other members of your party went to Adams. Following there, you took a Greyhound bus and eventually split with your party, passing the dispatch case onto one Specialist Serena Coulson for delivery. You then engaged a Transport Creeper outside of the Capitol, where you were injured. Specialist Coulson, however, arrived at the Capitol and has not been seen since."

"Except for the last part, ma'am, that's a fairly accurate story of what went on."

Her sharp eyes pierced at me. "Are you disagreeing about the status of Specialist Coulson in the Capitol?"

"Ma'am, I'm afraid I know nothing of what happened to Specialist Coulson after she left. I'm not in a position to add to that."

Her expression remains unchanged, like she's evaluating if I'm giving her a hard time or not, and then some hidden switch clicks on and the President's Chief of Staff smiles at me. "That sounds fair, Sergeant. So let's return to your escort of Mister Manson. What were you told about your mission and what Mister Manson was carrying?"

I want to take a deep breath before proceeding, but I know better than to show this sharp and dangerous woman how frightened I am. So I give her my best sixteen-year-old boy smile and say, "Ma'am, I'm afraid I can't answer that question."

Her smile hasn't changed position but the warmth contained within has become icy indeed. "And why is that, Sergeant Knox?"

"Because you're not my commanding officer, ma'am."

"I'm the Chief of Staff to the President."

"Ma'am, you're not in the chain of command. My apologies."

The smile is gone. "I can get you a ranking officer in here to tell you to cooperate. Would that work?"

I recall Cloutier's words. "Ma'am, I was tasked by my commanding officer to do a classified mission. I'm operating under his orders and direction. I will need to hear from him before I can discuss my mission with you."

She looks at me, anger still in her eyes, smile frozen to her face, and I try to keep my gaze focused on hers. Long seconds seems to drag by. She rearranges some of the papers in her lap and says, "Then I guess I'll have to arrange for your commanding officer to communicate with you."

"If that won't be much trouble, ma'am."

She briskly stands up. "No trouble at all, Sergeant. In the meanwhile, I've arranged your discharge from the hospital and your transfer to a local hotel."

"I'd rather be discharged to a local army post."

The smile now has humor about it. "Sorry, Sergeant, it's already been arranged. You have nothing to say about it."

Then she leaves, and I feel like throwing up, having gone up against the most powerful woman in the nation.

Riley, the more talkative of her bodyguards, comes in, carrying my assault pack and a black clothing bag, which he puts on the bed and unzips. "There you go, young man. Fresh uniform and your assault pack. It was left unclaimed in your bus from Adams. Time to get dressed."

He stands there and I say, "I'm going to have to ask you to leave."

Riley shakes his head. "I was told to stay in here until you get dressed and packed."

I shrug, get back up on my bed, stretch my legs over the clothing bag. "Then it's going to be a long wait. I don't get dressed in front of an audience."

Riley narrows his eyes. "You're in the damn army. When did you get so damn shy?"

"Not shy around my buds," I say. "I make an exception for hired guns."

He says, "I can make you get dressed."

I don't blink, reach over and pull my brand new uniform bag over on my lap. "In these clothes here?"

Riley blinks. "That's right, you snotty kid. Those clothes right there."

"*Molon labe*," I say.

"Hunh?"

I say, "This snotty kid is a commissioned sergeant in the National Guard, attached to the United States Army. I've had years of education in the military arts and sciences. *Molon labe*. That's what King Leonidas of Sparta said to the Persians as they massed in Thermopylae."

I sense his confusion and hesitation. I go on. "The Persians demanded the Spartans surrender and give up their weapons. The king replied by saying, '*Molon labe.*' Come and get them. So that's what I'm saying to you, Mister Riley. You want my clothes to dress me? Come and get them."

The air in the room crackles and I sense Riley is evaluating his options, and I'm under no illusions. If he decides to go forth, it's going to get bloody and violent in a matter of seconds. But I'm gambling Riley is going to back down.

He does.

"You got five minutes, kid."

"It's Sergeant Knox," I reply, but he leaves, and I decide not to press him.

I get up, close and lock the door. I strip off my hospital pajamas, wash up some in the private bathroom that I'm fortunate to have, and then I get dressed in the clean utility uniform that was provided to me. I grudgingly admire Tess Conroy and her crew, for my uniform is correct in all particulars, from my name to my rank to my unit badges. But I have to add one more thing. From the pillow I undo the Purple Heart and put it in the right place on my uniform.

After getting dressed, I put my assault pack on the bed, go through and see that everything's pretty much in place, except for my journal, which I had passed over to Serena back in the rain by that steam-powered Greyhound bus. My souvenir from my first Creeper kill is there as well, on a chain, and I slip it around my neck, and my blessed rosary beads go in a pocket.

My throat suddenly thickens. But no photo of mom, dad and Melissa. That's gone.

Gone forever.

I have a desperate fear that at some point—without that photo—I'll eventually forget what Melissa and Mom looked like, but I push that thought away. A problem for another time, a long time down the road, for I got more serious problems, staring right at me in my face.

I look over. The door's still locked. I go to the nightstand and take out my Beretta, check to see it's loaded, and it is.

"*Molon labe*," I repeat, and put the 9 mm pistol in a side pocket of my pack, zipper it shut.

Outside in the hospital hallway, Riley is waiting for me. My pack is over my shoulder and Riley says, "You clean up nice, kid . . . Sergeant."

"Nice to be back in uniform," I say.

He goes one way and I go another. He turns quickly and says, "What the hell are you doing?"

"Saying so long to some buds, that's what."

I go through the corridor doors, past the patients' rooms and the nurse's station, and make my way to my old room. But when I go in there's a surprise: Slim and his fellow platoon members are gone, but the beds are occupied with new patients. The bandaged and burnt and stitched faces turn in my direction as I stand in the door.

My friendly nurse Carrie—the one who located Thor—passes by and I ask, "Where's Slim and the others?"

"Off to a rehab center," she says. "We're short of beds, always are. You know how it is, Randy."

"Yeah," I say, picking up my pack. "I know how it is."

I catch up with Riley and he's standing in front of an open sliding door. I hesitate before going in.

"This is an elevator, right?" I ask, eyeing the tiny room inside past the sliding doors.

The sliding doors start to move and Riley holds out a large hand to block them. They bounce back. He says, "That's right, Sergeant. What's the problem? Haven't you ever been in one before?"

The door slides back again. I say, "Sure. A few days ago, when I was admitted here. But I was pretty drugged out. Don't remember it much."

Riley said, "Happens, don't it. Come on, Sergeant, let's get a move on."

I step inside, swallow. A moving room that goes up and down, held by cables I can't even see.

The door slides shut, Riley pushes a button. There's a lurch and I feel queasy, as we get lowered through the building. Lights on a panel flash. "One of the nurses, she told me the reason the hospital has power is because of some sort of shielding."

"That's right," Riley says, large hands clasped before him. "The white coats have come up with shielding that protects some power lines and generators. The killer stealth satellites can't detect it."

"Then how come it's not everywhere?"

"Expensive stuff," Riley says. "Only the high priority places get it. Like the Capitol. That's how things work, Sergeant."

The little room comes to halt, and the doors slide open. If I was by myself, I'd push some of the buttons to go for another ride, but instead I follow Riley out into the lobby.

An Excerpt From the Journal of Randall Knox

Dad late last night for dinner. No phone calls, no message from a runner, nothing. So I kept supper warm the best I could—potato soup with a side of old bread from the dining facility—and when he showed up, he sat down at the dinner table, slumped, and didn't say a word as he slurped the soup and ate the bread. I thought he might go to sleep right after that and I didn't like that idea. Usually when he works late and goes to sleep, that's when the nightmares start. Lots of moaning, trembling, and harsh whispers of I'm sorry, I'm sorry, I'm sorry I screwed up. And I know he's dreaming about Mom, because he's got some guilt about how the two of them got separated when the war started.

But tonight Dad surprised me when he said, dessert? Sure, I said, and I grabbed a salvaged can of Hershey's chocolate syrup, that I split with dad, both of us spooning out the syrup after I cut open the top. Tasted okay but a bit stale. When we were done Dad sighed, stretched out his legs and said, you know, Uncle Malcolm can be a jerk in so many ways, but sometimes, he knows his duty.

Really, I asked. Dad said, I'll tell you, but between us, all right? Sure, I said.

Another sigh from Dad. He took off his glasses, the pair with the tape holding one of the arms, and he said, your uncle got an urgent phone call from both the governor and the mayor of Concord. Protestors were marching on the Capitol building. They were worried the protests would get out of hand. Wanted your uncle to send over a platoon or two to keep order. He refused. Said he would only deploy them if there was immediate danger of a riot breaking out, people getting hurt or killed. Mayor and governor are P.O.'d, but colonel held firm. If the protests were peaceful, troops would stay on post. Gotta give him credit for that.

Dad just sat there as I cleaned up, and I said, what were they protesting about?

Dad said, martial law, upcoming elections, that sort of thing. Politics.

I laughed. Politics. Don't give a crap about politics.

Dad's mood changed. You know your history? And I said, c'mon, Dad, got an A last term. And the term before that. Dad said, you know about Trotsky? Sure, I said. One of the leaders of the Bolshevik Revolution. Head of the Red Army. Worked with Lenin and Stalin. And Stalin later had him murdered in Mexico when he was in exile.

Dad nodded. Not bad. But Trotsky's known for a famous quote about war. Somebody said to Trotsky that they weren't interested in war, and Trotsky said, well, war is interested in you.

His voice got sharp. You might not be interested in politics, Randy, but politics is definitely interested in you.

CHAPTER TWENTY-SEVEN

I'm put in a nearby hotel that was once a Hyatt and is now called Capitol Arms, and this place is apparently not a priority, since I have to walk up four flights of stairs to get to my room. A sweaty boy of about ten or eleven, wearing a baggy dark blue uniform, insists on carrying my pack up all four flights of stairs. In my room, he points out the bathroom, the television— "Works fine," he says. "Gets three channels. Can you believe that? That's why this is one of the best places in the Capitol"—and then he picks up a telephone by the bed.

"This works, too," he says proudly. "You can call down to the front desk, and some hours, you can actually order room service."

"What do you mean, room service?"

The kid goes to the door, and I give him two pre-war quarters. "You can call the kitchen and you get food brought up to your room. Costly, though."

"Thanks," I say, and after he leaves, I go to my bathroom and wash my hands and face. The water is nice and hot. I come back to my assault pack and look at the television. A real television that works, all for me.

I sigh. No time for entertainment.

From my assault pack, I take out my Beretta, strap it to my waist and go down the four flights of stairs, taking two steps at a time.

After spending a few minutes at the front desk, I'm outside of the hotel, watching the traffic go by. There are bicycles and horses, but still, I've never seen so many gasoline-powered vehicles moving around in one place. All of them pre-war, but most in good shape, with repaired bumpers or fenders or side panels. Fords, Cadillacs, Chevrolets. My dad once went to the Capitol for an intelligence briefing with the Joint Chiefs and when he came back, he said seeing all the pre-war cars was like taking a time machine back to his childhood. The sidewalks are crowded, the most well-dressed and well-fed population I've ever seen, but the place sure is hilly.

A boxy yellow car comes up, pre-war and gasoline powered, with a black and white checked pattern along the sides and a B ration sticker on the windshield. The driver rolls the window down and calls out, "Sergeant Knox?"

I go to the rear door, open it up. "That's me."

Then I hear laughter, a familiar voice. I turn and three men are exiting the hotel, bulky, large, scarred here and there but still in good humor. They're wearing civvies but it takes less than a second to realize they're military, and it's not because of their bearing and haircuts.

It's because the lead soldier is Captain Ramon Diaz; the Special Forces officer I met on the train.

I run after them, but the crowd blocks me; and when I get to the corner, they're gone. I look up and down the streets, clench my fists, and then race back to the hotel. Think about going inside and back to the front desk, ask the clerk about Captain Diaz. Was he staying there? Did the hotel know him? Did—

A horn blares out. It's the driver of the taxi cab, who's got on a light yellow cap with a brass shield in the center. He says, "Are you coming or what?"

"I want to go into the hotel for a couple of minutes. I need to check on—

He interrupts. "Sorry, soldier. I've got a schedule to maintain. I got a dozen fares lined up for the rest of the day and I'm already behind. So step in or walk away, your choice."

My dad. I just saw the captain who knows where my dad is and what kind of trouble he's in, leaving my hotel.

But I had something else important to do. I got into the rear of the cab, which smells slightly perfumed, and the cabbie starts driving even before I close the door.

⊕ ⊕ ⊕

It's only a ten-minute drive, which is great, because my eyes widen at seeing little plastic numerals flip by on the dashboard, indicating the increasing fare, and thank God, we get to our destination before the numerals outnumber what I have in my pocket. I pay and remember my dad saying something about taxi drivers being tipped, and I take care of him, and he takes care of me by giving me an active military discount.

In a few minutes, I'm in the back of a building that's filled with the smell of urine, fear and medicines, and there's lots of barking nearby. I'm in an empty room with tile flooring and three plastic molded chairs, and I stare at my feet. And wait. And wait.

The door pops open and a gaunt old woman in light green surgical scrubs come in, but actually she's being dragged, and tears come to my eyes as I see who's doing the dragging. It's my Thor, my good old Thor, and I fall to my knees. He yelps and the veterinarian unsnaps the leash and Thor stumbles over. He has a green cast on his right front leg, fur around his head and ears have been burnt off, the left side of his torso has been shaved off and he has a wide bandage wrapped around his midsection.

I grab him and gently hug him, bury my face in the side of his head. "Oh, you stupid brave, dummy," I whisper into him, trying to speak through the tears. "When are you ever going to listen? Hunh? When are you ever going to listen?"

Thor licks at the side of my face and with a sweet old lady voice, the vet gives me a run down of his injuries: broken front right leg, burn injuries, and severe lacerations on his side.

I lift up my head. "Can I take him now? Can I?"

The vet smiles and gently shakes her head. "Too soon, Sergeant. He needs a week of care, at least."

I scratch at Thor's head and he licks and licks my hand and then my face. "Okay . . . I just . . . I just miss him, that's all."

She kneels down on the dirty floor, scratches him as well. "Of course you do. You're a dog person. I can tell. Just like me. Just like so many others. Can't imagine what it's like to be without a dog. Has he been yours for a while?"

"Two years, since I got to Recon Rangers," I say, noting Thor's brown eyes seemed filmy, from the painkillers, I'm sure. "When the training started there were six of us . . . we had six dogs to choose from, and Thor . . . he chose me. Funny, hunh? He looked at me and came running right over. We've been together ever since, training and missions, and in between, lots of swimming and ball tossing."

She smiles, keeps on gently stroking my boy's fur. "Dogs . . . in some ways, they're a mystery, in how their ancestors bonded with ours. But in other ways, they're so transparent. They're pure innocence. They want to be loved, to be rewarded, to be part of the family . . . or pack. All they ask in return is to be fed, watered, taken care of, and when the time comes . . . to let them go peacefully and without pain. That's our duty, you know. To take care of them to the very end, to make sure they're not afraid and alone."

Her words strike something inside of me, as Thor's brown eyes stare at me, his face showing joy. My throat refused to move. She says, "And how do we repay them? We train them, we send them into battle, to be cut, stomped or charred. Poor creatures. And when they die on our behalf, we quickly find another one to take their place."

I kiss the top of Thor's head. "Nobody can ever take Thor's place," I manage to stammer out. "He's one of a kind. He'll . . . he'll play with kids, jump into bed with me, and when he smells a Creeper, he goes all out to protect me."

I look over at the veterinarian. "You take good care of him, all right? You take good care of my Thor."

The vet pauses for a long, long moment, and she starts talking again, her voice no longer sweet. She says, "Ten years ago, I was a volunteer at an animal shelter in Pompton, small town on the Hudson River. The war had just started and it was all so confusing. No power, no TV, no Internet. I could see smoke where West Point was burning. The Creepers had hit that right away from space, along with Annapolis and Colorado Springs, and so many other military targets. Didn't know much of what was going on. Then one of the low-powered AM radio stations that was still broadcasting reported on the tidal wave that had hit Manhattan."

I'm still rubbing Thor's head and I stay quiet. She falters, goes on. "We all knew that the wave that hit Manhattan was coming up the Hudson River. We didn't have much time. I could have gone with my husband and kids . . . but I went to the animal shelter instead. Using a bicycle, of course. No cars were running. No one was there. They had all left. Who could blame them? I did, at the time . . . but later, who could blame them? It was cold, raining. The river was rising fast and I didn't have much time. I opened up the cages and tried to get the cats and dogs out, so they could make a run for it. Some did, but the water came up so fast we were cut off. Luckily the shelter had a flat roof. I got the dogs and cats that were left up on the roof . . . got bitten and scratched plenty of times. But I got them up there, by God, I did. The water eventually came up to my ankles but I kept it together. Took a couple of days for the water to drop enough so I could scrounge some food from the shelter . . . that's what we all lived on, for week, soggy cat food and dog food."

She finally looks at me one more time, talks again, her voice thick. "Never did see my husband and kids again, but I saved those strays. So yes, Sergeant, you can count on me to take care of your dog."

"Thank you, ma'am," I say, ashamed. "I guess I can."

After a few more minutes of tugging and tussling with Thor, I promise him another visit, real soon, I go outside and hitch a ride back to the hotel. I'm lucky enough to get a ride with a grocer's wagon, bringing in deliveries to one of the Price-Chopper supermarkets in the Capitol. At the hotel I go into the lobby, head straight for the front desk, and Riley gets up from an upholstered chair and blocks me.

"Sergeant, glad to see you're here," he says. "Where the hell have you been?"

"Out visiting a friend," I say. "And if you'll excuse me, I need to go to the front desk."

I move to go around him but he steps in front of me, puts a large hand on my shoulder. He leans in and says, "You got the drop on me back at the hospital room, I'll give you that. But that was at the hospital, with docs and nurses around. Here, you're in my element, Sergeant. Don't push me. When I was younger I was chasing Taliban up and down mountains in Afghanistan, and when I rotated out, they sent me to chase hajis in Iraq. So don't get ahead of yourself."

His hand is gentle on my shoulder but I can feel the strength in it. "All right, what do you want?"

Riley pulls his hand away, smiles. "Good job. Look, Sergeant—see, I'm not calling you kid, am I—we can get along just fine. Here's the deal. Tess Conroy requests your presence in just under an hour, and you need to be gussied up. In your room is a full-dress uniform for you, because the good lady is going to put you on display."

"What the hell for?"

Riley grins wider. "You're the most famous soldier in the East Coast, you knucklehead. How many other soldiers are out there who've killed a Creeper with their frigging bare hands?"

"I had a knife."

"Yeah, in your hands. Tess Conroy wants to put you on display, so be a good sergeant and run upstairs and get dressed, and I'll take you there."

I look past his bulky shoulders to the front desk. "Where am I going?"

He tries to act surprised. "You don't know? You really don't know?"

"That's right," I say. "I have no idea."

Riley gently grasps my upper arm, sends me in the direction of the stairs.

"You're off to the New White House, my young friend," he says. "To see the President."

In my hotel room I move around slowly, like I've just woken up and I'm not sure where I am and what's going on. Sounds funny, but sure, I know where I am—the Capitol Arms Hotel—but I sure as hell don't know what's going on. I'm off to see the President . . . me? Randy Knox, from Ranger Recon? Randy Knox, who was nearly orphaned at six, has gone cold, starved, been wounded and injured and lives most days with dirt under his fingernails and with his stomach grumbling from not having enough to eat?

That Randy Knox is going to see the President?

I start getting the shakes, like I'm out on a Creeper mission, and I sit down on my carefully made bed. Like Riley had promised, a perfect-looking Class A uniform is laid out, with all unit badges, ribbons and medals in proper fashion. I run my hand across the uniform, feel so out of place, so much like an imposter. The shaking eases and I jump when the phone rings. I reach over and pick it up.

"Knox," I say.

"Sergeant, it's Tess Conroy," comes the sharp, confident voice. "I do hope you're not wasting my time up there, so be a good boy, get showered, dressed and get down to the lobby as soon as you can."

I can't think of anything to say, so I hang up the phone, and strip and go take a shower.

The shower is clean white tile and has a fresh bar of soap in the dish. I unwrap the soap and breathe deeply of the scent, and then turn on the water. It comes out nice and hot and fierce, and I can't help myself, I giggle. Plenty of hot water, no timing chit, fresh soap, and best of all, I can shower by myself. I go in and despite the orders from the Chief of Staff, I take my time, and I wince as I soap around the burn wound on my shoulder. The water also stings my face, hands and the back of my neck, but I'm used to those kinds of burns.

The water goes on and on until my fingers get wrinkly, and after I get out and towel dry, I carefully remove the still-wet bar of soap, pat it dry and then re-wrap it in the paper wrapper it came in. I then go out to my room and slide it into one of my pack pockets.

I finish drying off with a towel—and I have a temptation of larceny, wondering if the hotel would miss one of these towels—and the television catches my attention. I go over to the stand and turn it on, and it hums for a moment, and then the screen snaps into focus, a black-and-white picture. I sit down on the bed, the blankets turned down, and start watching an episode of something called *I Love Lucy*. There's a scene of a woman with big eyes and thick lipsticked lips, and she and a friend are working on some sort of assembly line, trying to keep up with a fast-moving belt containing lots of candies. I laugh out loud as I see her and her friend stuff the candies into their mouths.

I reach over, switch a channel. I get something called C-Span, focusing on some sort of Congressional debate. I turn another channel, and it's a test pattern. So I go back to the *I Love Lucy* episode and get dressed, looking around the room.

I'm tingling. Something's wrong. Something's not right.

I look around the room, in the closet, in the drawers, and then back to the bed, where the blankets have been turned down.

They weren't turned down when I stepped into the shower.

I edge around the bed, examining it, and the pillow is out of place. I slowly put my hand underneath the pillow, touch something that feels like leather. I run my hands around the object, not feeling any wires or batteries. Paranoid, I know, but the other day I saw a Creeper that wasn't a Creeper, flaming and lasing a train because of either

Mister Manson or Buddy Coulson, the quiet boy with a recording device for a brain. So I wouldn't put it past someone to put some sort of an IED in my bed, maybe something that'd be triggered by the weight of my head on it.

I sit back. Feels like a leather object. Contradicting all of my training, I know, I whisper, "To hell with it," and I pick up the pillow.

Revealing my journal.

CHAPTER TWENTY-EIGHT

"I'll be damned," I say, not whispering this time. From behind me and with my good ear, I hear a man in a Spanish-accented voice call out, "Lucy, You got some 'splaining to do."

I pick up my journal and inside the front cover is a handwritten note on a slip of light yellow paper. It says, "*Your talents are being wasted in the Army, Randy. Well-done. But be careful. Trust no one.*"

I bring the journal up to my face, catch a scent of Serena's perfume. Somehow she or someone she's with brought this back up to my room while I was in the shower. Not bad. A professional job. Very professional.

I look at the note again.

Trust no one.

"Tell me something I don't already know," I say, and then I tear up the note in half, quarters and eighths, and while watching a television show nearly a century old, I put the scraps of paper in my mouth and carefully chew and swallow them all.

Outside in the hotel's corridor, carrying my pack, there's a woman in a black uniform gently pushing a wheeled cart with brooms and towels and buckets. She spots me and I suddenly ask her, "Ma'am, is there another way to the lobby besides the main staircase?"

She smiles, like she's telling an old favorite joke. "There's the elevators, soldier, but you step in those shafts, you're going to the lobby faster than you probably want."

"True enough," I say, smiling back at her and she relaxes and says, "Here, I'll show you a back stairway. Dumps you out near the front desk."

"Perfect," I say.

I go down the narrow and dimly lit staircase, feeling pretty exposed as I go out into the lobby. I see Riley sitting in a big chair, staring at the main staircase, and sitting next to him, all alone on a long couch, is Tess Conroy, glasses on, looking at a collection of papers on her lap. Neither of them is looking over in my direction. I stroll over to the front desk and ask the nice elderly man there if he could store my assault pack for a while. I have to repeat what I say twice for him to hear me, and he motions me to the back of the counter, where I deposit my pack among some suitcases. He gives me a receipt. He's short, squat, with a fringe of black hair around his bald head, and eyeglasses hanging from a thin chain about his neck.

At the front desk, I feel my back tingling, like Riley or Tess is staring right at me, wondering what I'm doing, and I press ahead. "Excuse me, I was hoping you could tell me if someone is staying here. A Captain Ramon Diaz, from the Army. D-I-A-Z."

The clerk purses his thin lips, goes through a small metal file box, shakes his head. "No Captain Diaz here, I'm afraid."

I put both of my hands on the polished wood of the counter. "Anybody at all registered as Diaz?"

He shakes his head again. ""fraid not."

To the rear I hear Riley's voice. "Sergeant Knox! Over here!"

I say, "Well, anybody in the Army? Who do you have here that's in the service?"

He looks up in disbelief. "Sonny, we're smack dab in the middle of the Capitol. I'd say about half of the people staying here today are in the service. What, you want me to give you a damn list or something?"

Or something, I think, and I turn around and Riley is standing right there. "A problem, Sergeant?"

"No problem at all," I say. "I was just complimenting them on their hot showers."

He looks me up and down, and sighs. "When I was your age, I was—"

I push past him. "Spare me," I say. "I've heard it all before."

⊕ ⊕ ⊕

With Riley, the other bodyguard from the hospital and Tess Conroy, we go out through the lobby and out into the afternoon. It's cloudy and threatening rain. No big surprise. A pre-war black Cadillac comes by and stops. There's no ration sticker on the windshield. Riley opens the rear door and I follow Tess in. The interior is huge, looking like it could fit four or five people. There's a wide and luxurious seat, dark blue carpeting, and another seat facing the first. The windows are darkened in an odd way, so you can see out but people can't see in.

I sit back and look around, and Tess sits across from me. She has on a black formal gown that reaches down to mid-calf, and some sort of white wrap around her shoulders and bare upper arms. Riley sits next to me and the other guard slams the door shut, goes to the front, and we're off.

Tess says, "Excited?"

"Confused," I say. "Why am I going to see the President?"

With a pen, she makes a check-mark on a paper in her lap. "To be honored, of course. That knife fight you had the Creeper has been in the news for days. Like it or not, Sergeant Knox, by the end of the day, you're going to be very famous indeed. You and one other."

I look out at the streets and buildings, seeing what looks to be electric lights in lots of the windows. Looks like the Capitol is doing way better than the rest of the country in recovering. I'm sure dad would tell me that this was a great surprise, with his usual wry tone of voice.

"Who's the other person? Another soldier?"

A paper goes from her hands to the seat next to her, and she picks up another. "No. A Colonel Victor Minh, of the Air Force. He's getting the Medal of Honor for helping destroy the Creeper's orbital battle station. An astronaut."

I have to repeat the words she's just said to understand them. "An astronaut? He's an astronaut?"

She bites her lower lip, like something on the paper in front of her has just ticked her off. "That he is," she says. "Apparently the last one. So he's getting the Medal of Honor." Tess looks up. "You're getting the Silver Star. A nice way to honor those who kill the Creepers in orbit, and those who kill them on the ground."

"That's impossible!"

"Why's that, young man?"

I work to find my voice. "Awards like that are only given out after months, maybe even a year or two of investigation. Witnesses have to be interviewed, after-action reports need to be examined, everything checked and re-checked."

"You're probably right, Sergeant Knox, but your Commander in Chief thinks otherwise. And so do I."

The Cadillac maneuvers through an open wrought-iron gate, guarded on either side by Marine guards in dress blue. There's a small knot of protesters on the sidewalk, being kept away by uniformed cops. I see one sign: NEGOTIATE NOW, END THE WAR. And then another: WE DESERVE A PREZ, NOT A DICTATOR.

"And, Sergeant Knox?"

"Yes, ma'am?"

"When the ceremonies and speeches are over," she says, raising an eyebrow. "You and I are going to have a serious talk about Specialist Coulson, that dispatch case, and her possible whereabouts."

I feel a rush of panic for just a moment, wondering if Tess or Riley could catch Serena's scent on my hands, from where I had picked up my journal. I keep my voice calm and say, "That would be fine, ma'am."

She chuckles, picking up her papers. "Don't try lying to me, son. I've had years of experience you can't hope to match."

There are other pre-war cars parked here as well, with a couple of fine-looking carriages with matched black horses. Men and women are slowly streaming to the front entrance of an ornate three-story house, made of red brick. There are lots of uniforms, gowns, and fine suits with white shirts and tiny black bowties. Gas lamps and electrical lights are on, and I stand still, trying to take it all in.

Riley is standing next to me, seems friendly for a moment.

I ask, "Why do they call it the New White House? It's all red brick."

Riley says, "Tradition. Besides, some in Congress and the Administration thought calling it the Red House would sound too socialist or communistic or something like that. In any event, it's the New White House, though supposedly, the place is on loan to the President. It actually belongs to the Governor of New York."

"Where does he stay, then?"

Riley says, "Who cares? Come on, don't want to keep everyone waiting."

I try not to look too stunned or overwhelmed as I go into the New White House, with Tess Conroy at my side, who's busy waving and talking to people, shaking hands with some of them, pausing for a few words. Some of the people nod knowingly in my direction, and I freeze for a moment when a three-star Army general growls at me and shakes my hand.

"Christ, kid," he says, "when the books finally get written about this war, you and your kind are going to make the previous Greatest Generation look like amateurs."

Considering what that generation was up against, all earth-bound enemies, maybe he's right, but I don't press the point. "I appreciate that, sir, honest, I do."

There are so many electric lights from the ceilings and walls it hurts my eyes, and after passing through a security checkpoint, with Secret Service men and women giving the guests quick pat-downs, we're brought into a large ballroom. Music is being played and there are rows of chairs, facing a raised platform and podium that bears the Presidential seal, and at the rear, are round tables with white tablecloths.

Waiters and waitresses carrying trays are going by, and my mouth waters as I see the food. I eat, and eat, and eat, sometimes having to ask the serving people what exactly I'm eating. There's scallops wrapped in bacon, stuffed mushroom caps, bits of steak on skewers with vegetables, and it seems every time I finish something off, another tray is presented to me. One thing, though, I turn down, and it's some sort of sour cream with toast points and fish eggs. Fish eggs! Over the years I've eaten and scrounged for lots of food, sometimes opening up rusted tin cans with the labels worn off to see if I was going to be dining on hash, or beets, or beans, but I'll be damned if I'm going to eat fish eggs.

There are cold drinks as well, beers and iced teas and coffee, and I try sipping some red wine, and find it too strong, and go with a nice chilled glass of Coca-Cola. Based on the last time I'd sipped a Coke, it's nice not to have to share this time.

Then everything snaps into a greasy focus, and I don't feel so good.

Back up at Ft. St. Paul, who knows what's on the dining facility menu tonight, and Abby . . . good ol' Abby. If she had been here, she'd be eating right next to me, but she'd also be finding a way to gather up some of the food to bring to back to the barracks.

But me?

I'm just stuffing my face with all of these civilians. Suddenly I want this whole foolishness to be over, to confront Tess Conroy and get her off my back, and then get back to the hotel and see if I can't track down Captain Diaz. Find out where my dad is, why he's in trouble. Maybe Dad's in the Capitol, or nearby. Good. Track him down, see what's going on, and then get the hell to Ft. St. Paul and get back to work, killing Creepers.

I turn and bump into a plump woman with white hair, teased up in an elaborate hairdo, and a cheery looking face with light pink makeup on her cheeks. She's wearing the same kind of formal dress that the other civilian women are wearing, and she looks vaguely familiar.

"Sergeant Knox?" she asks, sticking out her hand.

I shake the hand, feeling some strength but smoothness, no calluses or worn ridges, as she announces, "Congresswoman Julie LeBlanc, from the Second District. Your district, if I'm not mistaken."

"Yes, ma'am, that's right," I say, seeing she has a young male aide standing closely behind her, holding a notebook close to his side.

She pumps my hand a few times. "Darn proud to see you getting recognized this afternoon. You richly deserve it. A few more boys like you and we'll lick those Creepers for good, eh?"

I pull my hand away, resist an urge to wipe it on a napkin. "If you say so, ma'am."

She winks and pulls in close to me, and her tone of voice gets harder. "Just a word of advice, son. I know Tess Conroy has her eyes on you, so play it safe. She's a powerful woman, and you don't want to cross her. You be bright and do what she says."

The delicious food I've eaten earlier is threatening to crawl up my gullet, so I give her an enthusiastic nod, which seems to please her, and she wanders off; and I do, too, to get away from the flattery and the oh-so-polite threats. There are snatches of conversation, and I try not to listen, but it's hard not to.

". . . the EPA is still at work, if you can believe it, about damn carbon emissions . . ."

"... Governor Franklin's got her panties in a bunch I hear, but she's learning Kansas ain't Albany ..."

"... so I managed to get an increase for my idiot cousin from the Fertilizer Distribution Board ..."

All this talk, all this blather, and not one word about the war, about the military or the Creepers.

Music is still playing in a corner by the raised podium. I go check it out. Marines in fancy red and gold dress uniforms are playing something that sounds like Sousa, and I remember an old history lesson, back at the fort. These Marines are the official band for the New White House, and are called the President's Own. I maneuver around a heavy-set woman and man, knowing they had never suffered through the famine years, and I enjoy the music, keeping my good ear tilted toward them, until I look closely at the Marine musicians.

All of them have scarred faces and healed burn tissue, and all of them are blind.

CHAPTER TWENTY-NINE

The music suddenly stops and there's a gentle touch on my shoulder. A girl my age, wearing formal dress Army uniform with the rank of lieutenant and a brassard over one shoulder, signifying she's a presidential aide, whispers to me. "Excuse me, Sergeant. You need to sit up in the front row. It's all straight forward. The President will present you with your award first, and then Colonel Minh, and then the party will resume."

I just nod, let the pretty Army lieutenant lead me to a seat that has RESERVED printed on white paper and taped to the back of the chair. I sit on the chair, hands on my thighs, still not believing this is going on. My buds back at my barracks would probably wet themselves laughing at thinking Randy Knox would be here and at this event.

Murmurs and voices as the assembled guests take their seats, and there's a bit of Sousa music and then applause, as Tess Conroy goes up to the stage and stands in front of the lectern with the Presidential seal hanging from it. She's smiling widely and raises her hand, and the applause dies down. There's a microphone set in the middle of the podium, and she leans into it like it's her best friend in the whole wide world, and she says, "On behalf of the President and the New White House, I welcome you this afternoon to this awards ceremony. We honor today two special servicemen who have gone above and beyond to serve their country, their fellow citizens, and the people of the world. One such serviceman is a young infantryman, who used his skills and bare hands to prevent the murder of hundreds of our fellow citizens."

With that, the audience starts applauding again and my face and ears burn, almost as bad as being near a rampaging Creeper, when I realize all of these adults are applauding me. Sixteen-year-old Randy Knox, in the New White House, about to meet the President, being applauded and honored.

I feel like throwing up.

I take some deep breaths, and Tess gives me a little wave, and I smile and nod in return. Man, oh, man.

When the applause drifts away, she says, "Then there's another serviceman, an Air Force pilot and astronaut, a legend who was nearing retirement age, but who still volunteered for one last dangerous mission, a mission he joined with other dedicated volunteers, to take the fight to the Creepers in outer space, in their own safe harbor, where they were hunted down and destroyed!"

Cheers and whoops and hollers at that, the applause really heavy now, and I join in, looking around, trying to spot the famous Colonel, but I can't make him out. The applause goes on and on, and Tess just lets it go on until it dies away, and her smile gets even wider.

"This afternoon, before I introduce the President, I have an announcement to make. A very important and special announcement, one that is currently being released to news agencies here and around the world."

The large room suddenly gets very quiet, so still and silent even with my bum ear I can hear a fat man next to me slowly breathing. Tess milks the moment, looking around the room, like she's trying to catch everyone's eye, and then, speaking slowly and deliberately, she says, "This morning, at nine A.M., the Joint Chiefs of Staff reported to the President that as of six P.M., last night, a task force led by the brave men and women of Bravo Company, the Two-One Sixteenth Calvary, of the Idaho National Guard, successfully broke through the Interstate Seventy MLR—Main Line of Resistance—in Colorado, and have held their positions. Relief convoys are now on the move along the Interstate."

I can feel the tension in the room, rising and rising, like we're all inside some steam kettle, ready to explode, not quite believing what we were hearing, and Tess says simply, "Ladies and gentlemen, the siege of Denver has been lifted."

⊕ ⊕ ⊕

The cheers, whoops, whistles and applause are deafening, and even I join in the celebrations, and we don't have much time to process that amazing piece of good news, when Tess dramatically steps back, holds out an arm, and announces, "Ladies and gentlemen, the President of the United States!"

The Marine Band strikes up "Ruffle and Flourishes," and that's followed by "Hail to the Chief," and from a door behind the stand and podium, the President slowly comes out, waving and smiling, as the applause tries to overwhelm the music. He looks older than the photographs I've seen over the years, and that's easy to believe. Poor guy has the hardest job on the planet, one he never really wanted.

When the war started and the Creepers' satellites started hitting targets from orbit using particle beams and weapons rods, the sitting President, Vice President and Speaker of the House were all killed within days. What was left of the National Command Authority responded the best they could, and in those confusing first couple of years of the war, we went through nearly a half-dozen Presidents, as the Constitutional line of succession was stretched beyond recognition. There were also some times when we didn't have a President: if you're the Secretary of Agriculture, next in line to the presidency, and your predecessors were killed by Creepers, do you take the job or retire to a hog farm in Iowa?

Our president now, though, has been in the job for nearly seven years. When the war started, he was an Assistant Secretary of Defense, and as the war went on, he was the highest surviving Cabinet member who agreed to serve as president. He was easily re-elected back when I was twelve, when the opposing party only put up token opposition from the governor of Rhode Island, a role to be taken later this year by the governor of Kansas. I'm close enough to see his tanned and wrinkled skin, his fine dark suit with white shirt and red necktie, his combed thick white hair, but it's his eyes that get my attention. They look so very tired, like the poor man hasn't had a good night's sleep in nearly a decade.

The applause finally dies down and the President comes to the podium, grasps both sides with his hands. He smiles and I note a flag pin on his lapel. It shows the American flag, with black mourning bands draped along the pole, denoting the start of the war on 10/10.

When it's quiet in the room, he looks around and keeps on smiling, and then the mood of the room changes. There's a cough, a quiet whisper, and I feel horrified for him, wondering what's going to happen next. It seems like nobody knows what to do, or what to say, with the President standing still in front of his podium with the round presidential seal fastened in its center. Tess Conroy is in the corner with the military aide, hands clasped tightly in front of her, and finally the President speaks.

"My friends," he starts, and then he stops, his voice raspy. "My dear, dear friends . . ." He looks down at the podium for a long moment, and raises his head. There are tears in his eyes. "This is a wonderful day, is it not? Just a few short weeks after our brave Air Force destroyed the alien orbital battle station, we receive the glorious news that our fellow Americans in Denver have been saved. It has been such a long, discouraging and hard road for all of us, here in the United States and around the world . . . but that promise I made on the day of my inauguration, in paraphrasing another president elected during perilous times, that I would 'pay any price and bear any burden, to secure victory for our people and our planet,' my friends, it seems that promise is finally being fulfilled."

More whoops, cheers and applause, and it seems to energize him, and he nods vigorously and waves again, and Tess Conroy looks like she's relaxing. When the quiet comes back, the President says, "So this afternoon, it's appropriate that we come together to honor two of our brave servicemen, one so very young, and one so very experienced, who have led, and who will continue to lead us, to our final and complete victory, so help us God!"

So another round of applause and I'm starting to get fidgety and nervous, like the time I went up to the oral boards for my promotion to sergeant, and Tess and the military aide join the President, and Tess slips a sheet of paper into the President's hands. Having something to read strengthens his voice, and my face and hands burn with embarrassment as the President starts talking about me.

The language is both flowery and formal, as the President reads the official declaration of what happened that night by the bridge near the swamp, where a rag-tag group of civilians and cops and yours truly went up against a Creeper Transport. As the words are spoken, I feel even more warm and uncomfortable. What I recall from that night is being scared out of my mind, knowing with some certainty that it would probably be my last battle, for Serena was right in noting why I had sent the dispatch case, my journal, and Thor along with her. I remember being wet, muddy and terrified as the Creeper Transport lumbered through the swamp, heading right towards me.

The brave soldier mentioned in the President's reading—a young man who was full of honor, sacrifice and devotion to duty—bears no resemblance to the scared teenage boy in uniform who was there that rainy night, but I just stare straight ahead and keep my mouth shut.

The sudden clapping of hands jerks me out of my semi-trance, and with Tess Conroy staring at me, I get up and make my way up to the raised platform. I nearly trip over my feet and I feel like I'm in an elaborate play, written and staged for my benefit. I shake hands with the President—seeing age spots on the back of his hand—and I'm gently turned to one side so photographers can take my photos. The military aide opens a small blue case, and the Silver Star is taken out, and the President pins it on my formal dress uniform, taking two tries to do so. Standing so close to him, I smell his cologne, see some sort of make-up on his face, and even his nostril hairs. He's smiling at me but damn, there's still something so very tired with his eyes.

"Congratulations, Sergeant," he says. "You've made us all very, very proud."

I shake his hand again and he propels me to the podium. "Do you have anything you'd like to say?"

Hell, no, is what I think, but I see the expectant look on his face, and I don't want to disappoint my commander in chief. I go to the podium and look out at all the people sitting in their chairs, waiting for me to say something wonderful and profound. I clear my throat and not daring to look at anybody directly, I say, "Thank you, Mister President, thank you very much."

I step back, almost bump into the President, and face still flushed, I get back to my chair as yet another round of clapping commences.

I'm so much out of place that I feel like I'm going to rise out of my chair and drift away.

The President reads from a second sheet of paper, about the exploits of Colonel Victor Minh, and I lean forward, not wanting to miss a single word, since this is the most information that's ever been revealed about the Air Force's low earth orbit attack. The President reveals that planning for the mission began nine years ago, and despite setbacks and accidents and failures, it continued, day and night, week after month, after year. "Using solid-rocket boosters salvaged from old space shuttle contractors, built at a secret high desert base in Nevada, a squadron of eight manned rockets was constructed."

The President looks up, blinks his eyes a few times, and goes on. Using old telegraph lines that went across the Pacific, cooperation was reached with surviving military commanders in Japan, Russia and China, where they launched diversionary ICBMs towards the orbital battle station. The killer stealth satellites easily destroyed those complex nuclear-tipped missiles, but the diversion allowed the simpler Air Force vehicles to reach orbit, where they destroyed the Creeper orbital base.

Another pause, as the President clears his throat. "The Air Force's 19th Orbital Attack Wing, the 'Retaliation Rebels,' was commanded by Colonel Victor Minh, who was the sole survivor of this daring mission. He is with us today, to receive the nation's gratitude and its highest military honor . . . honored guests, I present to you, Colonel Victor Minh!"

As one everyone stands up, applauding and cheering, again I join in, and the applause goes on and on, and the President looks expectantly to one side and then the other, and then looks to Tess Conroy, who's horrified. The applause dies away and there's a long, awkward silence.

Then from the left, a man approaches, getting up on the platform, stumbling, stumbling again, and he has on the uniform of an Air Force colonel, with medals and decorations. He walks with a pronounced limp, moving slowly now, and he cheerfully waves to the crowd, both hands scarred. He's of Vietnamese descent, his face also scarred with burn tissue, and he has a black eyepatch over one eye, making him look like an airborne pirate.

And above all, he appears to be drunk out of his skull.

He bows to the President, who steps forward and with the assistance of the military aide, drapes the light blue ribbon and gold medal around his neck. The President shakes his hand and Colonel Minh grimaces—I'm sure the burnt hand is still sensitive—but shakes right back. More applause and the President attempts to move Colonel

Minh away from the podium and microphone, but the last American to fly into space shrugs him off, and stumbles again, right in front of the podium.

When the clapping dribbles away, Colonel Minh is grinning widely, looking around at all of us, the expression on his scarred face saying "how about that, folks?" Then he belches and speaks into the microphone. "My God, what an honor . . . what an outstanding honor . . . if you had told me ten years back, when I was just a lieutenant, flying F-22s out of Nellis and trying to make sense of what the hell was going on when the war started . . . so many cities destroyed . . . so many of my friends burned out of the air . . . if you had told me that me, Vic Minh, son of boat people from a forgotten South Vietnam, would be here, meeting the President and getting the Medal of Honor . . . jeez, I would have told that you were full of shit . . ."

I laugh, but not many others sitting there do. Another belch and he presses on. "And it is an honor . . . you know? Good God, it is . . . but all this noble crap about sacrifice and duty and bravery . . . you know why I got this draped around my neck? Do you?" He flips the ribbon with one scarred hand and says, "'Cause I survived, that's why . . . Can't have a successful war without survivors . . . and finally, by God's teeth, looks like we might just win one . . . win one in the Gipper's memory . . . hah . . . just in time for election season and court decisions and all that nonsense . . ."

He lowers his head and tears come out of his good eye, and his voice, though slurred, gains strength. "Didn't have to be that way . . . you know . . . we could have prepared . . . could have been ready . . . it was a scientific certainty there was life out there . . . we even had some bits of evidence they were checking us out earlier . . . could have been easy to set up an early warning system . . . space-borne weapons up there . . . crap, so easy . . . but hey! Budget decisions had to be made . . . money to be spent on bridges to no where . . . corn subsidies . . . foreign aid to countries that hated us . . . and trying to get a Congressman or a Senator interested in preparing for an invasion, hell, might as well try to get a baboon interested in quantum physics . . . crap, we could have been ready and so many of us, God, so many of us wouldn't have had to die . . . get shot down . . . get burned like friggin' pork roasts . . ."

Out of the corner of my eye, I see Tess Conroy motion frantically to someone, there's a sound of someone snapping his fingers, and the Marine band bursts into a loud Sousa tune. The military aide gently takes Colonel Minh by his wrist and pulls him away from the podium with its presidential seal. More applause, subdued this time, and I look around at all the suits and neckties and dresses and plump faces, all of the people now standing up and milling about, and something clicks, and I want out of here.

So I get going.

I make it about three meters from the main ballroom doors before I'm stopped.

It's Riley, of course, as he blocks my way and says, "In a hurry, Sergeant?"

"Was thinking of finding a men's room."

He shakes his head. "Better think of something else. Like meeting up with Tess Conroy. Some stuff needs to get settled."

I'm thinking about going all out in a blitz, pushing by him, because he's cocky and confident and I might just make it, when Tess Conroy comes up, face pinched.

"Somebody wants to see you."

"I thought only you wanted to see me."

"I do, but this is going to take . . . precedence. Come with me."

Riley looks disappointed, like he was hoping I was going to pick a fight, but being obedient, I follow Tess through the crowd, with some calling out to her and she brushing them off, until we go through a rear door, down a corridor, and to an open door to the right, that leads off to a small balcony. Tess pushes me in the small of my back. "Go in there, talk to him for ten minutes, and then get out. Then you and I will meet. Got it, Sergeant?"

"Not really," I say, but I step forward anyway.

CHAPTER THIRTY

Out on the balcony the late afternoon air is muggy and the sky is overcast. I take two steps and stop. Standing in a corner of the balcony, leaning over a wrought-iron fence and smoking a cigar, is Colonel Victor Minh. He turns to me and in one hand he's holding a thick white coffee mug. He's still in uniform, the Medal of Honor tight around his neck, and black eyepatch in place. A small electric lamp on a near wall is lighting up the balcony. It seems like an awful waste of power.

"Hey, kid, how's it going?" he asks, taking a puff from the cigar.

Anybody else in uniform calling me kid, I'd bristle up like my poor wounded Thor, smelling a Creeper in the distance. But I'm in awe of this man, who's been in space, fought the Creepers on their home turf, and returned safely back to Earth.

"Doing fine, sir," I say. "You wanted to see me?"

"Sure," he laughs. "One famous serviceman to another, eh? I'm a damn hero for the ages. Ladies will be tossing their panties at me. Presidents and generals will salute me first. Schools will be named for me after I'm dead, and maybe even airports, once we get aircraft up and flying again. But you . . . What are you doing here?"

I'm not sure what he's asking. His good eye is boring right into me, and I say, "I killed a Creeper with a knife."

"Good for you, kid. A hell of a job. But again . . . Why are you here? To receive a Silver Star from the President? Bully and all that, but why the President? Why not your C.O., or your governor, or whatever congressman might be hanging around with nothing else better to do?"

I say, "Because they're trying to bribe me."

A crisp, smiling nod. "Good job, kid. Nice smarts, nice evaluation of the situation. You're young enough, when we get to flying again, maybe you should join with us. A nice real service. Pretty small now, but we'll grow eventually."

"No, thanks. I'm used to where I am. Don't particularly like heights."

"So there you go," he says, taking a deep swallow from his coffee mug. "Any idea why you're being bribed?"

"I got something the President's Chief of Staff wants. Classified information. I declined to give it to her. This whole ceremony with the President, the fine food and drink, all a bribe. Get me feeling good so I'll give her what she wants. What do you think?"

The colonel takes a deep drag from his cigar. The smell is rich and heavy, and I wonder how it tastes. "Could be. Also could be something else, nice P.R. of having a young buck like you and an old bastard like me being honored, the same time they announce the Denver siege being lifted, helps out the Administration during this whole election mess."

"What mess is that?"

He laughs. "Hell, boy, what do they teach you when you're not out running drills or going for target practice?"

I say crossly. "They teach me English, math, logistics, tactics, strategy, and military history from the Assyrians to the Third Gulf War last decade. Don't have much time for current affairs, except better ways to track and kill Creepers."

"Don't get so ticked off," Minh says quietly. "You see, kid, the President and his Chief of Staff have a problem coming up: it's called an election."

"Why do they have a problem?" I ask. "The President's term is up. Time for somebody else to have the job."

"Yeah, his term is up, but that's during usual times. Serve two terms and you're done. But these ain't the usual times. It gets funky, so bear with me, but ever since the second President declared Martial Law, a lot of laws have been suspended or ignored. Anything to win the war, right? So when our current CinC got into office, there was a compromise among what was left of Congress and the Supreme Court to let him serve two full terms. You sure you didn't notice that?"

"Maybe I did, but I've had other things to worry about. Like keeping my lieutenant happy and killing Creepers without getting roasted."

"So worry about this. The President's term is coming up, and he and his crew and Tess Conroy are trying to get the Twenty-Second Amendment repealed, so he can run for a third term."

"He looked pretty tired tonight."

"Sure he did, but a man gets a good taste for power, he tends to want to keep on tasting it. Along with his staff and his lackeys in the Congress. Maybe the Amendment will get repealed, maybe not. But having this ceremony tonight and announcing the relief of Denver, it sure does help his case, doesn't it. So maybe our commander in chief gets elected to a third term, and then a fourth. Think you'll remember that when you finally go home?"

"I think I will," I say, "and I think I'll remember something else. Like you don't look so drunk right now. You seem pretty sober."

That brings forth a chuckle and he says, "I meant to raise a bit of hell up there with the President, and I figured if I appeared cold sober, they wouldn't cut me any slack. But if I'm drunk . . . it's just the newest hero, breaking a bit under the strain. They had a part for me, okay, but I was going to do a bit of ad-libbing."

In the cloudy sky off beyond the balcony, there are three bright flashes of light illuminating the clouds, making them look milky white, as more space junk comes burning back to earth. Minh sighs. "What the President said back there, about our mission . . . he spoke the truth, mostly, about what happened. Right after the war started and the Creepers burned all the aircraft and most powered vehicles, we in the Air Force didn't have much to work with. But by God we got our orders: find a way to get up into low earth orbit and blast that orbital battle station, any way we could."

I keep quiet, knowing that when this night is over and I get back to my journal, I'll make sure to write down as much as I can remember.

The colonel says, "Did our best when the aliens revealed themselves. Minuteman missiles were launched, the Navy's sub force launched their own warheads, our classified satellite killers were sent up too, but the missiles never got more than a hundred-thousand or so feet up in the air. They were blasted before they could reach orbit. Way our white-coats figured, it was the electronics and complexity of the launch systems that the Creepers picked up on. That's why steamships and sailing craft and steam locomotives don't get disturbed. Too damn primitive. So we decided to go primitive, we did."

He coughs some and I hope I'm not running out of time from Tess' schedule. He says, "So we went to the old Morton-Thiokol factories in Utah, where they made solid-fuel rocket boosters for the space shuttle. Got the assembly line re-started, shipped the components by horse-drawn wagons to an abandoned base. I helped work on the crew capsule, which was pretty simple. One pilot and one warhead. Limited electronics. Manual controls. Nothing computerized, nothing to attract the Creepers . . . Couldn't even test the bastards. We had one chance, once chance only."

He stops, and his good eye is moist. I try to gently prod him. "The President said there were eight of you."

The colonel takes a slight puff from his cigar. "Eight went up. One barely got off the launch pad. Major Susan McLane. One of the best pilots I've ever known. Damn booster split into pieces as it went up, scattered her all over the Utah desert. No escape rockets or ejection seats. Didn't have time! Do you hear me, kid? They were pressing us, pressing us, no matter what others advised. We didn't have time!"

Softly I say, "I hear you, sir."

He takes a deep breath, turns and stares out at the buildings of the Capitol. "Seven of us reached space . . . God, you'd think we'd have time to look down at the Earth, get used to zero-gee, but we were in a hurry. The Russkies, Chinese, and Japs, bless 'em, had sent up the diversionary attack. Let us go right in. I was the commander of the squadron, herding all of those brave guys and gals to that damn Creeper orbital station. Big ugly thing, odd protrusions and shapes . . . dark and sparkly . . . our squadron sailed in . . . very little electronics . . . our brave space-borne *kaiten*."

I stay quiet. He turns away from the Capitol buildings. "You say you're educated, kid. Care to tell me what the *kaiten* are . . . or were?"

I pause, not quite believing what I was hearing. "The *kaiten* . . . they were Japanese sailors, back during the end of World War II. They operated one-man mini-submarines, designed to attack the Allied invasion force."

The colonel takes a final puff on his cigar, tosses it over the balcony. I watch the burning ember as it fades away. "A very polite answer, kid, but don't be so damn polite. The *kaiten* were a kamikaze force, since those mini-subs were nothing more than huge torpedoes. A one-way trip. That's why I got my ten minutes with you, pal, otherwise, as a drunk officer in the United States Air Force, I was going to tell everyone within reach that the other brave astronauts were kamikaze pilots. All volunteers. They launched knowing they were never coming back. And me? Their brave commander? I was sent along to escort them, to watch them, and report back. My capsule didn't have a warhead. It had a heat shield . . . and I came back and landed somewhere in Ohio. That was my damn mission. Before . . . I watched them all go in . . . we had old-fashioned radios, the ones with vacuum tubes, and I could hear them. Could hear them talking to each other and to me . . . got their last words. And for that . . ." He again flips the light blue ribbon and gold medal about his neck. "For surviving. I'm called a damn hero."

I find my voice. "You are a hero, Colonel."

"No more," he says. "Please, no more." He glances at his watch. "Besides, your time is almost up."

I remember something from his talk. "What did you mean, back there, when you said we weren't prepared? Said there was evidence we were being checked out."

He stares at me some more. "Oh, hell, not much of a secret anyway. For decades, right after World War II, there were unexplained sightings. I don't mean crap like the Roswell landing or people being brought up into space to get their butts poked. No, there's always been . . . unexplained stuff. Qualified air crews seeing objects that moved too fast. Radar and visual sightings that just didn't make sense. Even some gun camera footage . . . nothing provable, nothing that would stand up in court, but, by God. A warning. That we were being watched. Evaluated. Targeted. And what did we do? Nothing at all. For the cost of spare parts for one M-1 tank or an F-22 fighter, we could have put up an early warning system for the planet . . . but we didn't."

Minh takes one last sip from his coffee mug, looks down at it, and with one hard motion, tosses it over the railing, to join his cigar butt. "Sorry, kid, we let you down. Big time. The generation before ours was called the Greatest Generation, for taking on the Great Depression, fascism and communism. Our generation . . . we'll be known as the Stupidest Generation. We had everything handed to us, from wealth to knowledge to security . . . and we're giving you ashes and a graveyard and a big damn overdue bill."

The door to the balcony opens up. I turn and Tess Conroy is silhouetted there. His voice softer, the colonel says, "Go ahead now, kid. Do your duty. God knows I didn't do mine, even with this pretty ribbon around my neck."

CHAPTER THIRTY-ONE

With Riley escorting and Tess Conroy keeping a quick pace in front of me, I'm brought into an office somewhere deep in the New White House. It's spare, with a metal desk, two straight-backed chairs, and a door that shuts firmly behind us. There's no window, no bookcases, no photos on the wall, no telephone, not much of anything. I instantly know this isn't Tess Conroy's office; it's too simple. It seems to be an office for interviewing and grilling and demanding things, and Tess doesn't disappoint.

She sits on the other side of the desk, pulls open a drawer. "You've proven to be quite stubborn, Sergeant, but since you've just been honored by the President not more than a half hour ago, I'm willing to cut you some slack. So these are for you."

Tess tosses two envelopes across to me, and my heart nearly bursts, thinking they're from my dad. I pick them up and see both envelopes bear the return address of Ft. St. Paul, but the taste of disappointment is strong in my mouth when I see my dad's name isn't listed as well. Still, one name is Monroe—good old Abby!—and the other is my uncle, Colonel Malcolm Hunter.

"Couriers can move very fast when they have to," Tess explains. "I'll give you a moment to read them both, and then you and I will have our little meeting. All right?"

I feel like telling her we can have our little meeting right now, that I'll tell her everything and anything she wants to know about Serena Coulson, the dispatch case and her plan to meet up with her dad here. What do I care? All I want to do is to get out of here, see if I can't find

Captain Ramon Diaz and then get the hell back to Ft. St. Paul with my injured Thor right with me. I'm tired of secrets, of conspiracies, of the flattery and what not. Once upon a time I was just a simple soldier, a simple kid, and that's what I want to be now.

Be patient, ma'am, I think. In about thirty seconds, you'll get everything you want.

I open up the note from Abby. It says:

Dear Randy,

Sorry I didn't get a chance to see you off at the train station. Your departure was supposed to be very hush-hush, but I had to find out where you were going. I feel like a dope, the way I acted at the dance. You mean a lot to me and I miss having you and your smelly dog around . . . hah!

Get back to the post as soon as you can. I hear you've been a very brave Recon Ranger out there in New York State and I want to know all about it. We've got a lot of catching up to do, including dancing. (And I don't care if there's no Ranger Ball scheduled . . . you and I will do our own dancing.)

Under that she drew a little smiley face, and then signed it:

Love, Abby

I grin. Can't help myself. Abby's never signed a note to me before with that magic word.

Love.

I fold up the paper and grin at Tess, feeling the best . . . the best in . . . well, in a very long time. I think to myself, one more letter and then it's over, and then I tear open the second envelope.

It says:

My dear nephew,

I'm so proud to hear of what you did in responding to the Creeper Transport attack outside of the Capitol. I'm so glad to know that even when you're on a detached mission, you hold up the honor of the New Hampshire National Guard and the Recon Rangers.

Through channels I've heard of your interaction with Tess Conroy at

*the Capitol. Rest assured I fully anticipate that you will do your duty
and do what you must with the President's Chief of Staff, and fulfill all
aspects of your mission.*

*Once again, I'm so proud of what you did, and I'm sure my dear
brother-in-law—your father—would be proud as well.*

*All best wishes,
Your Uncle Malcolm*

While the first letter made me smile and forget the troubles I've
been in, the second letter does exactly the opposite. I wanted so much
to get out of the shadows, to get back to where I belong, but now I have
no choice.

My uncle's letter tells me that.

I slowly and carefully fold the letter back into shape, slide it into
the envelope. Tess Conroy looks at me expectantly. When I had met
with my uncle at Ft. St. Paul, when he had given me my mission
briefing, he had told me to cooperate with the President's Chief of Staff,
and to get the dispatch case into her hands. But he also told me to do
something else.

Now I have this letter in my hand from my commanding officer.
Tess continues to look hard at me. I put the letter down on the table.

"Ma'am, what is it that you wish to know?"

She nods. "That's more like it. Sergeant, what were you told about
your mission and what Mister Manson was carrying?"

"Ma'am, I was told by my commanding officer to escort Mister
Manson and the dispatch case to the Capitol. From there, I was to
ensure that Mister Manson and the case were to be delivered to
you."

"Go on. Do you know what was in the case?"

I answer carefully. "I was told that it was a message from the
Governor of New Hampshire to the President."

"Is that all?"

"No, ma'am," I say. "I was also told that if there was an unfortunate
. . . event, that I was to take possession of the case and make sure it
was delivered to you."

I wait, wondering if she was going to repeat herself by saying "is
that all," but she continues. "Yet you didn't do that, did you, Sergeant.

You chose to put that case in the possession of a young girl, and then go off to fight a Creeper."

"Ma'am, I had no choice in the matter. A Creeper attack was going on in my immediate vicinity. I had to respond. I made the best choice I could under the circumstances. I gave the dispatch case to—

"A young girl!" she interrupted.

"No, ma'am," I corrected. "I gave the dispatch case to one Selena Coulson, an Army Specialist. I ordered her to deliver the case to you."

"But she didn't, did she."

My hands are getting moist. "Apparently not, ma'am."

"Why was she coming to the Capitol? And why did she have her brother with her?"

Okay, here we go. "I don't know, ma'am."

"Do you know who she might be meeting in the Capitol?"

"I'm sorry, ma'am, I can't say."

"Does she have friends, family, any connection in the Capitol?"

"I'm sorry, ma'am, I can't say."

Her eyes flash at me. "Oh, come on, young man. Do you think I'm going to believe that?"

"You may believe what you wish to believe, ma'am, but I can't say why she was coming to the Capitol, what she was going to do when she got here, or who she was meeting."

"You're lying."

I keep my mouth shut. She says, "What is it, are you in love with her? A little hand-holding, a make-out session in the train or the bus coming over here?"

I still keep my mouth shut. The President's Chief of Staff goes on. "You think I have the time or interest to go back and forth with a boy like you? Do you? If you saw the dispatches and papers that cross my desk every day, you'd age ten years in ten minutes. Telegrams from the *Jefe* of Mexico, begging for food aid. Or the King of Brazil, looking for doctors. Australia asking us to increase shipments of the Colt M-10. Not to mention last month, we ended this damn war."

"With no disrespect, ma'am, I know a bunch of guys and gals back at the V.A. hospital who'd disagree with you."

She frowns sharply and says, "That dispatch case and that young girl are vital to the national security interests of the United States. Stop stonewalling, sonny, or you can't believe how difficult I can make things for you."

Something starts to stir inside of me. Anger? Disdain? Disgust? I don't know. I go on.

"I was just awarded the Silver Star from the President of the United States, ma'am," I point out. "I think it might be hard to do anything against me."

That gets her attention. "You stupid boy, I got you that Silver Star. Me! And nobody else! I gave it to you and I can damn well take it back."

I unhook the medal from my uniform, slide it over on the desk. "You can have it now," I say. "I just want to get back to my job."

She stands up, face scarlet. "Oh, you're going back, and sooner than you think, sonny. Does the name Fred Mackey mean anything to you? Fred Mackey of Purmort, New Hampshire?"

I have to think and then it comes to me. "Yes, he's a civilian that I . . . encountered during a Creeper mission a number of days ago."

"Correction, Sergeant Knox," she says, triumph in her voice. "He's the civilian you shot and killed during a Creeper mission a number of days ago."

My hands, my face, the back of my neck are all suddenly chilled, like a blast of Arctic air has come through the closed door. "The hell I killed him!"

"Oh, yes you did," she says. "I've seen the medical report from the New Hampshire hospital."

"I shot him in the leg! That's all that happened, and you know it."

She brushes past me, to the door. "What I know are three things, sonny. One is that you're refusing to cooperate with me, even after getting direct written orders from your commanding officer. The second is that you shot a civilian, one Fred Mackey, who later died of a massive infection, brought on by a gunshot wound that you inflicted on him. And the third is that in a few minutes, the MPs are coming here, to bring you back to Ft. St. Paul, where you're going to be court-martialed."

With that, she opens the door, goes through it, and slams it behind her.

I step up almost immediately, try the doorknob.

Locked.

⊕ ⊕ ⊕

I pace around the room. I've certainly gotten into it, but I had no choice. My uncle's letter had told me that. And knowing how Tess Conroy worked, I had a cold chill, wondering if Mister Mackey had really died of an infection, or something else. About the only good thing in her threat was me going back to Ft. St. Paul, which is fine. There I'd be among my uncle, my buds, and I'd be on a much more even playing field than this damn shadowy place. My pal Thor is getting good care at the vet clinic and I'll try hard to get him back, maybe by pressing our batman Corporal Manning to see what he can do.

As to Specialist Coulson and her scarier-than-hell brother, well, she'd have to figure what to do next out there in the Capitol without me.

The doorknob is unlocked and a man in uniform comes in. I'm expecting an MP, or even two MPs.

What I'm not expecting is Captain Ramon Diaz of the Special Forces.

He nods at me, wearing his Class A uniform, his face still burnt and ears misshapen. He shuts the door firmly behind him and sits down. I take the other chair, shocked and thrilled at the same time.

I say, "Captain Diaz, could you tell me where my dad is, what—"

"We're running out of time," he says, speaking quickly. "There are two MPs coming here to take you to the local stockade, and from there, a train to the east. So let's get to it before they arrive. You need to meet up with Specialist Coulson and her brother. Once you do that, follow her lead. Time is running out."

"But I don't know where she is!"

He glances at his wristwatch. "Minor detail. Now to get you out of here."

"I'm under arrest."

"Don't quibble. I've told the powers that be that I'd babysit you until the MPs arrive, do a bit of interrogation. So here I am."

To say my head is spinning would be like saying LEO is just a bit crowded. "How the hell did you get in here?"

A quick touch of a scarred finger to an emblem on his chest. "Diamond Eagle can open a lot of doors, either officially or unofficially. Including the one you're going to slip through. Sergeant, you need to escape, and escape now. Think you can get past me?"

My head feels thick, like I'm in math class, trying to figure out an unfamiliar problem. "A challenge, but if I do get past you, what do I do then?"

He reaches into a side pocket, takes out a hand-drawn map. "Follow this, you can get out of the New White House in five minutes and be back on the streets. The Secret Service worry about people getting in. They don't worry as much about people getting out. Plus you're a 'hero,' Sergeant, and only the Chief of Staff and a couple of others know the trouble you're in. The S.S. will probably hold the door open for you as you bail out."

From another pocket, he pulls out a set of handcuffs, which he clatters on the top of the table. "I took these in case you got out of hand. Come on, Sergeant, do I have to draw you another map? Get going, get past me, and hook up with the Specialist. She's waiting for you."

"Why me?"

His smile looks like a grimace on his scarred face.

"Because of all the men and women in the armed services, she says she trusts you the most. Seems you saved her from being killed in Massachusetts. True?"

"True, but where is she?"

"She got into your hotel room once before. She's a smart girl. She and her brother will be waiting for you there, but damn it, Sergeant, get a move on. You've got to get them to her father."

"What's the damn hurry, sir? And why are you here?"

He glances behind him, like he was trying to hear if the MPs are approaching. "Christ, sergeant, it's like this, all right? Some of us are trying to end this damn war, despite everything that's been going on out there for the past ten years."

"The President said the war's already over."

"Sure he did," the captain says. "And those of us that have bled, burnt and been blinded for this country want to make sure he's right, that he and his staff aren't blowing smoke up our collective asses. Maybe the orbital station attack was a success. Maybe it was a mistake. We don't know for certain. So get a move on!"

I pick up the handcuffs, juggle them in my hand, and say, "Where's my dad?"

"Sergeant—"

"Captain, you tell me what's up with my dad, or I'm going to stay here and let myself get arrested."

"Sergeant, there are a hell of a lot more important things to worry about than your father!"

"Sorry, sir," I say. "So says you. So where's my dad?"

He frowns, which on his face looks horrible, and he looks like he wants to knock me under the desk. "Sergeant, I answer your question, you get a move on. All right?"

I nod. "Fair enough," I say.

Captain Diaz says, "Sorry, Sergeant. Your father's under arrest. For treason. On his way to Leavenworth."

I stand up and slug Captain Diaz in the face.

I wince and shake my hand from the punch, and he does me the favor of falling back in his chair. I take my chair and bring it down hard across his shoulders and the back of his head. He curses at me and I grab a wrist, snap one end of the handcuffs there, and fasten the other to a desk leg.

Blood is running down the back of his head. "Christ, Sergeant, smartest thing you've done all day! Now haul ass!"

"What's the damn rush?"

He coughs. "The President says the war's over. Looks like the surviving Creepers disagree and want to prove it. Something's up and they're on the move, sergeant. To the Capitol. Tonight."

"My dad," I say. "Where is he now?"

"North of the Capitol," he says, touching his lips with his tongue. "Stockade at the Watervliet Arsenal. But forget him. Get out of here!"

I get out into the hallway, make sure the door is locked behind me. Should slow down the MPs some. I glance at the map, memorize the directions, and shove the paper in my pocket. I don't want to raise suspicions and bumbling around the New White House with directions in hand would do just that.

I move down the wood-trimmed hallway, take a right, and descend a set of stairs. My right hand hurts like hell, joining the throbbing in my shoulder from my Creeper burn. Men and women pass me by, all wearing lanyards around their necks with photo identification. Some of them glance at me with some curiosity, but I just nod at them like I belong and keep on walking. I feel like I'm in one of those dreams where you go into battle with all of your gear and M-10 in hand, only to realize you're not wearing pants and have no ammo.

Another set of stairs, a short hallway, and a door up ahead marked with a glowing red EXIT sign. According to the map, once I get through this door, I'll be out in a small park. Go through a park, go to a side gate, and then I'm out on the streets of the Capitol.

I'm about five meters away from the door when a hand grabs my shoulder.

I whirl around and there's a large, bulky man in a black suit with shiny areas on the knees and elbows, looking down at me. I recognize him right away. The second bodyguard who had accompanied Tess Conroy and Riley to my hospital room. Don't know his name but he's squatter and looks meaner than Riley. To get past him would take a pistol, an M-4 or a length of iron pipe, none of which I'm currently carrying.

"Sergeant Knox?" he asks, his voice a low-pitched growl.

I step back so his hand's not on me. If I can't fight, maybe I can flight. Dodge him and make a break for the exit.

"That's right," I say, evaluating, gauging, just seeing how I can get around this bulky armed man.

He moves his face muscles, revealing big yellow teeth. I suddenly realize he's smiling at me. He shoves a hand out.

"Congratulations," he says. "It'd be an honor to shake your hand."

"Sure," I say. My hand practically disappears into his and after a one-two pump, he reaches into his pocket, takes out a folded program from the day's ceremony, and presents that with a pencil stub.

"Could you sign this for me? To my son? His name is Travis, and he's enlisting next month."

I take the offered items and scrawl with a shaking hand, "To Travis, good luck in your service. All best, Sergeant Randy Knox, 2nd N.H. R/R."

I return the pencil and paper. "How old is he?"

"Twelve," he replies softly, looking at the program.

"Of course," I say, and he turns around, shoves the program back into his coat.

I walk by him, forcing myself to keep a slow pace, like I'm moving by without a care in the world, even though I'm expecting alarms to ring, lights to flash, or something to nail me between my shoulder blades if this bodyguard behind me gets the word that I'm not supposed to be out and about.

The door is in front of me. I push it open. Outside it's pouring rain. A beautiful night.

About a half-hour later, soaked through and with my right hand aching from punching Captain Diaz, I arrive at one of the service entrances of the Capitol Arms Hotel. I go through a kitchen area and after asking directions from a dishwasher, I get to the front desk. The same man as before is working there and I say, "Excuse me, I'm looking for my pack?"

He bustles about, his eyeglasses dangling down his chest, and I repeat myself, louder, knowing that when the MPs get into that locked room back at the New White House, they'll be racing right here after me.

The clerk turns from his paperwork, and I repeat myself for the third time, and he shakes his head. "Sorry, sarge, not here."

"Where did it go?"

A shrug. "Sorry. It's gone. You wanna make a claim?"

The MPs probably got here earlier, I think, and I just give him a quick wave, and go to the rear set of stairs, taking them two at a time. No assault pack. Means no spare clothes, no weapon, and no journal, damn it.

Out in the corridor, I make my way to my door. Get my key out, open the door, and I'm looking at Serena, who's standing there.

Holding my 9 mm Beretta.

Pointed at my head.

"Close the door," she says.

So I do just that.

CHAPTER THIRTY-TWO

With the door shut, I turn back to Serena, who's holding the pistol with both hands, staring right at me. She has on BDU's and so does her brother Buddy, who's sitting on my made bed. My assault pack is on the floor near the bed, so it's clear where her pistol came from.

"Randy, you've got to—"

I step forward quickly, grab the barrel of my pistol with both hands, shove it up hard. Startled, her hand moves with me and it's easy enough to push and twist the weapon out of her hand. With pistol now in my grasp, I give her a firm shove so she falls back against the bed. Eyes still on her, making sure she's not carrying any other weapon, I step back, now armed.

"Specialist, I don't have to do a damn thing. What's going to happen now is that you're going to answer my questions, and if you hesitate, if you blow me off, if I think you're dancing around, if you mention OPSEC, then I'm going to the telephone over there. I'll call the front desk and then we'll all be arrested together."

Her voice is firm. "Randy, please . . ."

"Specialist."

Her eyes are glaring at me. "Go ahead."

"Let's start simple. Thor. I told you to take care of him. What the hell happened?"

"The bus driver . . . he stopped at another checkpoint, a few minutes after we left. The door opened up and your damn dog ran out."

"My damn dog ended up nearly getting killed by a Creeper," I say sharply. "Lousy job, Specialist."

She stays quiet, lips pursed and trembling. I go on. "Your dad?"

Her voice tinged with desperation, "He's been arrested, Randy. I found out when I got here with Buddy. That's why I never delivered the dispatch case. I knew I'd be arrested, too. I didn't know what to do next."

I say, "But you knew enough to contact Captain Diaz. It's no coincidence he was on that train from Concord, was it. He was keeping an eye on you. When the train got attacked, I couldn't see him in the crowds. That's because while I was tracking down Mister Manson, he was getting you and your brother to someplace safe, away from the attacked train. Right?"

She nods. I go on, "That's why you didn't want to leave the next morning. You knew he was coming back to the rescue, along with the Quick Reaction Force."

"Randy, we're running out of time, and—"

"Yeah. And we're supposed to meet up with your arrested Dad. He's probably being kept at a stockade, up north of the Capitol, at the Watervliet Arsenal."

She opens her mouth, closes it, and then opens it again. "How did you know that?"

"Because my dad's been arrested as well. Another coincidence, eh? Both of our fathers arrested, both of them set to be transferred at the same time. My dad in Intelligence, your dad in Special Projects, up there at Jackson Labs."

I step forward, point my pistol for a moment at Buddy. There's an intake of breath from Serena. "Your brother's carrying a message. One for your dad, maybe one for my dad and Captain Diaz. It's something about a Creeper who's been interrogated up in Bangor, right? A Creeper that was captured by Captain Diaz and his guys. Special Forces are the only ones who have the guts and skills to do something like that."

Another reluctant nod from Serena. "What did they find out, Specialist? What's going on with the Creepers? Why the hell did they come here?"

"I don't know."

I go to the telephone on the nightstand, pick up the receiver, and she quickly says, "I don't know the details, Randy!"

The receiver goes back down on the phone. Serena says, "Your dad . . . he was part of the crew conducing the interrogation. Buddy recorded it, the way he does with his memory. The Creeper told him everything we've wanted to know for the past ten years: why they're here, why they're fighting us, and how we can end the war."

I recall what Captain Diaz had said. "War's not really over, is it."

"Why ask me?" she protests. "How should I know?"

I gesture with the pistol. "Then why not ask him?"

Exasperated, she says, "I can't! He'll only say what he heard during the interrogation if he hears a code phrase. My dad has the code phrase . . . and now he's in a stockade. Oh, Randy, what am I going to do?"

I go to my assault pack, quickly strip off my formal uniform, put on a set of BDU's, not caring if Serena's looking. When finished, I strap on my holster. My dad. In on this since the beginning. If he's involved, it has to be right. I'm not sure who to trust but I've always trusted Dad. I put the Beretta in my holster, take out my knife as well, strap it in place in my right boot.

"We three are getting out of here, now," I say.

Buddy is looking at the two of us, face impassive, and Serena goes around to the other side of the bed, picks up another familiar object.

"This . . . the dispatch case? What should we do with it?"

"Let's take a look, why don't we."

"You mean . . . break it open?"

"Why the hell not?" I ask. "I've had plenty of experience back in the Boy Scouts, breaking into homes and locked cellars." From my assault pack I take out the awl and screwdriver from the diner, and go to work. In a few seconds the plastic security strap is broken, and after that, so goes the lock.

Serena stands closer as I open up the case, me thinking about Mister Manson and how he had died so grotesquely to see it get delivered. Inside the case is a yellow cardboard folder. I take the folder out and it holds a sheet of thick creamy white paper, with the seal of the Governor of the State of New Hampshire at the top. Below is a handwritten message. I read it aloud.

"*'Tess. After our last phone conversation, it seemed the signal faded in and out at a convenient time for you. So I'm trusting my most valued aide to bring the message to your personal attention, so there is no misunderstanding.'*"

I pause, see Serena staring intently at me. I read more aloud. "*So let me make this is as clear as possible. If you want my support and that of my political organization for your boss in the first in the nation primary, I want out. Get it? I've been to the Capitol. I'm an old man. I'm tired of living here in Concord with little power, oil lamps, and crappy food. Get me in the Administration as a cabinet secretary, a special assistant, or czar. I don't care. Get me to the Capitol and I'll give your boss my state when the ballots come. My aide will wait for your answer, but don't wait long. Jack.*'"

Serena says, bitterness in her voice, "Nice to see our political leaders putting the people first."

I replace the paper in the folder, put it into the dispatch case. "Yeah. What a surprise."

I pick up my assault pack and gesture to her brother. "Well, now we know why the train was attacked. It was your brother. *He* was the courier with the vital message. Not one political hack bringing a demand to another political hack. Buddy was the one that was going to get killed, from an apparent Creeper. Nice set-up. Who would question that? Which explains something else. Tess Conroy interrogated me a while ago. Most of her questions were about you and your brother. Not the dispatch case."

Serena's shocked. "But . . . but why? In God's name, why? What Buddy has—"

I interrupt. "What Buddy has is something to screw up the official story, that by destroying the orbital battle station, the war was won. Maybe the Creepers don't agree. Maybe there's another damn stealth battle station up. I don't know. But with the official story being the war's been won by this President and his Administration, it clears the way for a third term for these folks. Maybe power is more important than a clear victory."

"Randy . . ."

"No more," I say. "Captain Diaz told me the Creepers might attack the Capitol tonight. We've got to go. *Now!*"

I open the door, look both ways. Corridor is empty.

I turn back and Serena is there, holding Buddy's hand. Buddy looks as blank as ever. Serena's face is pale.

Time to go.

We're halfway down the back set of stairs when we hear sirens coming from outside.

We blunder through some rear corridors, past maids and hotel workers who are bustling around. We go through a large kitchen and the smells of the cooking food almost compel me to stop and grab something, but I keep on moving. I'm scanning, looking, thinking, and there's a rise in conversation by the hotel's employees as we pass through.

". . . maybe it's just a Civil Defense drill . . ."

". . . my brother sent a courier over, told me to get the hell out of the Capitol . . ."

". . . but it's been safe here for years, why now? Oh God . . ."

There's a short hallway up ahead, crates piled up on either side. The door there leads to the outside and a rear parking lot, and from there—

From behind the boxes, a pissed-off Riley emerges, steps forward, and punches me hard in the chest.

I fall back against some crates, choking, coughing, trying to breathe, trying to catch my breath, failing at everything, my legs spread out, my back hurting where a piece of broken wood is pressing against my spine. Riley strolls up, kicks me in the ribs, and I cry out, roll to my side, eyes closed, everything hurting and burning and throbbing. I can't see Riley, but I hear him speak.

"Stupid boy," he says. "Like I told you, once I was in the Afghan mountains, chasing and killing Pashtun tribesmen whose ancestors had fought off the Russians, the British, and the armies of Alexander the friggin' Great himself. And you think you'd be able to get away?"

That earns me another swift kick in the ribs, but I hurt so much I can't say anything else. His hands are on me, stripping my pistol away and my boot knife. "Don't care how many medals you got or how many ribbons . . . you're just a damn boy, pretending to do a real man's job."

I snap out with my right hand, with luck hitting his face, and he only laughs. "Once went hand-to-hand with two Taliban on a mountain trail. Their bones are still bleaching in the sun, and you think you can hurt me?"

I hear him get up and I roll over on my back, and he's standing over me, grinning, holding my weapons in his hands. "So now I'm taking your girlfriend and her retarded brother to where they belong."

I kick out and get him in the left shin, and even with the fog of pain and the tightness in my chest, I'm happy to see him bounce back, pulling up his left leg. A flash of pain across his face and he ignores me, stepping past. I turn my head and Serena is there, on her knees, going through my assault pack, probably looking for a weapon, and her brother Buddy is standing with his back against the hallway.

"Come on, princess," Riley says, grabbing her shoulder. "Time to go meet your betters."

Serena tries to pull away and he grabs her again, harder, and pulls her up to her feet. My ribs ache, my chest is still so tight I can hardly breathe, and I pull myself up on my hands and knees, and then push off and throw myself against Riley's legs. I grab them and bite his rear thigh, and he curses and spins around, slamming a fist against my head, pain shooting out from my neck and shoulders. I'm back on the floor and Riley says, "Shit, kid, stay down or I'll slit your damn throat."

I hurt all over. The sharp tang of defeat is in my mouth. My dad worked with Serena's dad to get Buddy somewhere important, to stop a war that had killed so many, and I was failing the mission. I was failing my dad. I was failing . . .

Serena screams. Riley curses again, "This way, little girl, get your retarded brother lined up or—"

Another scream. A thud. Another thud.

I open my eyes. Serena is sitting down with her back up against the wall. Riley is on the floor, on his face.

Buddy is standing over him, holding a bright red fire extinguisher in his hands.

Serena's brother then leans down and smacks Riley once more time against his head.

His sister says, "Enough, Buddy. Enough."

The fire extinguisher slips from his hands, clangs on the floor, bottom stained with blood and hair.

Sirens outside are sounding louder and I slowly get up, weaving, my breathing easing up. Serena comes to me, holding out my Beretta and knife. I replace them, woozy, a wave of nausea rolling through. "Your brother is full of surprises."

She says, "He's not retarded. He's very, very smart. And loyal."

"He sure is."

I try to pick up my assault pack and it falls out of my hand. Serena grabs it and says, "I'll help you out but you're right, we've got to get moving."

She takes her brother's hand with her free hand, and we go down the hallway, pop open the exit door and we're outside, in the rear lot of the hotel. The sirens are sharp in the night air and in the overcast sky, I see flares from other parts of the city rising up and disappearing into the clouds, brightening them briefly with flashes of orange, red and yellow.

The lot is nearly empty, save for abandoned cars that have been pushed to one side. Serena bumps into me, dropping my pack. "Oh, God, Randy . . ."

"The Capitol's prepping for an attack," I say. "It's going to be hell out there on the streets."

Serena says, "Randy, what are we—"

I grab my assault pack. "Let's roll," I say. "Follow me."

The door behinds us slams open a couple of more times, as male and female employees of the hotel race out. I move quickly out from behind the hotel, looking around, trying to think things through, recalling my training: adapt, adjust, overcome. Nice words to use out in the field when you're tracking a Creeper, but here, in an urban environment? Not many options. Not many avenues of escape. Plenty of places to hide, but we weren't going to hide. Somehow we were going to get the hell out.

What to do?

Around the corner, we come to a street. A crowded two-horse carriage rattles by. Another set of sirens starts howling. More flares sputter up into the air, sending messages to Civil Defense cadres and Army or Marine detachments out there, prepping for an attack. From all of my training and experiences, I should be linking up with an Army or National Guard unit to do my part, but not this time. Outside forces are at work, are plotting, are making life and death decisions for the country and the whole damn planet, and this quiet boy and his beautiful sister are key to whatever those decisions are going to be.

To stop all this fighting and dying and burning.

A Chevrolet Impala is roaring down the street, one headlight burnt out, and I say, "Hold on, Serena. Keep Buddy still."

I step out into the street, Serena yelling at me, and I pull out my Beretta and draw down on the speeding car, quickly firing two shots. The Chevy screeches to a halt, slewing sideways, and I get to the driver's door, yank it open. A man in a dark tan suit and wearing thick black-rimmed glasses looks up at me and screams, "What the hell do you think you're doing?"

"Requisitioning your vehicle," I say.

The man says, "I know my rights! You can't steal my car without a writ or warrant!"

I push my pistol against his cheek. "My writ is signed by Mister Beretta. Good enough for you?"

"Damn Army," he says, swearing at me, and he gets out and says, "I hear the damn bugs are attacking. You know what you're doing? You're gonna kill me by stealing my car."

"Then get in the back and shut your mouth," I say. "I won't leave you behind."

"What? So you can drive me into a damn ambush?"

Serena says something and like a fool, I turn. Out of the corner of my eye I see the driver grab something from his coat pocket. I whirl back and he has a small automatic pistol in his hand, coming up to me, and I slam my Beretta down on his hand. He shouts and grabs his hand, and I kick his pistol under the car.

I lower my Beretta, push the muzzle against his chest. "You had a chance. You've lost it. Get running or I'll drop you right here."

He starts crying. "Damn Army . . . you're gonna get me burned . . . damn Army . . ."

He sobs more and turns and runs, his gait awkward and clumsy. Serena says, "Randy, you should go after him. Make him come with us. After all, we're stealing his car and—"

"Specialist, shut up," I say. "I gave him a chance. He didn't take it. Get in the front. Get your brother and my assault pack in the rear. Move!"

She pulls the driver's seat forward and gently propels Buddy into the rear, followed by my assault pack. I get in the front and she races around, opens the passenger's side door, and climbs in as well. The interior smells of old smoke and wet leather and dirt. There's a loud sound of something hitting the pavement over and over again and a brown and white horse races by, its eyes wide in fear, the empty saddle bouncing on its back, stirrups flying.

I run my hands over the steering wheel. I feel the hot breath of danger on my neck. The engine is idling. The keys are still in the ignition. There's a shift stick on the column. I look under the steering wheel. Three pedals are lined up on the floor.

Serena says, "For God's sake, what are you waiting for?"

"Trying to remember how to drive this damn thing," I shoot back. "Do you know how to drive?"

"How in hell would I know how to drive? Don't you?"

"Had a lesson or two last year, and that's it."

Another flare launches up into the air, followed by another.

I take a breath. Think, think, think. That lesson had been given by a master sergeant who was an expert mechanic in the motor pool, and who insisted that everybody should know the ins and outs of driving. Knowing that driver's licenses were awarded each year by lottery once you turned sixteen, I didn't think I'd ever find myself in this position, sitting behind a steering wheel.

"Well?" Serena demands.

"It's got three pedals," I say desperately. "That means it's a standard, not an automatic."

"What's the difference?"

"Automatic is a hell of a lot easier," I say. "Just shift and press the accelerator and go. But most of the cars and trucks that survived the 10/10 attacks were standards. A lot more confusing."

She turns and looks out the rear window. "Randy . . . looks like there are people out there. Breaking into a couple of stores."

"So?"

"So stop lecturing and get driving!"

I grab the shift handle, try to move it. Something starts grinding.

"Randy!"

The pedals. Think. One to the right, the skinny one, that's the accelerator. Makes you go. One in the middle is the brake. Makes you stop. And the one in the left . . . helps you change gear, that's the one, that's . . .

"Hey!" A fist is pounding on the glass. "Get out of the car! We want it!"

I just see a clenched fist and thick wrist. I shove the clutch down with my left foot, work the shift lever, push the accelerator, and—

We're off!

"Damn," Serena whispers.

The speed goes up until there's a high-pitched whining, the engine laboring, and Serena says something and a rock or brick bounces off the car roof, and a bit of memory comes back to me, and I shove the clutch in again. The engine whines. I move the lever. A grinding noise. I push the clutch in harder, shift, hit the accelerator and now we're moving right along.

I turn to smile at Serena. "All comes back, Specialist."

"So glad to hear it," she mutters, still looking out the rear.

We're driving along now and I manage to work out how to shift the gears, using the brake, clutch and accelerator, and it's an incredible sensation, having the power of the Chevrolet under my control. The roads are filled with people moving, people running, people on bicycles, a few other pre-war cars and trucks sputtering along, and a number of horse-drawn wagons. A couple of steam-powered Army trucks roar by as well, going to whatever rally point they were assigned to. I check the street signs as we speed along and after a few minutes, Serena says, "What's the plan?"

"To get the hell out of the Capitol," I say. "Then find a safe place for you and your brother."

"How are we going to do that?"

"One thing at a time, Specialist," I say. "Need to get out of town first."

She stays quiet for two blocks, and says, "Aren't we deserters, then?"

"No."

"Randy, please—"

"My uncle's in on it, isn't he."

Another pause. I'm sure the almighty God of OPSEC is fighting to keep her mouth shut, but she gives in and says, "From the start."

"Thought so," I say. "That's why I was assigned to protect you. Not Mister Manson. You."

"That's right," she says. "But that was back then."

"No worries," I say. "I got a note from him a while ago, telling me to keep on with the mission."

"Really? He really said that?"

I swerve sharply to avoid a roadblock of tree limbs that's being built at an intersection by some young boys and girls. A couple more rocks are thrown at us as we speed by. "In a manner of speaking," I say. "The note said I was his 'dear nephew,' and that my dad was his 'dear brother-in-law.' I know my uncle. He doesn't believe that for a moment. But he told me in the note to fulfill my duty. Not my duty to deliver the package to Tess Conroy. My duty to protect and escort you. And that's what I'm going to do."

We drive on for a while longer, passing two more Army trucks and three Humvees, one flying a Marine Corps flag. Serena says, "You've passed a couple of interstate exits that would have gotten us out of the Capitol."

"Good eye," I say.

"So why didn't you take those exists? We could be miles away by now!

"I have something important to do," I say.

"Important?" She swivels in her seat and nearly shouts, "My brother has the key to maybe ending this war, getting us all peace and stop the burning and dying . . . what could be more important than that?"

Her words stab at me. I know she's right. I should be focusing on the mission, focusing on getting Buddy Coulson and his sister out to safety. That's my mission.

I speed up some more.

But there's one other thing that must be done.

The tires make a high-pitched screeching sound as I brake and go into a bumpy parking lot. The sound is just like you hear in those old black-and-white Bogart movies. A small wooden sign flashes by as we approach the building: HERO KENNELS.

Serena's voice is even sharper. "Your damn dog? You're dragging your feet getting us out of the Capitol to save your damn dog?"

I brake again, the car coming to a halt. "I am."

"Hell, a few minutes ago you stole this car from some guy that might be killed later because of you. Now you're putting us at risk to drive to a damn kennel. Randy, he's just a dog!"

I put the transmission into park, switch off the engine. "No, he's my partner. My best friend. I can't leave him behind. It's only right."

I grab the keys from the ignition and as I open the door, Serena calls out, "Why did you take the keys? I don't know how to drive."

I duck my head back into the opening. "Just following your suggestions, Specialist. Trust no one."

She makes to snap back at me, but my slamming the door cuts off her voice.

The door is wooden, with a number of glass panes. It's locked. A sign nearby says RING BELL AFTER HOURS. I ring the bell, again and again.

The door is still locked.

I turn, see Serena and Buddy still in the Impala. In the distance, more sputtering flares rise up into the clouds, marking assembly areas and displaying orders to reserve units and Civil Defense forces. Sirens are still sounding.

Back to the door, I hammer at it with my fist, again and again.

No answer.

Feeling the eyes of Serena upon me, I take out my Beretta, hold it by the barrel, rap the base against the nearest glass pane. It shatters with a satisfying crack, and I carefully snake my hand and wrist in, making sure not to cut anything on the broken shards.

There. Got the deadbolt in hand. Unsnap it, slowly draw my hand out, and I turn the knob.

Open!

Serena's voice behind me, from an open window: "Move your butt, Randy! We don't have time!"

I bite my tongue, thinking of lots of things to say to Serena, none of them polite, and the door swings open.

There.

I walk in, and go face to face with the business end of a double-barreled shotgun.

An Excerpt From the Journal of Randall Knox

Open House at the post yesterday, inviting in our Concord neighbors. Way to still try to smooth things over since the National Guard took over the prep school after 10/10. All visitors got a boxed ration kit, which I hear strained our supply chain but which my uncle thought was a good deal, to help relations.

Out on one of the playing fields, I was roped into doing demonstrations with Thor. Sent him out on various commands, and he did good, as always, with me slipping him dried pieces of venison when he was finished. Little crowd of families and kids watched me, lots of applause and laughs as Thor did his job.

Later I asked for volunteers, three brave boys. A bulky trio came up, jeans, torn sweatshirts, ragged boots, maybe in their early 20s. I have Thor stay behind and then I lead them out mid-field, and tell them what to expect. I give 'em each a Baby Ruth bar and they seemed okay with that, and the guy on the right, I slip him a fresh chunk of Creeper exoskeleton, from a successful bug hunt up by Tilton last week that the First Platoon completed.

Back with the crowd, I patted Thor on the back, yelled out: Thor, test! Thor streaked across the field, teeth bared, growling, and nailed the guy on the right in his chest, dropped him to the ground. I yelled Off! and more laughter and applause as Thor broke away, grinning, trotting like he was the best in the world. The guy that got knocked down took it pretty good, and I gave him another Baby Ruth bar and pocketed the exoskeleton piece, knowing it has to go back later to our Intelligence section.

By then, kids and moms and dads were around Thor, scratching his ears, rubbing his back, and my boy was loving the attention. A little girl with red hair, pigtails, said to me, he's a brave dog, isn't he? And I said, the bravest. Can I kiss him? she asked. Sure, I said, and she smacked one right on Thor's lips and whispered loudly, Thor, I love you.

Crowd laughed at that. Somebody with a camera even took a picture, and another picture after Thor licked the girl's cheek, making her scrunch up her face. I looked at the smiles and the little girl, and I went up to the photographer, slipped him two more Baby Ruth bars, asked him if he'd get me a photograph of my dog. Guy said, sure, as a souvenir?

Thor gazed up at me, tail wagging. I think about the other K-9 units in our company, in other units here and across the region. About how so many, desperate to defend their partners, have gone one-on-one against the Creepers and have been burnt to cinders. In the years I've worked with my boy, I know how he rolls. I know what his end will be, either next mission, or the mission after that. Before 10/10, most dogs died peacefully at a vet office, in the arms of their loving families.

That's not going to be Thor's fate.

My voice choked, I scratched my boy's ears and told the photographer, yeah, a souvenir. Something to remember him by.

Forever.

CHAPTER THIRTY-THREE

I stop moving.

A woman is holding the shotgun, pointed right at my face. She's old, thin, wearing light blue surgical scrubs.

She says, "Turn back now or I'll blow your damn head off."

I say, "Not so fast. I'm here to get my dog."

The shotgun stays straight, and then lowers. "I remember you. You're that Recon Ranger from New Hampshire. The one that took on that damn Creeper with a knife."

A tightness in my chest eases. "That's right. I was here a couple of days ago, checking up on my dog. Thor."

The shotgun lowers some more. "A hell of a way to make an entrance."

"Nobody was answering the bell."

"We're kinda busy out back. Didn't bother to answer. Then one of my girls told me somebody was breaking into the front door. That's when I came out. Some times, Coasties and other troublemakers, they break in, try to steal what drugs we might have."

I say, "Sorry about the door, but please, I don't have much time. I want to get my dog, Thor. He's a Belgian Malinois."

She says, "He's still pretty dinged up."

I step in. "I don't care. Lady, look, in case you haven't heard what's going on out there, the Capitol is about to be attacked. That's why I'm here. And you should get the hell out of here as soon as you can."

She turns her head away, slings the shotgun under her arm. "Can't talk about that right now. You want to get your dog? Guess that's best for him."

Then her voice is hopeful. "Do you have room for others?"

I shake my head. "'fraid not."

She shrugs with disappointment. "Then come with me."

The veterinarian leads me around a waist-high counter, to a door that leads out back to the kennels. The sounds of dogs barking and whining hits me solidly, like a clenched fist, as I go into a large room, lined on each side by cages. Injured dogs are back there, barking, leaping, others just looking up in trembling fear. There's German Shepherds, Belgian Malinoises like my Thor, and a mix of others, like Labrador Retrievers and English Springer Spaniels.

My heart clenches tight as I look closely at the dogs. All of them are hurt. Most have fur burned away, some have casts on their legs, and a fair number are either two-legged or three-legged, their stumps bandaged. A couple that whine the most seem blind.

I follow the woman to the end of the cages where Thor, my sweet Thor, spots me and starts barking, his sharp voice cutting through the din. There are other people back here, three girls, even younger than Serena, and they move quickly around, even though their faces are pinched with fear. All are carrying trays that have syringes and lengths of rubber tubing on them.

The woman grabs a leash, tosses it to me and above the din of the dogs, she says, "He's yours, but he should really get a follow-up appointment at some other . . . clinic. That cast should be taken off in another week, there's sutures to remove, and some follow-up exams . . . but I guess I can trust you . . . But tell you what. When you get out of here, don't take Interstate 60. Take a right just before the highway exit. That'll place you on Townsend Road. Runs parallel, goes up in the hills, but it should be safer."

I say to her, leash in hand, "Cripes, lady, you need to get out of here, too. The Creepers might start burning in any second."

She shakes her head. "I told you my story before, right? About what I did after the first attack, back near the Hudson River? What makes you think I'm going to leave these poor guys behind?"

At a counter at the far end of the room, the young girls are carefully removing the syringes and rubber tubing from their trays and placing them in a long row. One girl's hands are shaking so hard that she drops a syringe. The vet sees that I'm looking and she says, "We're just getting ready," she says. "We're gonna stay here and do our duty, Sergeant. Maybe the Creepers will pass us by. Maybe not. But if they're in sight and there's nobody around to stop them, then I'll make sure these dogs don't suffer no more. That's my job."

I can't talk, I can hardly see. I don't want to be here. Thor is still barking in delight and I open the cage, get the leash on him, and I have a race with him to see who can get out of this killing zone the quickest.

Outside I slow Thor down, pick him up, and take him to the car. Serena gets out and pushes the seat back, and I gently lay him down on the rear seat. Buddy scoots over and Thor turns and licks his face. Buddy smiles. I slam the door and race around to the front, throw open the door. I fumble around for a few agonizing seconds and find the key, insert and turn it.

A harsh grinding noise.

Damn!

Serena says, "What the hell are you doing, Randy?"

"Apparently not a hell of a lot, specialist," I snap back. "And it's Sergeant."

I remember something and push down the clutch and brake, try again.

The grinding noise is replaced by the sound of the engine turning, turning, turning.

Not starting.

Explosions off to the south. Serena whimpers.

I try again, push down the accelerator, my feet clumsy and colliding together, and—

Success!

The engine roars into life.

I switch on the sole headlight, work the lever to get into reverse, and back out of the parking lot. The dim light from the Impala captures a figure at the open door to the kennels, lighting up a young girl, staring at us as we make our escape.

"That girl," Serena says, as I put the car into first and speed out of the parking lot. "It looks like she wanted to come with us."

"No time," I say. "No room."

"Ran—I mean, Sergeant," she says. "What went on inside there?"

I shift into second, then third, and say, "Specialist, you don't want to know."

The old woman's directions are perfect, and I take a right onto Townsend Road, passing some old abandoned businesses, and then a few homes and farmhouses. Serena says, "Why aren't we taking the highway?"

"This runs right next to the highway," I say. "Probably safer. You know how Creepers like to use the highway when it suits them. With the Army and National Guard gearing up, with Creepers on the move, we could get caught in the middle."

She keeps quiet and I glance up at the rearview mirror. Thor is panting with contentment, and I slide a free hand back, trying to rub his snout. He spots me and leans forward, and licks and licks my hand.

A good feeling.

After a few minutes the road starts to rise up, and I don't see any homes or farms about, just farmland. "Specialist, keep a sharp eye. Don't want to blunder into a Creeper column."

"Got it."

We drive along for a few more minutes, Serena moving her head around. Over the sound of the engine I can make out Thor panting with happiness at being back with me. I reach overhead to where there's a small roof light that comes on when the doors open up. I luck out, since there's a little switch, which I flip on to illuminate the inside. "Specialist, look in the . . . that small door there . . . the thing there. Glovebox. Yeah. See if there's a map."

She opens a lid and pushes some papers around, and comes out with a folded map that says EXXON on the cover. "It's old but it's for this part of the state," she says.

"Good," I reply. "We're going to need it."

Serena closes the lid. "Why do they call it a glovebox anyway?"

I try to think of a snappy answer when the engine coughs, dies.

"Damn!" I push down on the accelerator.

Nothing happens.

We coast to a stop, then start to roll back. I hit the brake, turn the wheel, and we back into a stone wall. A sharp, grinding noise, and we don't move again.

Serena says, "Oh, Randy . . ."

The dome light is still on. I glance down at the dashboard, trying to figure out what I'm seeing, and to the right, is a simple dial that has an E and an F. There's a red needle, and it's pegged against E. Hadn't noticed it before, which made sense, since this is the first time I've ever driven a car.

"Out of gas," I say desperately. "We're out of gas. C'mon, time to bail."

Outside a steady rain is starting to fall. I can still hear sirens off in the distance, and another flare climbs up into the sky. We're looking down at the lights of the Capitol, and block by block, the lights start going out, as Civil Defense starts cutting power to the buildings. A pathetic gesture, since Creepers can attack day or night, but I know the feeling: better to do something than to sit still and do nothing.

I go to the rear of the dented car, put the key in the trunk. Serena is next to me, and I say, "If we're lucky, the driver's smart enough to have some spare gas."

It takes a couple of hard turns, but the key opens the trunk. A little light comes on, illuminating a spare tire, jack, and a dull red gasoline jerrycan.

I easily pick up the can.

It's empty.

"Some luck," I say.

We get moving on the road, Serena carrying my assault pack, holding Buddy's hand, and after a few hesitant steps from my partner, I can't stand to see him limp and wince. I pick up Thor and hold him to my chest, and my sad little squad rises up the hill, the dead Impala behind us.

My back and head still ache from the thrashing I got earlier from Riley, and Thor seems to gain weight with each passing meter. My breathing gets ragged and tired, and twice I call a halt, so I can put Thor down on the ground and catch my breath. Each time I do so he licks my hand and I rub his head and say, "Good boy, you're being a very good boy."

Serena comes over the third time I call for a rest, and she drops my assault pack and says, "Randy, I'm beat. That pack is too damn heavy."

"Suck it up, Specialist," I say sharply back. "I've got my hands full here."

From somewhere she produces a tiny flashlight, which she switches on, lighting up the wet grass and my boy Thor. He's on his side, panting some, and Serena aims the beam on the bandages around his torso.

"Randy, he's bleeding. Look."

I don't want to see it but I have to. My fingers gently press against the bandages, and Thor whimpers. Serena says, "The walking . . . the carrying . . . you're opening up his wounds, Randy."

Tears well up in my eyes. "It'll be okay."

Serena says, "Sergeant, it's not going to be okay. He's hurting. You know it. You're making it worse. And we've got to get my brother to the right people."

Thor raises up his head, looks at me, and then lies back down again. The rain is drumming against my back and exposed neck. Serena says, "Sergeant . . . we haven't even gone a kilometer. At this pace, we'll both collapse within the hour. You know it."

I bite my lower lip and stand up, and say, "Specialist, what I—"

The world behinds us explodes.

I grab Serena and pull her down, and she takes her brother down next to her. The earth rumbles, shakes, quivers. I roll over on my back and a bright bulb of light and flames is rising up over the Capitol.

A flash of light, as a hard bright line screams down from the cloud cover, striking the Capitol.

Another half-dome of destruction rises up, up, and up.

The noise hits me like a cement block against my chest. A roaring, thundering blast of destruction, followed by a hot breeze.

Another hard line of light.

And another.

And another.

Serena clambers over to me, grabs my hand. "Oh my God . . . oh my God . . . oh my God . . ."

My voice is strangled. "The Creepers . . . they're using their killer stealth sats. They can still use their sats in a coordinated attack! The bastards . . ."

"But their orbital station . . ."

Another hard line of light, and another half-dome of light and flames and smoke rises up. "Destroyed. Sure. We thought the station had overall control of the sats. But they're aliens, Serena . . . what the hell do we know about them after ten years? Sweet Jesus . . ."

I find myself on my feet. Look down on the burning Capitol. Look over at Buddy Coulson, sitting there quietly. Serena is next to me. "Thousands . . ." she whispers. "Thousands must be dead down there. Oh God, Randy."

Thor is rustling at my feet. I can't bear to look down at him. She says, "Do you think the President got out?"

"Don't know," I say. "If he didn't . . . they can always find another one. Come on, we've got to keep moving. The killer sats might want to widen their fire, take out the suburbs."

I kneel down, slide my hands underneath Thor, and he barks a sharp, high-pitched cry. I slowly withdraw my hands, settle back on my haunches. Serena kneels down next to me, gently touches Thor's head. My throat is thick and it's hard to breathe. Softly she says, "Randy . . . Sergeant . . . you've got your job, your responsibility. Something bigger than all of us. My brother . . . he has the key maybe to end this war, to stop the dying and burning and the destruction. If my dad, if your dad . . . if they hadn't been arrested, Buddy and me, we would have hooked up with them. Then the message Buddy carries would have been released. Then maybe this attack on the Capitol . . . maybe it wouldn't have happened."

I choke out, "Lot of damn woulds and maybes in that little speech, Serena."

She says, "You know I'm right. You know Buddy is so very important. I'm so sorry about Thor. But he's slowing us down. We've got to get moving. You know it. There are no other choices. You have to do your duty, Sergeant. Your country . . . hell, maybe even the whole damn planet, is depending on you."

Thor's breathing steps up. My throat still thick, snot running down my nose, tears in my eyes. Duty. My dad, doing something secretive, something dangerous, that has him arrested. The doomed Marines on that train, fighting even though their weapons were useless, being cut down, but not running away. Colonel Minh, flying an untested rocketship, leading a suicide mission. The vet back at the clinic, staying with her canine patients, doing what was right.

Duty.

My dad. My dead mom. My dead sister. Not even a photograph left to remember them by.

"Sergeant," she says. "The lower part of the hillside . . . it's on fire. Look."

I turn and see she's right. Even with the wet weather, the lower part of the hill is burning brightly, the wind coming at us, driving the flames and smoke in our direction. In the distance the flames are even higher and brighter, as the Capitol burns and burns.

We're near a pine tree with overarching branches. I gently slide Thor over to the base of the tree, he whimpering some. I try not to think of our missions together, the play times, the training, and the most recent fights, against Creepers and renegade Coasties. He lives to make me happy, to protect me, to do his job and his duty.

Duty.

I turn to Serena. "Get my pack. Start up the road with your brother. I'll be along."

"Sergeant, I—"

"Just do it."

She moves back, grunts as she picks up my assault pack. She takes Buddy's hand and they start up the road. I stroke Thor's head. He sighs and licks my hand.

I reach down for my pistol.

A while later I catch up with them, take my pack away from Serena and as we reach another crest of the hill, the rain has stopped. For the past several minutes I've been saying one prayer after another, praying for a savior, praying for a miracle, praying for something. But the only thing I see is that the road has widened and there's a dirt turnoff to the left, with a picnic area. I go to the nearest picnic table, dump my assault pack on the table.

Serena looks to me and starts to talk, and I interrupt her. "Shut up. All right? Just shut up."

I slump down, put my head in my hands, say one more prayer, once again seeking a miracle.

But no miracle occurs.

There's a grumble of approaching engines. Headlights cut through the gloom. I recognize the shape of the vehicles. Humvees.

No miracles. But the next best thing.

Marines.

I say to Serena, "Do you have that flashlight handy, Specialist?"

She fumbles in her large black purse. "Here, Randy."

She passes it over and I switch it on, start waving it back and forth. I slowly walk out into the road and call out, "Army sergeant here, guys! Army sergeant!"

A larger flashlight beam catches me and the lead Humvee grumbles to a halt. It and its two mates are a rarity; diesel-powered craft that somehow either survived the 10/10 attack, or were successfully salvaged afterwards with spare parts. The first Humvee is also flying a large Marine flag on a pole at the rear; being the few and the proud, the Marines hate being misunderstood for Army or National Guard units, so they fly their red banner with the anchor and globe as much as possible.

Doors open up and Marines fan out, expertly setting up 360-degree security around the trucks, and I'm conscious that weapons from the lead vehicle are pointing at me, and they are certainly locked and loaded. A voice says, "Identify yourself."

"Sergeant Randy Knox, Second Ranger Recon, New Hampshire National Guard."

"And those two behind you?"

"Specialist Serena Coulson and her brother Robert. Detached duty from the Jackson Labs, up in Bangor, Maine."

A Marine steps up to me, and I note his name—SINCLAIR—and rank, lieutenant. His helmet is large on his head and he looks to be about eighteen or so, exhausted, with heavy eyes and a faint stubble of beard. Two other Marines flank him. "You three sure are the hell far away from home."

"We sure are, Lieutenant," I say quickly. "Sir, if I may, where are you going?"

"Troy," he says. "Rally point after what just happened at the

Capitol. But we're in a hurry, Sergeant Knox, so if you excuse us, we—"

"Sir, we're in the middle of an emergency," I say. "Could I talk to you for a second?"

He offers a bitter laugh, waves an arm at the fires on the horizon. "Hell, buddy, look over there! Whole damn place is one big emergency, and we're hauling ass to get away from this one, so move it and—"

Another Marine steps to him. "Sir, I know this guy."

Sinclair turns, surprised. "Chang, you sure?"

"Not personally, but yeah, he's the guy who knifed that Creeper a few weeks ago. Remember?"

The lieutenant looks back at me. "That true?"

"Yes, sir, yes it is," I say.

He takes a breath. "All right, I'll give you a minute, and only that."

I ask him a question and he says, "Impossible. No room."

I ask again, one more time, and the other Marine chimes in, "We can do it, Lieutenant. It'll be tight, but we can do it. Christ, the guy nailed a Creeper with a damn knife. That's gotta count for something."

My heart seems to stop as I look at Sinclair considering his options. My hands feel worthless, the flashlight pointing its beam to the ground. The fires seem to grow larger in the distance.

"You got one minute, Sergeant Knox. One minute and that is it."

I'm so relieved I feel like sitting on the ground. "Thank you, sir. Sixty seconds it is."

Back at the picnic table I open my pack and toss the contents onto the table, spreading out the spare food, clothing and other gear. I pass the flashlight back to her and say, "How about some paper and a pen?"

"Sure," she says. "But what's going on with the Marines?"

"You just hold on," I say. With paper and pen given over to me, I flatten out part of my assault pack and scribble a quick note, folding it in three pieces. On the outside I write a special name, and from the beam of her flashlight, Serena reads out the name and address. "'Corporal Abby Monroe, Ft. St. Paul., N.H.' What's this all about, Sergeant?"

I shove most of the gear back in the pack, slide the pack over to her. "Those Marines are going to Troy. You and your brother are going with them. They'll protect you and take you to a USO office. You and your brother . . . you get to that USO office, quick as you can, and stay there. Keep a damn low profile."

I point to the letter. "Somewhere along the way, mail that letter. It . . . it'll mean a lot to me."

Serena looks up at me, eyes wide. "You . . . what are you doing? Where are you going?"

I make a quick blanket roll of my remaining gear, toss it over my shoulder. "Off to get our dads."

"Randy!"

"Serena, you and Buddy can't come with me. I've got to move light and fast. One of those Marines recognized me right away, and I'm sure more people will do so the closer they get to Troy. I'm a Silver Star recipient but I'm also a wanted soldier. You and your brother are still fairly anonymous. You get to Troy, hang tight. Captain Diaz told me our dads are being held at an Army stockade up at Watervliet Arsenal. I'm going to get them out, and them I'm coming for you and your brother, with our dads in tow."

"Randy, that's impossible! You just said too many people know who you are!"

"Right," I say. "But there's also chaos out there, with the Capitol being attacked. You learn anything in military history, Serena? With chaos comes opportunity. By the time I get to the arsenal, maybe my Silver Star will open some doors. Maybe word won't have gotten there yet about me and Tess Conroy. But you and me . . . we're going to do what it takes to end this goddamn war. I'm off to Watervliet and I don't know how, but I'm going to get our dads sprung, and then we're going to hook up Troy."

A horn blares from the first Humvee. She looks to me and despite all that's gone on, there's something about that face, those eyes, those sweet lips. I hope Abby would understand. I lean over and kiss her, and she kisses me back. "Duty. We've all got our duties to perform. I've lightened up the assault pack, that'll make it easier for you. Now go."

She slings my pack over her shoulders, takes her brother by his hand, and starts walking to the Marine unit. She looks back just once and says in a mournful voice, "Duty, then."

"That's right," I say, and wave to her.

And as I pick up my blanket roll, I walk away from the grumbling

Humvees, off to take care of one more obligation before heading north to the Army arsenal.

My feet hurt, my back hurts, and my eyes are burning and watering from the approaching flames. I find my way back down to the road and to a certain pine tree, and there's my boy, my partner, my Thor.

I sit down next to his still form. I rub his fur. The tears are really rolling out.

The flames are so near that I can feel their warmth.

"You and me, pal," I say. "You had my back all these years, and now it's my turn."

Thor lifts his head, sighs once more, and settles down next to me.

I sit still and watch the alien fires burn and burn, and then take out my pistol again, and pull back the hammer.

CHAPTER THIRTY-FOUR

Thor looks up at me, love and trust in his eyes, and he turns his head away, like he's making it easier for me.

My boy.

I lower the pistol to the base of his skull, and pause.

I can't.

I can't.

I lower the hammer back, rub his fur, and Thor sighs again, squirms some against me. I take in the approaching fires and the trees and the branches, and—

Adapt. Adjust. Overcome.

Fool.

I slowly detach myself from Thor, holster my pistol, and get to work. From the light of the fires it's easy to get what I need, which are lengths of narrow pine tree trunks or branches, whatever works. I manage to get two three-meter lengths and with my knife, manage to hack off the branches. I drag the poles back to Thor, who watches me with drugged interest as I remove a coat from my pack, thrust the poles through the coat's sleeves, and with a bit more work and tying together, I've made a travois, used by the Plains Indians to haul gear and people across their lands.

I'm hoping I've done a good enough job to transport a wounded dog. I pick him up and he whines some, and I rub his head. "Yeah, pal, I know it hurts. Just hold on."

I made a harness out of a spare belt and necktie, and with my thick blanket roll next to Thor, I pick up the travois, and start walking, going up the road. I have no firm destination in mind. I know I need to get to the Watervliet Arsenal, but Thor is also my responsibility. No one is ever left behind on the battlefield, and that especially includes our K-9s. The smoke gets thicker and embers fly through the air, like fireflies seeking some dry place to land and set fires.

I move steadily and slowly, the fires of the current capitol city for the United States of America burning fiercely behind me.

Thirty, maybe forty-five minutes later, there's a low grumbling of an engine coming up the road. I drag Thor and my gear to the side of the road, hoping it's another Humvee or military truck, something I can use to get the hell out of here, to get my mission back on track, find a place where I can safely leave Thor.

I see a single light. It comes closer. Reveals itself to be a sole headlight, attached to a dirty green and yellow John Deere tractor. It's hauling an open wagon, with high wheels, and two lanterns hanging from either side of the wagon's sides. The tractor slows and I stand there, note the wagon is loaded with people.

A woman's voice from the tractor's high seat: "Need a ride, soldier?"

I cough. Smoke is getting thicker. "Only if my dog can come along."

"Shit, yes," she says. "You think I'm gonna leave a fine looking boy like that behind? Jack, get off and give 'em a hand, and be quick about it. Not sure how much more fuel I got here."

I drag Thor over to the rear of the wagon, and a boy about my age comes over, in torn khaki pants and faded blue sweatshirt. He helps me lift up Thor to the wagon, where we lay him down on a bed of straw. I disassemble the travois, retrieve my jacket, belt, necktie and everything else, and I climb up into the wagon. Faces look up at me. Old men and women. Young boys and girls. Some with plastic bags of belongings or suitcases. A couple of the younger ones quietly bawling, being held by a friend or relative. It's crowded but I have enough room to sit at the rear, legs dangling free. Strangely enough, there's no talking, no whispering. Just the quiet realization among these fellow Americans that once again, they were refugees.

A burp and a belch from the tractor, and we start moving.

Some time later the tractor is going through wide pastureland, with farms out beyond the road, past barbed wire fences and posts. Some motorized traffic is humming along the road, most coming from the direction of Albany. We turn gently down a dirt lane, leading to a farmhouse and several outbuildings, the tractor and wagon bouncing such that the lights flicker and make long, odd shadows. All through the trip Thor is on his good side, awake but not moving, not making a fuss. I keep a hand on him all the way to the farm, stroking his back in long, soothing strokes.

When the tractor shudders to a halt, other people come from the barn, holding lanterns. A light drizzle starts to come down. I jump off the wagon and turn around, and help other people off, handing small boys and girls to their relatives or guardians. A farmhand with a straw hat and patched overalls says, "Get to the barn, folks. Get to the barn. There's water and some apples in there."

The driver of the tractor is helped off. She's a heavyset woman, also wearing overalls, but one leg is pinned up to the knee. From the lanterns she comes into focus as she limps over to me, leaning in on two metal canes. I'm standing by Thor and she says, "Oh, your poor puppy. What happened?"

"Creeper attack a few days ago," I say. "He was being treated at the Hero Kennels outside of the Capitol, but I got him out before the attack."

She brings a hand to Thor's muzzle, and he gives her a sniff and puts his head down. "Not sure how many people got out, but we did what we could," she says.

"Did you get orders from Civil Defense to go in there after the strikes?"

A brief laugh. "Oh, hell no," she says. "I saw there was trouble, and we went to help. What else could I do? That's what we Americans do, right? Head for trouble without waitin' for orders."

She turns and I realize she's wearing a BDU jacket with name WHITTUM and captain's bars on the collars. I say, "Oh, excuse me, Captain. I didn't see your rank."

She laughs again, leans in on her canes. "No worry—" and she peers closer to me "—Sergeant Knox, I've been on the inactive reserve list since losing a leg and getting some of my innards rearranged. I wanted to re-up, but the all-knowing command thought it'd be best for me to get back to farming, so that's where me and my boys are. But that doesn't mean we sit on our behinds when there's a Creeper attack."

Thor squirms some, probably trying to get a comfortable spot. I say, "Ma'am, I need to get to the Watervliet Arsenal as soon as I can. It's near here, isn't it?"

"Just a handful of klicks," she says. "Your rally point?"

"You could say that."

She looks to Thor. "And what about your boy?"

I stand, frozen. I had rescued him from the kennels, had come close to snuffing him out over an hour ago, and now he was here, wounded and alive. But what I had to do . . . my dad and Serena's dad. Somehow get them out. See what can be done with Serena and Buddy and his all-important message. Exhaustion and fear both settle into me, and before I can say anything else, the former captain says, "If you want, you can leave him here."

"Really?"

"Sure," she says, this time gently stroking Thor's head. "I love dogs. The company I was in . . . we had two K-9 units assigned to us, and they must have saved our collective asses a half-dozen times by alerting us that Creepers were on the move. You can trust me, Sergeant. We'll take good care of him . . . until you come back. A day, a week, a month. It don't matter."

I flashed back to the swamp after the Creeper battle, where I had threatened those two men with death if they didn't take care of my boy. I had meant it back then, boy, had I meant it. But looking at the calm eyes of the woman before me, I know that no threats are necessary.

"I owe you a lot," I say.

She shakes her head. "No, no you don't. Just think of me paying back a big-ass debt."

"Thank you."

"Fair enough," she says. "Now, let's get you to your rally point."

"Just a sec," I say. I go to my boy Thor, rub his head, let him lick my face, and a few minutes pass this way, as I whisper to him. "My boy," I say finally. "Be good. Always be good."

The woman's name is Andrea Whittum, and she assigns her other son Billy to bring me to the arsenal. It's only an hour or so before dawn, and I want to get there when it's still dark, for one can always do more when things can't be easily seen.

Billy is about my age, dressed in filthy jeans and a leather jacket. He rolls out an old Italian Vespa scooter, painted yellow, and I sit on a little square leather saddle as we roar away from the farm. My blanket roll is on my lap, pistol holstered at my waist, and Billy has a shotgun in a sling at his side.

I close my eyes as we go out on the road, and Billy opens the throttle wide. Not as much traffic as before, and on the southwestern horizon is the orange glow of Albany burning. The passing wind and the high-pitched whine of the Vespa's motor makes conversation impossible, which is fine, because I'm running through plans and options as we get closer to the arsenal, located near the western banks of the Hudson River.

The farmland gives way to more houses and suburbia, and buildings within the town of Watervliet, and we're on a side street off the main drag of 10th Street, when Billy brings the Vespa to a halt. Traffic is heavy with deuce-and-half trucks, Humvees, and horse-drawn wagons. National Guardsmen and regular Army personnel trot by us, heading to the arsenal. Some civilians stand on their scraggly lawns, watching the activity. He pulls his goggles up from his face, skin reddened from the drive.

"'Bout as close as I can get," he says. "Don't want to get any closer, in case some smart-ass Army guy wants to seize my scooter for the good of the nation. Assholes."

I swing off the rear of the Vespa, and Billy adds, "No offense."

"None taken." I grab my blanket roll and Billy says, "Go down one block, take a left, there's the main gate. Can't miss it."

I offer him my hand, and he gives me a quick shake back. "Thanks again, and tell your mom the same."

Billy pulls his goggles down. "Glad we could help. You be careful, all right?"

I say nothing as I start walking. Don't make promises you can't keep.

I join in the lines of the other soldiers, reporting to the Watervliet Arsenal. I follow Billy's directions and the gate is up ahead, on the left. It's old, with dark gray stone, with a road leading in and a road leading out, with an enclosed stone and glass gatehouse in the center. Black wrought iron fence stretches on both sides. I get closer and it's—

Chaos. Just like I had hoped. Vehicles are trying to get out, MPs are trying to direct traffic, and uniformed men and women are streaming in. The arsenal has been building artillery pieces here for about two hundred and fifty years, and it's still doing so today. There's also rumors of research laboratories located on the campus, looking for easier and better ways to kill Creepers, but I don't care. I just want to get in.

Which I do, running alongside a couple of other troopers, flashing my military ID at a young and overworked female MP corporal with a flickering flashlight, and I'm on base.

I keep on trotting, pretending I know where I'm going. The roads are in pretty good shape, and from gas lanterns and other lights, I make out brick buildings that look to be centuries old, with newer buildings built right alongside. There are also little parks and displays of some of the howitzer and artillery pieces that they've built over the years.

Overhead is netting and camouflage. It's still a puzzle why this arsenal and several other military facilities across the country were never hit during the opening days of the war, and I was taught back at Ft. St. Paul that it was probably due to the relatively primitive nature of the work being done here.

Primitive or not, there's a lot of traffic on the move, and I feel itchy on my back and hands, like I'm entering one giant bulls-eye.

Up ahead at an intersection, another MP corporal—this one a boy about twelve or thirteen—takes a quick break from directing traffic. There's a gas lantern at his feet and I trot up to him and say, "Corporal! Where's the base stockade located?"

His helmet's too big and his eyes are wide with terror, but he gives me a snappy salute and points up the road. "Two blocks this way, Sergeant, and it's on your right. Small brick building, sign out front."

"Thank you, Corporal."

I turn and stop trotting. I start running instead.

Sirens are beginning to sound.

Exactly two blocks later, past large administrative and workshop facilities, I come across the stockade, just as described. It's a small, two-story old brick building that looks like one of the original structures from when the arsenal was founded, and the windows are barred. It's a simple flagstone path up to the front door, and there are lights inside. I drop my blanket roll, advance and open the door.

A lobby area, with scuffed tile floor, some plastic chairs. There's a small office area with metal desks, some flickering gas lights, and a woman corporal, about thirty or so. She's sitting by herself, hands folded, eyes darting back and forth, back and forth, looking down at some papers. Her uniform is neat and clean, but a couple of sizes too big. Her red hair is cut short. Off to the rear of the office is a door made of metal bars.

"Corporal."

No reply.

"Corporal!"

She looks up, startled. "Oh. Sergeant. Sorry. Didn't hear you come in."

I take a deep breath, start out with my rehearsed story. "Corporal, I've been tasked by the Chaplain's Office to do a personnel inventory of the prisoners here before any transfer."

"A personnel inventory?" she asks. "What for?"

"To make sure the Chaplain's Office records match who's actually being kept here."

"I don't have—"

I make a point of checking my watch. "Corporal, the Creepers have just burnt Albany. This base may be next on the target list. I've got a butt-load lot more important things to do, so you better give me the sixty seconds I need to check on your prisoner population, or there'll be hell to pay."

She opens a desk drawer, comes out with a thick key, attached to a block of wood. "Sergeant, no offense . . . go back there and knock yourself out. We had exactly two prisoners earlier today, a couple of old guys, and they're gone."

A hammer of ice hits me straight in the chest. "Gone . . . where the hell are they?"

"An MP transport picked them up about thirty minutes ago. Four MPs came in and took them out. Off to the train station at Schenectady. Heading west."

She tosses the key to me. "Go take a look . . . and don't be surprised if I'm not here when you come back. My relief was due two hours ago and I'll be damned if I'm gonna sit here and be zapped into charcoal."

I grab the key and go to the metal door, insert the key, give it a twist. Sirens are still sounding, and there's the sound of engines roaring by. The door opens up. I get into a tiled corridor. I start down the hallway, looking left, looking right. Severe looking cells, made of stone and stainless steel, with drains in the center, and their own gated doors, and steel toilets and washbasins.

And every one of the cells I pass is empty.

Empty!

"Damn it to hell," I whisper.

I turn and go back to the stockade's office.

It's now empty as well.

I'm all alone.

The sirens outside wail and wail.

CHAPTER THIRTY-FIVE

Outside of the stockade I stumble around, find a bench, sit down, my blanket roll on the ground, and I allow myself a good cry. The dark sky is lightening up and I don't care. For months I had kept alive the hope that my Dad was alive and well, and during those long months, I had reoccurring fantasies of what it would be like when we finally got back together. There would be laughs, hugs, handshakes, back slaps and a long night back at his quarters, talking and gossiping and catching up on our missing half year apart.

I pick up my belongings, start walking away from the stockade. Now I knew where he had been, where Serena's dad had been.

And I had missed them by thirty minutes . . . not even a damn hour!

The sirens have stopped their wailing. Part of me hopes that's a good sign and another part really doesn't care.

But the arsenal's roads still have traffic, from Humvees to horses, and I'm ignored as I walk, lost in what I have to do. Get safely out of here. Get to Troy, see if I can find Serena and Buddy at the USO. From there . . . ?

Work it through, one step at a time.

It's getting lighter. With all of this about me, I'm still thinking about Abbie, back at my home base. Poor wounded Thor, hopefully not thinking I've abandoned him. And the people I've met, from Colonel Minh to Captain Diaz to—

A cluster of Humvees up ahead, around a barracks or a

maintenance garage. Soldiers are gathered in small groups, talking and smoking, and they're not soldiers, no.

They're Marines. And one Humvee has a Marine flag, flying off a pole on the rear bumper.

I quicken my pace, go up to the nearest group, and ask for Lieutenant Sinclair. I'm directed to an area on the other side of the building, and there he is, bent over a picnic table, looking at some maps with two other lieutenants. I step forward and he spots me, smiles.

"Hey, it's the sergeant from New Hampshire," Lieutenant Sinclair says, genuine surprise in his voice. "How the hell did you get here?"

"Long story," I say. "Sir, if I may, have you already been to Troy and back?"

He shakes his tired head. "No can do, sergeant," he says. "The bridge over the Hudson is blocked with a massive pile-up, happened right after Albany got smacked. Goddamn civilians. We're tryin' here to figure out the best way to get up there."

"Your passengers . . . the specialist and her brother . . ."

A shrug. "Last time I saw, they were back there in the garage, taking a breather."

"Thank you, sir."

He goes back to the maps. I go into the garage. Humvees and other vehicles in various stages of repair are clustered closely around the floor. There's shouts and the whine and buzz of tools, overhead gaslights flicker, making strange shadows. I take my time and after a few minutes, I find them both: Serena and Buddy, sitting in a corner, all tucked in behind a large red tool box on casters, like they're trying to hide. Serena has her arm around Buddy and her face shows me that she's been crying. My pack is nearby.

She looks up and bursts into tears, and I put a finger to my lip. "Zip it, Specialist," I say. "We need to get out of here, but we need to do it quietly. Come on."

I extend a hand and she grabs it, as I help her up, and Buddy stands up as well, and maybe it's the flickering lights or my own exhaustion, but it seems like he's awarded me with a brief smile.

"I was so damn worried," she says, brushing her BDUs clean. "I wasn't sure when the Marines could get to Troy, didn't know if we'd be picked up by the MPs, but—"

"Enough," I say. "We need to get going."

She picks up my knapsack and says, "The only thing that went right is that I got your letter to that Abby posted."

"Thanks."

Serena shoulders my pack. "Our dads? Did you find them?"

"No," I say. "They've been transferred. I was about a half-hour late."

"Oh, Randy . . ."

I offer her a tired smile. "What? You think that's it? You think I'm giving up?"

She takes Buddy's hand. "I'm sorry, I don't understand."

"Our dads are being taken to the train station in Schenectady," I say. "You think they're going to get there and get on a train right away? Some express train to Leavenworth? Chances are, they'll have to wait, and while they're waiting, we're going to scoop them up."

We start out of the maintenance garage and Serena keeps pace with me. "Just like that? You think the MPs will give them up, just like that?"

"Why not?" I ask. "I can do anything I want. I've just gotten the Silver Star from the President of the United States."

Serena murmurs, "At least he did something useful before Albany got hit."

Outside of the garage the sky is graying out nicely. I go back to the squad of Marines, looking here and there, until I see the Marine I'm looking for: Private Chang, the Marine who had spoken up for me back at the burning hillside. His helmet is off and he's washing his face from a basin balanced on the hood of a Humvee. Other Humvees and tied up horses are tangled around the parking area. A haze of smoke is in the air. One Marine says to another, "Listen up, bud, you catch that smell? That's Albany burning."

His mate says, "How the hell can you tell?"

"Burning chickenshit and red tape, how else?"

Chang recognizes me again and says, "Hey, Sergeant, didn't expect to see you so soon."

"Me neither," I say, Serena and Buddy trailing behind me. I go up to him. "Look can you do me a favor?"

He shrugs. "Depends, I guess. What's going on?"

I make a point of looking around the crowded area. "How about we go someplace a bit more private?"

Another shrug. "Up to you." He dries his hands on a gray towel, grabs his helmet and M-10, and I follow him to the rear of the garage. There are oil drums filled with scrap metal and broken parts, some low trimmed shrubbery at the rear by locked Dumpsters. He turns, putting his helmet back on, tightening the chin straps. "What's up?"

"Private, after what you did for me back in Albany, I hate to do this to you, but I need a Humvee, along with an M-10, rations, and an M-4."

Chang starts to laugh and stops when he sees I'm not in on the apparent joke. "Sure. Why not. Let's go see my ell-tee, fill out some paperwork, and we'll send you on your way. Even give you some Hershey bars to pass out to any civvies you meet. Bet we can get you out in five minutes or less, if you say pretty-please."

I move fast and sure, slipping out my Beretta, cocking the hammer. I don't point it at Chang, but I don't try to hide it. "Private, I owe you one, but I really need that Humvee and those weapons. Now."

Chang stands still. He's about my age, and in the quickening light burn tissue and scars on his neck become visible. "Or what. You going to shoot me?"

"It's a thought."

Now he laughs for real. "Go ahead. Put me out of my misery. I've been fighting those damn bugs, off and on for five years, and just when we're told the war's over, time to get back to civvie life, time to relax, Albany gets smoked. War's back on. Think I'm gung-ho for that shit again?"

I point the Beretta at a leg. "Or maybe I just put a round through your knee, cripple you for the rest of your life."

His smile is wider. "Why not? Get me disabled, get me out of the Corps. Oh, yeah, and my platoon will hear the gunshot, see me on the ground bleeding out, and you won't live to get to a stockade. Gotta do better than that, Sergeant."

I don't move. He's got me trapped, damn it.

"What's the deal then?" Chang asks. "You looking to bail out? Head off to the Catskills or something, become a deserter? With a Humvee and military-issued weps?"

The rumble of a Humvee starting up startles me. Each second I'm spending here, means another second wasted while my dad and Serena's dad get closer to the train station. So, tell him the truth? That me and that scared young girl and quiet boy I'm escorting have the keys to ending this war? Tell him the truth? Chang's eyes are staring right at me, no fear, not much of anything.

Tell him the truth.

"I'm after my dad," I say. "And the specialist's dad. They were in the arsenal's stockade, and now they're being shipped to Schenectady. We haven't seen them for nearly a half year."

Chang's expression changes. "Your dads . . . they're alive?"

"Yes."

"And you're trying to get to them?"

"Yes."

His eyes and expression soften, like a hard candy or something, exposed to sunlight. "My dad . . . he'd been in the Corps, years before. When the war started, he got me and Mom and my two sisters, he got us out of Cincinnati, one of the few diesel buses still running . . . he had on his BDUs and his gut was hanging out, but he was off to the war . . ."

He snaps to. "Last time I ever saw him. You want to get to your dads? Should have told me right away. C'mon."

After a few minutes, Chang leads us to the end of the parking lot, to the last parked Humvee. He tosses me his M-10, along with a bandolier of five egg-shaped rounds. "Going into harm's way?"

"You know it," I say. I open the doors and Serena gets into the front, and Buddy is in the rear. There's a jumble of packs and equipment, and Buddy squirms his way in. Chang steps away, comes back with an M-4. "Best I could do. You've only got one magazine, so don't waste your shots."

I make sure the M-4 is in safe, give it to Serena. Chang ducks down and looks at the console, and says, "This baby's old, has been converted to electric, and I don't know how much of a charge you got, and the transmission's cranky as hell. Best I can do, Sergeant, wasn't gonna let you take one of our better ones."

I shake his hand. "Appreciate it."

He gives my hand a hard squeeze. "Get the hell out of here."

"How are you going to explain this to your lieutenant?"

Chang laughs, waves an arm at the busy and confusing parking lot, the road in front of the garage, the sounds of shouts and yells and engines, the *clop-clop* of horse's hooves. "Fog of war, how else? Now, git."

I go.

✦ ✦ ✦

The interior of the Humvee stinks of sweat, burnt things, and gun oil. The set-up was pretty simple. An ON/OFF switch for the electric motor, and a sliding shift lever on the transmission lump between me and Serena that had four markings: P, D, N and R. Much, much easier than that old Impala I had struggled with back in Albany.

I flip the switch on, catch a low hum, and I point something out to Serena: a faded bit of scratched graffiti, above the old dials that didn't mean anything and near an old-fashioned ball compass: BAGHDAD OR BUST.

"What does that mean?" I ask.

"It means this thing's older than you and me put together," she says. "Randy, please, drive."

I flipped the selector to D, and with a soft surge, we go out of the crowded parking lot.

"Look at me," I say. "Driving twice in two days."

"Goodie for you," Serena says, arms crossed.

I speed up as we approach the main gate, and the MP there just waves me on. I turn right and join the rest of the traffic getting out of the arsenal. Serena says, "You know how to get to Schenectady?"

"Nope."

"You got a map?"

"Nope."

"Then how the hell do you plan to get there?"

"Ask someone who knows."

It's full morning when I arrive back at the farm where I had departed some hours ago, being driven out on a raspy Vespa scooter, and the dirt driveway before the barn is crowded with horse-drawn wagons and one battered Ford pick-up truck that looks to be nearly a century old. I park at an open spot near the barn and get out, jostled by some folks going in and out of the barn. I spot Billy Whittum and he fetches his mom, she's coming out of the barn, on crutches, looking much more tired than from before.

"Sergeant," she says. "Looks like you've been at your rally point and back. Good for you, but if you're looking for breakfast, sorry, we're all out."

"No, ma'am," I say. "Just directions, and then I'll be on my way."

She looks at me, and then the Humvee. "I see. You're coming up in the world . . . where are you going?"

"Schenectady."

"What for?"

I feel like a dick, but I can't do anything else. "Sorry, ma'am. You know how it is. OPSEC."

She sags some in her crutches. A passing breeze tosses the loose pant leg where her stump is and she says, "OPSEC. Terrible bitch, ain't she. Billy! A piece of paper and pencil."

Leaning onto the hood of the Humvee, she laboriously draws out a map, and she passes it over. "Anything else?"

Time, time, time. But I say, "Yes. Thor."

Andrea seems to understand. "Sure. This way."

'This way" is an attached stall at the side of the barn, and God love my boy, I hear him whine as I approach. He knows I'm here. Behind me I see Serena get out of the Humvee, hurrying over to us. I go into the stall and Thor lifts his head, smiles, starts panting and wagging his tail. He's resting on a dog bed made from a large canvas sack stuffed with something, resting upon soft hay, and I motion him to stay still. Behind me Andrea joins me and he says, "We changed his dressings and the pup didn't give us no mind at all. Ate some dinner scraps and drank right up. That's one fine boy you got there, Sergeant."

The rest here has done Thor well. His eyes are bright and shiny. Serena joins us and says, "Randy . . . I mean, Sergeant, we really have to get moving."

"We certainly do," I reply. "And we're all moving together."

"Sergeant . . ."

I want to look at Serena but my eyes are filling, and I don't want her to see that. "Back in the Humvee, in the rear. I'm sure I spotted a collapsible stretcher. Bring it back."

My boy's tail thumps and thumps, and damn it, how does he know what I'm thinking?

"Thor's coming with us," I say.

A few minutes later Thor is in the rear of the Humvee, and Buddy smiles in enjoyment, and rubs and rubs his head, and Thor licks his hand in response. I fold up the collapsible stretcher and shove it in where I can, and return to the front of the vehicle. I turn the Humvee around and head out to the end of the driveway. To the south are columns of smoke and the orange glow of fires out of control, at our nation's latest capitol.

Serena raises her voice. "How are you feeling?"

"On top of the world," I say. "Now let's go get our dads."

In a while we're on Route Seven, also known as the Troy-Schenectady Road, and Andre's directions are clear and to the point. The road is four lanes, with a turning lane in the center, with deserted office buildings and complexes on each side, overgrown trees, abandoned cars in parking lots and dead traffic lights at some intersections dangling low. There's a detour she's noted that I take—due to a long-ago bridge washout that's never been repaired—and there's a backup due to an Oldsmobile that took out a farm wagon. Now we're on a typical narrow country road, houses and farms off at a distance, untrimmed trees and brush closing in on each side of the road. On-coming traffic is relatively heavy, with horse-drawn wagons, some folks on bicycles and two old cars passing us. One car honks and a couple of people wave.

I wave back and start puzzling out the map. Serena says something but I'm too focused on the map, so she has to say, "Sergeant, damn it, will you listen to me?"

I'm startled. "Yeah. What's up?"

She points out the grimy windshield. "The traffic. Haven't you noticed it?"

Heatedly I say, "Yeah, I have. They're refugees. What's the problem?"

Serena says, "Refugees? Heading in the direction of Albany?"

I feel like an idiot. I slow down. Another horse-drawn wagon rattles by, the farmer in front holding the reins yelling something at us.

"Specialist."

"Yes."

"Make sure you're ready with the M-4. And get that M-10 within easy reach."

She says nothing and does as she's told. I look back and Thor is stretched out on Buddy's lap, and Buddy is rubbing and rubbing his head. Serena rests the M-4 across her lap, and props up the M-10 and a bandolier of rounds next to her seat. I slow down the Humvee, lower the driver's side window. Behind me Thor whimpers, and then sets off a low growl that makes the back of my hands and neck itch.

"Randy," Serena says, voice strained.

"Quiet."

The road turns and then slopes to the left down to a four-way intersection. The smell of burnt things suddenly assaults us. At the crossroads, a statue had once been erected of a Civil War soldier, standing bravely in a tiny grass square, and the statue is on the ground, shattered and smashed, the granite stand cracked wide open. At the right a dirty white pick-up truck is on its back, both doors open, one of them gently swinging back and forth in the morning breeze.

"Oh, Randy . . ."

A bus is on the other side of the small intersection, pushed over to the side of the road. It's been shattered and burnt. The windows appear barred, but the glass is either broken or melted. The scorched and torn open frame is on four flat and melted tires. On the rear of the bus the white letters A R M Y are blackened.

I don't remember putting the Humvee in park. I'm outside, on the cracked and old pavement, M-10 in hand, bandolier over my shoulder, looking, evaluating, moving slow, sniffing the air.

Cinnamon.

I move closer to the destroyed bus, sensing Serena next to me. She stays with me and—

A burnt body on the ground, arms out-stretched. Another one a few meters away. Uniforms burned away, boots and helmets only recognizable. And huddled over a half-melted steering wheel, the charcoal-black arms of a headless driver leans to one side.

Serena screams and screams.

CHAPTER THIRTY-SIX

I grab her arm, give her a shake. "Sort it out. Knock it off."

She sobs some more. I let go of her, take a glance back to the Humvee. Buddy is at the near open window and Thor has raised his head. He's sniffing the air, whining. Unlike the attack on the train the other day, this is no fake Creeper assault.

The stench nearly knocks me back, but I force myself to go closer. Besides the two bodies on the ground, and the headless driver, I find another body in the wreckage, halfway out the door. The roof of the bus has been torn off.

Serena's sobbing goes on. Thor barks. I step carefully around the bus, M-10 still at the ready.

"Specialist!"

She sniffs and rubs at her eyes with her fists. "What?"

I take a deep breath, go back to the Humvee, grabbing her elbow. "There's four bodies there. Four."

"So?"

"Three of them have helmets on their heads. And the other one is behind the wheel. Our dads aren't there. I was told four MPs were in the transport. Four."

I give her another firm shake. "You hear me? They aren't here!"

I roughly push her ahead of me, thinking, looking again. No sign of Creeper trail in the near woods and fields. The bastard must have come down the road, and returned the same way. I get into the Humvee, leave the M-10 over my lap, slam the door. Think. Think. Serena gets in and closes her door and I turn left, drive down the road slow, turning to make sure Thor's head is out the open rear window, sniffing.

"Where are you going?" Serena asks.

"Nowhere. Anywhere."

"Randy . . ."

I don't look to her but keep on talking as I do down the road. "Don't you get it? The Creeper attacked the bus. The four MPs were killed on the scene. Our dads . . . they've been captured."

She starts sobbing again.

My hands are cold, my feet are cold, and I feel like I'm going choke in fear and frustration. How far down the road should I go? Would Thor pick up the trail? And how long ago was the attack?

I spin the wheel, make a bumpy U-turn, head back to the intersection. Nothing much has changed. I take a left. Serena's stopped sobbing, but she's staring out the window. Thor's panting. I can't smell anything.

One more road to take.

Are we too late?

Are our dads still alive?

Another U-turn, this time I speed up, and make a final left.

Thor starts barking and whining after we've gone about a hundred meters.

I speed up.

And stop. Creeper sign to the right, a fence post torn free, grass burnt, saplings tossed aside, and I flip the steering wheel and accelerate, and we plow across the field, and Thor's barking increases.

Cinnamon. That damn smell.

The field comes up across a section of woods, and the going gets rough, and I can't go any further. I slam the Humvee to a halt, switch off the engine, grab the M-10 and say, "Specialist! With me!"

She bails out without a word and is at my side. My breathing cuts at me, as I curse and run and stumble through the broken trees and branches, forgetting all my training about moving slow, moving sure. All I know now is my dad is up there, as well as Serena's, and I'm not going easy, not going slow.

More smell of burnt things, ashes. Serena's shouting something and

I ignore her. A broken branch tears at my face, the slashing pain making me tear up, but I press on, and press on.

The woods suddenly thin out, and end. All before me are ashes, burnt buildings, destroyed military equipment—105 mm howitzer, M-1A tank, an overturned truck—a broken stone wall, and a pockmarked landscape. A Battle Creeper is on the move about fifty meters away, firing away bursts of flame from its arms, herding two human figures before it.

Herding the two humans to the dull blue-gray dome marking a Creeper base.

I whirl, grab the M-4 out of Serena's hands. "Stay put!"

She yells again and I run harder across the broken and burnt field, stumbling, falling, picking myself up, running past a long trench with bones and uniform scraps jumbled together, ammunition boxes, melted barrels of heavy weapons. I run and run and run. The two men are in tattered uniforms, heads bent down. Hard to tell which one might be Dad.

I stop, flop myself down on the scorched earth, ignoring the M-10. The Creeper is moving away from me. I don't have a target solution, I don't have a target, I don't have anything at all. I need the damn thing to turn around!

I flip the safety off, bring the M-4 up to my shoulder, squeeze off one round, then two, and another. Aiming right at the rear of the main arthropod.

The Creeper keeps on moving, spurting out bursts of flame, keeping the humans in check.

I'm ignored.

I stand up, fire off three more rounds.

"Right here!" I scream. "Right over here, you bitch! Turn around and take me on! C'mon! Are you scared? Hunh? Scared?"

Two more rounds from me.

Two more bursts of flame the alien's arms. The Creeper ambles on.

Something is going on with the Creeper base.

A sliver has appeared in the smooth surface.

An opening is beginning to dilate.

My dad and Serena's dad. One of the two men tries to move and screams as a flame scorches his right side.

They're close to going inside the base and never coming out.

"Oh, Dad!" I sob.

I throw myself down to the ground again, where I'll have a better shot, recall the shouts of my DI from years back:

Nobody left behind.

Nobody captured.

Nobody.

I wipe at my eyes, and again. I bring up the M-4, bring the familiar stock against my shoulder. The barrel wobbles. I take a breath, settle down, aim through the sights.

There. Clear shot to the man on the left.

Is it Dad or Serena's father?

What difference does it make?

I'm not going to let a fellow soldier get into that dome.

Clear shot.

I start squeezing the trigger, the sights not wavering, the man clear in my eye—

A noise to my right. A shout. A clicking, whirring, sputtering sound.

I can't help myself.

It's Buddy.

Buddy!

And he has his hands around his mouth, and he's yelling something that sounds like gibberish. Clicks, whirs, sputtering and spits.

Up ahead the Creeper has stopped.

It starts to move.

I drop the M-4, take the M-10 off my back.

The opening to the dome gets longer and wider.

The two men have fallen to their knees.

I open the breech of the M-10, take out a round, click it from the safe position, go pass the ten-meter setting, and set it onto the twenty-five meter position.

The Creeper is now facing me, its two forward weaponized arms extended up and out, the main arthropod rising up.

I slam the breech shut.

Bring it up. Something sparking emerges from both of the alien arms.

BLAM!

I quickly eject, grab another round, spin it to the same twenty-five meters, and—

BLAM!

The second chemical cloud bursts just as the first one is spreading, and I'm grabbing another round, when the Creeper starts shaking, its arms extending up, legs collapsing.

I don't stop.

Eject the second cartridge. I flick the setting for the third round to fifty meters, slam it into the breech, and fire off one more round.

BLAM!

My shoulder throbs and tomorrow it's gonna hurt like a son-of-a-bitch, but the last round flies out and over the dying Creeper, descends, descends, and hits the ground, bounces once, and rises up and soars into the Creeper base, as the dilation begins to close.

I don't see or hear anything after that, and then the Creeper base is now back to one smooth surface, and I'm pretty sure my Colt round has exploded inside the base, but who knows for sure.

I yell to the dome. "Courtesy of Second Recon Rangers, assholes!"

The chemical cloud has drifted away, and the two men are coming my way, limping, one holding up the other. I pick up the M-4 and sling it and the Colt M-10 over my shoulders. Buddy is still standing there, a quiet smile on his face.

"You," I say, voice shaking. "What the hell did you say back there?"

The smile on his face doesn't change a bit. I walk the other way.

My Dad is on the left, black-rimmed eyeglasses with one stem tape repaired, limping. He has on plain BDUs. His face is black with soot and smoke. He's holding up another man, also in plain BDUs. Serena's dad, I'm sure.

He stops, and Serena's dad stops as well. He's breathing hard, and parts of his uniform have been scorched away.

Dad takes a breath. "Doctor Coulson, may I present my son, Sergeant Randy Knox?"

An Excerpt From the Journal of Randall Knox

The other night my squad and a few others had choir practice. Sounds cute, don't it, but it's something we need to do to blow off steam and just be teen boys for a while. We get leave and such, but there's not much for us to do in Concord, and the USO does what it can, but sometimes, a bunch of us just wander off to an empty stretch of woods on our base and kick back. That means a fire gets lit, some stolen chocolate bars get eaten, and if we're real lucky, some trooper has some 'shine smuggled in from trading with the local farmers.

That night there were about a half-dozen of us, and I'm always pleased that I get invited. Officially, of course, I'm in charge, but I know enough to forget my sergeant's stripes back at my barracks. But I do step in if things get out of hand.

The fire was roaring along nicely, a bottle of 'shine was passed around, and after a discussion of the cutest girls in the outfit—and I'm secretly pleased to see Abby made the top five—we get to a familiar subject: what would you do personally to end the war, if you could?

There was the typical—swim across the still-drowned island of Manhattan, go up against a Battle creeper naked save for a jockstrap and a dull spoon, that sort of crap—and a bunch of pretty obscene suggestions that made us laugh and laugh.

Then somebody asked Harrison, "Hey, Harrison, what would you do?"

And we get quiet then, because Harrison was new. Oh, he's not a rookie—he's got the burnt scar tissue and other wounds to prove it—and he's a year older than me, but still a private. Word was, he was with a Vermont unit that got roasted a few months ago, and the higher-ups

313

decided to transfer the survivors around New England instead of keeping them in Vermont.

Harrison's got dark hair, cut high and tight, and his left eye droops. He stared into the fire and quietly said, "I'd kill you, Mac, that's what I'd"

There was some uneasy laughter at that, and Harrison's voice gets louder. "No, I'm not foolin'. If somebody told me that I could end this friggin' war by killing you, I'd waste you, Mac."

He turned his head, going from one trooper to another. "Or you. Or you. Or this entire goddamn squad, I'd frag you all if it meant ending this war."

Silence after that, until I declared choir practice over, and for once, nobody gave me any grief.

CHAPTER THIRTY-SEVEN

I give my Dad an awkward hug, try to say something but I can't because I'm crying and my throat is so thick it threatens to gag me. He says, "M'boy, it's been a long, long time, but let's get out of this killing zone."

My throat clears. "Hold on, Dad, just for a sec, hold on."

A humming noise and from another section of the woods, a Humvee bounces out, driven by Serena. I'll be damned, she found another way to get to this battlefield. She maneuvers the Humvee up to us, and gets out, and Serena is with her dad, all over him. Smart girl, she's also taken a first aid kit and canteen from the Humvee and starts working on her father. Thor leans his head out of an open window, barks with happiness, and then his barks get sharper, being so close to Creeper sign. I yell, "Thor, settle!" My Dad takes the canteen and takes a deep swallow. Buddy, however, is still standing there, a self-satisfied smile on his face. Serena's dad leans against my dad, and Serena starts tugging away Doctor Coulson's burnt BDU blouse, tugging open the first aid kit.

"Randy . . ."

I interrupt him, "Dad, what the hell just happened here? Buddy . . . what the hell did he just do?"

Doctor Coulson gasps as Serena's fingers work on him. "He . . . he talked to that Creeper . . . I think he told him to turn around . . ."

"Dad?"

"Randy, we need to go."

I've always listened to my Dad, have always followed his advice and counsel, but now, on this torn-up battlefield and the trenches behind me, with skeletal remains, uniform scraps and broken weapons, and the dead Creeper in front of us, it's all changed.

"No," I said. "Not until I know what's going on. You and Doctor Coulson and Buddy . . . you've been communicating with the Creepers."

"We have," he says, taking another long swallow. "After years and years, we've made progress . . . and once we got a fragile line of communication established, I bet you can guess the first question, right?"

Sure. Topic A at every bull session every service member has taken part in during the past decade. "Why are they here?"

Another moan from Doctor Coulson, but Serena doesn't let up. Dad says, "Randy . . . why do wars break out?"

I give him the textbook answer. "Population expansion. Shortage of resources. Perceived security threat."

"True enough," he says, rubbing at his blackened face again. "But would a star-faring civilization really resort to war to address excess population? Or a shortage of resources? And we pitiful people here, who can't even travel in our own solar system, we'd be considered a threat? Really?"

No answer on my part, for this topic has been discussed at every military gathering for the past decade. Dad says, "So what other explanation for a war that doesn't make sense? What have we seen in our own history, Randy?"

The answer comes right to me, as silly as it sounds, and an answer that's always been hooted down during bull sessions. The Crusades. The Thirty Years War in Europe. The Jihads. "Religion?"

"A very odd answer," he says. "But millions of people have died on this planet because of disputes over which god to worship. And remember the missionaries who went into colonial Africa and South America, spreading the Word. And when they were imprisoned or killed, their sponsoring empires took that as a *causi belli*, and did what they did."

"The Creepers . . . they're here, fighting to convert us?" Even though the words come out of my mouth, I still can't believe them. Even Serena looks up from her medical work. Doctor Coulson is still standing although his head is slumped, and his son Buddy continues to ignore us all.

"Yes . . . that's the whole point of why they're here," Doctor Coulson says, head still bowed. "Kill and kill and kill until we accept their belief system. Until we learn to talk to them and convert. And Buddy . . ."

No wonder he can speak the lingo. He's learned it. He's adapted to it.

"He's . . . a convert?"

Doctor Coulson slowly raises his head. "My son . . . yes, he's the first. That's why they've been here, all these years. To beat upon us, kill us, until we convert to their . . . belief system. Or religion. Or whatever you want to call it."

I stare at the closed dome, at the killed Creeper exoskeleton. A waft of cinnamon comes over me. Standing here out in the open is an insane thing, but I've seen a lot of insanity in the past ten years.

"Buddy's the first then, right? And the Creepers know it? And converting us . . . that's their 'mission accomplished,' right? Killing is their evangelizing?"

My dad stays quiet. Doctor Coulson says, "That's . . . that's a good analysis, Randy."

"And as far as you know, Buddy's the only one in the world?"

Serena still works on her dad. My Dad just looks at me. Doctor Coulson says, "The only one."

I take my Beretta out, push it against the base of Buddy's skull, and with my hand firmly grasping his collar, the M-10 and M-4 bouncing on my back, I frog-march him away.

Towards the Creepers' dome.

As I remember that long-ago choir practice with my squad.

What would you do to end the war?

There's shouts, yells, movement behind me and I say, "You stay behind or I swear to God, I'll blow off his head, right here! Understand? Leave me be!"

Buddy doesn't put up any resistance, and strange, I know, I don't hear much but what I do hear is Thor barking at me, back at the Humvee. For God's sake, I hope my pal stays behind, because things are going to get goddamn interesting, pretty quick.

The ground is scorched and crusty earth, and I swerve around the collapsed exoskeleton, and the closer I get to the dome, the more my legs start shaking. Not many men or women have gotten this close to a Creeper dome and have lived to talk about it, and I sure as hell didn't think upon getting up this morning that I'd be joining that elite group.

At some point the sight of the dome freezes me, filling up most of my view in front of me, and I turn. Dad is there, and so is Doctor Coulson, leaning on Serena, and I don't think about the expressions on their faces.

"Doctor Coulson!" I yell, still digging my pistol into Buddy's neck. "I want you to tell Buddy to talk Creeper talk, and you better translate, word for word, what I'm going to say, or you're going to lose your son, and all of us are going to become charcoal in the next sixty seconds. Got it?"

He slowly nods, and I go on. "Doctor Coulson, tell Buddy to tell the Creepers to open up their goddamn dome."

Serena and Dad both shout "No!" at about the same time, but Doctor Coulson says, "Buddy! Authorization Pappa Bravo Pappa! Tell them . . . tell them to open the Dome."

Buddy is practically hanging off my hand, but he raises his own hands up and shouts again in that clicking, sputtering, whirring noise, and by Jesus and all the souls of the departed, a line appears in the dome, and it starts to widen. There are gasps behind me but I press on, although as the gap in the dome gets wider, I'm so goddamn scared I think I'm going to piss my pants.

I jerk Buddy closer, and as I yell out my words, Doctor Coulson repeats what I say, and Buddy talks in the Creeper language as well. It's like a game of telephone and I hope we're getting the damn thing right.

"I know why you're here . . ." I yell. "A holy mission for you . . . I understand . . . and now, here's your first convert, your first prophet to us . . . but here it ends . . ."

I pause, my hands shaking. "We have fought you . . . and fought you . . . and fought you . . . for ten of our years . . . your orbital station is destroyed . . . we have shown you . . . that we will never surrender . . ."

I jerk Buddy forward and Serena screams. "So here is your prophet . . . your convert . . . but if you do not surrender, if you do not stop fighting, if you will not submit to us . . . I will kill him . . . right here and now . . ."

From the corner of my eye, I see Doctor Coulson is trying to get to me, supported by Serena, but my Dad is in front of the two of them, blocking them both.

"I know you follow us . . . you know who I am . . . I am the fighter who killed one of your own . . . with just a blade . . . who climbed up on your warrior and struck it dead . . . and I have no fear of killing your prophet, your chosen one . . ."

My heart is one solid roaring thumping, and I yell out again, "Your warriors, they are to come out now . . . do you understand me? Now! They are to come out and surrender to us . . . or I will kill your prophet, the one you have fought so long to create . . ."

My eyes are filmy and I don't know what the hell is going to happen, but I flash back to that photo of mom and my sister, burning and fading way, and by Christ, if I can end it here and now, that's what I'm going to do.

"Now!" I yell.

Pause. Wait.

"Now!"

Movement.

Oh-so-familiar *click-click* sound.

God, what am I doing?

A Battle creeper comes out, followed by another one. I think I just might pass out. Another Battle creeper emerges, until eight are lined up, right in a skirmish line, not more than ten meters away. I've never seen so many Creepers bunched up like that, right out in the open.

The stench of cinnamon nearly knocks me to my knees.

I kick at Buddy's legs, push him to the ground. Another scream from Serena, followed by shouts from my Dad and Doctor Coulson as I unlimber my Colt M-10, set a round for ten meters, load up my M-10 and bring it up to my shoulder.

BLAM!

And I kill the Creeper on the far left.

CHAPTER THIRTY-EIGHT

"Doctor Coulson!" I yell out. "Remember, word for word!"

And I go on, though I feel like I'm going to pass out, but Buddy's collar is firm in my sweaty grasp.

"You moved too slow!" I yell to the dome, bringing up Buddy and pointing my pistol at his head. "I mean what I say . . . I want your surrender . . . the surrender of all Creeper forces . . . or your prophet dies . . . and you'll never convert any of us! You'll be a failure . . . and you Creepers . . . in this dome . . . will be blamed by your fellow fighters . . ."

More stuttering sounds from Buddy, and I wait, and I wait. My legs are about to give way. The Creeper on the left has finished its shuddering and is on the ground, dead.

The other seven are very much alive.

The smell of the cinnamon is still overpowering and almost gags me. I can make out the clicks and whirs from inside the seven exoskeletons. Inside each of those deadly shapes is a live, flesh-and-whatever Creeper, looking out at me, a teenage boy, each of them with the ability to smoke me down in less than a heartbeat.

God knows what their alien minds are thinking.

I jerk Buddy's collar again.

"Surrender!" I yell. "Now!"

The Creeper on the right starts to lift up its arms and I close my eyes. I've seen so much in the past ten years that I have no guts or desire to see what's going to happen next. I just hope it's goddamn quick, that my Dad survives, and that poor old Thor will be able to escape as well.

Click-click.

Click-click.

From behind me, Dad says, voice shaking, "God preserve us."

I open my eyes.

It's something I've never seen before. All seven surviving Creepers are stretched out on the ground, flattened, their weaponized arms folded behind them, in a form of submission.

Of surrender.

I let go of Buddy and he stands there. Still a quiet puzzle, still an enigma. "Boy," I say to him, "what the hell did they do to you?"

He turns his head to me, silent yet there's a look there, beyond the faint smile, in his haunted eyes.

A look of . . . triumph? Of power? Of revenge?

I reach out, take his hand. He doesn't protest. I need to see something else. I bring Buddy closer to the line of the outstretched Creepers. Serena is still screaming at me.

We get closer. The sound of the machinery inside the exoskeletons is louder. Behind them is the opening to the dome. I see flickering lights and dark shapes moving within there. What's back there? What's hidden away?

A job for somebody else. I'm so scared now it's a fight to put one foot in front of me.

We get closer still.

A whining noise gets louder.

The Creepers are on the move.

Away from Buddy.

Away from their new prophet, away from their convert, they slide back, still with arms down, still in submission.

I stop, manage to catch my breath. Buddy stops with me. I kiss the top of his sooty and sweaty head, not able to say anything after all the years of burning and fighting and drowning and dying, dying, dying. I take his hand and gently usher him back to the Humvee and Serena, Doctor Coulson and my Dad, and Serena runs up to me and clobbers me to the ground, swearing at me at every moment.

Dad helps me up, and I rub at my cheek and jaw, and I taste blood in my mouth. Scorched dirt is smeared on my hands. I look back. The Creepers haven't moved. Serena and her dad are clustered around Buddy, hugging him, stroking his hair, kissing his cheeks. I still can't believe what I've just done—or seemed to have done with this young boy—and I say to my Dad, "Why were you both charged with treason? Because of Buddy?"

He manages a smile. "Not because of Buddy. We've kept that secret . . . until now. No, we were charged with treason for unauthorized diplomatic discussions with the enemy. We were barely talking with the Creepers and we were supposed to let the Secretary of State—who needs a staff to find his shoes in the morning—take over the negotiations. Wasn't going to happen."

I rub at my moist eyes. "The President's people didn't want negotiations," I say. "They wanted the orbital station destroyed, so the President can declare victory before the next election. And you and Doctor Coulson and Buddy . . . had to be put away, or killed, so the truth about the negotiations would never come out, along with Buddy's . . . conversion."

My father says, "How many does it take to make war, and how many to make a peace?"

"One to make war," I say automatically. "Two to make a peace."

"True," he says. "The President declared the war had been won, and that peace was at hand. The Creepers obviously disagreed . . . until now."

I look back again at the open dome, at the flattened and unmoving Creepers. It's like a scene from some fantasy movie, if fantasy movies were ever going to be made again. "What now?

"Now?" my Dad asks, and then laughs, hugs me. "You tell me. You've just ended the Creeper war. You and Buddy! What do you think, Randy?"

What to think. What a question. Ten years of fighting and dying and burning and starving, to end here, in a field somewhere in rural New York? Where are the triumphant generals? The speeches? The signing ceremony? The bands? The celebrations?

"I don't know," I say, realizing just how filthy I am and how much I stink. "I've never trained for anything like this."

Dad laughs, hugs me again, and then we all slowly walk back to the Humvee, Serena looking at me now with some sort of forgiveness in her eyes, and now I think, do we have to do this again, one dome after another? Should we leave? Should we stay and alert any QRF's in the area about what's just happened?

What to do. What to do.

At the Humvee Thor has his head hanging out the rear window. I undo the door let him out, and he leaps on me and drops me to the ground. My boy is on top of me, barking and licking my face, and I hug him and plant my face in his fur, and I whisper, over and over again, "We've won, pal . . . we've won . . . we've won."

More happy barks, and then something else comes to me.

"No more fighting," I say, gently weeping with my dog in my arms. "You're gonna live forever, boy. Forever."